MOLLY GREEN has travelled the in a score of different countries which often became her new place of work. On returning to England, she set up an estate agency business which she ran and expanded for twenty-five years. Eventually, she sold her business to give herself time and space to pursue her dream to write novels. She has since moved to a village outside Lewes in East Sussex and writes her novels from a railway carriage in the garden, and hopes her new rescued cat, Betsy, will in time stroll over to keep her company.

You can keep up with Molly at mollygreenauthor.com

Also by Molly Green

The Dr Barnardo's Orphanage series:
An Orphan in the Snow
An Orphan's War
An Orphan's Wish

The Victory Sisters series:
A Sister's Courage
A Sister's Song
A Sister's War

The Bletchley Park series:
Summer Secrets at Bletchley Park
A Winter Wedding at Bletchley Park
Wartime Wishes at Bletchley Park

Courage for the Cabinet Girl

The Wartime Librarian's Secret

MOLLY GREEN

avon.

Published by AVON
A division of HarperCollins*Publishers*
1 London Bridge Street
London SE1 9GF

www.harpercollins.co.uk

HarperCollins*Publishers*
Macken House, 39/40 Mayor Street Upper
Dublin 1, D01 C9W8, Ireland

A Paperback Original 2025

1

First published in Great Britain by HarperCollins*Publishers* 2025

Copyright © Denise Barnes 2025

Denise Barnes asserts the moral right to be identified as the author of this work.

A catalogue copy of this book is available from the British Library.

ISBN: 978-0-00-867957-6

This novel is entirely a work of fiction. References to real people, events or localities are intended only to provide a sense of authenticity, and are used fictitiously. All other characters and incidents portrayed in it are the work of the author's imagination.

Set in Minion Pro by HarperCollins*Publishers* India

Printed and bound in the UK using 100% Renewable
Electricity at CPI Group (UK) Ltd

All rights reserved. No part of this text may be reproduced, transmitted, down-loaded, decompiled, reverse engineered, or stored in or introduced into any information storage and retrieval system, in any form or by any means, whether electronic or mechanical, without the express written permission of the publishers.

Without limiting the exclusive rights of any author, contributor or the publisher of this publication, any unauthorised use of this publication to train generative artificial intelligence (AI) technologies is expressly prohibited. HarperCollins also exercise their rights under Article 4(3) of the Digital Single Market Directive 2019/790 and expressly reserve this publication from the text and data mining exception.

This book contains FSC™ certified paper and other controlled
sources to ensure responsible forest management.

For more information visit: www.harpercollins.co.uk/green

To the late and very great Queen Mary, mother of George VI, who 'did her bit' in the Second World War.

Chapter One

Bath, September 1942

Esme Donaldson poured a cup of tea from the little blue-and-white china teapot for two that the uniformed waitress had just brought to her table. She sighed. Freda was late, but it had given her time to absorb the opulent surroundings of the magnificent Pump Room interior with its ornate classical ceiling frieze and the Corinthian pilasters set in rows against the walls. Her gaze wandered to the left of the room towards a curved alcove where the sun shone through stained-glass windows above, flashing coloured lights onto the three fish jumping in the water from the spewing Roman fountain. She knew beyond that window was the extraordinary sight of the Roman baths below. Normally, she would stroll over and gaze down for some minutes, taking it all in, but today was different. Once Freda arrived in her usual flurry, she'd be impatient if Esme wasn't sitting at the table and hadn't already ordered.

Sparkling light from the crystal chandelier above played on the cutlery and glasses on tables set out for lunch. Three musicians were performing on the stage in front of her. She didn't recognise the piece, but it sounded like Mozart. She closed her eyes for a few moments and let the music wash over her until it came to an end.

'So, my darling, will you marry me?'

Her eyelids flew open. For a wild moment, she'd thought someone was directing the question to *her*. Now, she glanced across to a nearby table where a young couple sat, their eyes fixed upon each other, their hands entwined. Esme held her breath. They looked so happy, so much in love, it made her gulp.

'Yes, Dickie, I will.'

'Oh, Shirley, you've made me the happiest man in the world.' He leaned over the table and kissed his new fiancée on the lips.

Esme averted her gaze, trying to blink back the tears. But it didn't work. She put her hands to her face as the tears streamed down her cheeks, squeezing through her fingers as the couple left, his arm around her shoulders. Witnessing such a happy pair should not have upset her. It was more than two years since Anthony had died suddenly of a brain haemorrhage, and she thought she was over the worst. But his death *wasn't* only the worst. He'd been so excited when she'd written to tell him the most wonderful news . . . She took in a juddering breath. Nausea gripped her stomach. If he'd had to die, at least he hadn't known what had happened later to their precious baby. Swallowing hard, she told herself she mustn't break down . . . not in public . . . not in here.

Unconsciously, she fingered the little gold locket he'd given her before he'd been sent abroad, a tiny photograph in each side – one of her, and one of himself smiling directly at her. She'd wished at the time he'd removed his RAF cap so she could see his eyes more clearly. But she only had to visualise him standing in front of her, the hazel eyes shining with love for her. Now, she felt the curious glances from one or two of the diners. She was causing a spectacle and her sister still hadn't arrived.

I need to get out of here.

Forcing back another sob, she was about to stand when she felt a warm pressure of a hand on her shoulder and the gentlest squeeze. She looked up through tear-filled eyes at the blurred vision of a uniformed man. He didn't say anything but simply pressed a large white handkerchief into her trembling hand.

'Thank you,' she mumbled and after dabbing her face, looked up. But he'd disappeared.

'Ah, there you are.' Freda's clear tones rang out as she approached the table, now the only one with a free seat. She glanced at the table before she removed her jacket and sat down. 'I see you've ordered tea for me as well, though it'll probably be cold by now.' She gave Esme a flash of a smile. 'Ask the waitress for a fresh one, there's a dear.' Pulling out a cigarette from a silver case, she lit it with a matching lighter, blew out a long cloud of smoke and leaned back in her chair. 'Oh, I needed that.' For the first time she regarded her younger sister properly. 'Why on earth are you crying?'

'Probably the start of a cold.' Esme sniffed and wiped her cheeks with the handkerchief. She folded it and put it into her handbag.

'Don't forget, Esme dear – I always know when you're not telling the truth.'

A sigh escaped Esme's lips.

'Stupid, I know, but I've just witnessed a romantic scene at the next table and it brought back memories, that's all.'

Freda clicked her tongue.

'For heaven's sake, Esme, you really must get over Anthony. You're thirty-one. The trouble with you is, you're so damned choosey. In your opinion, no one ever comes even close to him. And that's nonsense. If you're not careful you're going to let an opportunity go by to marry someone else and die a bitter, childless widow.'

Esme flinched. 'Thanks, Freda. I knew I could count on you.' She brushed a stray tear away.

Freda patted her hand. 'No one can deny you went through a

rotten time, but you can't keep harking back to the past.' She took a puff of her cigarette. 'You still have Bill Watson who's mad about you, but no man sticks around forever, just hoping. He'll give up waiting and when he does, I hope you don't regret it.'

Esme raised her eyes to Freda, imploring her to understand.

'I shan't regret anything,' she said. 'He's a very decent man, but I don't feel the same about him.'

'What's wrong with him? He has his own dental practice, owns his own house and could support you in a style I'm sure you'd soon enjoy becoming accustomed to. I doubt you'll do better.' Freda paused for breath.

'He can be stinking rich for all I care,' Esme said, realising her sister would never understand her. 'And besides, I don't find him in the least attractive.'

'Why not? He hasn't run to fat, he's kept his hair and I presume his own teeth – if not, he ought to, being a dentist,' she finished with a chuckle.

'He's too old, for a start.'

'Not too old to have babies.' Freda gave a knowing grin. 'But *you're* getting close to an age where it becomes more difficult, if not inadvisable. Look what happened—'

No, don't bring that up . . .

'Freda,' Esme interrupted, 'please stop lecturing me. You might be ten years older, but it doesn't give you the right to tell me what I should and shouldn't do, and definitely not who I should marry.' She wouldn't tell Freda she'd already said goodbye to Bill or her sister would never stop reprimanding her. She drained her cup. 'Let's change the subject. Tell me what my nephews have been up to.'

A waitress brought them a pot of freshly brewed tea and the two women chatted for a few minutes about Freda's boys, Felix, at seventeen, and Bobby three years younger.

'They're doing well at school and thank goodness the war should be over before Felix is called up.' Freda tapped the end of her cigarette into the silver ashtray. 'He's such a baby.'

'Well, I hope he doesn't have to go, but the way it's dragging on . . .' Esme trailed off. She didn't want to alarm her sister.

'I don't want to think about it.' Freda's pale blue eyes gazed at Esme. 'How's the job going in that fusty, dusty place you work?'

'That fusty, dusty place, as you call it, is where I'm happiest. I love helping people choose the right books – they're mostly all women who want an escape from all the bad news and worrying about feeding their children.'

'But it's not the place to meet eligible men,' Freda said firmly. 'Any man worth a second glance is not going to spend time mooching round a library, for goodness' sake.'

'Freda, can't you understand? I don't *want* to meet an eligible man. I'm happy as I am.'

'Then why did you go all soppy over that interlude with the romantic couple just before I came?' Freda demanded.

'Just nostalgia. Nothing to do with the present.' Her sister was well meaning, but Esme was desperate to stop her from harping on about marriage. She drew in a breath. 'Anyway, how was Dad?'

'Hmm. I think he's getting more than he'd bargained for with Muriel when he married her,' Freda said. 'Mind you, I only stayed last night – I clash too often with her – so I'm going back to Reading when I leave you.' She looked at her watch. 'I must rush, dear, so I can catch the 3.35.' She stubbed out her second cigarette and bent to kiss Esme's cheek. 'Why not give Bill a chance?' She patted Esme's arm.

'Say hello to Kenneth and the boys,' Esme said, ignoring her sister's last question, but Freda had already given an airy wave and whirled off in a flurry of smoke and perfume.

It was just as well she didn't see her sister more than once a month, Esme thought, as she briskly covered the short distance to the library. Her sister had always been bossy but really, sometimes she went too far. Esme knew it was mostly due to Freda having to step in as the role of mother when their own mother had died far too early from an aggressive cancer. Esme had barely been six. But at least Freda had escaped a year later when Dad had hired Muriel as his housekeeper.

Rebuilding was already in progress in one of the nearby streets after the destruction of a ruthless attack Bath had endured in April. It had come completely out of the blue, because the city authorities had thought Bristol, being a port, would be the target. But apparently, Göring had ordered the Luftwaffe to bomb the cathedral cities by following the Baedeker tour-guide series for German tourists. Bath was the first to be chosen. Horrifyingly, they had managed to destroy nearly two thousand buildings in two nights.

As Esme approached the Bath Lending Library building, her heart lifted as it always did. How she loved the Doric columns forming an exterior colonnade, the beautiful Regency windows, the lofty interior ceilings and the shelves brimming with books on every possible subject, together with a good selection of escapist fiction that she'd mentioned to Freda. They were probably more vital than the non-fiction, as at least those with a happy ending might give a boost to people's morale in this terrible war. No, the library with all its characters coming in and out was anything but dull and had saved her sanity when Anthony had died.

In a lighter mood, she walked through the grand entrance. Miss Lewis looked up from the counter.

'Ah, there you are, my dear. When you've taken your coat off, I'll go for my break.'

'Yes, of course.'

The staff were supposed to clear their breaks with Esme, the assistant librarian, but Miss Lewis had been there far too long to worry about such niceties. It was much more the other way round. Esme gave a wry smile as she removed her coat and hung it in the cupboard in the back room.

'Have you been busy?' she asked when she came back.

'Varied.' Miss Lewis bent her head to retrieve her bag from under the counter. 'I'll be off then.' She was about to open the door when she looked round. 'Oh, I nearly forgot – Mr Greenwood asked me to send you in when I'm back.'

Esme raised her eyebrows. 'Any idea what it's about?'

'None.' Miss Lewis turned to go. 'But he looked serious.'

She could have told Miss Lewis that Mr Greenwood's looking-serious expression was fairly normal. Well, Esme would know what it was soon enough. Maybe it was to do with Penny Baker, who wasn't working out as a trainee library assistant quite so well as expected. But Esme was sure that with a little more guidance, Penny would blossom in time. Anyway, she'd be willing to give the girl a fair chance.

The next hour was taken up with several people taking advantage of their lunchtime to bring back and borrow books.

'Do you have the latest Agatha Christie?' Mrs Bolt, one of Esme's favourite ladies, tottered in, leaning on her walking stick. 'It's about some pigs.'

Esme chuckled. 'That would be *Five Little Pigs*.'

'Yes – that's what I said.'

'I'm afraid it's out and there's a waiting list.' She looked at Mrs Bolt's crestfallen expression. 'But I'll add your name to it,' she quickly added.

'Thank you, dear.'

'May I help with anything else? There are plenty of other murder mysteries on the shelves.'

'No, dear. I'll just read an old one of hers over again. My memory is so bad it will be just as fresh as the first time – and the second!' Mrs Bolt smiled, showing nicotine-stained teeth, and limped towards the door, almost bumping into Miss Lewis.

'Right, Mrs Donaldson, you'd better go and see what His Nibs wants.'

Esme knocked on the door marked PRIVATE. Mr Greenwood was not a man who liked interruptions from the public and had therefore removed the brass plaque: Librarian. He'd only been here a few months but had already made changes – and not always for the better, Esme decided.

'Enter!'

She opened the door to be greeted by a barrage of smoke. Mr Greenwood was sitting behind his desk smoking, an unlit cigarette perched on the side of the ashtray ready to be the next one lit when this one was stubbed out.

Esme cleared her throat.

'I believe you sent for me, Mr Greenwood.'

'Yes.' He didn't catch her eye. 'Please take a seat, Mrs Donaldson.'

For the first time, Esme felt a flicker of unease. She shook herself. She was imagining things.

'I expect you want to know why I've called you in,' he said, stating the obvious, 'so I'll be perfectly direct.' She waited. 'I need to make a change to the staff.'

With relief, Esme said, 'You're probably thinking of Penny, but I'm sure with a little more time—'

'No, it's not Penny I'm concerned with – it's someone more senior.'

'Surely not Miss Lewis. The library couldn't function without her.'

Mr Greenwood peered over the top of his spectacles.

'Not Miss Lewis, I'm afraid, Mrs Donaldson. I am forced to give *you* notice.'

Esme's stomach squeezed.

'B-but why?'

'We can't afford you. It's not what I want, it's what the war has dictated. I'll need someone – two more even – but as volunteers to work on the counter. So they'll have to be financially independent and unless I'm wrong,' he regarded her, 'you are not financially independent.'

'No, I'm not.' Esme's voice was almost inaudible. Then she pulled herself up and this time her voice was firm. She looked him squarely in the eye. 'But there *must* be another way. Maybe I could work for a lower salary. It would be difficult, but I'm willing to take a reduction.'

Mr Greenwood shook his head. 'It's a generous thought, but it won't be nearly enough. The council have directed me to cut more corners.' This time he looked straight at her. 'You're a good worker, Mrs Donaldson, and I'll be pleased to give you an excellent reference, but until then I'm afraid that this Saturday will have to be your last day. Anything beyond that would have to be on a voluntary basis.' He drew in a final puff of his cigarette and tossed the end into the ashtray. 'However, I hope to see you from time to time when you come in to borrow a book.'

Esme rose to her feet.

'You might not know this, Mr Greenwood, but I've been here two years and it was the library that saved my sanity when my husband suddenly died and I was distraught. It's my whole life now.'

'I'm really sorry, Mrs Donaldson.' He stood to let her out.

She looked round the library numbly. People were browsing on the shelves just as normal, but it wasn't normal anymore. Well, she must leave with dignity. It wasn't as though she'd done anything wrong. It was simply economics – directly caused by that damnable, hate-ridden little Austrian, Herr Hitler, with his nasty black square of a moustache.

* * *

'Mr Greenwood should have got rid of me instead,' Miss Lewis said, when Esme told her the news. 'I'm older than you and I've got a bit of savings.' She peered at Esme myopically through her glasses. 'I daresay you rely on your wages.'

It was true. Because Anthony's death was not attributable to the war, her widow's pension was only a fraction of his wages. She tried to save, but it had been difficult to manage on the two pounds ten a week she'd ended up with from the library and pay the rent and food and bus fares. And that wasn't even counting a visit to the cinema or a pair of lisle stockings now and again.

Miss Lewis broke into her thoughts. 'Have you any idea where you might try?'

'Not really. But I'll get the *Chronicle* and see if there's anything.'

A middle-aged, harassed-looking woman came to the counter and put two books down. Miss Lewis stamped them and handed them back with a 'Thank you, Mrs Robbins,' then turned to Esme. 'Try *The Lady* magazine. They have pages of vacant situations – and I'm sure Mr Greenwood will be only too pleased to give you an excellent reference.'

Chapter Two

That evening, Esme opened the door of the large Victorian semi-detached house where she lived. Thoroughly dispirited, she trudged down the long hallway which led to a steep flight of stairs. Tiredly, she mounted them and unlocked the door to her small flat, one of several squeezed into the imposing house. It had been convenient for her work at the library, but now no longer.

A chill met her even though it was still warm outside. She closed the door behind her and curled up in her most comfortable chair – one she'd bought in a second-hand furniture shop for a few shillings. She sat there thinking, her mind in a muddle, trying to find a solution. If the library in Bath was having to pull in its horns, then she probably wouldn't have much luck anywhere else. And besides, she didn't want to move. She loved the city and all it had to offer. Except for the first few weeks after war was declared, the cinemas and theatres remained open. And in Bath there was always something on – a concert, an art exhibition, a lecture. But how could she stay in her flat? She had the rent to pay. It was reasonable at fifteen shillings a week but not if there was no money coming in.

I don't know what to do or where to go, and who would need a librarian in wartime anyway? After all, it's not considered a vital service for the wartime effort so other libraries are probably cutting down on their staff to allow them to go off and fight. The councils might not have the means to keep funding them when everything is focused on beating the enemy.

An overwhelming sense of helplessness swept over her. She put her hands to her head and sobbed her eyes out, thankful no one was around to stare at her and ply her with questions. After a few minutes she became furious with herself for breaking down the second time in two hours. She wiped her tears on the back of her hand and sniffing, she reached down for her handbag to pull out a handkerchief. It was twice the size of hers. Where . . . ? Then she remembered. That man. He hadn't spoken a word but had put a comforting hand on her shoulder and made her take his handkerchief. Turning the piece of white cotton over, she saw embroidered in blue: JBP. Would that be James Bartholomew Palmer – John Benjamin Pattison – Jack . . .

Stop this! You're being perfectly ridiculous trying to think what his initials stand for.

After all, she was never going to cross paths with him again. But it had been such a thoughtful gesture. She gave a wan smile. There were still some decent people in the world. She'd go and make herself a cup of tea and have those two strips of KitKat she'd saved for a special occasion. Well, she'd make this next change in her life a special occasion. And first thing was to put the kettle on. There'd be no opportunity to look for another job until Monday.

As it was, Saturday at the library was much busier than usual and she had no time to think about anything except helping people choose their books, putting the ones that had just been returned on the correct shelves, cataloguing some new reference books the family of a book collector who had just died had given them, and generally tidying up the files and other paperwork. There had been two difficult borrowers who'd become irritable when the books they'd asked to be reserved hadn't come in yet, and an infant who wouldn't stop crying, but mostly people were pleasant and some very grateful.

'I like a good murder,' an old lady with a heavily wrinkled face told her. 'When you live alone it takes your mind off the bombing.'

Esme hid a smile at the lack of irony in the old lady's remark.

At ten minutes to five, she emptied the wastepaper basket and made sure everywhere was neat and tidy. In the back office, she washed up the cups and saucers in the sink and wiped over the worktop. With a last look round, she knocked on Mr Greenwood's office.

'Mr Greenwood, I've left everything ship-shape, so I've just come to collect my pay packet and say goodbye.' She paused. 'I've enjoyed my time here very much.'

Mr Greenwood looked up, barely meeting her eye. She guessed he felt awkward. He opened the middle drawer of his desk and pulled out a small brown envelope.

'I've put a pound extra in from my own pocket . . . and this.' He handed her the envelope and a larger white one. 'That's your reference,' he said. 'You've been a good worker and I'm really sorry to lose you.'

She gulped. 'I'm sorry, too.' She made him catch her eye. 'Well, I'll be going then.'

He nodded. 'Good luck, Mrs Donaldson.'

Tears pricking at the back of her eyes, she quickly left his office. Outside, she drew in lungfuls of air, trying to calm herself. She'd loved her job. And Mr Greenwood wasn't a bad boss. But it was Miss Lewis whom she'd miss most. Miss Lewis who had shown her how a library works – the correct way to do the cataloguing, the gaps the library needed to fill, particular subjects and favourite authors, reserving books from other libraries for borrowers' requests – oh, and so many other little details that kept the library updated and running smoothly. If it hadn't been for Miss Lewis giving her all the training and then encouraging her to put her name forward to Mr Greenwood for the position of Assistant Librarian – a promotion Miss Lewis assured her she didn't want herself – Esme would never have achieved the title.

And now it had ended. Swallowing hard, Esme began the walk back to the flat. She wouldn't be able to call it home for much longer.

Sunday dragged. She filled the time with reading, cleaning the flat, washing her smalls and making a simple supper, all the while thinking that surely she'd find a suitable job this coming week. If only she could join one of the forces and do her bit for the war effort, but her heart, already scarred as the result of suffering from rheumatic fever as a child, had never recovered since she'd been caught up in a terrible bombing raid in the London Blitz, two years before. It had nearly taken her life. In truth, it had taken so much more. And even if she could pass a medical, joining up might present her with another problem – they could transfer her miles away, even as far as Scotland. Her father was getting noticeably worse by the month though he would never admit it and Muriel was not a natural nurse. Esme grimaced, remembering only too well how her stepmother had treated her when she was only seven and the first signs of the disease had appeared, admonishing her for being lazy when the little girl had complained of tiredness.

The following morning, Esme dressed carefully. She chose a navy straight skirt and a cream, short-sleeved, buttoned-through overblouse, its narrow belt emphasising her neat waistline and the scalloped collar deep enough to show the gold chain of her locket. After putting on a jaunty straw hat edged with a bright pink ruffle and navy court shoes, she took a last glance in the mirror.

She nodded, satisfied she gave a good impression to potential employers that she was serious about her search for the right job, but not look so dull that she'd be disregarded.

The weather was still warm, but today was heavily overcast. Just like her mood, Esme thought grimly, as she walked by the half-dozen shops that still had their windows boarded up from the Luftwaffe's appearance in the spring. The one on the end had taken the full brunt, leaving it simply a shell of its original structure. Thank heavens most of the bombs had narrowly missed the very heart of the city where the people feared the ancient Roman baths – some two thousand years old – would be obliterated in seconds. She scolded herself. If she went looking for a job with that despondent attitude, she wouldn't get very far.

'Sorry, miss, we're not hiring staff at the moment,' the owner of the local bookshop told her that morning when the shop hadn't long opened. 'Why don't you try the library? They have notices for people wanting jobs and leaflets with all sorts of information. You could join up.' He gave her an approving look. 'You'd look good in uniform, if I may say so.'

It was no use explaining the library was the last place she wanted to visit in order to gather information – at least at the moment. Maybe when it wasn't quite so raw . . .

'Thank you, I'll do that,' was all she said.

She'd pick up a copy of the *Bath Chronicle* having heard that sometimes newspapers advertised various jobs available and take the advice of Miss Lewis about looking in *The Lady* as well. With any luck, something might come of it.

With the two publications folded into her shopping bag, Esme decided she couldn't bear the thought of going back to her empty flat for lunch. She knew it was an extravagance, but she had a strong urge to be among people. On impulse, she darted into her favourite café, the Gryphon, modelled on a Lyons Corner House in London. The place was packed. If she could find a vacant seat, it would be just what she needed – people chattering away to their neighbours, filling the space with noise as they enjoyed their lunch break. She spotted a table on the far side with only one other diner, a young woman smartly dressed in a maroon-and-white suit topped by a bright yellow hat angled precariously on the side of her head. She was smoking and reading what looked like a letter, but as Esme approached her, the woman viciously stubbed out the cigarette. There was something about her manner that troubled Esme, who stopped, hesitating. Had the letter brought bad news? Too late. The woman had seen her. She looked up and smiled, but Esme detected the trace of tears in deep grey eyes. Best act naturally, she told herself.

'Would you mind if I joined you?'

'Not at all. I feel rather selfish sitting at a table for four, but it was the last one.' Her voice was refined.

'Well, I promise not to disturb you.'

'Don't worry about that.' The woman folded the letter and put it in her bag. 'I'll be glad of the company.' She passed the menu across the table.

Welsh rarebit and a pot of tea at one and tuppence wouldn't break the bank, Esme thought, as she pulled out the magazine and newspaper, putting the *Chronicle* and her handbag on a spare chair. *The Lady* would be easier to read than the unwieldy newspaper. She flipped over the pages. It was an excellent magazine, but she didn't often indulge. Today was different. There were articles on how to bring your hat into fashion by just adding a flower or a feather or a ribbon, 'Make-do and Mend', new ways to cook potatoes, and a fashion page. She'd read them later but turned to the end pages, her eyes skimming the columns of Situations Vacant for anything interesting. One caught her eye – teaching a young handicapped child at home, but it would mean going to Shropshire, and she couldn't do that to her father. She'd have to concede that *The Lady* wasn't the best place to look for a job unless you had no encumbrances and could travel anywhere in the British Isles.

'May I be very rude and ask if you're looking for a job?' the woman opposite broke into her thoughts.

Esme looked up and forced a smile. There was something about the woman's face that looked familiar.

'Even from upside down, I can see you're reading the Sits Vac in *The Lady*,' the woman continued, 'which is a good place to look if you don't mind going anywhere in the country.'

'That's just what I was thinking,' Esme said. 'The trouble is, I love living in Bath with all its history and architecture . . . and it's near my family home.'

'I'm not far from Bath and agree it's a beautiful city.' The woman paused. 'I'd better introduce myself. I'm Stella Stratten.' She fixed her gaze on Esme. 'And you are . . . ?'

'Esme Donaldson. How do you do?'

'How do you do, Esme Donaldson?' Stella Stratten balanced her cigarette on the ashtray and held out her hand. Esme briefly took it but before she could respond, the woman continued, 'Well, one shouldn't answer that question if one is brought up properly but now we've introduced ourselves, I can say that I don't do very well.'

'Oh, dear, I'm sorry.'

Stella Stratten flicked a strand of blonde hair off her face. 'I'm sure you don't want to hear about my woes – you've probably got enough of your own if you're looking for work.'

'What can I get for you, miss?'

Esme glanced up at the waitress who had just appeared. 'Welsh rarebit and a pot of tea, please,' she said, then caught the eye of the woman opposite. 'Are you having anything?'

'No. I'll have the bill, please.' Stella Stratten returned her attention to Esme. 'I was about to ask where I might have seen you before.'

'I was going to ask you the same question,' Esme said. 'I work . . . or I *used* to work,' she corrected herself, 'in the library. I was the Assistant Librarian.' The title stuck in her throat. 'Are you one of our members?'

'Yes, I am. Of course – that's where I've seen you. I didn't think I could mistake that lovely chestnut hair of yours. And the way you always wear it in a perfect victory roll.' Stella Stratten looked thoughtful for a few moments. 'I haven't been in lately because I've not been able to concentrate much on reading these days.' She caught Esme's eye. 'Assistant Librarian? You're probably like hairdressers – people tell you all sorts of secrets.'

'Not really.' Esme couldn't help smiling at the young woman's blunt manner. 'You're not allowed to speak in libraries unless very quietly and it has to do with books.' She paused. 'Though it doesn't always work and I do get to know people's tastes quite well after a while.'

'Yes, I imagine you do.' The woman frowned. 'So what happened to your job?'

'I was given notice. They're cutting down because of the war.' Esme tried to keep the bitterness from her tone.

'That's too bad.' She threw Esme a sympathetic glance. 'Isn't this war bloody awful?'

Esme was taken aback. She'd heard men swearing plenty of times but coming from such a sophisticated-looking woman was quite startling.

'It's certainly dragging on longer than I thought it would,' she said.

More people were coming into the café. The waitress brought Esme's tea and cheese on toast and popped a bill in front of the young woman who dropped a shilling and a sixpenny piece in the saucer. A waitress came over immediately and cleared her dirty crockery.

'What are you looking for exactly?' Stella Stratten said, leaning towards Esme.

'Well, I doubt I'll get another job in a library,' Esme said, 'and I really love that work. The thing is, I don't want to move too far away as I have an elderly father who's not in the best of health.'

'Oh, I'm sorry to hear that.'

'Do you have parents nearby?'

'No. My parents were killed in a road accident five years ago.'

'Oh, dear. How awful for you.'

Miss Stratten nodded. 'It wasn't easy. But you have to get on with your life. I was only twenty-one. Just got the key of the door, as they say. It was grim but the war makes you realise how precious life is and that you have to make the most of every day.'

'It certainly does.' Esme hesitated. She wondered if Miss Stratten was in the forces. 'Do you do any kind of war work?'

Stella Stratten's fair eyebrows pulled together in a deep frown. 'I did, but I've just been offered a job as a switchboard operator.'

She gave a smile that didn't reach her eyes. As though it wasn't really what she wanted, Esme thought.

'Somehow I don't see you as a switchboard operator,' Esme blurted.

'No? Well, that's what I'll be. It's a complete change from what I *was* doing . . . nursing.'

So that explained it. She'd been in a reserved occupation. But had something gone wrong that had made her leave? Looking across at Miss Stratten, Esme saw her mouth tighten as though she wasn't going to elaborate.

'Well, you certainly have the right accent for it.' She smiled, trying to soften the sudden tenseness, then added, 'Oh, dear, I hope that didn't sound ill-mannered, Miss Stratten.'

This time Stella Stratten chuckled. 'Not in the least – and do call me Stella.'

'Well, then, Stella, I wish you luck in your new job.'

'Thank you. You, too, Esme.' Stella took her cigarette from the silver holder and stubbed it into the ashtray. 'Look, why don't we keep in touch. I know quite a few influential people so I'll look out for anything interesting that comes my way that I think you might like.'

'That's most kind,' Esme said. 'And I'd like to stay in touch.'

'Here's my card.' Stella sprang to her feet and dropped a white card with black lettering by Esme's plate. 'Must fly. Don't forget – keep in touch – I mean it. I might be able to help.'

She was gone. Esme watched her leave. She smiled. Stella Stratten was certainly a force to be reckoned with. Without looking at Stella's card, she slipped it into her handbag. Quickly, she paid her bill, then realised she'd left the *Chronicle* on the seat and turned back to pick it up. She'd scour through the newspaper that evening. Until then, she'd promised to see her father this afternoon. Then she pulled a face. That would include having to speak to Muriel.

Chapter Three

Muriel had arrived at the house nearly a year after Esme's mother died, to start work as a housekeeper. A year later, she and her father had married. Esme had never recovered from the shock of seeing another woman in place of her beloved mother whose image had gradually become more blurred over the passing years, and to Muriel's annoyance, she could never bring herself to call Muriel 'Mummy' or even 'Mother'. No amount of Muriel's insisting would change her mind. Freda only ever used the term 'stepmother' on rare occasions when she had to introduce her to someone and always managed to coat the word with derision. When Esme turned thirteen, she starting doing the same.

Muriel had lost her fiancé in the Great War and at twenty-five, with no widow's pension and no qualifications, she'd had to find domestic work. Her position in Bath as a live-in, all found, housekeeper/surrogate mother to two girls was paid better than most jobs going at the time. Now approaching fifty, and when in a pleasant mood, she was a good-looking woman, but more often her features were drawn, ready to pounce whenever something or someone didn't suit her. No one ever measured up to what she thought they should or should not do. Worse, the new stepmother had been jealous from the start of the attention Bernard Grant had given his two daughters. She'd tried to set the sisters against one another but instead it had strengthened their bond, even though they were so unalike in character and so far apart in age. Furthermore, Muriel never stopped letting Bernard know what a disappointment he was, buried in his newspapers and history books and never giving her any attention. It was the one thing she couldn't control. Esme often wondered why her father had married her.

'To look after you girls,' her father had answered when she had him on his own for once after he'd helped her move into her flat.

'Freda didn't need any looking after,' Esme said. 'She'd taken the place of Mum by then. And when Muriel came, all on her best behaviour, Freda decided after a few months she could leave me in safe hands.' Esme looked directly at him. 'I remember being terribly upset that I only saw her occasionally after that, but when I was older I realised she had to live her own life.'

'Well, *you* needed someone.' Her father lit a cigarette. 'And Muriel was the best of the women who answered the advertisement.'

'But that was for a *housekeeper*,' Esme argued. 'You didn't have to *marry* her.'

'I felt I did.' Her father went quiet for several moments. Finally, he said, 'It was her suggestion. She said you, especially, would feel more secure because you were still only seven.'

Yes, Dad, she would want you to marry her, but not because of me. It would be for her own financial security.

But she couldn't tell him that.

'And you admit she's looked after you – and fed us well.'

Esme sighed. 'Yes, she's a good cook. But her manner changed as soon as she got a ring on her finger.'

Her father drew his brows together. 'I admit she can be a bit forceful. I expect it's because she never had children of her own and doesn't always quite know how to handle them.'

Esme grimaced. 'Well, at least she's saved some poor little child from suffering the same fate as me.'

'Look, Esme, it's no use going over old ground. She's not a bad sort. And you've now got your own life to lead.'

'But I worry about you.'

He looked surprised. 'Well, don't. She keeps me fed and watered.' He hesitated as though wondering whether to say more. 'You know that no one will ever take the place of your mother, don't you?'

'Yes, Dad,' she said softly, going over to kiss his forehead. 'I know.' She paused. 'I'm sorry.'

'I am, too,' he said gruffly. 'You don't know how much.'

Esme knocked on the door of her old home, irritated not for the first time that Muriel had insisted she give up her key when she moved into her flat. Her excuse was that if the flat got burgled and they found her previous address, it was only one step away from their house being burgled as well. Esme had been too flabbergasted to argue, though she noted that Freda had refused point-blank to give up hers, even though she now lived miles away in Reading.

As usual, Muriel opened the door. She gave a twist of a smile.

'Oh, Esme. Come in. Bernard's in the sitting room . . . with his newspaper,' she added pointedly. 'I'll make some tea for us.'

'How is he?' Esme said as she stepped into the kitchen.

'Hmm. Maybe it's best for you to judge.'

Her father's eyes lit up the instant he saw his daughter. He folded his newspaper.

'Hello, love. You're earlier than I expected. Come over here where I can see you.'

She dodged between the leather pouffe, two mismatching stools, and a low table piled with paperwork.

'Hello, Dad. How've you been?' She bent to kiss his cheek, feeling guilty that she hadn't been to visit him for a week as she sat down in one of the nearby armchairs.

'About the same.'

'Have you been to the doctor?'

'What's the point? He'll only say it's my age.'

'What, sixty-nine? Nonsense.' She looked at him directly. 'I wish you'd go and see him.'

'I will if it gets worse.'

'The news was bad today,' he said, glancing at the newspaper still on his lap.

'Oh no. What was it?'

'The *Laconia* – one of our passenger ships in the Atlantic. A U-boat sunk it.'

'Oh no. How dreadful. How many were on board?'

'Getting on for three thousand,' he said. 'A mixture of civilians and soldiers and hundreds of Italian POWs. The captain of the U-boat went to their rescue and saved something like a thousand passengers, though they'll *all* be POWs by now.' He shook his head. 'Frightful business.'

Esme tried to imagine injured people fighting for their lives, then giving up and drowning in freezing cold water. She shuddered.

Muriel came into the room with a tea tray. She pushed aside a pile of papers on the low table using the tray as a shovel. Some of the papers fell off the end, but even when she'd set the tray down, she didn't bother to pick them up. She poured out three cups of tea and placed one on a saucer and handed it to Bernard.

Esme saw his hand tremble as he took the tea, making some of the liquid slop into the saucer. No, she couldn't suddenly leave Bath to go miles away and hardly ever see him. She had to find a job close by so she could call in frequently to make sure Muriel was looking after him properly. Her father's illness probably stemmed from shell shock in the Great War. And now there they were, right in the middle of *another* world war. It didn't seem possible.

Her father took a swallow of tea and pulled a face.

'There's no sugar.'

'There's half a teaspoon,' Muriel shot back. 'I'm trying to wean you off it – it's difficult enough to make a cake now and again which you seem to enjoy, what with all the sugar and butter and egg rationing. The least you can do is cut down in your tea.'

'It just doesn't taste the same, dear.' He looked at her. 'Do we have enough supper for Esme to stay?'

Esme watched as Muriel hesitated. 'I daresay I could eke it out.'

'Oh, please don't bother,' she said quickly, not missing her stepmother's expression of relief. 'I have some leftovers at home.'

She didn't, but she wasn't prepared to take any portion away from her father. He was thin enough as it was. The conversation became stilted with Muriel's presence and Esme was sure her father felt it, too. She hung on for another half hour and then rose.

'I'd better be going.'

'Why were you so early today?' her father asked suddenly. 'You don't normally get here until half past five.' He looked straight at her. 'Is everything all right at the library?'

Esme startled. He was sometimes quite intuitive. She hadn't wanted to mention anything until she was offered another job, but the way he was staring at her, she had to placate him somehow.

'Oh, they let me off a bit earlier today as I've worked a few hours extra this week.'

That bit was true, at least.

Her father nodded. ''Long as you're all right.' He stood up. 'I'll come and see you out.'

'Oh, don't bother, Dad. I can see myself out.' She paused and smiled. 'I did live here once upon a time, remember?'

'Yes, I remember,' he said quietly. Then stumbling, he fell back into his chair.

She kissed him goodbye and turned to Muriel. This was always the embarrassing bit because she couldn't bring herself to kiss her stepmother. She couldn't remember ever kissing her when she was a little girl except when her father had made her.

'Goodbye, Muriel. Look after Dad, won't you?' Then she hastily added, 'And yourself, of course.'

Muriel gave a tight smile and nodded.

Esme didn't have long to wait at the bus stop. Sighing, she chose a seat downstairs as it was only a few stops. The bus was already crowded but she squeezed next to a plump lady with a bulky shopping basket on her lap. Every time the bus went round a corner, the lady leaned right in, the wicker of her basket pressing into Esme's side.

Puffing out her cheeks with relief that she was home, Esme plonked her handbag on the kitchen chair and hung up her jacket. Home. But it wasn't going to be home for much longer. If she'd mentioned losing her job to her dad and Muriel, he would have immediately said she could come back and live with them until she found something. She could just picture Muriel's expression of undisguised displeasure.

She opened a cupboard and peered in. There wasn't much food there. Saturday had been her last payday and she'd have to think very carefully how to spend it. How she would have loved a fried egg. But with the rationing, she was only allowed one egg a week and she'd eaten it on the first day she'd bought it. From her two ounces of cheese, carefully weighed by the greengrocer, she was left with a pathetic thimble-sized piece – even melted on toast it wasn't nearly enough to be a satisfying supper.

In the end, she fried a thick slice of Spam and ate it with two small boiled potatoes. As she sat down to eat the unappetising meal, her eye fell on the *Chronicle*. The front page was the usual war stuff. She couldn't bring herself to read it at this moment. Totally dispirited, she turned the pages, only reading the headlines until she came to the Situations Vacant. But to her disappointment, there were only three local jobs for women – two in catering and the third looking after eight-month-old twins while the parents worked.

She swallowed hard. Two babies. No. She couldn't look after babies – not when she'd lost her own precious one.

Thoroughly miserable, Esme finished the meagre meal and crunching an apple, she rose to switch on the wireless. Until she'd heard about the *Laconia* this afternoon, the news had been a little better lately but there was nothing more to raise her spirits. Even the dance music that followed failed to inspire her.

Quite out of the blue, the image of Stella Stratten floated in front of her. What an attractive woman she was, in looks and personality, although it was still surprising that she'd accepted what sounded like a mundane job after working in a hospital. Yet Esme had rather taken to Stella, who'd insisted she keep in touch. Esme drew her mouth in a determined line. Well, she'd do just that. In fact, she'd write the letter now so at least Stella would know where to contact her if anything turned up.

She found the card tucked into her handbag and read it for the first time. And gasped.

Stella Stratten
Redcliffe Manor
Bath

Redcliffe Manor! It was such a grand house it didn't even need the village it stood in to be included in the address. She recalled how Stella spoke so beautifully, so she was obviously part of the family.

Esme had cycled past the wrought-iron gates numerous

times, admiring the vast mansion. She'd noticed a lot of building going on there since the beginning of the year, judging by all the workmen and lorries delivering construction materials. The last time she'd noticed several furniture vans, one behind the other. Strange that a new building was going up when Redcliffe Manor was so enormous and there was a war on, although there was no sign of any extension at the front or side. They must be extending round the back where there'd be a wonderful view over all their magnificent grounds. She'd heard that quite a number of country estates had been requisitioned by the government since the war started and she wondered if this was what was happening at Redcliffe Manor.

She took her fountain pen and notepaper and wrote her address at the top, then began:

Dear Stella,

It was very nice to meet you today and I was sorry we didn't have longer to chat. I hope you don't mind my writing so soon, but you hinted that you might possibly come across a position that would suit me and I didn't want to waste a moment.

As I said, I have two years' library experience in the Bath Lending Library and was promoted to Assistant Librarian in May. I love the work but am willing to try anything so long as it stretches my brain. I speak passably good French but only a smattering of Italian that I've picked up in Renaissance history. I get on well with most people (good training in the library!) and like being busy.

If you happen to come across anything which you think I might be interested in, I'd be very grateful if you could write to the address above. I will have to give up the flat at the end of the month and go back to live with my father and stepmother and they are on the phone – Bath 315, so you could try me there from the beginning of October. I'll send you their address if I haven't heard from you. In the meantime, if I find something suitable, I will, of course, let you know immediately.

I can't thank you enough for your offer of help.
Yours sincerely,
Esme Donaldson

Esme read over the letter and hoped Stella would realise she was keen. As for now, she needed to carry on looking for a job herself.

Chapter Four

A week passed and Esme heard nothing back from Stella. Surprised and a little disappointed, she told herself it had merely been a pleasant chance meeting and that she shouldn't expect too much of people. These days everyone had so many problems to cope with. But her evenings were long and lonely because the end of the month was drawing near and she still hadn't told her father and Muriel she'd lost her job. She'd hoped she could find something else before saying anything to them and have Muriel chivvying for her to take anything . . . *anything* to stop her from having to go back home to live. The truth was that Esme couldn't stand the idea any more than Muriel would.

Esme had tried in the other two bookshops to no avail, and also Clarks shoe shop, the most popular one of the three in Bath, even though the window displayed only a handful of different designs.

'Footwear is more difficult to come by than clothing,' so the manager had told her, as he explained that they weren't busy enough to warrant another assistant. She'd even asked in the Pump Room if they needed another waitress. The manageress, a tall bony woman, had looked down her long thin nose at her.

'What experience have you?' she demanded.

'Well, I haven't done this kind of work before,' Esme said, 'but

I have a good memory for faces and I'm sure I could pick it up easily.'

'Hmm.' The woman took a step closer and scrutinised her. 'Didn't you used to work in the library?'

Oh dear. Was she going to combat this remark every time she applied for a job?

'Yes, but the council has had to cut corners, so I was given notice.'

'Hmm,' the woman grunted again. 'We have a certain class of customers in here, Mrs Donaldson, and they expect to be waited on by professionals. We're extremely busy every day, and I haven't time for anyone to train you. What's more, I'm sure if something you really like the look of turned up, you'd be handing in *your* notice.' She gave Esme a piercing look. 'Isn't that true?'

It was no use pretending she'd always wanted to be a waitress. The woman was absolutely right in her assessment. All Esme could do was thank her for her time.

Today, she'd come home for a jam sandwich at half past two. It would hold her until supper time. This weekend she would have to tell her landlord she was leaving and start packing. She swallowed hard as she looked round what had been her little home. Her salvation. She wiped the crumbs from her mouth and at that moment she heard the rattle of the letter box.

If there's anything for me, don't let it be a bill.

She trudged downstairs to the communal hall, then over to the long table against the wall where the residents found their post. One thick creamy-white envelope caught her eye and she picked it up. Yes, there was her name and address written in beautiful italic writing. She took it back upstairs and sat on the sofa and opened it, removing the matching sheet of paper. Her eyes darted to the signature and she was gratified to see that it was indeed from Stella.

14th September 1942

Dear Esme,

By pure chance your letter came at just the right time. I've made some enquiries and here's the news which I hope very much will interest you. Redcliffe Manor requires a librarian!!! Charlie, who's been doing the job up to now, though not qualified has a great knowledge of books and did his best but he's gone off to fight the Boche. The position would be perfect for you because the family would give you your own quarters to go with it. Yes, I know what you're thinking – that you're not a fully-fledged librarian, but there can't be that wide a gap between the two posts. That said, I took the liberty of telling Sir Giles Carmichael, the owner, a little fib – I said you were the librarian at Bath Lending Library. He was most interested and asked me to tell you to come and see him. He can be rather fierce – but on the whole, he's not a bad old stick.

You need to write to him without mulling over. If you agree on a date, let me know when you're coming and I'll try to make myself available to meet you.

Fingers crossed.

Stella Stratten

P.S. I hope you haven't already moved! If so, hope this gets redirected.

Esme took a deep breath. Stella was presenting her with the most marvellous opportunity, yet in doing so had told the owner an outright lie. Esme would either have to uphold the lie or say that Stella must have misheard, which as well as being untrue, would be totally unfair, especially as her new acquaintance was only trying to do her a favour by putting her in a good light.

By the following morning, Esme still hadn't made up her mind if she should contact Sir Giles Carmichael. In the end, she berated herself for being so woolly. She'd write a short note saying she'd be pleased to meet him at his convenience without any mention of library titles and length of service. It was always better to see someone in person when you're telling them something slightly awkward.

She didn't have long to wait. A typed reply came back the following morning asking if she could come for an interview at ten o'clock on Monday 21st September – not long before she'd be moving out of her flat. When she thought about it, she decided to get the move done right away so she was settled and ready for what felt like an important interview that might drastically change her future.

And she still hadn't mentioned anything about coming back home to her father and Muriel. She'd better go and see them right away and break the news.

'Wonderful news, love,' her father said, giving her a hug. 'And stay as long as you like.'

To Esme's surprise, Muriel didn't say much. She just shrugged and said she'd have to get the guest room prepared.

That's my old room. Is that what I am now – a mere guest?

But all she said was, 'There's no need for you to be put out so I'll freshen it up when I arrive.'

'If you insist,' Muriel said stiffly. 'The bed's made up but the room will need dusting and sweeping.

At least Dad's delighted I'm coming home for a while.

* * *

On the day Esme planned to move back to her old home, Muriel had made herself scarce.

'She's had to go into town,' her father explained when Esme arrived with her luggage.

She couldn't help an inward sigh of relief. She'd decided to take her suitcase with clothes and toiletries on the bus and then tomorrow, after the interview at Redcliffe Manor, she'd go back to the flat and fill it again with her books and family photographs and come back by taxi. Another phase of her life at an end.

She swallowed. She mustn't get maudlin. And any rate, she had an interesting interview to look forward to.

'Have you thought about what you're going to do now?' Bernard said when she'd unpacked the case and come downstairs.

'I have an interview tomorrow at Redcliffe Manor to work in the library.'

Her father whistled a breath. 'My, my. You'll be going up in the world if you land that one.'

'I'm not bothered about going up in the world – I just want to do something interesting, and as I love books, there can be no better place for me than to work with them all around me.'

'No, I suppose not.' Bernard took a few breaths as though he were hesitating. Finally, he said, 'I'm quite glad we have a little time on our own, Esme, as I need to talk to you.'

He looked serious. Esme's heart did a tumble.

'Go on.'

'It's like this.' He leaned back in the armchair and closed his eyes. 'I'm not doing too well at the moment. The doctor is trying different tests, but he thinks I have Parkinson's disease. And it's going to get worse – maybe sooner than I'd like.'

Not Dad . . . please.

He opened his eyes.

'I'd suspected it, even though it was still rather a shock to have it confirmed.'

'And it wasn't anything to do with when you were in the trenches?'

He shook his head. 'There's no telling. But I usually manage to get through those nightmares. This is beyond my control.'

'Oh, Dad.' She rose to her feet and went over to him, putting her arms around his neck. 'What can I do to help?'

'You have enough to do, love. I want you to carry on and enjoy your life. If you do that, you'll make me very happy. And I'm not going to pop off just yet,' he chuckled.

She kissed the top of his head.

'But when I do,' he continued, 'I want you to know about this house. Your mother had a small inheritance from her uncle when he died, and that was enough to put down a deposit. Over the years between having you and Freda, I paid off the mortgage. But when your mother became terminally ill, we decided to put the house in yours and Freda's names but that I could live here as long as I wanted. I think she had a suspicion I might marry again for the sake of you girls . . . and she was right.' He sighed. 'Anyway, when the house is sold, you'll have enough with your half to buy a flat of your own. And all your mother's and my possessions you girls can sort out between you.'

'So is Muriel not down for anything?'

'There's a tidy sum of money put aside for a housekeeper who stays at least ten years. That meant you would have been in your mid-teens and wouldn't need to rely on anyone in the same way. And of course Muriel has been here much longer than that.'

'Have you changed the will at all since then?'

He shook his head.

'Does she know about these terms?'

Her father hesitated. He didn't quite look her in the eye. 'Yes. When we got married, she wanted me to change the will to include her officially with the two of you as beneficiaries of the house, and I'm afraid I led her to believe I had.'

'Dad!'

He had the grace to look a little ashamed.

'I know. But I can't stand any rows with all that I'm trying to cope with. But so long as I know you and Freda will be well taken care of, I can die a happy man.'

'Oh, Dad, don't talk like this.'

'But it'll happen. I'm in for a rocky time.' He sighed. 'But I need to talk to you about Muriel.' He paused. 'I know there's no love lost between you two girls and Muriel, but there's nothing I can do about it . . . and I do understand.' Bernard stopped, this time to light a cigarette. He blew out a stream of smoke, then continued. 'I have to remember that she stepped in when there was no one else. Your sister was still only seventeen and the last thing I wanted was for her to have to take over and look after you. She had her own life to live. But you were such a little mite and I had my job that took me all over the place. Being a journalist was the only way I knew to earn a reasonable living.' He cleared his throat. 'You might not know it, but I was seriously thinking of putting you in an orphanage.'

She sucked in her breath. 'No!'

'I'm sorry, but that's how desperate I was. It was a lifesaver when Muriel answered that advertisement.'

'Well, I suppose I have her to thank for saving me from that horror, at least.'

He nodded. 'Yes.' He cleared his throat again, then drew on his cigarette, inhaling deeply. 'Anyway, I've left her a fair bit of cash, but it's not excessive as most of my earnings after expenses went into the house. But I'm relying on you girls to see that she's all right and has a roof over her head. We don't know how long this war will go on, but I wouldn't rest easy if I thought you'd abandoned her.'

'No, Dad. You know us better than that. We wouldn't.'

'That's all I want to know.' He looked at her. 'You know how much I love you both, don't you?'

'Yes, and we feel the same for you.' She leaned over and kissed his forehead. 'Did you talk to Freda about all this?'

'Not yet. I haven't seen her for nigh on a month. She always has the excuse of the boys. I'd like to see my grandsons more often but—' He broke off.

'I'm sure she'll bring them more regularly now she knows you're so poorly,' Esme said, hoping it would prove to be the truth.

Chapter Five

The mild weather had continued well into September. On the morning of her interview, Esme decided to wear the sand-coloured dress she'd made at the beginning of the war before clothes and fabric rationing were introduced. She was a decent seamstress, but this had been a labour of love with its shirt collar and pleated short sleeves which matched the box-pleated skirt.

She glanced at her watch. Oh dear. She'd spent too long on her hair, trying out a new upswept hairstyle instead of her usual victory roll she liked for work. Still in her brassiere and cami-knickers, she hurriedly added her suspender belt, then rolled up one stocking over her knee to her thigh and hooked it on the belt, twisting round to make sure the seam was straight. *Good.* Swiftly, she began to roll up the other. *Oh no!* The dreaded feel of a ladder began to crawl from the ankle up the side of her leg. It was her last pair of nylons. Freda had given them to her on her birthday in March and she'd kept them all this time for when she needed to look her best.

Furious with herself for not taking more care, she took both stockings off and flung them on the bed. There was only one thing for it. She reached in her small cosmetic bag for her eyebrow pencil and twisting her neck round, she carefully drew a straight line down each calf. When she'd finished, she hurriedly pulled her dress over her head and buttoned it up. To give it the final professional look, she slotted a narrow black patent belt through the waist loops which showed off her figure to perfection. Her best black patent court shoes would complete the outfit. At the last minute she picked up a light jacket. She was ready.

Esme had always cycled for the joy of being out in the air and close to nature, but she didn't want to turn up for an interview with her new hairstyle looking as though she'd been dragged through a hedge backwards. No, the bus wouldn't take more than twenty minutes and she'd catch one in good time to make sure she wasn't late.

The bus turned out to be one of those pulling a trailer with a gas cylinder on the back to save petrol. As it was full downstairs, she grabbed hold of the rail as the bus rattled its way forward and climbed to the upper level where there were two empty adjoining seats at the front. Another jerk and she practically fell into them. As they trundled along, Esme imagined the impending interview. She still hadn't made up her mind whether to come clean and tell Sir Giles Carmichael that she wasn't actually a fully qualified librarian but that she was doing most of the work her old boss had done. But if he asked outright, she'd be forced into the lie. If he didn't ask, she'd always worry that he'd find out later and be furious. Maybe dismiss her from the household. She drew in her lips. That would be too humiliating.

It struck her that she'd never opened the letter of reference Mr Greenwood had given her. Feeling apprehensive about the way her old boss might have worded it, she took the envelope out of her bag.

To Whom It May Concern.

Mrs Donaldson worked at Bath Lending Library from October 1940 to September 1942. She was initially engaged as a library assistant and six months ago was promoted to Assistant Librarian.

I have always found Mrs Donaldson to be an honest worker, diligent and very good with staff and borrowers. I am sure she will do well in whatever capacity you see fit to place her.
Yours faithfully,
C. A. Greenwood

Esme sighed. Her title was there in black and white. The only thing to do was to play the interview by ear and just hope Sir Giles Carmichael wasn't as fierce as Stella had described. And if he didn't ask her for a work reference, then she wouldn't produce it. Still lost in her thoughts, she glanced out of the window, admiring the open green spaces with sheep and cows contentedly grazing. Although she loved the city – and Bath was a very special one – it would be good to get away from all the fumes and give her lungs a chance to breathe in some country air.

There certainly wasn't any sign of country air in the stuffy confines of the bus. Suddenly she wrinkled her nose. What on earth was that smell? It wasn't from the cigarettes where only the upper-level passengers were allowed to smoke. It was something far more onerous. Oh Lord – was it gas?

Surely Hitler hasn't started gassing us.

Why had she been so stupid as to have stopped taking her gas mask with her when she left home just because nearly everyone else did?

She shot up from her seat and turned to face the other passengers.

'Can anyone smell gas?' she bellowed, her finger on the bell, pressing it frantically to stop the bus.

There were shouts of alarm. People began to scramble to their feet to make for the stairs, but the entrance was so narrow they were stumbling over themselves in their panic and were stuck.

'Where's the bleedin' conductor?' one of the passengers called out.

The bus jerked to a screeching halt. She heard the conductor shout to people to leave the bus immediately. Then he yelled up the stairs:

'There's a gas leakage! Put all cigarettes out! Keep calm and come down one at a time!'

Esme felt her throat close up. She grabbed a handkerchief from her bag and held it over her nose as she clutched the handrail down the winding stairs. The driver standing outside took her arm and helped her onto a narrow path at the edge of a field.

'What happened?' a plump woman with a basket on her arm demanded.

'Stand right back, everyone,' the driver ordered, removing his cigarette and stamping it out underneath his shoe. 'There's been a gas leak from the pump which feeds the engine.' He jerked his head to the back of the bus to the trailer holding the gas cylinder. 'I'm afraid this bus is going nowhere.' He looked round. 'Anyone going to West Harptree can walk – it's not more'n a mile away. Those travelling further will have to wait for a substitute bus.'

'How long will that be?' demanded a frazzled-looking woman holding onto a sobbing child.

'However long it takes,' he answered with a cynical smile.

Esme reckoned it could be at least half an hour's walk, as Redcliffe Manor was on the far side of the village. She should be there on time, but she wouldn't feel as composed as she'd been when she'd left home this morning. Glancing down at the handkerchief she'd used against the gas and was still clutching, she noticed again the initials: JBP. Whoever JBP was, his handkerchief had 'saved' her twice already. This was the third time.

Resolutely, she began to walk briskly towards West Harptree, taking in lungfuls of air every few steps. It was further on foot than she'd anticipated and she was conscious her hairpins had begun to loosen in the breeze. She could feel some strands tickling her cheeks. But at least the village was just ahead. She still had a quarter of an hour in hand so she should just make it. She walked past the shops and pubs, relieved to think she knew the way to Redcliffe Manor as it was no use looking for fingerposts nowadays. Country folk were in the habit of changing the direction of the signs or removing them altogether, also many of the names of towns on station platforms – all to confuse the Germans, should they invade. But walking was different from cycling. On her bike, she enjoyed bowling along the narrow country lanes, spotting the different wildflowers depending upon the time of year, but on foot this morning she stumbled more than once. If only she hadn't worn her court shoes. They were quite unsuitable for country walks and without stockings she could feel a tightness at the side of her toes in the right-hand shoe.

Beads of perspiration formed on her forehead and crossly she brushed them away with her sleeve. The road was becoming more uneven. Then round the next corner was a pair of magnificent wrought-iron gates facing her. And looming in the distance was the impressive estate beyond. Esme stopped a few moments and blew out her cheeks. She'd made it. She opened one of the heavy gates and carefully shut it behind her, then gazed down the long gravel drive slicing through what looked like acres of beautifully mown grass. Her heart sank. It must be a quarter of a mile.

Gingerly, for a few steps, she picked her way, heels digging and wobbling among the tiny stones. She mustn't fall over. That would be the end. *Ouch!* She stopped suddenly, the side of her right foot now protesting. It was impossible. She couldn't go a step further. Glancing round, she couldn't see anyone else in sight except a gardener with his back to her, who was tending one of the borders.

Impulsively, she side-stepped onto the grass, then whipped off her shoes. Oh, the bliss of that soft carpet, the gentle moisture from the grass seeping between her toes, cooling and comforting her poor sore feet. Impulsively, she pulled the hairpins from her new upswept hairstyle and stuck them in her jacket pocket. She half ran, heart beating fast at the thought of the impending interview and that she'd be arriving late, hot and dishevelled. The interview seemed doomed before it had even begun. Then she gave a mental shake and drew a breath, slowing down.

As she came within reach of the house, she bent down and was about to slip her feet back into her shoes and join the gravel coach circle at the top of the drive when she heard the faint rattle of small stones. Jerking her head, she stood up and blinked. Some way away was a tall man, smartly dressed in a dark olive-green belted jacket and light-coloured trousers, staring down at her bare feet. Even from this distance, she could tell he was grinning. There was nothing for it. She had to keep on walking towards the house. When she was about to step into the grand entrance porch with its coat of arms, he raised his peaked cap to display a head of dark, close-cropped wavy hair.

'Beautiful day, ma'am.' His voice was slightly husky and there was a soft accent.

Ma'am? An American? What on earth was *he* doing here?

'Yes, isn't it?' she managed to say, trying to look nonchalant, as though she always carried her shoes rather than wearing them.

He nodded, still smiling, and put his cap on as he turned away.

Just her luck. He must think her one of these eccentric Englishwomen he'd heard about.

Forget it, her inner voice admonished. *For heaven's sake, put your shoes on and concentrate on that interview.*

But all she could see was the attractive American grinning at her.

To take her mind off him, she looked up at the solid Elizabethan mansion surrounded by formal gardens, then glancing at her watch, saw it had just gone ten. There was no time to stop and admire anything. Conscious she was late, she bounded up the five shallow stone steps to the front porch and took hold of the door knocker, then banged it firmly three times. At once she heard footsteps. Seconds later the door opened. Standing there was not the maid Esme had expected, but a solidly built woman, probably in her fifties, in a plain, charcoal-coloured dress with no-nonsense permed grey hair, her expression askance as she looked Esme up and down.

'No representatives,' she snapped, beginning to close the door.

Esme took a step back.

'I think you've made a mistake,' she said in the tone she used when dealing with a difficult member in the library. 'I'm not delivering or selling anything. I have an appointment with Sir Giles Carmichael.'

'Oh.' It was the woman's turn to move back. She held the door wide. 'Well, in that case, you'd better come in.'

Esme stepped inside the lobby, still a little flushed from the encounter with whom she thought of as an American officer. The woman closed the door behind them, then led the way into a vast hall. Before Esme had the chance to admire her surroundings, the woman said in a slightly less abrupt manner:

'And whom shall I say is calling?'

'Esme Donaldson.' Esme hesitated, then said, 'I hope I'm not being impolite, but may I ask your position?'

'I'm the housekeeper – Mrs Morgan.' She picked a non-existent piece of fluff from the top of her dress. 'I've been here for the last thirty years but for how much longer with all these newcomers, one can only guess.'

She sounded resentful. Esme couldn't help feeling a little sorry for the woman dealing with what sounded like a sudden influx of strangers.

'It's a madhouse in here nowadays,' the woman said, as though she were bursting to get out her complaints to anyone who would listen, 'what with young girls cavorting with the Americans, I don't know what the world—'

'I'm sorry, Mrs Morgan, I'd like to see Sir Giles right away.'

Mrs Morgan bristled into action.

'You'd best wait here and I'll tell him you've arrived.'

She gestured to a pair of chairs by the fireplace, obviously antiques and rather uncomfortable-looking, and vanished.

Esme decided to wander around the enormous hall, admiring the tall chimneypiece with its carved marble reliefs of Grecian women, and the chandeliers – unlit now, but what must they be like when they were? The ceiling rising high above her was relieved by decorative wooden arches spanning the width of the hall with several tables against one of the walls holding vases of flowers and copies of Greek and Roman busts on pedestals. She walked up to what she guessed were portraits of the family, in awe of the clothes and jewellery the women wore. But by the look of the dusty spaces below the paintings, they must also at one time have held another row. She frowned. Were the owners worried that if an invasion were to happen, priceless works of art would be stolen? And what did Mrs Morgan mean about this being a madhouse with the girls cavorting with the Americans? Was the American she'd just met anything to do with it? Well, there was no sign of any girls now, but it did sound rather intriguing. She allowed herself a smile. At least it didn't sound a dull place to live in.

There must be an American camp nearby and Mrs Morgan was finding it difficult to control these young girls who seemed to have descended upon the housekeeper, though why they should be Mrs Morgan's responsibility, goodness only knew.

Esme was deep in thought when a voice from the doorway startled her.

'Mrs Donaldson?'

She whirled round to set eyes on a towering figure of a man, dressed in an immaculate grey suit, perfectly cut to his narrow build. A thatch of white hair, white moustache and full white beard framed the hawklike face thrust forward as though he depended upon it to lead the way.

'Sir Giles?'

He nodded but remained in the doorway, one hand leaning against the architrave, the other holding a stick. As she walked over to him and held out her hand, he propped his stick against the wall and took her hand awkwardly for a second before letting it drop, then consulted his pocket watch.

'Thirteen minutes late,' he announced.

'I'm so sorry,' Esme said. 'There was a gas leakage in the bus and I had to walk the last mile, but I've actually been here for ten minutes.'

He harrumphed, eyes fixed on hers, staring. After an uncomfortable few seconds, as though deciding what to do with her, he said, 'You'd better come into my study.'

She noticed a significant limp as he walked but it didn't seem to slow him down as he ushered her through a door marked STRICTLY PRIVATE. A stale smell of tobacco wafted into her nostrils as she looked around his study. An ornate fireplace seemed the only decoration in an otherwise plain, masculine room. The walls were oak-panelled and an outsized mahogany desk stood under the window with a wooden filing cabinet to one side and a set of bookshelves to the other. Glancing out, she had a sweeping view over the grounds and distant countryside. Her eyes fell on his desk, dismally cluttered with paper, files, pencils and pens, silver-framed photographs, paperweights and three piles of books and magazines. In an adjacent desk, equally filled up, was what looked like an ancient typewriter. If so, who used it? Surely not Sir Giles.

He nodded towards a chair on the other side of the desk.

'Take a seat, won't you?' he said, lighting his pipe.

It was then that she noticed two of his fingers on his right hand were missing. Did that mean he had been injured, possibly in the Great War? Was that also the reason for his limp?

He caused his pipe to make little popping noises until he was satisfied he had it going, then began to shuffle through the mountain of paperwork. 'Now, where's the blasted thing?'

'What would you be looking for?' Esme said, wondering how he could find anything on his desk.

'Your letter.' He sat back in his chair, pipe dangling from the side of his mouth, steepling his hands. 'But matter not – you can tell me in your own words about your library experience. Don't leave anything out. If it sounds all right, I'll describe the position. If not, I won't waste my time . . . or yours.'

She wouldn't let him see she was nervous. Not so much of him, she told herself, even though his eyes seemed to pierce right through her, but of having to uphold Stella's fib (as she preferred to call it) about being a librarian so she would stand a chance of being offered the position here at Redcliffe Manor.

After briefly outlining her work and managing not to use the actual title of 'librarian', Esme paused, watching Sir Giles, but she could tell nothing from his expression as to whether he would seriously consider her.

'Hmm.' He tapped his pen on a spare inch of the green baize desk covering and fixed a startling blue gaze upon her. 'You seem to have the necessary experience for working in a public library, though you would soon realise the library here is in a mess and I want it sorted. I would also require you to do some typing.' He paused and sent her a steely look. 'I imagine you can type.'

'Well, I did go to night class years ago but I'll be very rusty as I haven't had to use a typewriter in years. She held his gaze. 'What sort of typing would you need doing?'

He looked away. 'My biography,' he said gruffly.

He sounded almost embarrassed. Maybe he wasn't quite so confident as he made out, particularly when it came to writing his life story.

'I'm sure that wouldn't be a problem if you're not in too much of a hurry.'

'I don't know about that at my age. It's best I don't dilly-dally in anything.' He paused. 'But before we go any further, Mrs Donaldson, you haven't mentioned your husband. Is he in the forces?'

'I'm a widow,' Esme said, her hand automatically fingering her gold locket. Oh, how she hated that word. It didn't seem right for someone only thirty-one, but of course there were thousands of women in the same position, some of them even younger, and many of them having the worry of children. She bit her lip.

'Was he killed in the war?'

'He died in the war but not by the Germans. He was a radio engineer in the RAF and two years ago had a sudden brain haemorrhage.' She swallowed hard. 'I never set eyes on him again.'

Sir Giles nodded. 'I'm afraid these things happen.' He drew on his pipe. 'Children?'

Nausea threatened in her throat. She swallowed hard. He gave her a sharp look. Finally, she managed to push the word out. 'N-no.' She waited, hardly daring to breathe. Instinctively, she knew she would dearly love this position. It would be something different – using her previous library experience but working for just one gentleman and typing his memoirs in such gracious surroundings yet still being close enough to her father to keep an eye on him. He *must* offer her this job. She was the right person. She knew it.

'Have you brought your references – professional and personal?'

Inwardly, she groaned.

'I'm sorry, I didn't think to bring a personal reference.'

Buried between the tangle of white beard and moustache, she saw his mouth tighten. Then it relaxed. 'No matter. I respect Miss Stratten's judgement – she's a distant cousin of mine – and she highly recommended you.'

Should she admit she'd only met Stella once over a coffee? Before she could own up to this, Sir Giles said:

'And the professional reference.'

Drat!

She took the envelope from her handbag and passed it to him. He studied it, his forehead in deep furrows for what seemed ages before he looked up.

'It clearly states that you were an *assistant* librarian in the Bath Lending Library. Does this mean you lied to Miss Stratten?' Without waiting for her answer, he added, 'I need a librarian, not some assistant.'

She had to stand firm. Not let him intimidate her or she'd be in for a rough ride – that is, if he didn't dismiss her straightaway. 'I think she might have made that assumption.'

There was a long pause.

'Sir Giles, I really want this job. I know I'm experienced enough to do whatever it takes to bring the library into order. Mr Greenwood was more than pleased with me. I would just need to know what the problems are to start with.'

He fixed his gaze on hers for a few seconds, then drew deeply on his pipe. Esme felt she was sitting on the edge of a precipice. She couldn't bear such an opportunity to slip away, all for the sake of a title. But she had said all she could. Anything more might irritate him further. She crossed her fingers and waited.

Sir Giles took a few more puffs, then cleared his throat.

'Well, I'm willing to try you out . . . soon as possible,' he said finally. 'You'll be on a month's probation and a month's notice. Mind you, I'll know in a week if you're any good or not. If I keep you on, you'll be paid six pounds every month, all found. If you live out, it will be eight.' He looked at her. 'That suit, Mrs Donaldson?'

'Oh, yes, sir. It would suit very well.'

'In or out?'

For a moment she didn't understand what he was referring to. *Ah. Of course.*

'I'd like to live-in and could start this coming Monday if that would suit you.'

He nodded, and without consulting a calendar, said, 'That'll be the 28th.' He stroked his beard. 'Before you leave, I'll get Mrs Morgan to show you your quarters, but for now, you'd better come and have a look at where you'll mainly be working.'

Considering Sir Giles's age – he must be nearing seventy – he clipped along the passages at a nifty speed with his stick despite his limp, Esme thought as she followed him. Leaving his stick at the bottom of the beautiful oak staircase, he held onto the balustrade and slowly mounted the steps which forked in the middle up to a second level. From the long landing, he opened a door where a cruder set of narrow stairs opened onto a second landing with a gently sloping ceiling. Several doors led off to what Esme presumed were the servants' quarters. Surely the library wouldn't be up on this level. It would be most inconvenient for Sir Giles with his gammy leg every time he wanted a book.

Sir Giles opened the last door facing the end of the corridor and gestured her through. She gasped. Before her stretched an enormous library containing what looked like several thousand books, many of them placed higgledy-piggledy over mahogany shelves that were covered in a thick layer of dust. She wrinkled her nose. The room smelled of stale tobacco from men's pipes and had an unloved air about it. It wasn't going to be a very pleasant place to work in, she thought with disappointment, until she could arrange for it to be thoroughly cleaned. She drew in a breath. If the books were this disorganised, heaven knew what sort of state the catalogue system was in.

'I hardly ever come here now. It used to be my favourite room where I'd spend hours – sometimes all day. Getting a bit tricky these days.' He tapped his leg with his stick. 'Charles, the previous chap, left us in great difficulty when he went off to join the Army. As you can see, he wasn't the tidiest so there'll be plenty to do.' He sent her a fierce glance. 'Put you off, does it?'

'Not at all,' she said. 'I love being busy and getting stuck into something really interesting. And I'm sure this is exactly what I'd be most happy doing to pull it round.'

'Good.' He hawked his throat, then regarded her. 'I hope you're strong, Mrs Donaldson, because the first job I want you to do is to move the library to the ground floor!'

Back in her flat, after pinching herself that she'd been offered the position that she so wanted, Esme came down to the practicalities of the mammoth task in front of her. She certainly couldn't move a whole library on her own or she'd be a physical wreck by the end. Perhaps Sir Giles didn't mean her to. There were bound to be people around the estate who could help. And Stella. Strange how the Manor seemed to be her family home. That was a revelation, finding out she was Sir Giles's cousin. A pity Sir Giles hadn't shown Esme what room his cousin worked in when manning the switchboard. And why on earth did Redcliffe Manor need a switchboard? That bit didn't make sense.

Her topsy-turvy thoughts turned again to Sir Giles. He couldn't be blamed for wanting to move his massive collection of books, not with that limp. No doubt he realised he was getting older and might not be so good on his feet in a few years; a library on the ground floor would suit his needs far better. And she would have the satisfying job of seeing it through.

He hadn't told her what room he'd earmarked for the great event. Maybe he hadn't yet decided. She couldn't help feeling a frisson of excitement at the thought of all those books waiting for her to dust and catalogue and rearrange logically in their new home downstairs.

Mrs Morgan hadn't appeared again to show her where her bedroom would be, but it didn't much matter in a mansion such as Redcliffe Manor. The main thing was that Sir Giles had offered her what she considered an extremely prestigious position. If she wrote straightaway to thank Stella for the introduction and posted it first thing tomorrow morning, she might with luck receive it on either of the two later deliveries that day – at any rate, it would be well before Monday.

Chapter Six

Esme took the precious photograph of her father and mother in happier days from her dressing table in her bedroom at her old home. Her mother was slightly turned towards her husband and smiling up at him. Esme held the frame and stared at the laughing young woman, but although the black-and-white photograph was in focus, Esme couldn't for the life of her recognise the woman as her mother. It was the one thing that upset her. Surely as a child of six, she'd been old enough to keep a picture of her mother firmly in her head.

The other was of Freda, about twelve, and herself as a toddler in the garden. Freda was standing behind her, her hands on the little girl's shoulders, and they were both giggling at something – probably the photographer, Esme thought now with a smile, as she wrapped the two silver-framed photographs in newspaper and tucked them among her clothes in her suitcase. Not that there was a huge variety of clothes. But where she was going, she wouldn't need fancy evening dresses or even her two worsted suits she'd worn most days in the library. It wasn't as though she'd be meeting the public every day, and lugging boxes of books up and down three staircases – well, she'd need really comfortable shoes for that job.

It crossed her mind that trousers were the answer. They'd be so much more practical. More women were wearing them nowadays although she heard that some men accused them of losing their femininity. She clicked her tongue. It was sensible, that's all. Well, there wasn't time to buy any now, but she was determined that the next day she had off she would at least try on a pair and see how they felt.

It had been a very casual interview in many ways. She had no idea what hours he expected her to do, if she had a day or one-and-a-half days off, if he wanted her to start moving the library straightaway or get to know its layout first, if he was ready for her to begin typing his memoirs . . . there were so many questions and few answers. But it was bound to fall into place once she was there.

She put her sponge bag and the last two books on top of the contents of the somewhat cumbersome leather suitcase her father had lent her – first to move into her flat and now to move to Redcliffe Manor. *Hmm. Quite a difference between the two.* The case was bulging and she'd probably have trouble clicking the locks together. The only thing missing was her bicycle that she stored in the shed at her old home. She'd need that as Redcliffe Manor was so isolated but that would have to wait until she visited Dad on the bus next time and could cycle back.

Thinking of Muriel, Esme gave a wry smile. Muriel had looked so relieved and happy that her stepdaughter had found a new post that was 'all in' and had been really pleasant this last weekend. Her father, on the other hand, had looked glum.

'I'll be sorry to see you go, love,' he'd said. 'I've enjoyed having you here these few days and I wish you could have stayed longer.'

'You know I like my independence, Dad,' Esme said. 'And it's going to be a new experience that I think I'll really enjoy.'

'Yes, I think you will.'

'And I should be able to see you almost as much as when I lived in Bath.'

Her father shook his head. 'I doubt it, love. I think you're going to be well and truly occupied – at the start, at least.'

The sound of a taxi blowing its horn interrupted her thoughts. Hurriedly, she sprang up and shifted the suitcase onto the landing with her foot. She'd ask the driver if he could help her down with it.

'Pleased to oblige, miss,' he said, raising his cap and climbing down from the cab. He was back in a trice, the suitcase now safely in the boot.

Her father hugged her.

'Good luck, love. I'll be thinking of you.' He looked at her seriously. 'I hope you won't be lonely. It's going to feel very different living and working in the depths of the countryside.'

'I'll enjoy it and there are plenty of people around not to be lonely.' She kissed his cheek. 'Thanks for everything, Dad. And take care of yourself. Rest more.'

He smiled. 'Be sure to do the same,' he said, his eyes gleaming wet.

'I'm looking forward to visiting you, Esme,' Muriel called out as the driver came to Esme's side to shut the cab door. 'I've always wanted to see inside that house.'

Muriel had made it perfectly clear that she wasn't coming to see *her*, Esme thought, but to satisfy her curiosity. It wasn't unexpected but her stepmother might have been a little more tactful. She shrugged. Nothing she could do about her.

Thankfully, the journey to Redcliffe Manor was without any dramatic event this time and twenty minutes later the taxi pulled up outside the main entrance. The driver took her case right up to the front door. Esme paid him and he kindly waited until the door opened. This time a maid answered, and Esme heard the crunch of gravel as the taxi disappeared up the drive.

'Mrs Donaldson,' Esme said. 'I'm expected.'

'Please come in.' The maid, a slight young girl, hardly more than sixteen by the look of her, stepped forward and took the handle of the suitcase.

'No, it's too heavy for you,' Esme protested. 'I can manage . . . really.'

'Not up the stairs, you can't, madam,' the girl said. 'One of the maintenance men will be here in a minute. Leave it in the hall and I'll show you your room.'

Where the staircase split in two, the maid took the right-hand fork and halfway along the landing she opened a door. Esme gasped. A pattern of huge yellow roses trailed up the walls of a bedroom bigger than her whole flat. It was much lighter than she'd imagined, due to the huge window. Drawn towards it, she looked out at the rear of the mansion, then blinked. Partially obstructing what should have been the most breathtaking view was a river with a linking bridge to a series of ugly grey huts beyond.

From where she stood, they stretched the whole width of Redcliffe Manor and couldn't have been more than a couple of hundred yards away from the back of the main house. What an eyesore. Why would Sir Giles have allowed anything like this to be built? She stepped closer to examine it. Darkly clad scurrying figures emerged from one of the doors facing her. Then a man dressed in uniform came to the door and stopped one of them to speak. After a minute or two she nodded and he walked on. Esme wondered what it all meant.

Well, she'd find out soon enough.

'Will this do for you, madam?' the maid asked when Esme hadn't said anything.

Esme glanced round the room. It smelled slightly of stale smoke, but it was beautiful. She turned to the maid.

'Oh, yes. It will do very nicely, thank you.'

There was a knock at the half-open door and an elderly man appeared with her suitcase.

'I'll leave it just inside,' he said, and disappeared.

Esme turned to the maid and smiled. 'I'm sure I'll see you from time to time, so what is your name?'

The girl smiled shyly back. 'It's Dolly.'

'Have you been here long?'

Dolly shook her head. 'Not long. A fortnight today.'

'Well, I might have to ask you where various rooms are until I find my way round.' Esme smiled. 'But meantime, can you point me to the bathroom?'

'Yes. It's just two more doors along the passage. It's just for the staff.' Dolly hesitated. 'Would you need anything more, madam?'

'No, it's fine, Dolly, thank you.'

'Then I'll be off.' The maid bowed her head and shut the door behind her.

Esme peered into the dark recess of the musty-smelling wardrobe. Her clothes would soon take up that odour, she thought, wrinkling her nose. She'd have to leave the wardrobe doors open before she unpacked her clothes. But the first thing was to open the sash window to let some air in the room, which didn't feel it had been lived in for some time. With difficulty, she managed to push up the sash a few inches, but any further was impossible – it wouldn't budge. Then she set out all her toiletries on a shelf near the wash basin. Next were her books. Finally, she put the photograph of her mother and father in their youth on the little square table by her bed. She was just about to tidy her hair in the mirror above the basin when she heard a tremendous clattering of feet and loud voices and giggles on the landing outside her door. These must be the girls the housekeeper was talking about. Full of curiosity, she pulled the door open and stepped out, nearly knocking one pigtailed girl over as they stampeded by in their navy-blue hooded capes, the light from the window showing flashes of crimson lining.

'Why doncha look where yer goin'?' the pigtailed girl yelled over her shoulder.

'I'm sorry, I—' But the girl, no more than thirteen or fourteen, had disappeared with her rowdy friends.

Really, there was no need for such bad manners. Dismissing the child's outburst, Esme wondered where she was supposed to go. Well, as Sir Giles had mentioned she'd be mostly in the library, she'd have a look in there. Perhaps that's where he was expecting her. But no one was there. She'd try his study. After knocking on the door and hearing no response, she turned the handle, but it was locked. Since the crush of girls had noisily rushed by her bedroom door, the house seemed eerily quiet.

Dying for a cup of tea, she decided to make a tour of some of the ground-floor rooms until she found the kitchen. As she walked along one of the corridors she heard the clanking of crockery. She must be near the pantry. At that moment, another maid came out of a door nearby carrying a tray set out with a coffee pot and a plate of biscuits.

'Excuse me, but can you tell me where the kitchen is?' Esme said.

The girl jerked her head to the adjacent door. 'In there.' She hurried on.

Esme knocked and gingerly opened the door to a large kitchen. A solid-looking woman, presumably the cook, in a wraparound white apron and cap, was removing two enormous pies from the oven. She placed them on the large pine table in the middle of the room and the smell of blackberries and apples wafted towards her. A young girl was peeling a mound of potatoes and another, a little older, was chopping cabbage.

The cook, if that's who she was, looked up as Esme stood in the doorway, her face red and glowing from the heat.

'Oh, I do hope I'm not disturbing you,' Esme said, 'but I've only just arrived and I'm not sure where I'm supposed to be. Sir Giles doesn't seem to be anywhere around.' She caught her eye. 'Would you have any idea where he is?'

'None. He don't tell us none of his whereabouts.' She eyed Esme up and down. 'You'll be the new teacher then.'

Esme shook her head. 'No, I'm not. I've come to help sort out the library.'

The woman snorted. 'They say they're short of a teacher. Sounds to me more important than tidyin' up shelves in the library.'

Esme bit back a retort. Instead, she said:

'Are you the cook?'

'So I'm told.' There was no humour in her answer.

Why is this woman being so difficult?

Esme set her jaw. She wasn't going to play to whatever resentment the cook obviously felt. Perhaps she was overworked and didn't have enough help. Esme tried to swallow but her mouth was completely dry.

'Would it be possible for me to make myself a cup of tea?' she said.

Cook pursed her lips. 'No, Lil will make you one.'

Esme looked around the kitchen. There was a vacant chair by the side of the girls, who'd stopped working to listen for a few moments and then hurriedly continued peeling and chopping the vegetables. 'Could I sit in here for a few minutes?'

'I'm afraid not.' Cook threw a glance at the kitchen maids. 'Lil, make Miss—' she glanced at Esme.

'Mrs Donaldson.'

Cook threw a glance at the kitchen maids. 'Make a cup of tea for Mrs Donaldson and she can take it to the pantry.'

It was obvious to Esme that the cook was put out by her

appearance. She felt awkward hovering while the younger maid poured her a cup of tea and put a lump of sugar in the saucer, then handed it to her with a shy smile showing badly crooked teeth.

'Thank you.' Esme smiled back. 'May I know both your names?'

'Janey,' the girl said, then pointed to the elder girl. 'And that's Lil.'

Esme smiled at Lil, who didn't respond but gave a quick nod and made herself busy putting the cabbage into a huge saucepan.

'Cook, may I ask you something?' Esme said as she was about to go to the adjoining pantry.

'Yes?' Cook stood with her hands folded over her considerable bosom.

'What are all those huts I can see from my bedroom window?'

'Which room have they given you?'

'The one with huge yellow roses on the wallpaper.'

'That'll be the Yellow Rose Room.' Cook gave another sniff. 'It's a Yanks' hospital.'

Esme raised her eyebrows. 'An American hospital built in private grounds?'

The woman's mouth twisted into a grim line. 'That's what it is.'

'I wonder how they had permission.'

'I expect it'd be the War Office,' Cook answered, 'same as the school. Sir Giles didn't have no say in that. He told us we was lucky to still have our jobs because the War Office allowed him to stay in his own home, but he was reduced to four rooms instead of seventy-four.' She gave a sardonic smile. 'He were that shocked but he soon knuckled down – I'll say that for 'im. I reckon he'd rather have the school than a ton of evacuees landin' on 'im.'

And with that she reached under the kitchen table and drew out a huge Pyrex basin from the overladen shelf of bowls and serving dishes. Esme hid an amused smile. It was obviously the end of the conversation.

She sat on the only chair in the pantry, an uncomfortable narrow one with a hard back, sipping the lukewarm cup of tea, musing on Cook's last remark. *Hmm. Intriguing, to say the least.* She was determined to find out more. After all, this was to be her home. She needed to know what was going on – who were the people around her, especially those who stayed there at night. As for now, she'd go back to the library and have a closer look at the way it was laid out – maybe get to grips with some of the problems – by which time, surely Sir Giles would have put in an appearance.

Chapter Seven

'Ah, there you are!'

Esme startled at Sir Giles's booming voice. She'd been sitting in one of the leather armchairs in the library with an index-card box on her lap, trying to work out the estate's cataloguing system. Someone, many years ago, had kept meticulous files and catalogued the books under the Dewey decimal classification system used nationally in libraries. However, in later years, whoever had been the librarian – Charlie? – must have attempted to try a different, newer way of grouping the subjects. Unfortunately it hadn't completely obliterated the old method, so it was in a complete muddle.

She sprang to her feet.

'Oh, Sir Giles, I'm sorry, I did look—'

He flapped his fingers to silence her as he came in and sat opposite her on the other leather armchair.

'No matter – you're here now.'

His tone sounded mildly irritable. Esme bit her lip, wondering if she should explain she'd been here several hours looking for him. But by his expression, she thought better not to.

'Have you had a look on the shelves to see how they're classified?'

'Yes,' Esme said. 'I did wander round. But there's a lot to take in.' She glanced round the room. 'And you certainly have some wonderful volumes.'

'Many are very valuable.' He gave her a piercing look under bushy white eyebrows. 'Did you notice there are many first editions?'

'I haven't touched anything as I wanted to wait until you came, so I thought I'd have a look at these index cards to try to work out how the books are categorised.' She caught his eye. 'Perhaps you could walk round with me and give me a general idea of how you like things assembled.'

'Couldn't find a damn thing when Charles was here,' he grumbled.

'Maybe he just hadn't explained his system.' She certainly wasn't going to get into any conversation about an ex-staff member whom she'd never met.

His mouth tightened. 'Hmm. I don't think so. I don't think he knew himself what the system was – if it ever existed.' He gave another of his sharp looks. 'That's what I have *you* for. Sort it out. Make it logical so I can find things.'

'Do you have some particular interests?' Esme said, feeling a little out of control.

'Interests? *I'll* say I have. We'll start with the weather, shall we, and move on to wildflowers, trees, birds, architecture, history—' He stopped. 'Well, that's a big subject in itself. That includes works of art – particularly the early Renaissance – the Tudors . . .' He gave a wry smile, showing large, stained teeth. 'Will that do to be going on with, Mrs Donaldson?'

'I have a feeling you've only just scratched the surface, Sir Giles,' she said, smiling back.

'Hmm. You're probably right.' He paused. 'Have you been round the house yet?'

'No. I didn't want to miss you when you came in. I did try the study, but it was locked so I took the liberty of making myself known in the kitchen and had a cup of tea in the pantry.'

'In the pantry?' Sir Giles repeated. 'You don't have to sit in the pantry.' He frowned. 'Who said for you to go there? Was it one of the kitchen maids?'

'Um, no.' This was awkward. She hadn't really got off to a very good start with Cook as it was, so she didn't want to make it worse. 'I just thought I'd be out of the way in there.'

'Well, I won't have it. You're to have your coffee in the library or the study if you happen to be working with me. And you'll be in the breakfast room in the mornings – that's just reserved for the staff – and the dining room for lunch and dinner. Mind you, you'll have to share that one with the two teachers and the schoolgirls.'

'Oh, I don't mind that one bit – I'd like it.' She paused. 'Is it an actual girls' boarding school here?'

'Yes. The Royal School for Daughters of Officers of the Army.' He gave a sardonic smile. 'Bit of a mouthful, isn't it?' He touched his beard as though to emphasise it. 'Their school was in Bath, but the Admiralty requisitioned it, so the Ministry of War informed me they were to come here. They gave me all of two days' notice.'

'Did you mind them all descending upon you?' Esme asked curiously.

'I did at first.' Sir Giles gave a slow smile. 'And Mrs Morgan nearly went berserk with all the extra work and Cook was put out because they'd brought their own. She wasn't having another one in what she regarded as *her* kitchen and told me she could manage perfectly well with a couple more kitchen maids – and as you can see, she does. And when I became used to it, I decided I quite enjoyed a bit of young life around the place. I've been on my own since my wife died more than five years ago and it felt like a morgue here before they came.'

'Oh, I'm so sorry you lost your wife.'

He flapped his hand. 'No matter. Comes to all of us in the end.'

'And those outbuildings I can see from my bedroom—'

'It's a military hospital – the USAAF.' When she raised an eyebrow, he added, 'The United States Army Air Forces. And that encampment of Nissen huts on the left is where the medical staff and the orderlies live – not the doctors though. They're in the hospital.' He smiled. 'Redcliffe Manor has become a very busy place these last few months.' He paused. 'Now, where were we?'

Esme would love to have asked more about the hospital. She would when she got to know Sir Giles better.

'I was hoping you might show me the rest of the house, particularly the room you want the library moved to.'

Sir Giles looked vaguely round. 'I'll need my stick.'

'I didn't see it when you came in.'

'Perhaps I left it in the study . . . where I thought you'd be.' His expression was like a petulant schoolboy.

'Let me go and have a look for it,' Esme said.

'I'll come down with you. Can't use it on all those stairs anyway.'

She hurried in front of him and back to the study. Ah, there it was, leaning against the desk where he'd stood. She grabbed it and caught up with him at the foot of the main staircase. He wore a strange expression. She wondered what on earth he was thinking, although instinctively she felt his bark was worse than his bite. Was he testing her? Seeing if she was willing to do other jobs beyond library work and typing his biography? Well, she wouldn't mind that. But were they going to get along? She sighed. Only time would tell.

Sir Giles proved to be an excellent guide as he led her from one magnificent room to another, giving her a potted history of the architecture and the lives of the people who'd lived at Redcliffe Manor. He showed her the beautiful ornate drawing room with its carved ceiling, boasting not one, but three marble fireplaces, so large they were more than a match for the long wall they occupied. Next was the banqueting hall – now used as the school dining room since Redcliffe Manor had hosted the school – with a beautifully polished walnut table that would seat twenty-eight, Esme quickly calculated. Four small tables were placed near the window. Peering down at the diners was a double row of portraits on two of the walls, and Sir Giles patiently explained who these people were. They then toured through three informal sitting rooms – one of them being a staff room – the breakfast room and another library, more modest this time, that Sir Giles called the Red Library, owing to its burgundy flock wallpaper.

'The girls are allowed to come in here and borrow a book but I'd want them to go through you so you could watch that it's returned,' Sir Giles explained when he led her to a morning room near the kitchen but now used for storage. 'So far, not one of them has ever bothered.' He shook his head. 'A great pity,' he murmured.

Upstairs again, he limped past several doors – the girls' dormitories, he said – and finally they were outside a room where she could hear muffled voices from within. This time Sir Giles knocked before he opened it.

A man with flame-red hair, not plump but well built, of perhaps her own age, looked round from writing on the blackboard as they entered. Roughly twenty girls in their early teens sitting at their desks eyed them. He laid his piece of chalk down. The room fell quiet. Esme noticed the same girl she'd nearly knocked over, sitting at the end of the front row and watching them with narrowed eyes.

'Good morning, sir.' The man, obviously their teacher, glanced at Sir Giles, then looked meaningfully at Esme.

'Good morning, Kingsnorth. I've brought our new librarian to meet you.' Sir Giles stepped to one side to allow Esme visibility. 'This is Mrs Donaldson. She'll be living in.'

'Russell Kingsnorth,' the red-haired man said, coming forward and holding out his hand. 'How do you do, Mrs Donaldson?' He shook hers warmly, letting his eyes linger on hers for a few seconds. 'Welcome to Redcliffe Manor. I hope you'll be very happy with us.'

'Oh, I'm sure I will,' Esme said, a little disconcerted under his gaze.

'Anything I can do to help, just let me know.'

'Thank you, Mr Kingsnorth, I will.'

Esme turned to Sir Giles, who was regarding this brief interlude. She could swear that underneath the thick white beard, his lips would be turned up in – well, maybe not amusement, but at least cynical enjoyment. She hoped she was right.

'That used to be another bedroom,' Sir Giles said when Esme had shut the door behind them. 'But as you can see, it's now a classroom.'

'How many girls were evacuated here?' she asked.

'I believe about fifty. Many of them went back to their families, which was a good thing as I wouldn't have coped with any more.' He paused. 'These girls seem to have settled quite well considering they've not even been here a month.'

'They couldn't be in more beautiful surroundings.'

'I doubt that enters their heads,' he said. 'Mrs Morgan has to keep a tight rein on them because they've already broken a valuable vase and spilled coffee on one of the antique Persian rugs.' He glanced at her. 'I asked one of them the other day what they thought of the portraits. She answered, "It's all right, sir, they're not bothering us any longer – we're getting used to them."' He gave a deep-throated chuckle.

Esme smiled, then said, 'Do you think it might be wise to

remove some of the valuable items – perhaps put them in, say, the morning room?'

'I've had the most valuable pieces – some furniture and silverware and china – moved into the stables as I'm told the buildings are perfectly dry and they shouldn't come to any harm. But mostly I want to leave things where they've been for centuries. Those girls need to be educated in the finer things of life, so they recognise quality when they see it. Most of them come from decent backgrounds – I'd call them good middle class – but they haven't lived in country estates like this, as far as I'm aware. So even if only one of them learns to appreciate beautiful furniture, paintings, rugs, books,' he looked at her, 'then it will be reward enough.'

What a kind-hearted man. He was more solicitous than she'd originally judged him. She hoped he'd be proved right and the schoolgirls wouldn't damage anything more.

'Well, Mrs Donaldson, what room do you think would work for a library?' he cut into her train of thought.

'One of the sitting rooms might work, although I doubt any of them would house more than half your books and furniture.' She looked at him. 'You'd have to condense it.'

'Hmm. Yes, I thought that could be a possibility, though I don't like the idea of getting rid of anything. But I suppose I could store . . .' He trailed off, sounding uncertain.

'Have I seen all the rooms?' Esme asked.

Sir Giles shook his head. 'No. I closed three-quarters of the house when my wife died five years ago, and even more when war was declared. They didn't have any heat in them so what was the point? Of course I had to reopen a large number of them when the school came.' He waited as if she might contribute something to the conversation, but she remained mute. 'There's another classroom for the younger girls run by Miss Lonsdale – I'll take you to meet her tomorrow. Then the sick room on the first floor but we won't go in there because two of the girls have mumps – the last thing we want to catch.' He eyed her. 'Have *you* had it?'

'Yes,' she reassured him. 'I have.'

'Good, but we'll steer clear.' He paused. 'I haven't shown you the Muniment Room.'

'Oh, where the family-history papers are stored?'

He gave her an approving nod. 'And other important documents. Come with me, Mrs Donaldson. Downstairs again.'

Once back on the ground floor, and with the aid of his stick, he moved swiftly along the main corridor, then rounded the corner to the left. He stopped and took a bunch of keys from his pocket, chose one and unlocked the first door they came to.

The Muniment Room was significantly larger than the sitting room, Esme noticed, with tall windows overlooking the eastern side of the house. There were display cabinets and high-level cupboards, some with glass doors and some with their contents hidden behind solid wooden ones.

'I think this is the room that would make a perfect library,' she said, impulsively turning to Sir Giles. 'Don't you?'

'I do indeed. I just wanted you to confirm it,' he said brusquely.

Chapter Eight

Esme spent the next hour or so with Sir Giles walking round the attic library. He pointed out the various subjects he was interested in – dozens, it seemed. But when she looked more closely, she could tell there was real disorder. A number of the classic novels were interspersed with non-fiction volumes. It was clear that there would be plenty of work to keep her occupied. In a way, it was good that the library was to be moved because then she'd be starting almost from scratch and could set up the new location exactly as he wanted.

'What do you think?' Sir Giles broke into her thoughts. 'Overwhelming job, is it?'

'Nothing that can't be resolved.' She smiled, hoping he'd be reassured. 'I can't wait to get started.'

He took his pocket watch from his waistcoat and peered at it, then put it away.

'You'll probably need some lunch to give you the energy to start,' he said, and for the first time she noticed a twinkle in his piercing eyes.

'Where do you have your lunch?' she asked.

'Study, library, bedroom sometimes . . . wherever I happen to be at the time.' He looked down at her. 'But you, Mrs Donaldson, will be having yours in the dining room and I've already told Dolly to make a place for you. It's coming up to one o'clock, which is the second sitting, so you'd better go now and I'll expect you here promptly at one forty-five.'

I think we might be all right, Esme thought happily, as she walked back to the dining room. She opened the door to the sound of boisterous schoolgirls who were jostling for a chair at the long walnut table with Russell Kingsnorth at the head. He immediately caught her eye and gestured towards the one empty chair next to him. The girl with the pigtails who'd spoken so rudely was facing the portraits and turned to see who their teacher was looking at. When she saw it was Esme, she pulled a face and turned her back to carry on eating.

Strange girl. She obviously doesn't approve of me, Esme thought, with an inward shrug.

Glancing round the room, Esme looked for other possible places to sit. She certainly wasn't going to squeeze onto the redheaded teacher's table. Then out of the corner of her eye she recognised a familiar figure. *Stella!* She was already seated at one of the smaller tables by the window and was looking up and waving at her. Esme threw Russell a smile of apology and made for Stella's table.

'Oh, my goodness. I hoped I'd run into you soon and there you are.' Stella gestured to the far end of the room. 'Lunch is over there but hurry. I'm due back in a few minutes and I want to have a natter before I go. I'll save this seat for you.'

'Thanks, Stella. How lovely to see you. I'll be quick.'

Esme picked up a tray and joined a short queue where an aproned woman put a portion of shepherd's pie and cabbage on a plate, then a small bowl of Spotted Dick and thick custard together with a cup of tea on her tray.

Esme wove her way through the tables back to Stella.

'It's my first day,' Esme said, 'so it's nice to see a familiar face – and a smiling one at that.'

'It must feel all of a haze to you at the moment,' Stella said sympathetically when Esme had had a chance for a few mouthfuls of her lunch.

'It is. But I'm sure I'll soon find my way round and get used to it.'

'And how do you find Sir Giles?'

'Well, I was a bit anxious on the interview and also this morning, but by the time he told me to go and have some lunch, I felt we'd reached not exactly an understanding' – she was hunting for her words – 'but that we were going to rub along. And I did remember what you said – that he could be a bit grumpy but was all right underneath.' She chuckled. 'At first he was irritated because he felt we'd led him up the garden path because I wasn't a qualified librarian, so I had to convince him I was perfectly capable of doing the job.'

'He'd respect you for sticking up for yourself,' Stella commented.

'Possibly. But changing the subject, Stella, where do you work that you can come home for lunch?'

'I work here.'

Esme's eyes widened. 'Why on earth would they want a switchboard at Redcliffe Manor?'

'Well, not exactly here . . . I'm in the American hospital outside. You've probably seen the conglomeration of buildings – more like huts really, from some of the windows.'

'Yes, I can see it clearly from my bedroom window.' She paused. 'Sir Giles mentioned you were his cousin.'

'Only a second cousin and that's one removed, if you can work it out – I never can.' Stella hesitated, and her expression became serious. 'Remember that bombing raid we had last April?' Esme nodded. 'Well, the hospital in London where I used to work took an explosion and although it didn't cause as much damage as it might have, my dearest friend, Julie, who was also a nurse, was badly injured.' Stella's eyes filled with tears. 'She hung on for a few weeks – I used to visit her nearly every day – and then—'

Esme saw Stella take a great gulp.

'—well, she died on the fourth of June.'

'Oh, Stella.' Esme reached for Stella's hand and gave it a gentle squeeze.

'That letter I was reading when we met in the café was from her mother, who I still write to.'

'I'm so terribly sorry. It's dreadful to lose a friend so young.' Esme hesitated. 'But you didn't continue nursing.'

Stella shook her head. 'I did for a week or two, but I wasn't concentrating on the job. I think they thought it was only a matter of time before I made a serious mistake. So one of the doctors wrote me a sick note to say I was to have a few months off to prevent me from having a nervous breakdown.' She sighed. 'That's when Sir Giles kindly took me in.' She reached for her handbag and brought out a packet of cigarettes. 'I feel right as rain now but can't face going back – if they'd have me, that is – and at least here I'm still in a hospital atmosphere.'

Esme was curious. 'And do you like your job?'

'I do so long as they keep me busy.' Stella gave a throaty chuckle and her eyes now sparkled with mischief. 'Especially now the director of the whole shebang is on the scene. He's gorgeous – the classic tall, dark and broodily handsome – and it seems all the other women who work there think the same.'

'Oh. Is he American?'

'Yes, all the doctors and nurses are. People like cleaners and cooks are mostly English – plus yours truly on the switchboard.' She giggled girlishly.

'Mmm, I smell romance in the air,' Esme said with a grin. She suddenly felt more light-hearted than she'd felt these last two years. She'd secured the job as librarian, Sir Giles seemed to accept her, she had an incredible roof over her head, and now it looked as though Stella was going to be a staunch friend. Life had definitely taken a turn for the better.

'You must come over and meet some of us,' Stella was saying, breaking into her thoughts. 'And I'll introduce you to Colonel Parker.'

'Is he the gorgeous director?' Esme laughed.

'He is. So it's hands off,' Stella said, putting a cigarette between her lips and lighting it. Even though her voice was light-hearted, Esme sensed a serious undertone.

'You don't have to worry about anything like that with me,' she said. 'I'm not at all interested in men.'

Stella glanced at Esme's left hand. 'Oh, Esme, of course – your wedding ring.' She gazed at Esme. 'Is your husband abroad?'

'He was. But he died two years ago, just before he was due to come home on leave.' She swallowed. How many hundreds of times had she had to say those words.

Stella's jaw dropped. 'Oh, Esme, how unfair. This blasted war. I'm so sorry, but at least he died fighting for our country.' She looked straight into Esme's eyes. 'You must be very proud of him.'

There they go again. Always taking it for granted that he'd been killed by the Germans.

She wouldn't tell Stella any further details concerning Anthony. It was no one's business. Not for the first time a spike of guilt shot through her. Was she being dishonest by not telling the truth when people so kindly enquired about him? Oh, it was so difficult to know.

'Yes, he was a lovely man,' she said with perfect genuineness. 'But I'm very happy on my own, so the coast is clear as far as your Colonel Parker is concerned.'

'Not quite mine . . . not yet, anyway.' Stella gave a rueful chuckle. She glanced at her watch and shot to her feet.

'Goodness, the time. I must go.' She blew a kiss in Esme's direction and was out of the door in seconds, leaving Esme to start on her pudding and custard.

The afternoon passed pleasantly. Sir Giles said he was going for a nap and asked her to continue looking through the files that catalogued the books and make any notes and suggestions. He wanted to work on his memoirs later and didn't want to be disturbed and Esme was happy to comply. She could carry on quietly, knowing she had his permission to tackle the mountain of work.

'We'll start moving the stuff downstairs tomorrow, once you've acquainted yourself with the layout,' Sir Giles had stated. 'Or rather *you* will. I don't want to do anything which might put my back out.'

Never mind my *back*, Esme thought, with a wry smile as she recalled his words. She'd been bending down to take note of the larger volumes on the lower shelves and now she stood up and stretched her spine, extending her arms above her head. She wrinkled her nose. *Oh, for some fresh air.* She loved the smell of books but when it was obvious no one had dusted them for years, becoming musty from absorbing smoke from pipes and cigars and cigarettes, the odour was overpowering. Hoping that Sir Giles wouldn't be annoyed that he hadn't been asked, she marched over to the sash window and pulled it up several inches.

There was a light knock at the door. Esme opened it to see Lil bearing a tray with a cup of tea and two Huntley and Palmer oat biscuits.

'Lil, you angel! How did you know I was longing for one. Did Cook ask you to bring it up?'

Lil gave a knowing smile. 'No, Mr Kingsnorth did. I took him one in the staff room and he asked me to bring a cup to the library for you.'

How thoughtful. Then Esme remembered how the teacher's eyes had lingered on her for longer than was polite. *Hmm.* She must be careful not to give him any ideas. Smiling gratefully at Lil, she took the tray and set it on an intricately carved Indian table with a copper surface next to the leather armchair.

'First supper is five-thirty to six-fifteen and the second one is six-thirty to seven-fifteen,' Lil told her.

'I'd prefer the second sitting.'

'Then I'll ring the bell five minutes before, madam.'

When the door had shut behind the young maid, Esme sank into the armchair and picked up the cup and saucer. She took a sip of tea and pulled a face. It was lukewarm. But she mustn't grumble. It was wet and more or less quenched her thirst. She nibbled on a biscuit, newly rationed, all the while wondering how on earth she was going to move several thousand books, some of them extremely heavy, down three flights of stairs on her own.

The supper bell jangled through Esme's tired brain. It had been a tedious job trying to work out the jumbled system for the books. Another thought struck her. She must ask Sir Giles if he was aware that moving the present library into the Muniment Room would need some more thinking. Luckily, one of the walls was lined with oak shelves which would take perhaps a thousand books, but that would be only a fraction. And in the meantime, where would the display cabinets go? Yes, it was an enormous room by most people's standards, but this was a mammoth undertaking and would need some sound preparation. But how to be tactful. He might be perfectly aware of what needed to be done and had, in fact, started the wheels turning already. Well, she'd tackle him after supper.

That night, her first at Redcliffe Manor, Esme lay on her back on the enormous feather mattress, looking up at the ceiling. She noticed quite a crack and a stain which she'd not seen before, but it looked old, so presumably wasn't any kind of threat. *What a day.* She rubbed the side of her neck, then the other, thinking about Sir Giles and when he'd seemed to have approved of her. It was firstly when he mentioned the Muniment Room and perhaps realised she would be knowledgeable enough for the task, even if she was only an assistant librarian, and the second time when she'd felt certain the room would make an ideal library. He'd been testing her – she was certain. She'd heard the word 'muniment' before but had learnt its true meaning when one of the regular borrowers in the Lending Library, Mr Franklin-Brown – an elderly gentleman, beautifully spoken – had raised his cap and asked if she had a book of a certain country house, as he wanted to take notes of his ancestors. His own home, he'd explained, had been recently bombed, completely destroying his study and all the documents and other important paperwork he'd been working on for years.

'If there's a chapter on the Muniment Room, that could help tremendously,' he'd said.

What a piece of luck that she'd asked what that had to do with armoury. He'd given a hearty laugh, then apologised when a woman browsing along the shelves turned to hush him.

Dear Mr Franklin-Brown, Esme thought, as she switched off her bedside light and grinned in the darkness. *You didn't know it, but I believe you've saved my reputation.*

Chapter Nine

The following morning, Esme sleepily opened her eyes to what looked like a garden of yellow roses. She blinked. *Where on earth . . . ?* And then she remembered. Her new home was Redcliffe Manor. It didn't seem possible.

She reached for her watch on the bedside table. Ten to seven. Later than her usual time. She supposed she'd been extra tired from trying to take in everything that went with a new job surrounded by unfamiliar people – except, of course, Stella. Esme smiled to think Stella hadn't wasted any time finding a potential boyfriend since her job had begun as a switchboard operator. She just hoped this Colonel Parker was a decent sort.

Her mouth felt dry. She wished she'd asked if it was all right to make a cup of tea in the kitchen when she was up in the morning. And what time breakfast was. Well, this morning she'd splash some water on her face in the basin in her room, dress and wander downstairs.

Stella was the first person Esme set eyes on as she came to the bottom of the main staircase. *Good*. She would have the answers.

'There you are,' Stella said with her usual wide smile, though Esme noticed her eyes looked tired and a little bloodshot. 'I'm just going into the kitchen to make tea.'

'Will Cook mind?'

Stella's eyes went wide. 'Are you joking?'

'No. She was a bit funny with me yesterday when I wanted one.'

'She'd better not pass any comment on me.' Stella opened the kitchen door. 'Morning, Lil. Mrs Donaldson and I have come to make a cup of tea.'

Lil nodded. 'I've just made a large pot and I'm about to take Cook her early tray. You can help yourselves.'

'What time does Cook come in?' Esme asked.

Lil glanced up at the wall clock. 'Not for another half hour. But she'll want this first – I'd better go or she'll haul me over the coals.'

Stella poured two cups of tea and set them on the pine table while Esme pulled up the two kitchen chairs.

'Sugar?' she asked Esme.

'No, thanks. I gave it up as soon as it was rationed. I actually like it better without, now I've got used to it.'

'I have to have a bit of sweet first thing.' Stella put half a teaspoon in her cup and stirred. She looked at Esme. 'Did you sleep all right?'

'I did. But it was quite strange waking up this morning – for a few seconds I had no idea where I was.'

Stella smiled. 'I think you'll enjoy it here – and Sir Giles is bound to keep you busy.'

'Stella, do you know his plans for the library?'

She frowned. 'He's always grumbling that he has to go up three flights of stairs to get there and one day he'll move it.' She looked at Esme. 'Why? Has he said anything to you?'

'Yes. I don't think it would hurt for me to tell you, but he wants it moved to the Muniment Room.'

Stella raised an eyebrow. 'Oh, I can see that room would work perfectly.'

'I agree, but it's not set up for a library. It would need loads more bookshelves for a start. And he thinks we're going to start moving the books on Monday.'

'That doesn't give you even a week to prepare.'

'I know.'

Stella looked thoughtful for a few moments while they sipped their tea.

'I have it,' she squeaked. 'The hospital!'

'What about it?'

'There are still some final building works going on. All they have to do is let a couple of their carpenters come over this week and they'd have it done in no time.'

Esme grinned at her beaming friend.

'That's a marvellous idea.'

'And who better than I to ask Colonel Parker if we could borrow them,' Stella said, chuckling with delight.

Esme gave a burst of laughter. 'Isn't this just an excuse to talk to him? Although I admit this will definitely be for a valid cause.'

At that moment Cook bustled in.

'What is this nonsense going on in my kitchen?' she demanded, her mouth a grim line. 'Oh, it's you, Miss Stella. You should know better.' She waved her arms. 'Be off, both of you – I've work to do.'

'Now, now, Cook,' Stella said, going up to her and to Esme's astonishment, giving the woman a hug. 'We're making plans to help Sir Giles.'

'Hmm. Let's hope he welcomes your interference.' But Esme noticed Cook's mouth had relaxed into a slight smile.

'Seriously, Stella,' Esme said, when she and Stella had left the kitchen, 'do you think Sir Giles will mind that we've "interfered", as Cook called it?'

'Not at all. He expects that if he gives out an instruction it's for other people to decide how to go about it. So long as it's what *he* wants rather than what *we* want, he'll be happy.'

'Will you ask the colonel today?' Esme said.

'As soon as breakfast is over – and I have my lipstick freshly applied,' Stella said with a wink.

Breakfast was a simple affair: porridge, toast and marmalade, and tea.

Now well fortified, Esme climbed the stairs to her room to clean her teeth. Then she pulled back the eiderdown and blanket and sheet to air the bed, folded her pyjamas and laid them on top of the two pillows, deciding to make the bed later. For now, she wanted to tell Sir Giles what Stella had suggested, to be sure she had his permission.

Sir Giles was already seated behind his desk with a pile of papers in front of him covered in writing. He'd already lit his first pipe but thankfully, she quite liked the smell of fresh tobacco. He looked up.

'Good morning, Mrs Donaldson.'

'Good morning, Sir Giles.' Esme hesitated. 'Are those papers part of your biography?' She nodded towards the pile of handwritten notes.

'Partly.' That expression again – almost embarrassed.

'Have you actually finished it?'

'Not quite. Not sure how to end it. No one wants to read about old people.'

'You'd be surprised,' Esme said. 'And I know that from experience in the library. Younger people love reading a long and interesting life story. I bet even some of the older schoolgirls would enjoy it. So I do hope you'll carry on with it.'

'If you say so.' His eyes gave him away with their twinkle.

'Would you like me to start typing them?' Esme said. 'It will help get my speed up if I do even a little every day.'

'That sounds sensible,' he said briskly, handing her a wodge of paper. 'You can start as soon as you like.'

This was the time to mention the move. 'Sir Giles, I know the Muniment Room will be perfect for the library, but as we said earlier, it will have to be modified.'

He peered at her. 'What do you suggest?'

'Stella and I have been discussing it over a cup of tea this morning and she suggested asking the director of the hospital if we could borrow a couple of carpenters to do the alterations.'

'Hmm. Stella is brighter than I've given her credit for,' he muttered. 'But it's not that straightforward. It's not a question of a couple of chaps knocking up some shelves. An ordinary carpenter wouldn't do at all. It needs someone with an artistic eye who understands Elizabethan architecture and doesn't smash into the cornice, for instance. Someone who can work with the architectural features, not against them.' He drew on his pipe. 'We're only custodians of these fine country estates, Mrs Donaldson, and have a responsibility to see that when we die, our descendants can enjoy them as we have.'

'Yes, I do see that,' Esme said. 'But this will be a permanent move, won't it?'

'Oh, yes,' came the firm answer. 'The attic was a nonsensical place for the library in the first instance, if you ask me. I do have a third library – the Old Library – downstairs that I haven't shown you. That might also need some attention but that's the least problem at the moment. I keep that one locked because it has some extremely rare books, so I don't want the schoolgirls to get their hands on them.' He glanced at her. 'As Stella is working at the hospital, is she willing to approach Colonel Parker and ask if he might be able to help?'

Esme held back a grin.

'I'm sure she'll be more than happy to approach him,' was all she said.

Esme caught up with Stella at lunchtime. The same rowdy group of girls was sitting at the table with Russell Kingsnorth. He half rose from his chair when Esme passed by, but she merely smiled and hurried over to where Stella occupied the same table by the window.

'I have some news,' she said when Esme was back with her lunch plate.

'You've had a word with the illustrious Colonel Parker?'

Stella grinned. 'I certainly have.' She gazed dreamily into the distance. 'What a lovely man.'

'Did he say he'd be able to send anyone?' Esme tried to bring Stella back to practicalities as she began to eat her lunch.

'Yes, and not only that – he said there's loads of timber left over from the small library they've already built at the hospital, so we can have whatever we need – at no cost.'

Esme hesitated. 'I don't think Sir Giles would be happy with any old timber,' she said. 'He'll undoubtedly use the same mahogany shelves already in the attic at present though there'll still be plenty of modifying to do.' She looked at Stella. 'But there is one thing he said when I spoke to him about it this morning.'

'What's that?'

'He wants someone who can go beyond being just a carpenter – more an artisan who appreciates the fine architecture and won't hammer and smash without any understanding of the house.'

'I think he's being perfectly fussy,' Stella said irritably. 'Does he want the job done or not?'

'Well, I understand why he's concerned. After all, it is a beautiful house and I think he feels a great responsibility towards it.' Esme took up another forkful of macaroni cheese.

'Hmm. Sir Giles can be a difficult man. Colonel Parker said he could send two carpenters tomorrow morning, and I'm sure they'll pass muster with him.' Stella rolled her eyes. 'And when they've finished dismantling and putting up shelves and such, they can box up the books and bring them down for you, so you won't have to do any of that lugging.'

'I think I'd prefer to pack them,' Esme said, 'and then I can label them and I'll know exactly what's in what box.'

'Yes, that's probably just as well, so you keep control, but let them help you.' Stella regarded her with a slight crease in her forehead. 'Look, Esme, I've done my bit, and as you're the one Sir Giles has talked to about what he wants, then I think you should be the one who can explain it to our colonel.'

'I don't mind doing that,' Esme said, thinking it would be fun to finally meet the man whom Stella seemed so crazy about. 'Where can I find him?'

'He'll probably be in his office having a sandwich.' She looked at her watch. 'I've got to get back to work, so why don't we go as soon as you've finished eating. If he's available, I'm sure he'll be pleased to have a word. But I'm sure you'll understand if I make myself scarce as I'm needed back on the switchboard.'

Ten minutes later, the two women walked across the parkland and over the bridge spanning not a river, as Esme had thought, but a series of narrow lakes to the hospital. Just as they were about to enter one of the buildings, Stella gripped her arm.

'Oh, there he is.'

Esme turned and caught her breath as he strode towards them. It couldn't be. Oh, but it was. The American officer, now without his cap, exposing his dark wavy hair, who'd seen her walking on the grass in bare feet when she was going for her interview. Who'd grinned. Who'd commented on the beautiful day. Watching him, she saw he was probably over six foot, and his Army jacket did nothing to disguise the breadth of his chest, the broad shoulders.

Don't let him recognise me. She comforted herself that she looked completely different from that first meeting – if you could call it that.

As he came closer to them, she saw his nose was strong, his mouth smiling. But the feature that caught her off-guard was his dark eyes topped by black brows. For one long moment that felt wrapped within a lifetime, he stared at her, his ready smile fading and those penetrating eyes fractionally widening. Her pulse beat painfully in her ears. No wonder Stella had her eye on him.

'Hi, ladies,' he said. 'Are you looking for anyone?'

That husky edge to his voice sent a shiver across Esme's shoulders.

That's down to too many cigarettes, she told herself crossly.

'Actually, we were looking for *you*,' Stella said under her eyelashes as she kept her eyes fixed on him. Sounding almost reluctant, she added, 'Let me introduce you to my friend.' She turned to Esme. 'Esme, this is the director of the new American hospital I was telling you about – Colonel Parker.' She looked back at him. 'Colonel Parker, Esme Donaldson.'

He held out his hand. 'Brad Parker.'

Her hand was lost in his. A spark shot up her arm and she hurriedly drew her hand away.

'Pleased to meet you, Miss Donaldson.'

To Esme's relief, he gave no indication that he remembered seeing her barefoot on the grass that day.

'Oh, it's *Mrs* Donaldson,' Stella corrected quickly.

Esme bit her lip. For the first time since Anthony died, she wished she hadn't had to make someone aware of her marital status. Or rather, Stella had done it for her.

He glanced at her left hand as though he needed to confirm it himself by seeing her wedding ring.

'Oh, my mistake,' he said, then added so quietly she was sure Stella couldn't have made out the words, 'I'm really sorry.' Seeming to collect himself, he said, 'Shall we go to my office and we can talk.'

He held the door open for both women to pass through. They stepped into a wide passage lit by powerful fluorescent tubes.

'Well, I'll leave you two to discuss the library,' Stella said, 'as I should get back to work. Pop in when you've finished your chat, Esme, so you can see me at work. I still get muddled up with the switchboard, terrified I'll put my lipstick in the hole instead of a plug. That'd be just like me.' She laughed, fluttering her thickly coated lashes at Colonel Parker, then addressed Esme. 'I'm at the end of the passage – door on the left marked "Communications".'

Esme noticed the colonel merely smiled politely before Stella disappeared. He turned to her.

'This way.' He indicated the right.

She walked with him along the passage, aware of his proximity as her heels clicked on the linoleum.

'I'm presuming it's about the house library.'

'Yes, that's right,' Esme said, managing to steady her voice. 'Sir Giles is concerned about a few things, so I'd like to go over them with you.'

'I'm right here.' He opened a door off the main passage and stepped aside to allow her to go in front.

It was a small, sparsely furnished, very masculine office. A modest desk was stacked with papers and files, all neatly piled but not leaving much space for him to work, she wouldn't have thought. A leather swivel chair was positioned behind the desk and two comfortable-looking spare chairs were placed next to one another, a couple of feet to one side. There were no pictures on the walls, only a large map of the West Country and an aerial view of Redcliffe Manor before the hospital was built. By the side of it hung a blueprint plan of the hospital design. Two metal filing cabinets jutted out from one wall near the window and bookshelves lined the other. She longed to walk over and inspect them properly – see what his reading material was, though no doubt it would all be medical stuff – but he nodded to one of the chairs.

'Do take a seat, Mrs Donaldson.'

He picked up a notepad but didn't sit behind his desk. Instead, he took the seat next to her, pulling it round to see her more clearly, then produced a fountain pen from his inside pocket.

'I'll make a note so I don't forget anything,' he said.

'You must have a lot on your mind with the hospital.' He was closer now. There was a cleft in his chin, which only added to his attractiveness. She gave herself a mental shake. 'Do you have any patients yet?' she asked him, desperate to sound matter-of-fact.

'We'll take our first twenty next week. We have pretty well all the medical equipment and the staff, so most things are in place. But there are always things you've overlooked so we've given ourselves a few more days to be perfectly ready.' He leaned towards her, his eyes warm with attentiveness. 'Now, what are Sir Giles's concerns?'

'He's worried that an ordinary carpenter wouldn't have the knowledge of a historical building like Redcliffe Manor.' She hesitated, not wanting to sound rude. 'He thinks just because someone's been a carpenter in the hospital building, which is only temporary while the war lasts, it isn't the best example to show him he has the required experience.'

Colonel Parker drew his brows together.

'I see.' He glanced at her. 'I think I can allay his fears. I propose to send Stanley Hicks and Herb Davis to do the design and work. They're both English. Stanley has an architect's background and has worked in several British country estates. Herb doesn't have quite that background but has a real love of old buildings and is an exceptionally talented carpenter – more like you'd call a joiner. I was very lucky to get them here and it's only because Stanley was too old to join up and Herb didn't pass the medical test because he has flat feet. But they both wanted to play their part, so they jumped at building a hospital for us. They haven't just done carpentry work here – they've built the whole darned hospital, with the help of some of our soldiers who've voluntarily done some of the rough work.' His eyes met hers. 'Do you think that answers Sir Giles's question?'

'I hope so,' Esme said fervently. She wished he wouldn't gaze at her like that. And she in turn couldn't take her eyes off him. It was as though she were mesmerised.

'Good.' He smiled, showing strong teeth. 'Anything else?'

'Yes. Any old timber – as he calls it – won't do. He'll use the existing shelves in the attic, but for any extra woodwork, he insists upon mahogany or oak. Many of his books are extremely valuable and he feels they should be displayed looking their best.' She paused. 'I have to say I agree with him.'

'So do I.' He jotted a few notes. 'All that will be dealt with by Stanley. He'll reuse what he can and if more timber is needed, he'll have the answer.'

'I'll pass that message on,' Esme said, glancing at her watch. 'I'd better go. I'd like to see where Stella is and then I need to get cracking with some work or Sir Giles will wonder where I've got to.' She looked at him as she stood up and he followed suit. 'He's not the easiest person to deal with . . . but you can't help liking him,' she added quickly, not wanting the colonel to think she was being disloyal.

'Yes, his heart seems to be in the right place.' He put the cap back onto his pen. 'Okay, let me take you to Miss Stratten, then do you think you can find your way out?'

'Oh, yes. And please don't come with me. I'm sure you're busy and she's told me where to go.'

'I wouldn't dream of not accompanying you.'

While they walked, Colonel Parker chatted about the canteen that had become operational. It sounded as though it was much better stocked than any British canteen or domestic kitchen. She gathered it had all been sent from America.

'We're short of so many of those things here,' she couldn't help saying. 'I don't mean particularly at Redcliffe Manor – we're probably luckier than most – but in general.'

He gave her arm the briefest touch. 'Any time you need something, you only have to let me know,' he said as they came to the last door. 'Okay, here's the Communications Room. You should find Miss Stratten in there.' His eyes met hers. 'I'll leave you to it, then, Mrs Donaldson.'

Esme swallowed. She placed a hand where he'd touched her arm – it had been so light, and yet it had felt as intimate as an embrace. She took in a breath to steady her nerves and knocked on the door, then opened it. Stella had her back to her and twisted round in her seat.

'Ah. Did you get it all sorted with the divine Colonel Parker?'

She felt a sudden warmth to her cheeks as Stella gave her a studied gaze.

'Yes, he seems very nice.'

'Hmm. Looks like you're already quite taken with him yourself, if I go by that flushed face of yours.'

'Don't be absurd, Stella. It's just warmer in here than in the passage, that's all.'

'I hope that *is* all,' she said. 'As I mentioned, I rather like him myself.'

Mentioned more than once, Stella.

'Don't worry,' Esme said, forcing a smile. 'He's all yours.' She made a pretence of looking at her watch. 'I can't really stop but I'll see you later.'

Stella nodded. 'I expect you can't wait to get started.'

Esme smiled. 'You're right.' She paused. 'Thanks, Stella. I really appreciate all that you've done.'

'Let's hope Sir Giles does as well,' Stella said, blowing her a kiss.

Making her escape, Esme wondered what on earth was the

matter with her. Why had she felt so irritated with Stella going on and on about Colonel Brad Parker? Then Stella accusing her of being taken with him herself, which of course was nonsense. She'd only just spoken to him for a few moments. But after Stella had told him she was Mrs, not Miss, and he'd politely acknowledged he'd addressed her wrongly, he'd added under his breath for her ears only: *I'm really sorry.* Did he mean that he was sorry she was married?

She scolded herself. She was behaving like one of the schoolgirls, trying to analyse those last three words. But she couldn't shake off a surge of longing. Squeezing her eyes shut, she admitted she was unbearably attracted to Colonel Brad Parker. She hadn't felt like this about any man since Anthony. And even then . . . She felt her cheeks warm at the memory of Brad's smile. She took in a jagged breath. She didn't want to upset her friendship with Stella, the very person who had found her the job which had led her to Brad. Added to that was the risk that any relationship with him could compromise her position at the Manor.

No, this overwhelming emotion must remain her secret.

Chapter Ten

'So I have Cousin Stella to thank for organising this, do I?' Sir Giles said, when Esme had told him she'd been to see Colonel Parker and about their discussion when she was back in his study ready to continue with his biography.

'You do really, Sir Giles.'

'Hmm. Perhaps I'll have a word with her. I also want a word with Colonel Parker.' He stroked his beard. 'It would be a good idea for you and me to have a meeting with him and the two carpenters – the sooner the better – so we can get the timing and cost agreed.' He chewed one of his charcoal biscuits. 'In fact, I'll strike while the iron's hot and ask when he'll be free to bring the carpenters over.' He looked at her. 'You'll be all right, won't you?'

'Yes, I'll just carry on with your memoirs.'

'How are you finding it?' Before she could answer, he added, 'Is it boring?'

'On the contrary,' she said truthfully, 'I'm finding it fascinating.'

He gave a snort as though he didn't believe her. 'I'll be back shortly.'

Esme turned to his biography again. She was relieved to see how quickly she remembered the keys on the ancient typewriter. But Sir Giles's handwriting was untidy, to say the least, so she had trouble deciphering it – caused, no doubt, by his missing fingers.

But she couldn't help feeling privileged to be asked to type his personal story and wondered if he hoped it would one day be published. If not, he hadn't mentioned any family – whether he and his wife had had children or there were other family members who might be interested in reading it.

Sir Giles had begun his life story right from when he was a baby, born in one of the dozens of bedrooms at Redcliffe Manor. He was an only child and appeared to have been totally spoilt by both his parents and grandparents, who gave him everything he wanted except the freedom that he craved. To escape their steel-like rules, he would go off on his bicycle with a picnic in the basket and his latest book, sometimes cycling for thirty miles before he felt he could stop and breathe freely, as he put it. She was sad to note that he was bullied at school because he hated sport and the headmaster would often haul him out of the library when he was supposed to be playing football. He'd end up with a good thrashing which, of course, did nothing to change his mind about sport.

Giving herself a break from tapping the keys, she skimmed the bulky manuscript to get an idea of his life after childhood and how much importance he gave each phase. Esme noticed he had different styles of expression. When he was passionate about something, such as reading the classics and learning about the natural world – how he loved sketching various animals, birds and plants – he wrote with ease and a spontaneity which drew her in. These were the parts she found most interesting. He'd even illustrated some of the pages, although how he'd managed to hold the fountain pen and sometimes a paintbrush steady with his right hand because of his missing fingers was hard for her to imagine. But his descriptive language of the different boarding schools he was sent to was often heavy-going and repetitive and there was rarely any reference to friendships formed. Her intuition told her he was a solitary being – perhaps by choice.

Strange. Esme stared at the sheet of paper, then checked the one before. He seemed to have left out an important part of his life. Now he suddenly had the two missing fingers but no explanation as to how it happened. She read more thoroughly the next few pages. There was no mention. But he did comment on how awkward some activities were these days and found drawing and painting a challenge.

Should she ask him why he hadn't explained about how he'd had some sort of accident? She hadn't really known him long enough to decide how he'd take it, but she couldn't help being curious. And so would other people be who might read it. But perhaps it was something very painful, very private, and decided not to say anything – not until she'd read and typed the whole manuscript anyway.

Esme found herself checking his work carefully as she typed, correcting his spelling as a matter of course, but sometimes condensing a repetition. She only hoped he would either approve or he wouldn't notice. The tip of her tongue showing in her concentration, she pressed on. The English language was not something to be mucked about with.

A quarter of an hour later Sir Giles was back. Esme looked up from her typing.

'Colonel Parker is with someone,' he said to Esme, clicking his tongue, 'and likely to be gone the rest of the day. I've left a message for him to bring the carpenters tomorrow morning.'

She felt a little thrill that she'd see Brad tomorrow, but she mustn't show any sign.

'It's probably just as well,' Sir Giles continued when she didn't answer. 'I'll be fresher in the morning.'

She typed steadily for another hour. The whole house was

eerily quiet. Dolly had mentioned the schoolgirls had gone on a hike. Long may it last. Esme was utterly absorbed in reading and typing Sir Giles's story when she heard voices outside the door. Turning her head, she saw Sir Giles, followed by three men... one of them Brad Parker (as she had begun to call him to herself), looking heart-stoppingly handsome in his uniform. She swallowed, fingers frozen in mid-air above the typewriter keys. He wasn't supposed to be here until tomorrow. Then she gathered her wits and smiled at them.

'Mrs Donaldson,' Brad Parker said, his voice making her head feel fuzzy, 'I've brought Stanley and Herb to meet you as they'll be doing the necessary work for the Muniment Room to become a library.'

'I'm Stanley,' said the older one, grinning and placing a hand on the shoulder of the sandy-haired man next to him, 'so he must be Herb.'

'Delighted to meet you,' Esme said, forcing her gaze from Brad Parker to the two carpenters.

'I've already shown them the attic where the library is at the moment,' Sir Giles said, 'and informed them I'd like a replica of that in the Muniment Room.'

'It won't be possible to do an exact replica,' Stanley said, 'because the shape is completely different and there's the fireplace we'll have to work around, but I'm sure we can make it look as similar as possible to the old one.'

'Well, do your best,' Sir Giles said gruffly.

'I'll sketch out a plan of how I think it would work,' Stanley continued, 'and if you approve, sir, we'll get cracking tomorrow as it will take us at least a week, maybe more, to get everything in place ready for the books to be moved.' He glanced at Esme. 'Sir Giles tells me you're in charge of the move, madam.'

Esme smiled. 'I believe so.'

'I'll send a couple of lads in to bring some boxes over right away to start packing, and when Herb and I are ready for them to be brought downstairs, we'll let you know.'

'That's marvellous,' Esme said. 'I'll mark them and all they'll need do is put them on the floor on the appropriate chalk marks I'll make for where I want each box to go and I'll unpack them at the other end.'

Sir Giles turned to the colonel.

'If you can give me an approximate idea of the charge, Colonel Parker, I'd be grateful.'

'No charge for any extra timber we might need for the shelves and any other materials as there's plenty left over at the hospital . . . and no charge for the labour.'

Sir Giles's bushy white eyebrows shot up. 'Nothing?'

Brad Parker smiled. 'It'll be my pleasure, sir. It's the least I can do when you've given us permission to build our hospital in such wonderful grounds.'

'Well, that's jolly decent of you.'

Esme saw from the corner of her eye, Sir Giles's worried frown fade.

'I'll get that sketch to you by the end of the day, sir,' Stanley said, 'and if the young lady could accompany us now to the new location, she can point out anything we might not have thought of.'

'You do that,' Sir Giles said, nodding to Esme.

Esme rose from her chair and Brad Parker held open the door for her to pass in front, giving her a small wink as if to say that everything had gone well with the meeting. As the four of them walked to the Muniment Room, she was grateful Stanley and Herb were with them. She would find it awkward to be alone with Colonel Brad Parker.

Stanley whistled through his teeth when he stepped inside the Muniment Room.

'This'll make a perfect library.' He looked at her. 'Do you know how many books there are to move . . . roughly?'

'I've calculated several thousand – at least five – maybe more.'

'Yes, that's probably about it.' Stanley narrowed his eyes and turned to Herb. 'Do you think there's room to incorporate enough shelves to take that sort of number, Herb, without disturbing all the wall cabinets?'

'No, definitely not.' Herb produced a packet of cigarette papers but saw Stanley frown and shake his head. He put it back in his pocket. 'Although this room's bigger'n the attic and has more floor to ceiling space, the cabinets will have to be positioned elsewhere. The window for one thing is triple the size of the attic one so that's taking up wall space in itself – and the fireplace is much larger.'

'Also we can't have the shelves too high up,' Esme broke in, 'because the library ladder isn't that tall and Sir Giles is not too steady on his legs.'

Stanley nodded. 'Fair enough. As it is, Sir Giles is going to have to think of another place for all his wall-hung cabinets but there should be enough floor space to keep the free-standing ones as they'd be a nice feature in the library.'

'The less you have to disturb anything, the better Sir Giles will like it,' Esme said with feeling.

Stanley opened the notebook he'd been carrying and drew a crude plan of the room and made a few notes.

'I'll turn that into a more detailed drawing,' he said, when she looked over his shoulder. 'Colonel Parker, can I ask you to drop it here this evening?'

'Be glad to.'

Her heart skipped a beat. So Brad would be calling at the house this evening. Maybe she'd see him. Stop and have a chat. She could ask him if there was anything more to do on the hospital building. Perhaps get an idea of how long he might be staying at Redcliffe

Manor. And then she collected herself. She mustn't be available. For one thing, it would look too obvious. For another, at his age and with those dark looks, he'd have a wife and children waiting for him in America. She wondered if Stella had thought that one through.

'Everything all right, Mrs Donaldson?' Sir Giles said, looking up when Esme went back to the study.

'Very much, Sir Giles. They're trying to work out a way to leave some of your display cabinets.' She wouldn't specify which ones.

'Hmm. If they have to go, then that's that.' He dipped his pen in the inkwell, and continued writing.

'I'll continue with your manuscript then,' Esme said.

But he either didn't hear her or was too engrossed in working out how to end his story because he didn't look up.

After supper, Esme decided to spend the rest of the evening in her room until Brad had been and gone. Then she could relax. As for now, she lay on top of the bed and opened the slim book she'd found in the library called: *Redcliffe Manor: A History of a Fine Elizabethan Estate.* She passed over the first flimsy page to the frontispiece. It was published in 1928 – a year before the stock market crash in New York. Maybe this was the reason Sir Giles was writing his memoirs, hoping it would be published, thereby bringing the history of the country house up to date. She'd just started to read the preface when she heard the doorbell ring.

She couldn't help it. Her heart fluttered. She knew it would be him. She opened her bedroom door and heard his voice in the hall.

'I have something for Sir Giles,' she heard him say. 'He's expecting it.'

'Please come in and I'll let him know you're here,' came Dolly's light tones.

Esme left her door slightly ajar. He hadn't taken a seat. She could hear his footsteps up and down the hall.

After a minute or two Dolly returned.

'The master is indisposed but he asked if you would kindly leave it and I'll take it to him first thing tomorrow morning.'

There was a short pause. Then she heard her name.

'If it's not too much trouble, would you please ask Mrs Donaldson if I could have a word with her instead? It's quite important.'

Esme bit her lip, waiting.

'I'll see if she's in.'

Esme quickly shut her door, then sat on her dressing-table stool brushing her hair.

Moments later Dolly gave a tentative knock.

'Come in.'

'Sorry to disturb you, madam, but Colonel Parker is downstairs and wants to speak to you as the master is having an early night.'

Before she could stop herself, Esme said, 'Thank you, Dolly. I'll come down. Tell him I won't be a minute.'

Dolly bobbed her head and shut the door behind her.

Her heart beating too fast, Esme glanced at herself in the mirror. Her face was flushed and her eyes shone brilliant under the light. Maybe a little powder on her cheeks would disguise how pink they looked. No, she was just prevaricating. There was nothing more she could do to put off the moment. Rising to her feet and determined to hold herself in check, she walked down the first flight of stairs to the landing. Brad Parker was staring up at her from below. Their eyes met for long seconds. Hating to break the spell, she slowly descended the main staircase in a daze, hardly realising one foot had touched the floor until she felt herself sway. In a flash, he caught her arm to steady her.

'I'm glad you were able to see me,' he said, his hand still on her arm.

She moved away, not trusting herself.

'Did Stanley give you his more detailed plan?' She managed not to stutter.

'Yes.' He held out a large brown envelope. 'I wonder if we could go to the Muniment Room so I can point out the various changes.'

For a breathless moment, Esme wondered if he was using it as an excuse to see her alone without risk of being interrupted.

Then she shook herself. Of course he wasn't. Sir Giles hadn't been available and Brad knew she was in charge of the move. That was all. Thankfully, Mrs Morgan hadn't let him in. *She* would have insisted upon taking the envelope and showing him out of the door. That thought made her smile and Brad smiled back.

'Yes, that's probably a good idea,' she said, leading the way. The only person they encountered was Dolly who stopped when she saw them.

'Would you be having a cup of tea or a mug of cocoa, madam?'

'Cocoa for me, Dolly . . . that would be lovely.'

The maid looked at the colonel. 'And for you, sir?'

'Make that two, please, Miss Dolly,' he said, smiling at her.

Dolly giggled. 'I'll leave it in the kitchen.'

With trembling fingers, Esme opened the door to what would be the new library. Brad Parker followed her and tossed the envelope on a nearby cabinet. He turned to her.

'Esme . . . may I call you that?'

'Yes, I'd like that.'

'And please call me Brad.' He gazed at her. 'Is Esme short for anything?'

'Esmeralda.' She ran over the syllables as though to get rid of them quickly.

His eyes widened a fraction. 'What a beautiful name. Does anyone call you that?'

'Only my sister when she's annoyed with me.' She smiled, trying to make a joke of it.

'Then I'd like to call you Esmeralda, but I promise it won't be because I'm annoyed with you, and not in front of anyone as it sounds so special.' He lowered his voice. 'Would that be all right?'

Her pulse raced.

'If you'd really like to.'

'I *would* really like to . . . Esmeralda.' His voice cracked on her name.

She was melting. He stepped towards her, his eyes dark with longing. Without realising what she was doing, Esme's arms were around him. He pulled her close, and even through his jacket, she imagined she could feel the beat of his heart. He was kissing her hair, her eyelids, her cheeks, her jawline . . . and finally, oh, finally, his mouth was on hers and he was kissing her with a passion that nearly sent her flying. She clung onto him as he steadied her, her lips parted, kissing him back. But just at that moment she heard the door squeak open . . . then a gasp. She froze as she heard it carefully close. Footsteps scurried away. Brad must have heard them too because he dropped his arms. Before she had time to wonder who had caught them in an embrace, Brad said:

'I'm so sorry, Esme.' His eyes were transfixed on hers. 'That was completely out of order. In the heat of the moment I'd forgotten you were married. Please forgive me.'

And with that, he made for the door, closing it softly behind him.

Esme didn't know how she crawled back up the staircases and into her room. Once there, she quickly got ready for bed, all the while aware of her burning cheeks. He'd kissed her. She'd wanted him to. She'd even been the one to put her arms around him first. How could she have been so bold? She'd never done anything like it in her life, and certainly not when she'd first met Anthony. Their romance had developed from a long friendship. This feeling she had for Brad was like a bolt of lightning, mocking her usual common sense.

He hadn't given her time to say she was a widow. All he'd done was take it for granted that her wedding ring meant she was married. She couldn't blame him for that, but if he hadn't been in so much of a hurry to get away . . . Oh, why hadn't she run after him? Called him to stop so she could explain. Was it because she'd kissed him back just as passionately? Then, as if a curtain had been pulled aside and she could see things clearly, she knew it was because of Anthony. She'd been so wrapped in this new feeling for Brad, she'd given Anthony no thought. But now she felt disloyal to him – to his memory. After all, despite what Freda said, it was still only two years ago. And she still missed him. So how could it be that she felt such a deep connection with someone she barely knew?

If she were honest, she missed Anthony's tender lovemaking. Maybe that was the reason she'd been so responsive to Brad – missing a man's arms around her. Missing having someone who loved her. But deep down she knew that wasn't it. She didn't want any man's arms around her – only Brad's.

It was going to be nerve-wracking when she next set eyes on him. Thank goodness she'd be dealing with Stanley and Herb regarding the new library and there'd be no reason for her to see him on her own, hearing him call her Esmeralda. With that small crumb of comfort, she closed her eyes. It was only then that she remembered about the cocoa Dolly had made them. She ran her tongue over her lips. She could just do with it. And then something else struck her. She hadn't picked up the envelope containing Stan's library room plan. Well, she wasn't going to retrieve it now and have someone question her as to what she was doing roaming around the manor at this time of night, letting herself into Sir Giles's private rooms. She gave a deep sigh. She'd collect it first thing in the morning before anyone else was up and clear away the two cold mugs of cocoa before Dolly came in, so as not to hurt her feelings.

Chapter Eleven

The first thing on Esme's mind when she awoke was the feel and taste of Brad Parker's kiss. Her body quivered and her cheeks grew warm at the memory. She resolved to put it away in a private part of her mind and concentrate on the job that Sir Giles had entrusted her with. And then she remembered the door opening – someone giving a sharp intake of breath. Who was it? It would be pointless trying to find out as she'd only bring more attention to herself about her and Brad in the Muniment Room. No, best to let it die a natural death and just hope whoever it was wouldn't start any rumours.

She glanced at her bedside clock. Twenty past six. She quickly washed and dressed and ran down the two flights of stairs to the kitchen, ready to apologise to Dolly. To her dismay, the bulky figure of Cook faced her, and on the pine table were the two incriminating mugs, still full of cocoa that the girl had made the night before.

'Come for the mugs, have you?' Her sharp eyes pierced Esme's. 'So you could get rid of them before I came down?'

'I'm terribly sorry,' Esme said, desperate not to allow her cheeks to flush. 'Dolly kindly made Colonel Parker and me the drinks yesterday evening, but to tell the truth, we got chatting about the ins and outs of the new library and forgot to collect them.'

'Hmm.' Cook stood staring, her hands on her hips. 'Forgotten there's a war on as well, no doubt, by this waste.' She nodded over to the mugs. 'I'll remind you that cocoa's in short supply, Mrs Donaldson.'

Cook was quite right. Esme had to save the situation from escalating. She glanced at the saucepans hanging on a rack and unhooked one of the smaller ones, then poured the contents of the mugs into it.

'I'll be happy to have this warmed up instead of coffee later,' she said, placing the pan on the sideboard. 'And Sir Giles loves cocoa so he won't mind . . . and I'm sure I can rely on you not to spill the beans . . . even the coffee beans,' she added, biting back a grin at Cook's pinched expression.

Cook merely grunted and began to set out her utensils and bowls ready for the day's meals. Esme beat a hasty retreat. Her stomach growled. She was desperate for a cup of tea and something to eat. Sir Giles was never down early. She'd have plenty of time to pick up Stan's envelope after breakfast.

She quickly finished eating in the breakfast room where no one else had joined her. Not wanting to waste any more time, she left for the Muniment Room, but the door was locked. Esme frowned. She'd only closed it behind her when she'd left last night. So someone – was it one of the maids who'd caught her kissing the director of the American hospital? – whoever it was, had locked it. This was embarrassing. Well, all she could do was present herself in Sir Giles's study and wait for any remarks.

Sir Giles seemed perfectly normal when he greeted her. But then he said:

'Have you the plan Stanley promised would be here yesterday evening?'

'Yes,' Esme said. 'As arranged, he gave it to Colonel Parker who dropped it in.'

'What do you mean, dropped it in? It was important. I didn't want him to hand it to just anyone. I wish I'd come downstairs myself.'

'It's all right, Sir Giles. He gave it to me.'

'Where is it then?'

Esme swallowed hard. She'd have to own up. 'It's in the Muniment Room.'

His blue eyes pierced through her with suspicion.

'Oh. Why's that?'

'He wanted to look at it in the room where the library is going to be, so I went with him.' Her heart began beating faster.

'And what did you both think?'

'We didn't open it.'

Sir Giles's forehead furrowed in deep recesses.

'But I thought that was the whole point.'

'I know. We just got talking about the best way to do the move. And when we left, I forgot to pick it up.'

'I see.' His expression was one of displeasure. 'Well, Mrs Donaldson, you'd better retrieve it then as Stanley and Herb will be here at any time.'

'I tried to, sir, but the room was locked.'

He nodded. 'Yes, it would be. I go round all the rooms we use downstairs every night and make sure the ones that need to be locked are. And the Muniments Room, as you might expect, is one I keep under lock and key when I'm not around.' He fished in his pocket and handed her a key. 'Take this.'

She took the key and made a swift departure. How could she have been so stupid as to not take the plan with her when she left the room? Her cheeks beginning to flush, she could only blame herself for being so carried away with Brad Parker that everything else had fled from her mind.

Maybe no harm's been done, she consoled herself, as she

unlocked the door. *Sir Giles will probably forget all about it when he becomes involved with the move.*

She opened the door and glanced over at the cabinet where Brad had tossed the envelope. She blinked. The top of the cabinet was completely clear. There was no brown envelope in sight.

Feeling sick to her stomach, she stepped into the room and searched. But the cabinet cases themselves were all locked. She glanced in the wastepaper basket but there were only a couple of white envelopes torn in half. There was nowhere else it could be. If Sir Giles didn't have it, then who on earth did? She'd been gone several minutes and Sir Giles would be wondering where she was. She couldn't put off the moment any longer.

Standing in front of his desk, Esme said, 'I'm afraid it's not there.'

'What do you mean, it's not there?' He raised his voice. 'Where is it then?'

'I don't know,' she said miserably. 'It was there last night.'

'Are you saying someone's picked it up?'

'It must be that.'

'Well, that someone has some explaining to do.' His fingers tapped on the desk. 'But I must tell you, Mrs Donaldson, I'm not at all pleased. This was a simple thing for the colonel to bring the plan here last night, and for it to be in your safe keeping until this morning.' He shook his head. 'I'm not sure I can trust you in the future to do any personal jobs for me – and that's part of the reason I hired you.'

'Sir Giles, this is not like me at all,' Esme protested. 'I'm sure it hasn't gone far. I'll find out who took it. But for now, at least we know roughly what Stanley intends to do.' She felt a stinging at the back of her eyes. This was all her own fault. 'I'll prove to you I can be trusted.'

'We'll see,' Sir Giles grunted.

There was a knock on the door.

'Enter,' Sir Giles called.

Dolly bobbed her head. 'Mr Stanley has arrived, sir, with two others.'

'Thank you, Dolly.'

She bobbed her head again and held open the door for Stanley and two youths, no more than sixteen, both grinning. One of them looked at Dolly and gave her a wink. She stifled a giggle and scuttled off.

'Have you had a chance to look at the plan, sir?' Stanley said.

'No, I haven't had sight of it.' Sir Giles's mouth was in a grim line.

'Oh, I gave it to the colonel as we arranged. Didn't he bring it over?'

'Yes,' Esme said, 'but somehow it's disappeared.'

'Not to worry – I made a copy.' Stanley produced a sheet of paper. He handed it to Sir Giles who studied it.

'You've taken down all the wall-hung cabinets.'

'We had to. We'll need every bit of space possible. But—' Stanley broke off and glanced round the study, then turned to Sir Giles. 'In my opinion, you could easily house them in here, sir, and I think you'll enjoy them every day if the study is where you spend most of your time.'

Sir Giles stroked his beard. 'I do at the moment, now I'm writing a book.'

'Well, shall we try it and see how you feel?'

Sir Giles nodded. 'I'll leave it to Mrs Donaldson's discretion.'

Esme felt a flicker of relief. It looked as though Sir Giles was giving her another chance.

'Right, sir. The boys are ready to work and have gathered a load of cardboard boxes so should we take them straight up to the attic?'

'Good idea. Mrs Donaldson will decide what books go in which boxes.'

'And when you've finished packing the books in one section, Herb and I will start dismantling the first lot of empty shelves straightaway.' Stanley turned to the boys. 'Right, lads, let's get going.'

In spite of their young ages, Esme realised the boys, Tom and Arthur, took the job seriously and that afternoon half a wall of books had been packed neatly in boxes and she'd labelled them by subject. She'd soon given up dusting the books one by one – it held up progress. Maybe one of the maids would help out when the books were all transferred to their new home.

The three of them worked methodically through the week, with Stanley and Herb dismantling the shelves, bit by bit, until there was only one small section on the right of the fireplace. One afternoon on the second week, Esme was on the fourth step of the ladder handing down the books to the boys when the next one she came to was an enormous atlas lying on its side. Using both hands, she tried to gently prise it from the shelf, but it was too cumbersome for her to manage it. She came down the stepladder.

'Tom, that next book is going to be really heavy. Do you think you can bring it down?'

''Course I can.' He flew up the steps.

'Be careful.'

But in Tom's exuberance and with the weight of the atlas, he pulled the book too sharply and overbalanced. Arthur tried to right the stepladder, but Tom crashed to the floor, and the book went flying.

Esme rushed to him.

'Oh, my goodness, are you all right?'

He scrambled to his feet. 'No bones broken,' he said cheerfully.

'Lucky I landed on that rug. Sorry about that. Hope I haven't damaged the book.'

Arthur had recovered the atlas and set it on one of the floor cabinets.

'It's still in one piece,' he said.

'I don't think we need pack that,' Esme said. 'Anything really heavy, we'll carry down individually.'

Tom bent down and picked up what looked like a thickly folded piece of paper. 'Oh, this must have been inside the atlas.' He started to unfold it.

'Tom!' Esme put her hand out. 'I'll take that. It could be someone's private correspondence.'

Tom's face reddened as he handed it over.

'Now let's get on with the task,' Esme said firmly as she re-folded the letter and tucked it into her pocket.

The next hour passed in silence except for a few grunts from the boys when they had to lug more weighty volumes.

'Phew!' Tom said, closing the latest cardboard box by folding over the four flaps. He stood up and stretched his arms above his head and gave Esme an exaggerated woebegone look before turning to his mate. 'Dry work here, innit, Arth?'

'Too right,' Arthur said.

'Is that a hint that you want a cuppa?' she laughed.

'Thought you'd never ask,' Arthur chuckled.

'Well, I don't want you two to die of thirst, so I'll go and see if there's anyone in the kitchen.'

She soon returned, Dolly following a couple of minutes behind carrying a tray of tea and a plate of biscuits, not before giving the two lads a smile, then a giggle as she left.

'Right,' Esme said firmly, 'Ten minutes, that's all.'

'Slave driver,' Arthur said, his mouth full of digestive biscuit as he grinned at her.

'No, it goes for me, too. We need to get this wrapped up and then tomorrow the boxes can go downstairs.'

Finally, the last box was labelled and stacked with the dozens of others along the sides of the walls, now bereft of most of their shelves that Stanley and Herb were busily fitting in the new library.

'We'll be off then, Mrs Donaldson,' Tom said. 'See yer tomorrow.'

'Thank you both very much,' Esme said. 'You've been good workers.'

'We'll be even better when we get a breath of air and can light up,' Arthur said cheekily when she hustled them out of the back door.

Esme blew out her cheeks. It had been another tiring week and she knew she must look a sight. Time to go upstairs to her room and freshen up before supper.

But as she wearily climbed the staircase, she couldn't help wondering what Brad was doing this very minute.

Chapter Twelve

Loud girlish voices and clanking cutlery and china met Esme as she opened the dining room door. She looked round at what had been the elegant banqueting room, imagining a dozen beautifully dressed, bejewelled and coiffed women and the same number of men handsome in their white tie evening dress. Now it was packed with schoolgirls all talking at once. Oh, if only there was some corner, some little back-room storage closet, even, that she could tuck herself into to get away from the cacophony.

Esme scanned the room, but every space seemed to have been taken. Then she spotted Russell Kingsnorth who caught her eye and stood up.

'Mrs Donaldson,' he called, 'please do come and sit at our table. The girls will love to have you and there's a seat here that's vacant.'

Esme forced a smile and walked over to his table, full of chattering girls. Once again, Bertha, the one with the pigtails, stared daggers at her from near where Russell indicated to sit. The girl certainly belied Russell's sentiments. What on earth was the matter with the child? What terrible deed was Esme supposed to have done?

'I'm so glad we have a chance to talk,' Russell said when she reluctantly sat next to him. He fixed his gaze on hers long enough for her to not exactly feel uncomfortable but more irritated. 'How are you finding us?'

'I'm enjoying the work,' she answered in a neutral manner, 'and everyone is helpful.'

'Even Mrs Morgan?' Russell grinned.

She couldn't help smiling. 'Mrs Morgan may take a bit more working on,' she conceded.

Russell roared with laughter. 'You'll be the first if you succeed,' he said. 'And you haven't met Hilary Fenton yet, have you?'

'No. Does she work here?'

'Yes. She's the housemistress for the girls and teachers. She's been away but came back yesterday.'

'Well, I've been buried in the attic all week, so it's not surprising I haven't come across her,' Esme said. 'I'll look forward to meeting her.'

'Sometimes looking forward to something can be disappointing.' He put another forkful of onion and potato pie in his mouth.

'Why do you say that?' Esme asked curiously.

'No comment,' he said, deftly changing the subject.

Back in her room, Esme took her skirt off ready to hang it up when she saw the folded letter sticking out of the pocket. Removing it to put on her dressing table so she didn't forget it in the morning, she could immediately see it was the best quality stationery. Should she open it and read it? No, it was private. But she did need to know who it belonged to, so she could return it.

Assuring herself she was only going to look at the salutation, she unfolded it. Immediately, her attention was drawn to the address at the top: *Redcliffe Manor, Bath*. It was dated 23rd January 1925 and began in beautiful italic writing: *My dear Giles*. She removed the top sheet and her eyes flicked to the end of the letter: *Your affectionate father, Lindsay Carmichael*. Quickly she refolded it and placed it on the dressing table.

Why hadn't Sir Giles kept the letter in a desk drawer instead of tucked into an atlas?

Esme bit her lip. It was obviously a private letter from a father to his son. But it wasn't even in an envelope. Anyone could have taken down the atlas and discovered it.

Should she put it back unread within the pages of the atlas? Or just give it to Sir Giles? She tried to picture his face. All she could see was his forehead creased in suspicion, then his cheeks flushed with annoyance, certain she must have already read it. There would be an awkward silence between them. He might even sack her for snooping. But oh, how she dearly wanted to read it. It just might help her to understand why Sir Giles sometimes seemed so morose – or snappy.

With heart beating harder that she was invading someone's privacy – her employer's, no less – and trepidation as to what the letter would reveal, she began to read:

23rd January 1925

My dear Giles,

It might seem strange that I am sending this letter rather than speaking to you, but now I am confined to my bed, I have had plenty of time to think about serious matters. Also, you can re-read a letter but it's more difficult to remember everything in a conversation and take note and you might need to re-read this.

Your mother and I were so proud of our three sons – George, Gerald and you, Giles. It was of course a huge disappointment when George married a French girl and moved to France. It showed us he wasn't interested in the estate, and I must now admit he never was. Next in line was Gerald, the practical one, who I always assumed would be the natural successor. He had always taken a keen interest in the Manor, but that wasn't to be either. It broke our hearts when your brothers were both killed in the Boer War. We have never recovered from the shock. But we put all our hopes for the future and Redcliffe Manor into you, our youngest son. Perhaps we were mistaken to do so, but I don't see what the alternative could have been. I know you didn't want to learn estate management but to your credit you followed the course and made a fair job of it.

Then came the Great War – a war to end all wars, they said. But to learn that my only son and heir was a conscientious objector was a deep shock to me. After all, you were still young at 34. I could certainly have used my connections to get you a decent job in the Navy and be somebody we could all respect and who would have made a useful contribution to the war effort. Imagine if everyone decided the same as you – we would have been overrun by the Germans!

I couldn't help thinking you were not the son I expected you to be – a man following in the footsteps of his father and taking an active role. Your brothers died heroes. But your refusal to go into the military was a bitter blow. You may take comfort that your mother was not so upset as I was. She said she didn't want to lose her third son and only living child. But I was brought up to believe the family name was of the utmost importance, so I'm afraid I told people you'd been sent away to fight. I couldn't stand the thought of them knowing you'd gone to prison for two years.

Then two nights ago you confided in me about your climbing accident last year. You faced a terrible decision but there was no other possible outcome and you cannot spend the rest of your life feeling guilty. Put this behind you.

Now you tell me you are content teaching history and, to be perfectly honest, you were extremely lucky to get a decent job given the circumstances, but they were short of teachers. Your school may not have gone into your background as carefully as they might have. But whatever you do, I strongly advise that you do not speak of that day in the mountains to anyone as it will continue to haunt you, *and on no account must you ever hint you were once a CO in the war. I do not want that shame brought upon the family.*

You were always a dreamer and spent too much time on your own. It is a pity you and Beatrice never had any children as the line dies out with you.

I hope you will understand me a little more after reading this letter. The doctor has given me only a few weeks so at least it's all out in the open now. I hope you will forgive me for any harsh words I have used to you in the past.

Your affectionate father,
Lindsay Carmichael

Esme blinked. How dreadful to lose both his brothers in another senseless war. She read the letter. Something else struck her. She'd heard a neighbour tell her mother that a young man she knew was a 'conchie' and what a disgrace it was that he wasn't doing his bit like all the other young men. Later, she'd found out it was what people called a conscientious objector – or CO for short. At the time, she hadn't thought much about it, except that perhaps they must be sensitive boys, or brought up to be very religious. And in a way, she could feel some sympathy for them. But Sir Giles being of the aristocracy – *oh dear*. No wonder his father had sounded so upset. His son had obviously refused to sign up when he'd been called upon by the government and instead had served a prison sentence. She couldn't help a sigh. His father must have been beside himself with shame. And then knowing his son was teaching schoolboys history when they'd only just come through a terrible war that Sir Giles hadn't fought in, thereby risking humiliation to the family, must have been a double blow.

She'd always assumed Sir Giles had lost his fingers in the Great War, but it seemed that something awful had happened since the war when he was mountain climbing. Was that when he had lost his fingers and given him a limp? She wondered what mountains his father was talking about and what had happened to cause such a dreadful outcome. There was so much more to Sir Giles than she realised.

Carefully, Esme folded it back, thinking that Sir Giles must now be not much more than sixty, though he looked more like seventy with his white hair and beard. Perhaps the accident had turned his hair white prematurely. She'd felt more than once while typing his story that he was bottling up something, and that it might be a cathartic exercise if he brought it out in the open and wrote about it in his memoirs. But how could she approach him without opening any floodgates?

The following day, Tom and Arthur worked tirelessly taking down the boxes of books to the new library. Esme was delighted to see most of the bookshelves in place ready for her to position the books where she and Sir Giles had directed them. Herb was giving them a polish and Stanley was fitting the last ones in the alcoves beside the fireplace.

'Everything looks very satisfactory,' she said to their beaming faces. 'And you've managed to keep the floor cabinets.'

'All but one,' Stan said, wiping his forehead. 'That's gone into the hall.'

'Now the *real* work begins when I put them into their proper categories,' she teased.

'Yep. And thank goodness it's *your* job,' Stan said.

'Do you think Sir Giles will approve?' from Arthur.

'I'm sure he will,' Esme said.

There was a tap at the door and Lil came in.

'Madam, the master gave me this for you.' She handed Esme a small, folded piece of paper.

Esme read that Sir Giles was tired and was going to have

supper brought to his room. And for her to go ahead with where she thought the books should go. It felt to Esme as though he was thoroughly fed-up with the project and had put it into her hands. She looked at Lil who was waiting expectantly.

'Tell him I've taken note and I hope to see him tomorrow.'

Lil nodded and disappeared.

'Let's get started unpacking,' Esme told the boys. 'We'll do an hour, then call it a day.'

Chapter Thirteen

Esme stood back and surveyed the new library. It had taken nearly five weeks instead of the week Sir Giles had first envisaged and tomorrow was the first day of November – a Sunday where she could draw breath. Tom and Arthur had left a few minutes ago and she'd given each of them five shillings, explaining it was from Sir Giles. She imagined they'd be straight down to the pub with their mates. Well, they were only young once and they'd worked jolly hard until late in the evenings and even at weekends. Everyone had backache from constant bending and stretching and lugging, but now the job was done.

She longed for Sir Giles to come and inspect it, but he'd developed a bad cold and frightful cough. His doctor decided it could turn into pneumonia, so in spite of the patient's protests, he had ordered complete rest.

'I'll leave it to you to finish the job,' Sir Giles had rasped when she'd brought him a hot lemon drink. He took a sip, then pulled a face as he handed back the glass. 'This needs at least two teaspoons of sugar and a good shot of whisky.'

There was no point in telling him that sugar was rationed.

'I'll see what I can do in the kitchen,' she said.

And that had been it. She'd simply carried on without any further direction from him, cataloguing and arranging his books logically in the Dewey system that couldn't be bettered so far as she was concerned.

We probably finished in half the time it would have taken if he'd been involved, she thought wryly.

But the problem of the letter from Sir Giles's father was still niggling away at her. Should she tell him now and get it over with – or wait until he was back on his feet. And if he questioned her, should she pretend she hadn't read it? But it wasn't in her nature to lie.

Nor is it in your nature to read people's private letters that are no concern of yours, her inner voice admonished.

I only did it so I might be able to help him, she argued.

She couldn't hold off any longer. She'd intercept Dolly and take him his hot lemon and whisky this very morning at eleven o'clock and own up.

To her surprise, Sir Giles was up and, although still in his dressing gown, was sitting at a table in his bedroom and opening a pile of brown envelopes.

'Good morning, Mrs Donaldson.' He smiled, showing his large yellow teeth.

His nose was still red and his eyes watery, but he sounded more chipper.

'Good morning, Sir Giles. Are you feeling better?'

'Much.' He took the glass from her. 'I'll drink this and get dressed and come and see how the library is getting on.'

'I'll see you down there, sir,' Esme said.

Good. They'd be in the new library, and she could show him what they'd done and what was still left to do and casually mention how they'd found the letter.

Sir Giles joined her a quarter of an hour later when she was sitting at one of the desks doing some cataloguing. He looked round the room. She felt his eyes missed nothing.

'Shall I take you round and explain where everything is?' Esme said, after a silence where he'd given no indication as to whether he approved or not.

'I'll go on my own when I feel up to it. Get myself acquainted with a new method, no doubt.'

'I hope you'll find your way around,' she said. 'I've recorded on the index cards the various subjects and how they're numbered.'

Is now the time?

She had the atlas on the desk in front of her. Mentally crossing her fingers, she picked up the two sheets of notepaper and walked over to him.

'Sir Giles, this fell out of one of the books when we were taking it off the shelf upstairs.'

He took it from her and unfolded the creases. Just as she imagined, he frowned, the blood draining from his face, leaving him sheet white. He sank into the nearest chair, hooking his walking stick over the arms, his eyes not leaving her face.

'Which book was it in?' His voice was hoarse.

She couldn't work out if it was the shock or his cold.

'That large atlas.' She nodded towards the desk where she'd been sitting.

'Bring it over here!'

With a heart as heavy as the book, she put it in his hands, noticing the difficulty he had holding it. He leafed through the middle pages, then glanced at the letter. She stood near his chair, waiting for the explosion.

'I haven't read this in fifteen years,' he said, looking up at her, his face expressionless, 'so I'm sure you will be far more acquainted with it than I.'

He knew. She swallowed.

'I'm sorry, Sir Giles. It was very wrong of me. I don't remember ever doing anything like it.'

'Then why did you?'

She might as well make a full confession. There was nothing to lose now.

'It was typing your biography.'

'I can't see what that had to do with it.'

'Well, sir, you'd started from birth right through your schooldays, and then learning estate management so you could take over Redcliffe Manor, but then I noticed there was a gap of a few years and I wondered why you left them out, especially as it would have been during the Great War. I thought that was where you had lost your fingers. And why you limped. But you never mentioned any accident. And then a few years later when you were teaching history, there was another gap. I had the feeling you were glossing over something important. So I'm afraid that when I saw it was a letter addressed to you from your father, I thought I might find some kind of answer and if so, persuade you to include that part of your life.'

'I see.' He sneezed and whipped out a handkerchief to blow his nose.

She was sure he didn't see at all.

'It sounds . . . well, I think it would make a very human story,' Esme fumbled for her words.

'What makes you think that?' Sir Giles's voice was perfectly controlled.

She had no idea what he was thinking or what he would do next. When he was silent, she said:

'Something happened in the mountains, and I wonder if that's where you lost your fingers.'

'You're right,' he said shortly. 'Frostbite. Toes as well. Lost some of those.'

Compassion filled her. But there was more to his story than frostbite. She must not mention the guilt on any account.

'I do understand if you tell me it's none of my business, Sir Giles, but—'

'No buts.' Sir Giles stared at her. 'Mrs Donaldson, you do realise this gives me reason to sack you for such an effrontery.'

'Yes, I do,' Esme said miserably.

Sir Giles stroked his beard. 'But you might be right.'

She startled. 'Sir?'

'Perhaps I've bottled it up too long.' He cleared his throat. 'I think we'll have a pot of coffee in my study and then I'll tell you what happened in the mountains. Maybe then it will be clear to both of us whether it should be included in my memoirs or if it should remain as the skeleton in the cupboard. But first, I'll show you where I was.'

While he was looking for the right place in the atlas, Esme went to the kitchen to ask one of the girls if she would bring some coffee for Sir Giles and her in his study. Ten minutes later, when Dolly had set the tray of coffee down on his desk and left the room, he told her what had happened in the mountains.

'And that night, as though it were my punishment, I was struck by frostbite in my hands and feet and eventually lost the two fingers and two toes in my right foot,' Sir Giles finished.

Esme's hand trembled as she picked up her cup of coffee, hardly noticing it had gone cold in the time it had taken Sir Giles to describe what had happened that fateful day when he'd lost his friend. Surreptitiously, she glanced at her watch. It had taken him through many hesitations and pondering long seconds before he was ready to resume his story and she felt as drained as though she'd been with him on the expedition to Mount Everest and had experienced everything he had. She needed something to moisten her parched throat. Sir Giles's coffee had also remained untouched as he regarded her with a grief-stricken expression.

'So now you know even more than I told my father that evening,' he said gruffly.

Esme was silent, too shocked to speak as she tried to gather her wits.

'Oh, Sir Giles, I can't tell you how very sorry I am,' she said, finally finding her voice. 'What an awful situation you were both in.'

He gave an almost imperceptible nod. 'But it doesn't make it any easier to bear.'

He wasn't going to allow himself to see it from his friend's perspective, Esme realised. There didn't seem anything else she could add to persuade him.

Her cup rattled as she placed it in the saucer. Her thoughts jostled into one another. He had confided in her. Could she possibly tell him what she truly thought he should do?

'I can't drink this,' Sir Giles said, eerily echoing her thoughts as he jerked his head towards the coffee pot. 'Would you make me a nice hot cup of Bovril, Mrs Donaldson?'

'Gladly.' She rose to her feet. It would give her a few minutes to think what to say.

But there was so much commotion in the kitchen, with Cook raging because the fish hadn't arrived as the fishmonger had promised, that Esme felt in the way of the maids who were peeling a mound of vegetables and trying not to take notice of the tirade. She made the two drinks and escaped as quickly as she could.

Back in Sir Giles's bedroom, she silently handed him his Bovril and quickly downed her tea, grateful for the hot liquid to revive her. She hoped it would do the same for her employer. After a minute, he looked up.

'You've been a good and loyal worker, Mrs Donaldson, so I've decided I'm not going to say any more about my father's letter.' He was watching her closely.

'I'll never do anything like it again,' she said. 'But please believe me, it was only that I felt you were deeply unhappy and thought it might throw a light on the reason so I might be able to help in some way.'

'Yes, you mentioned I should include the experience in my memoirs.'

'Only if it wouldn't upset you too much.'

He shook his head. 'If I'm honest, I feel a little better telling you – someone who's not family and wouldn't judge me.'

'Nobody should judge you,' Esme said. 'You did the only thing.'

'I like to think so,' he replied. 'But how do any of us know how we'd react until we're faced with it?' He shook his head. 'We'll leave it there. And if you think anyone would be interested to read that part of my life, well . . . I'll think about including it.'

'I feel very strongly they would,' Esme pressed on. 'It's a very human story which people will relate to – maybe not in a mountain accident, but how you lost someone dear to you—' She broke off, feeling the sting of bitter tears at the memory of the nurse only giving her a glimpse of her precious baby daughter. Sir Giles flashed her a glance but said nothing. Collecting herself, she added, 'And in a way, it would be a recognition of your friend's bravery if it were ever published. You could dedicate it to him.'

'Hmm. I hadn't thought of that.' He trumpeted his nose. 'I'd better get it written then – if only for the exercise of recalling it. But when he looked over to her, she saw his eyes glistened with tears.

Chapter Fourteen

Cataloguing the books in the library occupied most of Esme's days but she managed to make time to slip outside for air every afternoon and walk round the grounds now that autumn was in its glory. The leaves on the lime trees had turned yellow and the acers were the most wonderful deep red – brightening up the gloomy grey November skies as she approached the bridge that led to the military hospital.

Today, a red squirrel ran in front of her, then darted into the undergrowth near the bank. Once, she turned round and looked towards the hospital as she was making her way back to the Manor. In the Great Hall, she went upstairs to take off her hat, coat and scarf, and put them away, pinching herself once more to be working in such interesting surroundings, even if the bedroom radiator clicked and hissed. At least it kept the chill off.

But when she had even a few minutes spare, her thoughts strayed to Brad. How she wanted to tell him he hadn't kissed a married woman. And that she hadn't been unfaithful – not really. She bit her lip. If she were honest, she still felt guilty to Anthony's memory. Brad must have thought she was a loose woman to have kissed him back the way she did when she evidently had a husband fighting for the country. But how could she just walk up to him and tell him the truth? It would be too embarrassing for words. And then it would be his turn to be embarrassed, thinking she was only telling him because she wanted him to know she was free. But he'd only kissed her in the heat of the moment and she shouldn't take it in the least seriously. Oh, what a mess it all was.

The good thing was that Sir Giles, although quieter, seemed focused on his project to fill in the missing years of his life, and had begun to address her as Esme. She couldn't be more pleased on that front.

Today, the postman brought her a letter from Freda. It was a rare occurrence for her sister to put pen to paper, and she eagerly opened the envelope. It was dated 2nd November 1942.

Dear Esme,

I hope everything is going as you hope with your new position. It's the usual chaos here but we're all well, at least. However, I am very worried about Dad. I went to see him yesterday (sorry I didn't get a chance to see you as well, especially in Redcliffe Manor) and noticed a deterioration in these last weeks. Muriel is becoming more obnoxious than ever and makes it obvious she's resentful that she has to look after a husband who is older and has failing health. Was she really so stupid not to work that out before she married him? But no, all she could think of was that one day he'd leave her comfortably off and she wouldn't have to worry about looking after anyone else for the rest of her life.

I don't need to spell it out, but I'm horrified. She has no real love for him, any more than she does for you and me.

But first I need to meet you on our own. I'll come to Bath if you like, or even to Redcliffe Manor. That might be a better idea so I could see where you work. Let me know.

Freda

No 'Love', nor any sign of a kiss. Esme couldn't help a rueful smile. Freda's nature was to be direct without any sentiment. But her sister was right. It wasn't fair for Muriel not to help care for Dad when she'd insisted he marry her all those years ago. If only she'd been a loyal wife and loved him, Esme thought, but it was patently obvious that Muriel was nothing like she'd first portrayed herself to the family. Esme sighed. It was doubtful the woman would ever change.

Sir Giles was most sympathetic when Esme asked him about her next day off so she could help her sister settle a family matter.

'Let her come here one afternoon,' he said. 'Telephone her and say that she can come tomorrow, if you'd like. That way, you'll still have your full day off.'

The following day, Esme heard the crunch of gravel at just gone three o'clock and, peeping out of the window, caught sight of a taxi. The driver pulled right up to the front entrance and Freda stepped out. She was immaculately dressed as usual in a light-grey coat and cherry-red hat and could easily have blended in with any aristocratic guests who graced the dining table. Esme felt a twinge of pride on behalf of her sister and wished some of her confidence had rubbed off on herself.

There was a sharp rap and Esme hurried towards the door, just behind Dolly, who unlocked the huge oak door.

'Miss?' Dolly looked questioningly at Freda.

'I've come to visit my sister, Mrs Donaldson,' Esme heard Freda say.

There was a pause as Esme stepped into view.

'Ah, there you are, Esme.' Freda lightly pecked her sister's cheek. She looked her up and down with a critical eye. 'You look well.'

Esme smiled. 'I expect it's because I'm happy here.'

'Probably now you've got some decent food inside you,' Freda said.

'Yes, Cook is very creative at eking out the rations.' She stepped aside. 'Come on in, Freda. I'm longing to give you a tour of the house . . . as Sir Giles suggested.'

'I'd love to,' Freda said, looking pointedly at Dolly as though wondering why she was still loitering.

'Shall I bring you and your sister coffee in the new library, madam?' Dolly said.

'Good idea. In half an hour, thank you, Dolly.'

'You seem on very friendly terms with that maid,' Freda remarked when Dolly had disappeared.

'It's only natural,' Esme said. 'We all have to live together. It's like a family.' She put her arm through her sister's. 'Let me take your coat and then I'll show you round.'

'I'll keep it on, thanks,' Freda said. 'It's none too warm in here.' She gave an exaggerated shiver.

At that moment there was a pounding on the landings above and a crowd of schoolgirls flew down the stairs, loudly chattering and giggling. They halted a few yards away, throwing curious glances at Freda.

'GIRLS!' A woman's voice boomed from upstairs. 'Be quiet, all of you!' Immediately, the girls were silent, as though they'd been electrically switched off. 'Off you go outside! You know where to wait. I will join you in two minutes.'

Esme and Freda looked up at a tall woman, maybe in her mid-thirties, leaning over the balustrade. Her cascade of golden hair, swept up at the sides, was in sharp contrast to her tightly fitted black costume, relieved at the neck by the large bow of her bright pink blouse. She straightened and vanished from view.

'What's going on?' Freda said in a low voice as the girls rushed by and out through the entrance door.

'There's a school for Army officers' daughters here. The girls were evacuated from Bath after that dreadful bombing.'

'Well, I suppose they bring a bit of life to the place.' Freda stared as the last girl ran down the staircase, long, thin pigtails flying, then stopped abruptly midway. 'Who's that child pulling a face at us?'

Esme gave an inward sigh. Trust Bertha to cast a cloud over the normally pleasant atmosphere that she wanted to portray to her sister.

'Ignore her. She took a dislike to me on my first day.' She took her sister's arm again. 'Come on, Freda, they're probably on some kind of physical activity, so let's get out of here.' She pulled her away, hoping to switch Freda's attention away from Bertha.

'There must be some reason,' Freda commented as Esme led the way to the new library which everyone still called the Muniment Room. 'People don't take a dislike if they hardly know you unless you've done something to upset them.'

'I haven't done anything to upset her that I know of.'

But just as Esme opened the door, giving the same protesting squeak as it always did, something flickered through her head. That gasp of surprise when she'd been in Brad Parker's arms and they were kissing. Could it possibly have been *Bertha* snooping around at that time of night? And not being pleased with what she'd seen? But there wasn't time to dwell on it. Freda put her head in the door and went straight out.

'Very nice,' was all she said.

'Don't you want to have a proper look round?' Esme said. 'It's mostly what I've been doing since I've been here. It was a huge undertaking.'

'It's a library,' Freda said. 'Just like any other in these sorts of places, I would think.' She looked at Esme. 'Is there somewhere warm where we could go and have that coffee the maid promised to make?'

'Only the kitchen, and Cook wouldn't allow us to sit in there. Look, why don't I show you some of the rooms and my bedroom and then we'll come back to the library where Dolly said she'd bring it.'

Freda kept her coat on throughout the tour.

'I expect you're used to it,' she said, 'but we keep our house much warmer.'

Then you're very lucky, Esme wanted to say.

Back in the library, she saw that Dolly had already been and left a silver coffee pot and jug of hot milk with a few biscuits.

'This should warm you up,' she said, handing Freda her coffee. 'Now, tell me about Dad.'

'I don't think he's long for this world,' Freda said, without mincing her words. 'And Muriel's neglecting him. He told me on the q.t. that she often makes his lunch but otherwise leaves him to it. And when she's with him, she makes him feel it's his fault and that she's not there to be his nurse.'

'Oh dear, that sounds awful.' Esme looked at her sister. 'Has he really deteriorated that much in such a short time?'

Freda nodded. 'The doctor was there when I went. I had a word with him as he was leaving. He asked me if Dad had made a will. I said he had when they bought the house. It must have been the year before Mum died.' She fished out a packet of Players Please from her handbag and laid it on her lap without opening it.

Esme frowned. 'Did he say it was Parkinson's?'

'Yes. Apparently, Dad's had it for years, but it was undetected. Now the symptoms are getting more pronounced. Dad won't die of it, but it will eventually cause serious complications. He's already finding it's more difficult to swallow his pills. And he says the muscles in his arms and legs ache. That's making him feel very low in himself. And even more worrying – I think it's affecting the mentally as he's getting very forgetful.' She narrowed her eyes as she looked at Esme. 'I'm going to suggest something you're not going to like.'

Without knowing what bombshell her sister was about to make, Esme found she was bracing herself.

'Go on,' she said.

'That you give up your job here and go and look after him yourself.' Freda paused. 'You need to take that in so I'm going to light up – if that's allowed in here.'

Esme had noticed Sir Giles light his pipe when his books were in the attic. She nodded dumbly.

Give up? Go back to her old home where Muriel wouldn't be greeting her with open arms or scarper altogether, leaving her to nurse and cook and be a companion – a wife's job, surely. And not see Brad Parker again. Her heart squeezed at the thought.

'You know I'd help if I could,' Freda said, leaning back in the chair and inhaling. She made a face as she blew out the smoke and looked at the cigarette. 'Ugh. These are horrible. I had to pinch this packet from John.' She caught her sister's eye. 'Where was I?'

'Me giving up my job here,' Esme answered drily, 'because you have the boys and I don't have any children.' She nearly choked on the last word. 'That's what you were going to say, wasn't it?'

'Yes, I was.' Freda threw her a sympathetic look. 'Don't think I've forgotten what happened to you, Esme, and don't think I wasn't upset about it, because I was. You would have made a wonderful mother. You were very brave, but the truth is that you don't have any dependents so you must admit it makes sense for you to make sure Father's comfortable.'

Brave? Esme briefly squeezed her eyes shut. *I wasn't brave at all. But Freda was only able to stay with me a few days at the beginning because of the boys. After she'd gone back to Reading and I was alone, I never told her how I really felt – that I had nothing to live for.*

'Oh, yes, it's very sensible.'

Freda snapped her head round.

'You do see it, don't you, Esme?'

'I said I did.' It was her turn to watch Freda. 'The truth is, I don't want to leave here and that's the short answer. I love it. I'm happy in my work. I feel I'm doing something worthwhile and haven't by any means finished the job I promised I'd do.'

'I'm speaking about Father,' Freda said abruptly. 'Not some stranger. Not Sir Giles.' She looked round the room. 'You say you've moved the library for him. That's the main thing. He'll just have to hire another librarian – the easy bit, I would have thought. But keeping an eye on Muriel is far more important.'

'I know, but it's quite something to put this whole situation onto me,' Esme protested. 'Don't forget that he's your father too.'

'I realise that, but I haven't got the time at the moment. It's quite a journey for me these days and the train is always packed with soldiers. I feel guilty taking up a space when so many of them have to stand. Besides, you have more patience with Muriel than me.' She gazed at Esme. 'But you know I'll come as often as I can to visit you both.'

She met her sister's stare. 'I'll have to think about it.'

'Don't take too long,' Freda said crisply, 'or you might be too late.'

Chapter Fifteen

Even though she was pleased to see her sister, Esme was grateful that the taxi had come for Freda to take her to the railway station shortly after her suggestion about leaving Redcliffe Manor to look after their father. In fact, it had more the tone of an obligation. Freda had simply finished her cigarette and picked up her handbag. A quick peck on the cheek and a 'Sorry about this, Esmeralda, but it's the only way to make sure Dad's being looked after,' and she was gone.

Esme brushed aside a spike of resentment. Freda had insisted it was the only sensible solution – as though it were a foregone conclusion. It wasn't fair that she should be the one to give up her new life that she'd settled into so well, to go back home, under the suspicious eye of Muriel who would surely guess she was there to keep tabs on her. In any case, Esme was certain the woman would be on her best behaviour so it would be up to Dad to tell her exactly how she was when they were on their own.

It really was too bad. At the interview Sir Giles had said if it didn't work out, then notice would be a month, which might be too late for Dad. Either way, she'd be out of a job. She heaved a sigh. It was just too depressing even to contemplate.

Slowly, she walked back to Sir Giles's study in deep thought, to find her employer ensconced behind his desk, immaculately dressed as usual.

'Your sister didn't stay very long,' he commented, gesturing for her to come in.

'No, she was in rather a hurry.'

She wasn't going to tell him the main reason for her visit until she knew her own mind and exactly what she intended to do.

'I wanted to discuss something with you,' he said. 'It's about celebrating that the library has now been moved.' He looked at her. 'What do you think?'

'Sounds a good idea.'

'It can be a double celebration,' Sir Giles went on. 'The new library location and the completion of the hospital.'

Esme's heart jumped at the unexpected mention.

'I thought I should have a dinner party. Something modest. Invite maybe a dozen guests including some Americans. Obviously, Colonel Parker will be one of them.'

Just to hear Brad's name set Esme's heart beating faster. Sir Giles hadn't confirmed that *she* would be invited and she couldn't be so presumptuous as to ask him. But how she hoped he'd include her. His next words jolted her into the present.

'And as I've met Colonel Parker's right-hand man for the interior planning of the hospital,' Sir Giles went on, 'a Dr Charles Coates – nice chap – we could invite him. He's married to an Englishwoman who is also a doctor, so she must be invited. But you need to find out her name.'

'Of course.'

'We'll need to invite Stella, of course. And Dr and Mrs Samuel Brooke – he's my doctor – and the teachers here plus the housemistress, and should we invite the main chap who planned the Munitions Room – Stanley Hicks, wasn't it?'

'Yes.' Esme felt a flash of discomfort at the thought of Stanley's plan disappearing that night and still no evidence as to who'd taken it, though she had a good idea. 'I think we should as he worked hard to see it through. I know he's married, so I'll find out his wife's name, too.'

Sir Giles ran his finger down his nose. 'How many is that?'

Mentally, she quickly went through them. 'Eleven.'

'That should do it.'

'What date did you have in mind, sir?'

'Friday week. Seven thirty.'

If she were invited, he might change his mind when she subsequently gave in her notice, Esme thought wryly. She was about to open her mouth and get it over with but snapped it shut. She'd told Freda she'd sleep on it. And sleep on it she would.

But the following morning, Guy Fawkes day, when the schoolgirls and Russell Kingsnorth were building a huge bonfire with an effigy of Hitler ready to be put on the top, Esme was still undecided.

Her pride baulked at the idea. She didn't want to confront Muriel. Or go home for the foreseeable future. She genuinely loved working for Sir Giles and her mission to continue working on his memoirs. Only now did she think there was a good chance he'd include the fact that he'd been a CO in the Great War but explain his reasoning. And by describing the Mount Everest expedition and the subsequent accident, she was sure it would help him come to terms with what happened and finally shed his guilt. And then she stopped herself. Was she being absolutely honest? Was it really because she wanted to see Brad?

Well, it was no good dwelling on the reasons why she didn't want to give up her job. She had work to do, and she might as well write up the guest list so Sir Giles could decide who else to add. Then she'd have a good stint in the library doing some more cataloguing unless he had anything more urgent for her to attend to.

Taking a sheet of scrap paper from Sir Giles's wastepaper

basket, she started to draw up the list. He'd said about a dozen. She jotted down *Miss Stella Stratten, Russell Kingsnorth, Miss Anita Lonsdale, Miss Hilary Fenton, Dr & Mrs Samuel Brooke, Mr & Mrs Stanley Hicks, Dr Charles & Dr* . . . she must find out his wife's name, *Col. Bradley Parker* . . . She stopped, her pencil in the air. *Did* he have a wife? It was perfectly possible though he'd never indicated he was married. She couldn't bear the idea. If he was, then he was playing around by kissing her the way he had.

Why does everything have to be so complicated?

So far there were eleven guests. Twelve with Sir Giles. A baker's dozen with her. Was it tempting fate that she would be invited . . . Well, he'd soon alter things if he didn't approve.

She put the list on his desk at the same time he came through the door.

'Ah, good,' he said. 'Let's see who we have.' He looked up at her. 'Where's *your* name?'

'I didn't like to assume I'd be invited.'

'I don't know why. You must know that I depend upon you now.'

Esme momentarily shut her eyes. He couldn't have said anything nicer to assure her she was needed at Redcliffe Manor. But it made it worse for her to give in her notice . . . because with sudden clarity, that's what she knew, like it or not, she would have to do. But when to tell him?

'Thank you, Sir Giles. I look forward to it.'

Chapter Sixteen

Two days later, on her half day off, Esme caught the bus to Bath. As usual, the double-decker was crowded.

'More seats upstairs,' called the conductor.

Esme took a seat halfway along and was joined by a woman wearing a turban. The conductor sprinted upstairs and approached the new passengers, then came to the double seat where Esme was sitting.

'Where are you going, madam?' he asked the older woman.

'All the way to Bath,' she answered, giving him a thrupenny piece.

'Me, too,' Esme said, handing him the same.

He promptly rolled out a sixpenny ticket from his machine, tore it in half and gave one piece to each.

'Saving tickets,' he explained to their bemusement, as he moved towards the back of the bus to see to another passenger.

Esme glanced at the other woman and they both burst out laughing.

She was still amused thinking about the conductor's contribution to the war effort when she knocked on the door of her old home. Slow, shuffling footsteps came down the hall. Her father's. He opened the door and his face split into a welcoming smile.

'Hello, love.' He gave her a hug. 'I didn't expect you today. When you last phoned . . . no, it was your letter . . . your letter . . .

that's right . . .' he nodded, 'you said you've been busy, so . . . well, I wasn't expecting you.' He kissed her cheek. 'But I'm so glad to see you . . . so very glad, love.'

His voice was more hesitant, as though he were trying to find the words, and was unusually repeating himself. A wave of self-reproach washed through her. She shouldn't have left it so long to see him. Instead, she'd let herself get swept up into the world of Redcliffe Manor.

'Where's Muriel?'

Her father rolled his eyes. 'Shopping.'

'Will she be long?'

'No, she said . . . now what did she say?' He squinted at his watch. 'Oh, any minute.'

Darn it! She'd been hoping for a private conversation and to see at close hand how Muriel was treating him.

'I'll put the kettle on,' her father said, his head thrust forward as he shuffled along the hall in front of her. Esme watched him, shocked at the deterioration.

He had just struck a match to light the gas hob when Esme heard the front door open and Muriel's voice calling, 'I'm home.'

She came into the kitchen and seemed taken aback to see Esme setting out the tea tray.

'Oh, hello, dear. How nice to see you! Have you been here long?'

It was rare for Muriel to call her stepdaughter by any endearment.

'No, I've just arrived.'

'Oh, you might have been on the same bus.'

Muriel set the tone, being perfectly pleasant but never leaving her alone for one minute with Dad as she normally used to. It was as though she were already suspicious. But except for that giveaway grimace he'd made when she'd first asked where Muriel was, there was nothing Esme could glean of any bad treatment.

The woman was evidently on her best behaviour – so different from how Freda had described.

Well, she would gauge Muriel's true feelings when she announced she was coming back to live. And just as well that she said it in front of both of them. Then her stepmother couldn't accuse her of planning this behind her back. Whatever one said and thought, she was Dad's wife.

'Dad, Muriel, I need to ask you something.' At this, Muriel swung her head round sharply in Esme's direction.

'If it isn't an imposition, I'm coming back to live for a while.'

Esme watched Muriel's face carefully. It was a picture. Two red spots had appeared on her cheeks and her mouth had slackened in surprise – shock, even. Then her eyes narrowed.

'What's brought this on?' she said sharply. 'We thought you were happy with Sir Giles. I was planning to come and see you next week.'

'Two reasons,' Esme said. 'I'm sorry to be blunt, Dad,' she said, briefly turning to him, 'but Freda noticed you're getting a bit unsteady on your feet so I think Muriel will be glad of some help.' She turned her attention to her father's wife, but not before she'd seen out of the corner of her eye Dad wagging his head.

'And the other reason?' Muriel demanded through stiff lips.

The lie sprang easily to Esme.

'The job isn't exactly what I'm looking for,' she said. 'There's too much typing, for one thing.'

'I don't believe you!' Her father stared at her. 'You're always so enthusiastic when I ask you about it. And you get on very well with Sir Giles – or has he changed in his behaviour?'

'No. He's a nice, honourable man.'

'I don't want you to do this for me,' her father said with rare intuition.

'I want to help. It's not fair loading everything onto Muriel.' She glanced at her stepmother who had her arms folded over her stomach as though in disbelief. The woman obviously felt out of control and wasn't sure what to do about it. If it wasn't so serious, it would be laughable.

'Don't do anything foolish like giving in your notice,' her father said, seeming to find his words now he was patently upset. 'Will you promise, Esmeralda?'

It took her by surprise, as he only called her by her full name when he was serious or angry.

'I can't promise, Dad, because I've made up my mind – and I'm not going back on it.'

She didn't stay much longer. She could tell by her father's pale skin and the dark circles under his eyes that not only was he upset, but he was tired.

'Are you off already?' he said, grasping the arms of his chair to raise himself. But he wasn't strong enough and flopped back down. Muriel rushed to put him in a better position. 'Please, Muriel, I'd like to see my daughter off,' he told her firmly.

Esme hurried to the other side of the chair and between the two women, they pulled him upright.

'See how useful I can be,' Esme smiled, trying to lighten the heavy atmosphere.

Muriel gave a mirthless chuckle. Her father simply grunted.

As Esme opened the gate, she turned to wave, but it was only Dad standing at the front door with hand raised. She watched as he turned back into the house, his shoulders slumped in what looked like pure desolation.

But at least there'd been no obvious evidence at all that Muriel was neglecting him, Esme thought with relief. She'd write to tell Freda straightaway.

All the invitees responded that they'd be delighted to attend. Now, Esme's main thought was what to wear. She simply didn't have any elegant evening gowns, but she didn't want to appear as 'Plain Jane' either.

Clothes rationing was strict now. She needed eleven coupons for a dress – probably more if it was an evening dress – and she simply didn't have that many spare as her underwear would soon need replacing, and her sturdy shoes were in a dire state. There was nothing for it – she'd have to wear the black skirt from her two-piece suit and a pretty chiffon blouse of brightly coloured flowers which would have to pass for evening wear. She did at least have one pair of silk stockings that she'd been saving for best, and her plain black court shoes. But how she wished she had a beautiful gown to catch Brad's attention.

Three days later, Lil and another girl from the village laid the dining table under the watchful glare of Mrs Morgan. Esme spotted Stella in the Orangery, finishing off a table centrepiece that was already a blaze of gold and red foliage.

'That looks beautiful, Stella,' Esme said, amazed at her skills.

'It's only what I've collected in the grounds,' Stella said. 'Well, except for the artificial roses.' She stuck several claret-coloured roses in among the ivy where she'd let the leaves and berries trail off at the end of the long basket, then laid pinecones in small clusters around the edges.

'Can I do anything?'

Stella passed her two cream-coloured candles. 'You can wind some ivy around the base of them. I'll do the orange ones, then I think it's finished so perhaps you'll help me carry it through.'

'Yes, of course.'

'Sir Giles and his wife used to give marvellous dinner parties,' Stella commented, as she set the five candles into the decoration, 'but that all went when she died.'

'I don't suppose he had the same enthusiasm,' Esme said mildly.

'Probably not. But the house needs occasions like this. I doubt those schoolgirls appreciate these priceless antiques at all.'

'You're probably right,' Esme said. 'Sir Giles once mentioned that although they've come from good families, he didn't imagine they would have been exposed to these sorts of treasures at home.'

'Well, they don't know how lucky they are.' Stella gave her work of art a nod of satisfaction. 'Not quite the same as a glittering line of candelabra that they would have placed along the centre of the table, but I think Sir Giles was wise to have those sorts of valuables safely stored out of the way of those kids.' She sent Esme a curious glance. 'I'm told there are twelve of us, but you haven't mentioned exactly who's coming.'

'The teachers and the housemistress, his personal doctor and his wife—'

'Any Americans?' Stella's tone was casual, a pencilled eyebrow arched.

'Um, yes. Dr Charles Coates and his English doctor wife from the hospital.'

'And?'

Esme swallowed. 'I expect you're wondering about Bradley Parker.' Stella was waiting, a look of expectancy in her eyes. 'Yes, he's been invited,' Esme added.

'Good.' Stella beamed. 'I really like him . . . a lot.'

Here was Esme's chance. She bet her last shilling that Stella would have found out about any wife where Brad was concerned. Keeping her voice casual, she said:

'Don't you think at his age, you could be in for heartbreak?'

'What do you mean?' Stella demanded.

'He's likely to be married – probably even with children.'

There was a moment's silence.

Esme licked her lips, aware that Stella was watching her.

'Well, of *course* he has a wife.' Stella's eyes met Esme's.

Esme's stomach clenched at the way Stella had said it, so calmly, as though it didn't matter a jot.

'Really?' Esme's voice was hardly more than a squeak. 'He's never mentioned her.'

'Maybe. But I understand she stayed behind in America. So they can't be that happy or why wouldn't she come to England to be with him.' Stella paused. 'If he was *my* husband I wouldn't let him go off to a foreign country alone for goodness knows how long.' She gazed at Esme. 'Would you?'

Esme swallowed. 'That's beside the point, Stella, because even if they're happy as larks, she wouldn't be able to join him anyway. There happens to be a war on, in case you've forgotten, and every ship doing the Atlantic crossing will be strictly reserved for the military.'

'Oh.' Stella closed her eyes, then flicked them open. 'I hadn't thought of that. I thought because he was a colonel, he'd automatically be able to bring her.'

'No, it would be out of the question.'

For once Stella was silent.

'Does it make any difference that he might be happy and can't wait for the war to be over so he can go back to her?' Esme said, hating the idea but wanting to know exactly what game Stella was playing.

She stared at Esme. 'Why? Why do you want to know?'

'I don't want you to be hurt, that's all.'

Stella chuckled. 'You don't have to worry about me, Esme. I've got my head screwed on.'

To Esme's relief, her remark seemed to have satisfied Stella.

Chapter Seventeen

Of course he has a wife.

For the next few days, Esme couldn't get rid of the loaded words, no matter how hard she tried to ignore them. Brad Parker was married.

She quivered at the memory of Brad's lips on hers. She'd never responded to any man's kiss in such a passionate way and had surprised herself. But there it was. Well, she would certainly keep the truth from him that she was a widow. But she could not allow it to happen again. From now on, she was also married, as far as he was concerned.

But from her conversation with Stella the other day, Stella wasn't giving up. Esme sighed. It was no concern of hers. She had to forget him. Thank goodness she'd never given him the slightest indication of her feelings – except for that one kiss. At least going home to keep an eye on her father would put some distance between them. Yes, she thought, I must go home.

Already it was the day of the dinner party. What she must do was screw up her courage and tell Sir Giles she would have to leave by the end of the week. And it was best to face it now – before the dinner party so she wouldn't feel such a hypocrite. And let him know she simply couldn't appear this evening.

Resolutely, she knocked on his study door, and he looked up and smiled as she entered.

'Good morning, Esme. Is everything ready for this evening?'

She took a breath. 'Yes, Sir Giles, but I have some news and I don't know how to tell you.'

His smile faded. He looked straight at her. 'You're not ill, are you?'

She bit her lip. 'No. But I have to give in my notice.'

There. She'd said it.

'What!' His pen clattered onto the desk. 'What are you talking about? I thought you were happy here.'

'I am . . . very happy. I love my work . . . and working for you, Sir Giles,' she added quietly, hating to put her decision into words that would make it definite. She looked away, wishing she could think straight instead of battling with so many emotions.

'Esme, please sit down.'

When she'd seated, he said, 'Now what's happened to have caused this sudden change of heart?'

She drew in a deep breath, forcing herself to look him in the eyes. 'You may remember that my sister visited me the other day. I didn't tell you at the time, but she came right out with it and said Dad was becoming very frail and that I should be the one to look after him.'

'I thought you said he had a wife – your stepmother.'

'He does, but to tell the truth, she doesn't take care of him. Freda says she neglects him and that terrifies him as he really can't look after himself properly now.'

'But that's preposterous. She's his wife. It's her job. It's not yours. You're a grown woman with your life in front of you.' He drummed his fingers on the desk. 'Yes, by all means go and visit your ailing father, but don't give up your job here. There's still plenty of work to finish in the library and that's not even mentioning the books in poor condition which need to be rebound.' He looked directly at her. 'Besides, you're only about a third of the way through typing my memoirs.'

'I know,' she said miserably.

'Why can't your sister help?'

'She lives in Reading and she has a husband and two boys. They keep her busy, though she does visit Dad regularly.'

Sir Giles was thoughtful for a few moments. He shook his head. 'There has to be a solution to this.'

'There isn't one.'

He suddenly changed his tone. 'Why didn't you have the courtesy to tell me before this?'

Esme flinched. 'I hadn't made a definite decision until now.'

'And what's happened now that you've suddenly decided on the day of the dinner party?' Sir Giles demanded.

Warmth spread to her cheeks. *Dear God*. How to explain that she couldn't face Brad across the table.

'Esme, I want you to act as hostess tonight. In fact, I insist.'

He was practically ordering her. Oh, this was awful.

'Sir Giles, I don't think I should take on that role, knowing—'

'I can't do it on my own,' he interrupted.

Esme suddenly had a thought. *Of course!*

'What about Stella? She'd be a marvellous hostess.'

He shook his head. 'No. She's unreliable.' When Esme frowned, he continued. 'She had a rough time after the bombing raid in Bath last April and that's why she came to live here.' He stroked his beard. 'She almost had a nervous breakdown, you know.'

'She did mention something about it.'

'Please, Esme, do at least this one thing I ask of you. And then you can leave us for good the following weekend – that is, if that's *really* what you want.'

What could she say? He'd been more than kind to her. She tried to swallow the lump that had stuck in her throat.

'It's *not* what I want.' Her words were jerky. 'I don't want to leave. I love my job. But I *am* anxious about my father.' Tears stung at the back of her eyes. 'But I'll host the dinner party, if you're really sure you want me there.'

'I'm sure.'

Esme's stomach trembled with nerves as she changed for the evening. She'd already brushed her hair until it shone like a nut and powdered her nose and applied a crimson lipstick. She quickly put on her underclothes, zipped up the black skirt and slipped her arms into the chiffon floral-printed blouse. It was pretty enough, she decided, as she tied the two ribbons at her neck into a floppy bow, but nothing much out of the ordinary. Finally, she stepped into her black court shoes.

With a last glance at her legs to make sure her seams were straight, Esme pulled her bedroom door behind her. She'd have to do, whatever anyone thought. Sir Giles had asked her to meet him in his study. As usual, she knocked, then opened the door. He glanced up from behind his desk, then half rose as she stepped inside. Being so tall, even though slightly stooped, he cut a dignified figure in his dinner jacket and bow tie, sharply contrasting with his white hair and beard. But his expression was serious. Esme gulped. He'd been kind enough not to make her stick to the month's notice they'd agreed on her interview. She'd be leaving in a week and knew she would worry about how he was coping.

'You're looking lovely this evening,' he said unexpectedly.

She smiled her thank you. 'I don't have a special evening dress so I hope I'm not letting you down in front of your guests.'

He shook his head. 'You could never do that.' He gestured to the chair on the opposite side to his desk. 'I wanted to have a word with you about your leaving, so just sit down for a moment.'

'I'm really sorry, Sir Giles, but if you're asking me to change my mind . . .'

'I'm not asking you to. But I may have come up with a solution.'

Esme straightened her spine, wondering what was coming.

He looked directly at her. 'Why don't you invite him to stay here? We've plenty of room. You'd be around to keep an eye on him and your sister would be welcome whenever she wanted to pay a visit . . . and bring his grandsons.' He kept his eyes fixed on hers. 'What do you think?'

Her eyes widened. She hadn't expected anything like this. What a long way the two of them had come since her interview only a matter of weeks ago. His thoughtfulness reminded her of her father.

'I think that's an incredibly generous offer.'

'Then it's settled.'

'Not quite.' Esme gave him a rueful smile. 'There's Muriel to consider.'

'With what you told me yesterday, she doesn't sound as though she deserves any consideration.'

'She doesn't, but she would make things very difficult for him. He's got enough to contend with as it is.' She searched his face. 'It's such a kind offer, but I can't accept it. For one thing, he's going to get worse with whatever he has wrong with him.'

'There's a hospital right outside the door if he should need one urgently,' Sir Giles said. 'And if he needs permanent care, he'd be sent to one of the hospitals in Bath – St Martin's, most likely.'

'I wish I could say "yes" on his behalf, but I can't. I know what his answer would be. He couldn't bear to give up his independence and besides, he loves his home. It's where he and my mother lived before she died. It would kill him to leave.'

Sir Giles's face drooped with disappointment. Then he said:

'Have you heard the news this morning?'

Why is he changing the subject?

'No. But not another setback for us, I hope.'

Sir Giles nodded. 'You might say that.' He drummed his fingers on the desk. 'The Germans and Italians have marched into Vichy France. But Pétain always bent to Hitler's and Mussolini's instructions anyway, and only operated as a puppet government, so we probably won't notice much difference – just another creeping invasion. But whatever happens, your father would be safer here than in the city.'

'But Bath hasn't been bombed since April.'

'That's not to say it won't happen again. The Germans love to make a raid when one's least expecting it.' He steepled his hands. 'Well, all I can say is that the offer is there.'

Without even thinking, she walked round to his side of the desk and kissed his cheek.

'What was that for?' His voice was gruff.

'For being such a kind and considerate employer.' She looked at him. 'But I can still do one thing for you. Dad used to be a journalist and has a typewriter, so I can continue your biography while I'm at home.'

His face brightened. 'You would?'

'Yes, I'd be glad to. It would give me something really important to focus on. And before you say anything different, I'm going to finish it without any payment.'

'Oh, no, I—'

She held up her hand. 'But in return, I expect you to include those missing chapters . . . sir.'

She grinned to lighten her mischievous command and was relieved to see his mouth twitch upwards under his moustache.

'I'm coming round to the idea.' He checked his pocket watch, then stood up. 'I think we'd better go to the hall to greet our guests, don't you?'

Dolly had the job of answering the door and asking everyone's name, then repeating it to Sir Giles and Esme in a loud, clear voice. Esme's heart turned over as the first two guests stepped inside, accompanied by Dolly and Janey.

'Colonel Parker and Mr Carlisle,' Dolly announced proudly.

Brad, looking devastatingly handsome in his uniform, caught Esme's eye and nodded. It was the only hint of acknowledgement. Immediately, she wished she hadn't been persuaded to host tonight's dinner party. But it was too late. Mr Carlisle, a fair-haired young man with glasses, simply nodded.

'Good evening, Sir Giles,' Brad said, then turned to Esme. 'Good evening, Mrs Donaldson. Good to see you again.'

She gulped. She couldn't answer. Her throat had closed.

Brad turned to Sir Giles. 'I hope I'm not taking advantage of your generosity, sir, but I've brought with me Rudy Carlisle, an exceptionally brave patient of mine.'

'Of course not, dear boy.' Sir Giles turned to Rudy Carlisle. 'It's good to have you with us. Why don't you let Dolly take your coat . . . and the colonel's.' He turned to Janey. 'Would you ask Mrs Morgan to kindly set another place?'

Sir Giles led them into the larger sitting room, telling Dolly to bring in any stragglers. For now, Esme was grateful Brad chose a seat on the other side of the room. She helped Sir Giles pour the drinks and hand them to the guests who had all arrived, bar one. Then the door burst open and there was Stella, standing in the entrance and looking magnificent in a cream dress that fell to her ankles. The skirt was in the pleated style of an Ancient Greek goddess, with a wraparound, silver-beaded bodice, perfectly setting off her platinum blonde hair that was swept up by silver combs.

'Good evening, everyone. Sorry if I'm late. A whole lot of calls came in on the last hour at the hospital.' She sent a pointed look towards Brad, then gave him a seductive smile, her lashes lowered.

She looked as though she'd spent the last hour preening herself in front of the mirror, and now was making a beeline for Brad, Esme thought viciously, then scolded herself. She was being unkind. Just because *she* had made the decision that hers and Brad's fragile relationship could never go anywhere didn't mean she should judge Stella's intentions. After all, Stella had never made any secret about her hopes where Brad was concerned.

'What would you like to drink, Stella?' she asked.

'Oh, a sherry – dry, if you have it, darling.'

Sir Giles poured a glass and handed it to Stella, who graciously took it, her eyes still on Brad as she walked slowly towards him and sat next to him on the sofa.

'Colonel Parker,' Esme said, keeping her tone formal. 'May we offer you something?'

'Not right now, thanks,' he said. 'Maybe later at dinner. Unless you have an orange juice?'

'Oh, have a glass of champagne,' Stella chimed in, rising to her feet. 'There's hardly any alcohol in champagne,' she added, with a giggle as she took a coupe glass from the tray Sir Giles was handing round. She gave it to Brad, and Esme witnessed Stella making sure her fingers brushed against his hand.

He put the glass of champagne on the side table.

'Thank you, Miss Stratten.'

'Oh, less of the "Miss Stratten",' Stella protested, her laugh tinkling. 'Call me Stella. Everyone does.'

Brad gave her a nod that could have meant anything.

'And for you, Esme?' Sir Giles said.

'Nothing at the moment, thank you, Sir Giles.' After a moment's hesitation, she added, 'Maybe later at dinner,' echoing Brad's answer to the same question.

She had a feeling she'd need her wits about her tonight.

By the time everyone had been given his or her place at the dining room table, Esme was pleased to see that people were chatting together, although she noticed the two teachers, Russell Kingsnorth and Anita Lonsdale, were only speaking to one another. They probably felt they had little in common with all the others. Hilary Fenton, the housemistress, had captured the attention of Rudi Carlisle, who appeared mesmerised by the woman's sophisticated demeanour and had only given a brief nod to Esme when Sir Giles introduced her at the door, then had immediately turned back to Hilary.

They had just finished the hors d'oeuvres when there was a knock at the door and Dolly entered. She went straight to Esme.

'Beg your pardon, madam, but there's a telegram for you,' she said importantly, handing Esme a brown envelope.

'Me?' Her pulse beat rapidly. Telegrams usually brought bad news, particularly at this time of the evening. She looked at Sir Giles. 'Could I—'

'You can use my study to read it,' he said. 'I'll send for Dolly to give your plate to Cook to keep hot.'

Feeling Brad's eyes on her as he half rose from the table, Esme said, 'Please excuse me,' and quickly left.

Her heart thumping in her ears, she half ran along the corridors to Sir Giles's study. Sitting at the desk with the typewriter, she ripped open the envelope.

FATHER VERY ILL STOP ASKING FOR YOU STOP M

Chapter Eighteen

Esme sat at the desk feeling light-headed. She couldn't take it in. What Freda had warned her about Dad looked as though it had already happened. He was obviously seriously ill for Muriel to have sent a telegram. Did she send Freda one as well?

Bile rose to Esme's throat, choking her. She needed to go immediately. There was no time to pack anything. All she could think of was to phone for a taxi. Even then, she could be too late. Just like Freda had warned her. If only she'd packed up her things and stayed at Dad's when she went to see him only a few days ago, she would be there with him now. Her eyes filled with tears. She didn't want to go back into the dining room and say all this in front of everyone. It was too private – too upsetting.

Through her daze, she heard a light tap on the study door and then it opened. *Sir Giles. Thank goodness.* But it wasn't him.

'Esmeralda,' Brad said, hurrying towards her. 'Are you okay?'

She shook her head and handed him the telegram. As he skimmed it, she said, 'I must ask Sir Giles if I can use his telephone and ring for a taxi.'

He gently put his hands on her shoulders. 'You'll do no such thing. My automobile is parked in the drive and I can get you back to Bath in no time at all.'

She looked up at him, tears threatening again. 'Are you sure?'

'Of course. Leave it with me. Go and fetch your purse and coat and I'll tell Sir Giles quietly what's happened. Don't worry about saying goodbye to him. He'll understand.'

His voice was calm, soothing. It was such a relief to put herself in his hands. Not to have to think.

'I'll meet you outside the front door.' Brad gave her shoulder a gentle squeeze and disappeared.

Something clicked in her brain. His touch had felt familiar – like the same hand on her shoulder that time she was having tea in the Pump Room. *How very odd.* She shook herself. *Stop imagining things that aren't real.* She must concentrate, gather the minimum she needed and get back to Bath.

She ran up the two flights of stairs and into her bedroom. She scooped up her nightdress from the pillow and her sponge bag, throwing in her toothbrush, and stuffed them in an overnight case. Her coat buttoned up and she was ready. But where was her handbag? She looked frantically around the room. *Nowhere. It must be . . .* Dear God, she couldn't keep Brad waiting any longer. Dad was desperately ill and asking for her. She'd have to just go.

Of course! She rushed into Sir Giles's study, and there it was, under the desk where she'd left it. She grabbed the handbag and ran to the front door. But it was as though every ounce of strength had left her. She couldn't heave it open.

'What's going on, Mrs Donaldson?' came a woman's strident voice from behind.

She spun round. The housekeeper.

'Oh, Mrs Morgan, would you help me open the door, please?'

'Where are you off to at this time of night?'

'My father is very ill.'

'Oh dear, I'm sorry.' With a grunt, Mrs Morgan opened the door.

Esme shot through, aware that the housekeeper didn't close

it until Brad had settled her into the front seat of his motor car. Then he strode round to the driver's side and started the engine. A few moments later they were down the drive and on their way to Bath.

He drove cautiously and steadily in the blackout. She wanted to scream for him to go faster but she knew it was too dangerous. The car's headlights had the obligatory covers fitted over them, directing the now-dimmed light downwards, barely indicating where the side of the road was. He didn't say much, though he frequently glanced at her. Once, she gave him a tentative smile and he patted her hand. She peered through the windscreen, trying to fathom where she was in order to direct him once they'd reached the city.

Thankfully, after a couple of wrong turns on the smaller roads, she was at her old home.

'Thank you so much.' She touched his arm briefly. 'You must get back now.'

'I'm coming in with you.'

'No, you—'

'There's no argument. I'm coming in.'

On the doorstep, acutely aware of Brad's presence behind her, she rang the bell. It opened almost immediately and Muriel stood there.

'I just received the telegram,' Esme said in a weak, jagged voice she didn't recognise as her own. 'Am I in time?'

'Just about,' Muriel said, looking over her shoulder. 'I'm afraid your driver will have to wait in his cab.'

'I didn't come by taxi. Colonel Parker brought me here.' She turned to Brad. 'This is Dad's wife, Muriel. Please come in.'

Muriel stood aside, her lips pursed, while the two of them stepped into the hall.

'Have you called for the doctor?' Esme said.

'Yes, but he can't come. He's on an emergency. If he gets a couple of hours' sleep, he hopes to stop by in the morning.' She sniffed. 'Fat lot of good that will do. Bernard could be gone by then.'

Dear God.

'May I be of assistance?' Brad spoke quietly but with authority.

Muriel shook her head. 'Not unless you happen to be a doctor.' Her tone was tinged with scepticism.

'That's exactly what I am.' Brad's voice was unusually sharp.

There was a moment's pause of surprise from Muriel.

'Well, I suppose so, as long as you don't upset him.'

Esme bit back a retort as Muriel followed them up the stairs. Just before she opened her father's bedroom door, Esme turned to her stepmother.

'Does Freda know?'

'Yes. I sent her the same telegram.'

'Did she reply?'

'No,' she said shortly.

Esme opened the bedroom door, then turned to meet Muriel's eye.

'Please let me have some time quietly with my father.'

Muriel harrumphed and Esme heard her stomp down the stairs as she quietly took her place by the side of her father's bed, thankful to see he was still breathing with some regularity, though noisily.

'Dad,' she whispered. 'It's me, Esme.'

There was not a flicker of acknowledgement.

'May I take a look at him?' Brad said.

'Of course.'

He picked up the limp hand lying on top of the bed, put his fingers on Bernard's wrist and removed his stopwatch. After a minute, he turned to her.

'His heartbeat is irregular, so he needs to be constantly watched for the next forty-eight hours. Is that possible?'

'It'll be down to me,' Esme said, 'as I doubt Muriel will offer to take a shift.'

'Then you and I will do it between us in six-hour shifts and she can make herself useful and prepare our meals.' He glanced at her. 'Do you agree?' Esme nodded. 'Are you on the phone so I can let them know at the hospital that I'll be away for as long as it takes?'

'Yes.'

Esme gave an intake of breath. Why would he do something like this? She stole a glance at him, but he'd already turned towards her father again, gently putting his hand underneath the bedcovers.

'I can't drag you away from the hospital. They need you.'

'You need me more,' he said firmly, 'and there's no need to worry about the hospital – we have a team of doctors there.' He glanced at her. 'I'm sure your husband would have helped if he hadn't been posted abroad, so please let *me* help you. It would make me happy.'

Now's the time to tell him about Anthony, her inner voice whispered.

Esme stifled the idea. Nothing must get in the way of looking after her father.

'The telephone's in the hallway,' she said.

Two hours passed by and there was no change in her father. Esme's stomach rumbled embarrassingly. She felt the warmth creep up her cheeks. Brad threw her a sharp look, then said:

'You and I have had very little to eat this evening, so why don't you rustle up one of your famous English cups of tea and a few cookies – I mean biscuits – anything to get us through the night.'

'I'll go and see what I can find,' she said, relieved to be doing something. 'You will call me to come up if anything happens, won't you?'

'Yes, of course I will.'

She fled downstairs and into the kitchen. Thank goodness it was late now – gone eleven. Muriel must have retired to bed.

She prepared a tea tray and a few of what looked like Muriel's home-made biscuits, smelling of ginger. At least Muriel had one thing in her favour – she was a good cook. Esme poured boiling water onto the tea leaves in the pot, all the while thinking how surreal the scene was upstairs. They would need more than a few biscuits. She'd see if there was any cheese in the pantry. Five minutes later, Brad appeared and sniffed the air.

'Something smells good.'

'I've just made us some cheese on toast, although the cheese is a bit thin with all our rationing.' She looked towards the trays. 'Will you take one up and I'll bring the other?'

'No. He'll be okay for a while. It'll be easier having it here than taking trays up and down the stairs.' His mouth quirked as he looked at her. 'One patient is enough to deal with at the moment.'

Sharing cheese on toast – Brad picking the pieces up with his fingers and Esme, after a second's hesitation, following – and a pot of tea and sitting opposite him at the small table in the dim light of the kitchen seemed somehow intimate. Esme suddenly felt shy although it didn't stop her from stealing glances at him when he was concentrating on his snack. The dark wavy hair, the cleft in his chin and strong jaw. And his mouth. The mouth that had kissed her. Her body quivered at the memory. She had to force herself to think of his wife – anything – or she would give herself away. She took a swallow of tea, hoping the comforting drink would help to compose her.

He caught her eye. 'Did you ever realise I saw you before you started working at the Manor?'

Her cup rattled as she set it back on the saucer. *Darn it.* She hadn't thought he'd recognised her.

'When you came to Redcliffe Manor for what I think might have been your first time.'

'Um, yes, it was.' She sought her mind. How could she change the subject? But she could tell by the way his eyes danced that he wasn't going to let it go. It was no good. She'd have to brazen it out.

'I expect that was for an interview with Sir Giles,' he said. 'I recognised you straightaway when Stella introduced us, but I wasn't going to say anything in front of her.' He grinned. 'It made me laugh when you surreptitiously took your shoes off and walked on the grass barefoot right up to the Manor. You looked so natural in such a formal setting.'

She couldn't help smiling for the first time since they'd arrived. And now here he was, trying to take her mind off the seriousness of her father's health for these few minutes.

'Do you enjoy working for Sir Giles?' Brad said.

'Very much. But I had to give in my notice yesterday.'

He raised his eyebrows. 'Oh? Why was that?'

She briefly explained that she intended to come back and look after her father, although she didn't mention the will or how Muriel was behaving towards him lately.

'That's too bad.'

He put his hand over hers across the table. A current of electricity travelled up her arm. She felt, rather than heard, his sharp intake of breath as he abruptly took his hand away. But it was too late. The atmosphere was charged.

He wiped his fingers on the napkin Esme handed him.

'I'll go up and see how he's doing,' he said. 'You just finish your supper.'

'I'll be up in a minute.' She needed time to collect herself. It was too much with Dad dangerously ill upstairs, and Brad Parker here in her old home, taking on the role of his doctor.

Smashing into her thoughts came an insistent banging on the door. She glanced at her watch. *Gone midnight!* Time seemed to be all at odds this evening. Sometimes an hour flashed by in minutes when she was with Brad – but sometimes it felt the night would never end.

It must be the doctor, even this late.

She rose to answer it. Her sister stood there dripping wet.

'Freda! Goodness, come in! I didn't even know it was raining.'

'I forgot my key and I've been ringing the bell for at least five minutes,' Freda grumbled, leaving wet footprints on the lino as she followed Esme into the kitchen.

'I was upstairs with Dad,' Esme said. 'You were lucky to get a train this late.'

'I didn't start off late. I caught a train just before ten. It was packed. Thankfully, a soldier gave up his seat for me, but we hadn't been going long when it stopped. The guard said he'd find out what the delay was, but he didn't come back.' Freda looked at Esme directly. 'Anyway, I'm here now so how is Father?'

'He's very poorly. Brad said—' She bit her tongue hard. 'A doctor is with him at the moment. 'Would you like a cup of tea? There's still some in the pot.'

'Who's Brad?' Freda immediately pounced. When Esme didn't answer, she eyed the two plates and teacups. 'It looks like you and Brad, whoever he is, have had a cosy supper together.'

'Brad Parker is a doctor,' Esme said, annoyed to feel the familiar warmth at the mention of his name. 'He happened to be at the same dinner party tonight when they brought me the telegram and gave me a lift here. Then when Muriel said she'd called the doctor, but he couldn't come until tomorrow morning, he offered to take turns in watching him through the night.' She looked at her sister half defiantly. 'Well, you know Muriel would never offer.'

'Hmm.' Freda's eyes were full of suspicion. 'I won't bother with tea at this time of the night, but I'd like to see Father and also see exactly who this Brad person is.'

'He's a colonel in the US Air Force and director of the military hospital they built in the grounds of Redcliffe Manor.'

'Oh, very senior.' Freda stared at her. 'He must think a lot of you if he's come all this way.'

'He's just a very nice man – and I'm told an excellent doctor.' She wouldn't let on that he had a wife. It was none of Freda's business. She'd only start lecturing her about being careful not to fall in love with a married man. And they'd be wasted words because that could never happen.

'Let's go upstairs, then,' Freda said, 'and I can put my bag in my room.' She gave Esme a mischievous smile. 'I presume my old bedroom is still going spare.'

'Of course it is.'

Brad had his back to the door and was speaking softly to Bernard. He swung round at the sound of the two women's voices.

'Freda, my sister, has come to see Dad,' Esme said, quickly making the introductions.

'Good to meet you,' Brad said, moving away from the bed and shaking hands with Freda. 'And you'll be pleased that your father is awake but very sleepy still. He's rather agitated so try to keep him calm.'

'Father,' Freda said, 'it's Freda. Can you hear me?'

'Yes,' came a weak voice. 'Sit where I can see you.' There was a long pause as he struggled for breath. 'Is Esme with you?'

'Yes, I am,' Esme said, joining her sister. She watched as her father's eyelids flickered, then opened again.

'Call me if you need to,' Brad said. 'I'll be downstairs.'

When he'd left the room, Bernard weakly stuttered, 'Whassa time?'

'Late,' Freda answered. 'Gone midnight.'

'Muriel . . .' Bernard gave a despairing sigh. 'Wanted to explain—' He broke off.

'Father!' Freda bent over him. 'Father, speak to me!'

'Not now,' he said, his voice fading. 'In the morning.'

'Goodnight, Dad,' Esme said, but he was already asleep. She turned to her sister who was yawning.

'Sorry, sis,' Freda said, 'I can't keep my eyes open. I'll leave you and Dr Brad to it. But call me if there's any change.'

Chapter Nineteen

Freda surpassed herself by being up by seven to make porridge for everyone before Muriel emerged. Bernard was still sleeping. Esme had told Brad to wake her up at four o'clock in the morning to give him a few hours' sleep, but he'd insisted she get to bed and he promised to let her know if there was any kind of change in her father's condition.

'Freda's made us all porridge,' she told him after she'd cast her eye over her father and Brad had assured her he was no worse. 'Why don't you go and have some?'

'Have you had yours?'

'Not yet.'

'Has Freda?'

'Yes, because she'll probably leave shortly as she has to get back for the boys.'

'Then why don't you tell her to come up and have a few minutes with her father on her own and we'll have our breakfast.'

With Freda upstairs, Esme and Brad were finishing their porridge and toast as Muriel appeared.

'I see you've made yourself at home,' she said, looking pointedly at Brad.

'Dr Parker kindly stayed with Dad right through the night,' Esme snapped.

'Did I hear Freda come in?' Muriel asked, appearing to take no notice of Esme's annoyance.

'Yes. She's upstairs with Dad and then she's going back to Reading.'

'And you, Esme. You need to be getting back to Redcliffe Manor, don't you?'

'No, Muriel. As I mentioned when I was last here, I'm staying . . . to help with Dad.'

Muriel pursed her lips and pulled the door firmly shut behind her.

'She doesn't seem to be very sympathetic to your father's plight,' Brad said mildly.

'She's not. She thinks we've come to keep an eye on her to make sure she's looking after Dad.'

'And is she looking after him?'

'No, she's not. It's all pretence with her.'

Freda came into the kitchen. 'Father seems to be sleeping but his skin looks grey.' She glanced at Brad. 'Did he speak to you at all in the night?'

'He mumbled something about Muriel. I couldn't really make it out.'

'Do we know when the doctor's supposed to be coming?'

'No,' Esme said. 'Muriel just said in the morning.'

Freda furrowed her brow. 'I hate to do this, but Bobby's not been that well these last two days. I think it's only a cold but—'

'You must go home,' Esme said firmly. 'There's not much you can do here. And I'll ring you if there's any change.'

'You will let me know if you need me?'

'Of course I will.'

Esme walked with her sister to the bus stop.

'Keep me posted,' Freda said when her bus for the railway station came. 'I'd like you to know I approve,' she added, chuckling.

'Approve of what?' Esme said.

'You know full well.' With that, she kissed Esme's cheek and the bus conductor rang the bell as Freda swung onto the platform.

Yes, she did know full well, Esme thought. Freda could only be referring to one thing.

Back at home, Esme insisted Brad go and have a rest and told him where the guest bedroom was.

'Call me if you're worried at all,' he said, smothering a yawn.

Just then, Esme heard the slam of the front door. She went to the window and pulled back the curtain to see Muriel with her shopping bag walking down the path, then opening the gate. Good. Esme drew the curtain again and the house immediately felt peaceful without the woman crashing around the place. She turned back to her father. He had his eyes open and was watching her.

'Dad.' She hurried to the bed.

'Esme. Sorry. Socks. Want to explain.'

She took his hand. 'You don't have to explain anything, Dad. Just concentrate on getting well.'

'No.' His voice was firmer. 'Socks,' he said again.

'What about socks? Are your feet cold?'

He didn't answer but jerked his head from side to side, his eyes now wide and staring.

Should she call Brad? No, she'd let him be.

'Just rest, Dad. You can tell me about the socks later.'

She held onto his hand as he closed his eyes, taking in a jerky breath, then several more, each one sounding like a baby's toy rattle as though he was choking and desperate to catch his breath. Then he gave a long deep sigh and to her horror it felt as though his very lifeblood was draining away through his hand.

'Dad!'

His chest no longer moved up and down. She touched his face

with disbelieving fingers. *No!* He couldn't have. He was talking only moments ago about his socks of all things.

Numbly, she let his hand softly drop onto the eiderdown, shaking her head, desperate to take in what had just happened. Her mouth was horribly dry. She glanced towards her father's bedside table where his water jug stood. Hardly aware of what she was doing, she poured out some of the water into an empty glass, then held it to her lips, swallowing great gulps, willing herself to keep calm. She set the glass back on the table and it was only then that she noticed a small bottle behind his bedside books. It was practically empty save for a few little white tablets, but he or Muriel had forgotten to put the top back on. *Dad's medicine.* She picked it up and screwed it back on the bottle and glanced at the label: *Mr B Grant. One tablet three times daily after meals.* Peering at the tiny writing, she read the date – exactly a week ago. That was odd. The tablets were tiny. Even taking three a day for a week, he couldn't have used up anywhere near as many of the hundred it stated on the bottle.

She gasped aloud. It was as though someone had punched her hard in the stomach. She felt the blood drain from her face. *It's not true!* But the evidence was in her hand. Hardly aware of what she was doing, she put the bottle into her pocket and stumbled to the bathroom. Lifting the lid of the toilet, she knelt over the pan as she brought up Freda's porridge in sticky hard lumps. She retched again and again, feeling perspiration beading on her forehead, even though the bathroom itself was cold. She shivered, then tried to stand so she could rinse her mouth in the wash basin. But she swayed and sank to her knees again.

Footsteps behind her, then a hand on her damp forehead. His touch was soothing.

'Esmeralda. It's me. Is it your father?'

'Yes.' She felt she was choking. 'He's stopped breathing.'

'Let me check.' Brad shot off.

Disbelief engulfed her. It had all happened so quickly. Her father would never speak to her again. With a supreme effort she dragged herself up and hurried on shaking legs to her father's room.

Brad was holding a small glass mirror a couple of inches away from her father's mouth. Giving an almost imperceptible shake of his head, he closed her father's eyes, then turned round.

'I'm so sorry, Esmeralda.' When she didn't answer, he stood up. 'Do you want to be left alone with him for a while?'

'No.'

Gently, he led her to the nearest chair.

'Stay there and I'll get you some water.'

He went to the sink and picked up the glass holding some toothbrushes. Tossing them into the basin, he rinsed the glass, filled it with cold water and handed it to her.

She took a few swallows, then glanced down to his feet.

'You haven't got your shoes on.'

'No time. I rushed out when I heard you being ill.'

Had he been any other man, she would have died from embarrassment. But somehow not with Brad. Besides, he was a doctor. He was used to people in all kinds of states.

And then she remembered the empty glass bottle. Wordlessly, she drew the bottle out of her pocket and gave it to him. His brows shot up as he read the label and took in the significance of the date. He momentarily closed his eyes and muttered something under his breath. Then he looked her in the eyes.

'You know what this means, don't you, Esmeralda?'

'Yes.' She wasn't capable of saying anything more.

At that moment the doorbell jangled, startling her.

'I'll get it,' Brad said.

She couldn't have moved if she'd wanted to. Her legs were

leaden. She tried to swallow the sour lump that clogged her throat. Her father had done the unthinkable. She couldn't even bring herself to say the word.

There was a muffled voice from another man. Then she heard Brad say:

'Colonel Parker – a doctor and friend of Mr Grant's daughter. She's with him now, so do go up and I'll wait downstairs if you need to ask me anything.'

The sound of heavy footsteps thumped up the stairs. Esme looked towards the door to see Dr Humbert, his raincoat dripping as he came into the room. He acknowledged her and went straight over to the bed. It was only seconds before he sighed and twisted round.

'I'm so sorry I couldn't come last night. But from Dr Parker's assessment, particularly when he told me about the prescription, I don't think there would have been anything I could have done.'

'I know he was poorly, but he didn't have to commit—' She broke down, sobbing.

He took hold of her arm and sat her down in her father's easy chair. She could smell the tobacco her father always used in his pipe. He'd never light it up again. Tears streamed down her cheeks, her thoughts spinning out of control.

Dr Humbert put his arm round her shoulders.

'He was very ill, Esme. It was Parkinson's disease, which he'd had for several years but ignored – even denied – the symptoms. He only came to me when he couldn't hide them any longer. He was finding it difficult to keep his balance and he couldn't stop his hands trembling. When I diagnosed him, he wanted to know the prognosis and I said I was afraid it would worsen over time, but he might have two or three years. I didn't tell him by then he would likely be totally dependent on someone every minute of every day – too strenuous even for a devoted wife, I would say.

But he knew, because he told me he didn't want to burden you or your sister, especially you, Esme, when you'd lost your husband not long ago.'

'I feel so guilty,' she choked. 'I would have looked after him.'

'No, my dear, that's the last thing he'd want. The very opposite. He wanted you to start to enjoy your life again. And to carry out his wishes. That's exactly what you must do.' He glanced towards the bed. 'Unfortunately, one of the symptoms is depression. The realisation of the outcome would have been torture for him. But he's at peace now – and believe me, he wasn't before. That's what you must remember.'

'But what he did was against the law.' She hesitated, hating to say it, feeling disloyal to her father. 'And people will judge it as a shameful act. I couldn't bear—'

'No, my dear, there'll be no shame, I'll see to that. He died from his illness and that's all you need to tell anyone when they ask.' He looked at her. 'And don't worry about what happens now – I'll arrange everything. I had a great deal of time for your father. He was a gentleman.'

She gazed up into his warm grey eyes.

'Thank you, doctor,' she whispered. 'I'd better telephone Freda.'

'Oh, I'm sorry I wasn't here,' Muriel said when she came into the kitchen before Esme had a chance to telephone Freda. Her stepmother dumped her shopping basket on the table. 'I really never expected this to happen quite so suddenly.' She didn't meet Esme's eye.

Esme gazed at the woman, but her expression showed no hint of shock that her husband had died while she was out shopping.

'Of course, I've been watching him get worse every day,' Muriel said, adding pointedly, 'as I was the only one here to look after him.'

Dr Humbert had told Esme before he left that he would explain how her father had taken a turn for the worse, but not that in the end he'd taken his own life.

'Least said, soonest mended,' he said, to Esme's relief.

She'd insisted Brad return to the hospital where he was needed, that Dr Humbert was taking care of everything. He'd left – reluctantly – but not before he kissed her lightly on the cheek at the front door.

'Will you be okay here with Muriel?'

'Yes, I don't suppose she'll bother me. There'll be a lot to do now, sorting out his stuff.' She looked at him. 'It still seems unreal.'

'It will, for a while. It's natural.' He brushed her jaw with his finger. 'Call me if you need me – promise?'

He hadn't waited for an answer.

Why did he kiss her cheek? Why did he brush her jaw, leaving it tingling? A wave of anger unexpectedly pulsed through her. He was acting as though she meant something more to him than just a friend. Yes, he'd been very kind to support her with Dad and she'd always be grateful. But he was married and behaving as though he were otherwise. It was all too late – everything was too late. She couldn't have stopped herself if she'd tried. She might as well admit it. She'd fallen in love with Brad. But he must never know.

Chapter Twenty

Freda hadn't seemed very surprised when Esme had telephoned her that morning to break the news.

'Did he speak again?' Freda asked.

'A few words here and there. He kept saying "socks". I asked if his feet were cold, but he shook his head. He was rather agitated because I didn't understand him.'

'I expect he was under the influence of all his medication.'

She'd have to tell her sister the truth. Esme set her jaw.

'Be prepared for a shock, Freda.'

'Oh?' There was a sudden tension over the wire. 'Is it about Father?'

'Yes. Oh, Freda he . . . I don't know how to say this—' She broke off.

'Then don't. But I can guess. He took his own life.'

Esme gave a sharp intake of breath. 'How on earth did you guess that?'

Esme almost saw her sister shrug.

'Easy, really,' came Freda's clear tones. 'He had nothing to live for. Father was a proud man and dignified. He would have hated a long, drawn-out, painful ending, and could see Muriel wasn't prepared to care for him in a wifely way.' There was a pause and the line crackled.

'Damn!' Esme heard her sister say. 'Can you hear me?'

'Yes, I'm still here,' Esme said.

'Is Brad still with you?'

'No, he's gone back to the hospital.'

'Oh, that's a pity. Now you've only got Muriel.'

'Yes.' Esme suddenly remembered. 'How's your Bobby? Is he any better?'

'He seems to be improving,' Freda said, 'but I'll give it another day or two, if you don't mind, and then I'll come and give you a hand in sorting out his stuff.'

'I won't sort anything important without you,' was all Esme said.

When Esme mentioned Freda would be coming to help in a day or two's time, her stepmother's mouth thinned.

'I'd like to help but I have an appointment in the town.'

'Just carry on,' Esme told her. 'We won't get anywhere near finished but we can make a start. 'We'll sort his clothes and shoes and stuff and give them to the Salvation Army, so they'll be put to good use.'

Freda arrived two days later, just as Muriel left to go into Bath. Esme heard a muttered exchange of words and then her sister came into the kitchen, annoyance flushing her cheeks.

'Honestly, that woman . . .'

'What's happened?' Esme said, wiping up the last of the breakfast dishes.

'She said she had an urgent appointment. When I asked her what it was, she went bright red and told me it was none of my business and marched off.' She gave Esme a knowing glance. 'Well, we're not daft – we don't need her to confirm she was heading for the solicitors. . . to hear the terms of the will. Thank goodness Dad drew it up when Mum was ill and put the house in both our names. I wouldn't be surprised if Mum hadn't encouraged Dad to do it – without telling him, of course, but on purpose in case he married again and unwisely.' Freda clicked her tongue. 'Well, at least Muriel can't touch *that*.' She opened the kitchen door. 'Anyway, let's go upstairs and make a start on sorting his things.'

The sisters worked methodically, starting with the wardrobe. Soon there were various piles of jackets, trousers and shirts on the bed.

'I think that's it for the wardrobe,' Esme said, stretching her back. 'I'll tackle the chest of drawers with his underwear and socks—' She broke off, her hand flying to her mouth. 'Freda, you know Dad kept saying "socks" and I just thought his feet were cold.'

'Go on.'

Esme pulled open her father's top drawer of the chest. She glanced in. Nothing untoward there. Just a photograph album and braces and shirt-sleeve garters. She pushed it shut, then opened the middle one. There were his underpants and vests neatly folded, and by the side were his socks, each pair twisted together. She emptied the contents and threw them on the bed with his clothes, rifling through his socks as she did so.

'What are you looking for?'

'I don't know,' Esme admitted. She was just about to close the drawer when she noticed where the socks had been that the lining was very slightly raised in the corner. She pulled it away and there was an envelope. She picked it up and read in her father's scrawl: *Freda and Esmeralda*. She handed the envelope to her sister.

Freda's eyes widened. 'Goodness. So that's what he was trying to tell you. That he's written to us and must not have wanted Muriel to know, else why did he hide it?'

'Quite.' Esme's mouth was grim. 'Let's go downstairs and you read it while I put the kettle on.'

The sisters sat at the kitchen table and Freda, using a letter opener, removed the three sheets of notepaper.

'It's dated a month ago,' she said, 'and it's typed.' She glanced up at Esme. 'I suppose it's because he couldn't hold a pen. Good thing he learnt when he was a journalist.' She cleared her throat and began reading aloud.

'*My darling Freda and Esmeralda,*

'*You will now know I decided to end my life. The decision was not made lightly. I don't want you to feel sad about it in the least. When I met your mother, my life was transformed. She became the centre of my world. And then she had you, Freda, which was wonderful. We wanted another baby, but in the end resigned ourselves that you would be an only child. So it was with great excitement when you, Esmeralda, came along ten years later.*

'*We were a complete and happy family. But it wasn't to last. My world collapsed when your mother died. I've never got over it. It was bad enough for Freda at only sixteen, but alarming for Esme, a child of six. It was hard to find a housekeeper and Muriel seemed genuine when she said she'd find it a privilege to care for the two of you. Give Muriel her due, I think she did her best. But not having children of her own, it was too difficult for her in the end. And after she'd been with us a year, she pointed out that by devoting herself to me and my daughters, she had scuppered her chances of meeting someone whom she might have married. She said she'd grown fond of me, but if I didn't feel the same, and make her my wife, she'd leave. That meant another woman for you girls to get used to and I couldn't risk it. In retrospect, I should have discussed all this with you both. You were old enough.*

'*Dr Humbert gave me no hope that my condition could be stabilised. It was only going to get worse and I'd end up completely bedridden and unable to even feed myself. I couldn't picture a more ghastly ending. Muriel doesn't have the instinct for nursing and I didn't want to be a burden on either of you – Freda busy with her husband and my two delightful grandsons, and Esme, I hope with all my heart that you will find happiness with someone new in the not-too-distant future.'*

Freda looked at her sister and nodded as though to say she agreed with their father.

'So I decided to take matters into my own hands.

'I want to let you both know I am so proud of my beautiful daughters. Neither of you need feel any shame for what your father saw was the only way out.

'I'm truly horrified by events in this latest war and I hope for both your sakes that Britain and its Allies – both in whom I have great faith – will soon be victorious, and everyone can get on with their lives in peace. But I fear it's going to carry on quite a bit longer yet.

'The most important thing to remember is that I love you both very much. I always have and always will. Goodbye, my darling daughters, and forgive me for everything.

'Your ever-loving father.'

Freda looked straight at her sister. There was a few moments' silence between them. Freda was the first to speak.

'At least we understand a bit more about how he must have felt.'

Esme briefly closed her eyes, sad to think how desperate Dad must have been.

'If only he'd confided in us,' she said, 'we could have got him some psychiatric help.'

'I don't suppose it would have made the slightest difference,' Freda said, lighting a cigarette, for once seeming to forget it wasn't in its usual holder.

Esme and Freda were still upstairs, filling items for the Salvation Army, when they heard Muriel come in, her footsteps echoing on the lino to the kitchen. Then the sound of a gush of water into the kettle.

'I'm going down,' Freda said. 'I want it out where she's been.'

'Please don't,' Esme said. 'We *know* where she's been.'

'I want her to tell us herself.' She gazed at Esme in her challenging manner. 'She's going to be furious, no matter what. Are you coming?'

Esme sighed and followed her downstairs. Muriel was sitting at the table drinking tea and reading the newspaper. She looked up, her expression inscrutable.

'There's tea in the pot. I've just made it,' she said pleasantly.

'So what did Mr Wallace have to say?' Freda obviously couldn't resist asking, as she poured a cup of tea for Esme and herself.

Muriel gave a start. 'Why would you think I went to the solicitor's?'

'It stands to reason,' Freda said. 'You wanted to learn the terms of the will.'

'Yes, I did, as a matter of fact.' Muriel tossed her permed head. 'But Mr Wallace wasn't there, if you must know. He's going to be away for some time.'

'Oh, why's that?' Freda asked.

'Apparently, the receptionist said he'd been coughing for weeks. He said it was only a cold, but it was getting worse and he sometimes telephoned in sick. The doctor told him he had TB and he'd have to go to a sanatorium for at least six months to build up his strength.' She broke off to refill her cup. 'So that's where he is.'

'Did you speak to anyone else?' Freda demanded.

Muriel gave a heavy sigh. 'Yes, Mr Lake, his senior clerk. He's left him in charge. I thought this would all be dealt with in two or three weeks. It seems not. You might as well know it, but he says he first has to apply for probate, and that sometimes takes months.' She took a swallow of tea. 'Unbelievable, how slow these things are.'

Freda sent a quick glance to Esme, then looked back at Muriel.

'You might have given us the courtesy of inviting us to go with you,' she said.

'I didn't think it necessary,' Muriel said, looking away.

Esme was silent. There was something about Muriel's guarded expression that told her the woman was withholding something. Then she shook herself. She was seeing things that didn't exist. When Muriel had rinsed her cup in the sink and left the kitchen without another word, Esme said:

'If Muriel's seen the contents of the will, she doesn't appear to be that bothered her name *isn't* included with ours on the house.' She paused. 'In fact, all she seemed annoyed about was how long probate took.'

'Maybe she doesn't know the exact terms yet.' Freda creased her brow in thought. 'If it takes months I just hope Mr Wallace is back because I don't like to think it's in some clerk's hands. Anything could go wrong there.'

'I shouldn't think so,' Esme said. 'Mum and Dad's wishes are down in black and white and that's the end of it.'

Chapter Twenty-One

It was so good to have her sister's company, Esme thought, even though she could only manage two nights. Muriel had made herself scarce, almost as though she didn't want another confrontation with her husband's elder daughter, who said what she thought at all times.

After her sister went home, Esme kept out of her stepmother's way as much as she could, just coming down to make coffee or tea and having a meal. Occasionally, she joined her in the kitchen, but the conversation was stilted, and Muriel would normally be the first to disappear, which Esme much preferred. The funeral date had not been confirmed because of a backlist of burials. Each day crept slowly by. She hardly noticed as she was so caught up with the emotions of her father's death. On top of that, she felt she was letting Sir Giles down, though she was endeavouring to tap out his memoirs at odd hours on her father's old typewriter. Then there was the grim business of organising the funeral along with keeping Freda updated.

There's someone else I'm desperate to see, her inner voice whispered.

She mustn't dwell on him. He was married and could never be hers. But coming to terms with that reality only wrenched her heart further. When she wasn't typing, she buried herself in carrying on with the daunting task of clearing her father's things that neither she nor Freda wanted. Muriel had already told her she'd put the things she wanted to keep in her own bedroom. The woman hadn't offered to show her what she'd taken but Esme didn't have the energy to challenge her – not at the moment anyway.

A fortnight passed while she steadily sorted her father's things. This morning she decided to start clearing all his paperwork in the make-do study in the shed but because it had dropped to freezing point in the night she couldn't push the key into the padlock. Muttering a few choice words, she thought to tip the remains of the hot water in the kettle over it. *Ah.* The key slipped in and she unlocked it. She stepped inside and immediately the smell of dank wood invaded her nostrils. She'd get used to it, she told herself, but it was freezing cold. Her thick jumper and the layers underneath wouldn't be enough of a barrier to keep out the cold. She fetched her coat. It might have made sense to lug the files over to the house, but quite frankly, she wanted to have the least contact with Muriel as possible.

She smiled at the way her father used the workbench as a desk but at least he had an old filing cabinet that she hoped he'd kept in order and up to date. Keeping tidy had never been her father's strong point. She took the old kitchen chair he used and prepared herself to work through the piles of paperwork, throwing out as much rubbish as she possibly could.

She came to a cardboard folder marked *Personal*. She opened it to find a foolscap envelope containing her parents' marriage certificate and her mother's death certificate. Tears sprang to her eyes to remember how young her mother had been – not quite forty. Almost Freda's age. She couldn't imagine the death of her sister, so vivacious, who had always been so important in her life.

In another drawer was a photograph album. She'd take that into the house to have a look at it when she had time, but she couldn't resist opening it to glance at a page of photographs beautifully set out. The first picture was a newborn baby with Freda's name and date of birth in handwriting that she didn't recognise but instinctively thought must be her mother's. She chewed her lip. She'd ask Freda. There were several more of her sister as a happy toddler. She turned over the page and her heart contracted at a larger photograph of a slim, dark-haired young woman holding a baby. On the back, her mother had written: *Esmeralda at six months*. She'd never seen this photograph before. She stared at her mother's image. It was uncanny. Now, not much older than her mother was in the photograph, Esme could see she had her mother's nose, her mother's mouth and chin – almost an exact replica. Why had she never noticed this similarity before? But when she thought about it, she didn't remember seeing any photographs of her mother around the house, and it crossed her mind that it would have been Muriel who persuaded her father to put them all out of sight when they were married. And when she'd so often looked at the photograph she had of her mother and father when they were young, before any children arrived, it was their happiness of being together that had always caught her attention.

Dad had once said that her mother made a habit of always being beautifully turned out, no matter what the occasion. She wished with all her heart she could remember what her mother looked like in person, and not just gazing at a flat black-and-white photograph. Blinking back the tears, she decided she'd look through the rest of the album at a later time. For now, she needed to crack on. But a warm feeling had stolen around her heart. She felt closer to her mother than she ever had before.

It was going to be difficult to act normally with her stepmother, Esme thought, when she heard the postman the following morning. There was a brown envelope addressed to Mrs Bernard Grant. She took it to the kitchen where Muriel was making herself some toast. Muriel brushed her hands down her pinafore before she opened it.

'Your father's funeral is on the seventeenth of December,' she announced. 'A fortnight tomorrow.' She tutted. 'That'll be five weeks since he died.'

'I've been told the funeral director has been conscripted,' Esme said mildly, 'so it's left them very short in the parlour. But at least we have a date now.' She swallowed hard.

'That brings us nearly up to Christmas,' Muriel said, studying Esme, 'so I expect you'll be going to Freda's.'

Esme had no idea where she'd be, only that Muriel was the last person she wanted to spend Christmas with.

'I've only been to Freda's the last two Christmases since Anthony died and that was because it would feel more Christmassy with the boys. But this year I'm not sure where I'll be, but I *do* know I won't be spending it here.'

'With me, you mean,' Muriel said, eerily reading Esme's thoughts. 'You might as well say it, but let me tell you, my girl, if it wasn't for me, you'd have grown up in the orphanage. Your father didn't have a clue on how to bring up a six-year-old daughter.'

'Freda would never have let me go there,' Esme said firmly.

'She was only sixteen so she wouldn't have had a say in the matter.'

'Dad would, though.'

Muriel shook her head. 'Like it or not, it was me who rescued you.'

'I was barely seven by that time and didn't know anything about stepmothers,' Esme said, hating this conversation, 'only that I couldn't understand why my mother wasn't there anymore. And you never showed me any motherly love. On the contrary . . .' She stared at Muriel. 'Maybe it wasn't your fault as you'd never had children of your own, but it *was* your fault that you rarely showed me even kindness.'

'And it was your father's fault for taking any chance of having children away from me,' her stepmother snapped. 'It took me a whole year before he agreed to do the decent thing and marry me. But marry me, he did.'

Esme bit the inside of her mouth to prevent herself from saying what a mistake he'd made and that she was sure he'd soon realised it himself.

'So where *will* you be going for Christmas?' Muriel cocked her head on one side.

'I haven't decided yet.' Esme swallowed the last piece of toast, feeling it would choke her if she stayed any longer in Muriel's presence.

'Well, if you don't find anywhere, don't come running back here because—'

But the rest of the sentence was lost as Esme shut the kitchen door. She might not know where she was going for Christmas, but she knew where she was going today – to see Sir Giles and ask if she could resume working for him after the funeral.

Esme's heart leapt with pleasure when she stepped off the bus and walked towards the ornate iron gates of Redcliffe Manor. She'd barely set foot on the gravel drive when she heard the sound of heavy traffic behind her. Twisting round, she watched as six ambulances lumbered by, then turned into the next entrance reserved for the tradesmen but must now serve the new hospital. Brad had mentioned they only had twenty or so patients as it had only recently begun to function as a fully functioning hospital with a small operating theatre; now it looked as though things had stepped up since she'd been away.

As she hurried to the entrance, she could hear a scurry of activity from the rear. Ambulance doors clanged shut and sounds of muffled voices, but one rising above the others – firm and authoritative. A smile drifted across her lips. It was an American voice and in her imagination it was Brad, though she knew she couldn't discern it for certain. Her anger with him had already evaporated. She'd been reading too much into a few friendly kisses on the cheek and that one special kiss that many men might be tempted into when away from their wives for long periods. She'd simply put too many of her own feelings into a non-existent romantic connection.

Thoroughly annoyed with herself, she rang the bell. And there stood Mrs Morgan, her sharp eyes looking her up and down.

'Oh, you're back then,' were the words which greeted Esme. 'How long will you be staying this time?'

'I'm not sure,' she answered vaguely.

The housekeeper sniffed. 'I shall need to know to tell Cook.'

Esme gave her a sardonic smile. 'When I know, I'll tell her myself. But for now, may I come in?'

Mrs Morgan couldn't resist a tut of disapproval as she stepped aside.

'Is Sir Giles in?'

'He won't want to be disturbed.'

Just at that moment, Sir Giles came into the hall. When he saw it was Esme, his face split in two with his smile.

'Hello, my dear. How nice to see you. But why didn't you let me know you were coming?'

'I didn't know myself until an hour ago,' Esme said, breathing out her relief at his welcome and noting the triumphant look on Mrs Morgan's face had instantly been wiped off.

'Come to my study.' He glanced at the housekeeper. 'Mrs Morgan, would you rustle up some coffee for the two of us?'

He must have caught Mrs Morgan's pursed lips because his eyes twinkled as he ushered Esme to his study.

'It's rather noisy outside,' he said, pulling down the sash window. 'Lot of action going on at the hospital. They've taken a big influx of patients.'

'I thought so as I saw all the ambulances.'

He gave a deep sigh. 'It's been like this every day for the last week. Colonel Parker was telling me Herr Hitler is determined to hang onto Tunisia at all costs as it's a stronghold for the Axis forces. Apparently, the Germans forced the Americans back to Algiers in the latest combat, and unfortunately that meant many badly wounded soldiers needing care.' He glanced at her. 'I expect because of the American involvement, our Colonel Parker has opened the hospital to some patients who've partially recovered and are back in England.'

Even though her heart went out to those injured and the families of the ones who'd been killed, Esme couldn't control the quickening of her pulse at the sound of Brad's military name. She was aware that Sir Giles, perceptive as she'd often found him, was watching her.

'I keep wondering how much longer the war's going to drag on,' she said.

Sir Giles grimaced. 'By Colonel Parker's reckoning, there'll be a few more years to go yet.' He smiled at her. 'But you haven't come here for an updated bulletin – there's enough of that in the newspapers.' He cleared his throat. 'First of all, I'd like to say how sorry I was to hear about your father, as it sounded so sudden.' He looked straight at her. 'Is it too early to ask what you plan to do after the funeral's over?'

'That's what I wanted to see you about,' Esme said. 'I'm only here for the day as Dad's service is next week on the seventeenth, but I wanted to see you in person rather than on the telephone.'

Sir Giles frowned. What did that mean? Esme thought. She wasn't sure how to continue. It really was for Sir Giles to say if he'd like her to come back – or not.

When he didn't say anything. Esme had to break the silence.

'I wanted to know if your offer still stands for me to come back here and work for you.'

He regarded her with a serious expression.

'I've never changed my mind. You know that.'

Esme breathed out a sigh.

'I'm not always good at saying the right thing,' Sir Giles said gruffly, 'but it's not been the same here since you left.'

Warmth rolled through her at his words.

'Sir Giles, I do have a favour to ask of you.'

Sir Giles immediately became brisk, as though he were embarrassed.

'Go on.'

'I just wanted to telephone my sister that I'm here – I couldn't ring her because my stepmother never allows me a moment's privacy on the telephone.'

Sir Giles immediately got up from his chair and nodded towards his telephone.

'Help yourself,' he said. 'I'll leave you in peace. And take as long as you want.'

'Thank you, sir. You're very kind.'

He opened the study door to leave at the same time Dolly was about to knock with the tray of coffee. The maid only just managed to keep the tray upright.

'Well done, Dolly,' Esme heard him say as he passed by the young girl, at the same time removing his cup of coffee and taking it with him.

Dolly grinned as she set the tray on Sir Giles's desk.

'Will you be staying from now on, madam?'

She'd give anything to say 'yes'. But she'd have to face Muriel sooner or later. She smiled at the little maid.

'Not this time, Dolly, but the next time I come, I'm here to stay.'

'Very good, madam.' Dolly beamed, then gave a little bow of her head.

Esme picked up the receiver. 'Operator, could you please put me through to a Reading number?' She didn't have long to wait until she heard Freda's voice.

'Hello, Esme. What's up?'

'Just to tell you I left after breakfast and I'm back at Redcliffe Manor speaking in Sir Giles's study at the moment. He kindly let me ring you because there's no privacy when Muriel's around.'

'Has he asked you to go back to work for him?'

'Yes.'

'And?'

'I said I would.'

'Well, I suppose that's where your heart is,' Freda said, 'but not necessarily in the work.' When Esme didn't reply, Freda said, 'I'm talking about Dr Brad.' She gave a chuckle.

'I know you are, but don't read anything into that, Freda,' Esme said. She'd have to tell her sister or Freda would never let it go. 'I've found out he has a wife.'

The words choked in her throat. There was a silence. Then Freda said:

'Do you know for certain?'

'Yes. Stella told me. She works at the hospital, so she probably gets to hear all sorts of gossip.'

'Hmm. Could be that's all it is – just gossip.' There was a pause along the wire. Then Freda said, 'Does this Stella like him?'

Esme bit her lip. 'More than likes.'

'Since she has designs on him herself, she could be putting you off on purpose.'

'I don't know. But I'm not really surprised. He must be in his mid to late thirties, so it stands to reason he has a wife.'

'Not necessarily,' came Freda's cool tones. 'But it might be a good idea to find out once and for all.'

Chapter Twenty-Two

The war news from Tunisia was depressing. It all sounded a long way away. Esme frowned as she picked up the newspaper and read that the Allies might not be able to hold out much longer against the surprisingly strong combat troops of Germans and Italians. More injuries and deaths. She wondered how the American soldiers were doing at the hospital. If only there was a glimmer of hope that the war was coming to an end. But there was not the slightest sign.

Back once again at her old home, Esme had tried to keep out of Muriel's way as often as she could, taking her father's clothes and shoes to the Salvation Army and stacking any books to one side in her bedroom that she and Freda would be interested in. The remainder would go to the second-hand bookshops.

This evening, Esme folded the newspaper and sat for a few minutes in her father's armchair thinking about him and how desperate he must have been at the end. It was so sad. If only Muriel had been a loving wife and mother to her, how different everything would have been.

An abrupt shrill clanged into her thoughts and she rushed to the hall to pick up the telephone before Muriel grabbed it.

'Esme Donaldson speaking.'

The operator's bored-sounding voice came over the wires.

'Would you take a call from Colonel Parker?'

Esme's heart fluttered.

'Yes, of course.'

'Esmeralda?'

'Yes, it's me.' She warmed to hear her full name. The wires crackled, and then the line cleared.

'Are you okay?' His soft American voice was like a soothing balm to her jangled nerves.

'Not really,' she couldn't stop herself from saying.

'You sound as if you have problems. Is it to do with the arrangements for the funeral?' When she hesitated, wondering what to say, he added, 'Tell me. Maybe I can help.'

'I don't really want to talk about it on the telephone.' Esme kept her voice low.

'I understand,' he said quickly. 'Changing the subject, I happened to run into Sir Giles a little while ago and he told me you're coming back.'

'Yes, that's right, but not until after the funeral next week.'

'I was going to ask if you'd like to have dinner with me this evening. Give you a breather. I could pick you up and take you home afterwards.'

It sounded wonderful. Then she remembered the rationing.

'What about the petrol?'

He hesitated. 'Oh, you mean gas? We don't do too badly on gas.' There was a smile in his voice. 'Can you be ready in an hour?'

'Yes.'

'Okay. I'll fetch you at seven.'

She heard him put the receiver down. She should be excited about seeing him again. But she almost felt the opposite. Despite the rumours, she was in love with him. Simple as that. And now she was worried as to whether she should ask him if he had a wife. What would she do if he admitted he had and the woman was waiting for him in America? And if he said no, how would she know he was telling the truth?

Brad pressed his foot a little harder on the accelerator, not wanting to lose a minute that he could be spending in Esme's company. It wasn't surprising that she sounded blue, considering her father had died so suddenly, but he felt there was something more at the back of it.

Could it be anything to do with her husband? It was strange that she never mentioned him. Not even his name. Was it possible he'd become a POW? If so, she'd be very worried about how the Germans were treating him. And if they'd taken him back to Germany. Dreadful thought. Should he ask her about him? He'd wanted to so many times. He felt he knew her well enough by now, so what was holding him back? If he were honest, he was sure that the growing feeling between them was developing into more than friendship. It was on his part, anyway. Had done at the very beginning when he'd first laid eyes on her tiptoeing across the grass in bare feet. He'd presumed her heels had been digging into the gravel, making her unsteady. He smiled at the memory of the charming picture she'd made and how he'd been determined to talk to her. Find out if she was single. But to his utmost disappointment, she wore a gold band on her wedding-ring finger.

And even if she could push her husband to the back of her mind, she couldn't deny that he existed. So maybe she felt guilty that she'd begun to have feelings for another man – him. Especially when she'd kissed him back so passionately that time in the Muniment Room, no holds barred. It had nearly knocked him off his feet. It was as though his were the only lips she'd ever wanted to kiss and the effect was pure magic. Afterwards, he'd had to force himself to break the spell. Pull away from her. Apologise to her. Because he'd forgotten in the intensity of the moment – and so had she, it seemed – that she was married.

Brad groaned as he pulled up at a set of traffic lights, wishing he had time to light a cigarette. His imagination was running riot. Reluctantly, he realised he had to come to the most likely conclusion – that Esme felt nothing more than friendship for him. But he couldn't stop himself from thinking more – trying to work her out.

Maybe she and her husband had met at the beginning of the war and it had been a whirlwind courtship that would never have happened in normal life. He let the handbrake off and drove across the junction. The war had a lot to answer for. But if it hadn't happened, he wouldn't have met her. Unthinkable. He wouldn't even be in England, supervising the building and running of a hospital in the grounds of such a fabulous country house.

He didn't wish for her to be unhappy – not for one moment – but if she and her husband had made a mistake – for God's sakes, he'd made plenty – then perhaps there was some hope for him. He shook his head. It was no use ruminating. He'd know soon enough – with whatever she cared to tell him.

A few minutes later he drew up outside her house. He knocked on the door and it immediately opened. And there in the dim light of the hall stood the woman he thought about night and day, smiling at him.

Chapter Twenty-Three

The doorbell rang and Esme rushed to answer it. She already had her hat on. She could see Brad's outline behind the front door's stained-glass panels. He smiled as he stepped in, then bent to kiss her cheek.

Oh, if only . . .

'Are you ready?'

'Yes,' she said firmly, snatching her coat off the hook. 'I'm ready.'

'How was Muriel?' he asked when he'd settled her in the passenger seat beside him. This time it felt quite natural to be sitting by his side.

'I really don't want to talk about her. All she's waiting for is probate and how much Dad's left her. Freda and I don't even know that for sure.' Esme sighed. 'She's not an easy woman.'

'I could tell that when I was there with your father, but no need to say anymore, unless you want to, and that will be over supper and a glass of wine.' He smiled. 'I think we could both do with a little break from everything, don't you? And I know just the place.'

Esme had never been to this restaurant before – not that she'd often eaten out at restaurants when she was living near the centre of the city in her little flat. She and Anthony had enjoyed a meal on occasions, but he didn't like anywhere too fancy – or what he considered poor value.

'I prefer your cooking,' he used to say.

But Brad's choice of restaurant was rather quirky as it was over the top of an old bakery and from the outside, in the blackout, you couldn't tell it was a restaurant. But as soon as they stepped inside and were ushered up a wooden staircase, Esme could hear the hum of voices and sense enticing smells from the kitchen. The interior of the restaurant had already been decorated with coloured paper chains draped across the ceiling. A fir tree on a low table to one side of the room sparkled with tinsel and a mixture of baubles and red bows. She brought her gaze back to Brad.

'I've barely had a chance to think about Christmas,' she murmured as a waiter came to take their coats and hats and show them to their table.

'With all that's happened, I'm not surprised,' Brad said.

The waiter put a menu card in front of them, saying the special was a fish pie, and that he'd be back shortly for their order. In the meantime, would they like something to drink?

Brad caught her eye. 'Would you care for red or white wine, Esmeralda?'

'Red will probably make me fall asleep over the table,' she said, smiling.

'Better be white then,' Brad chuckled, looking up at the waiter. 'What do you have?'

'We have a few bottles of 1939 Sauvignon left,' the waiter said.

Brad looked at Esme and she nodded. He turned to the waiter. 'Then we'll have a bottle of Sauvignon, please.'

'Very good, sir.'

Brad turned his head to look round the room with its Christmas festoons. 'I suppose I'll have to organise some decorations for the wards – something I hadn't thought about.'

'Oh, yes, you must,' Esme agreed. 'It would cheer the patients up no end.'

'I don't suppose you'd come and help, would you?'

It flashed through her mind that Stella would certainly have something to say about it if she waltzed over to the hospital and started putting up decorations.

'What about Stella? She made the lovely table decoration at Sir Giles's dinner party.'

He hesitated, then said, 'I would rather you ask her than me.'

She hoped his hesitation was because he was reluctant to ask Stella any favours.

'There are several wards to do,' he went on, 'so we'll need more than two of you anyway. But everyone – the nurses and cleaners are working non-stop with all the new patients we've taken in recently. No one has a moment to spare.'

'What about the schoolgirls? I bet they'd love to help.'

'Mmm. Good idea. Can you arrange it?'

'I'll try, though the housemistress seems a bit of an ogre although I've never really spoken to her.'

His eyes twinkled. 'I'm sure you'll charm her – like you do all of us . . . in an unpretentious way,' he added when he saw her raise an eyebrow.

She couldn't help smiling as she looked across at him. He was only two feet away from her. She couldn't help it. Her eyes dropped to his lips – the shape of them. She could almost feel that kiss and willed herself not to blush.

'Is anything wrong?' Brad said in that husky voice she loved.

'N-no, nothing.'

Catching her breath, she was relieved when the waiter appeared to take their orders.

'Esmeralda?'

'The fish pie, please.'

'Make it two,' Brad told him.

The waiter nodded and disappeared, soon returning with their wine.

'Good health.' Brad raised his glass to hers. 'That's what you British say, don't you?'

'Among other expressions,' she smiled, touching her glass with his.

'Do *you* like Christmas?'

His question came completely out of the blue. He was studying her as if her answer was important.

Esme's face clouded. 'It's really for the children, isn't it?'

He was looking at her intently. 'You know you've never mentioned children before.'

Dear God, how was she going to answer that?

It didn't sound as though he was talking about children in general but questioning her as to whether she had any herself. His gaze was still fixed on her. She had to say something.

'Muriel plainly didn't like children and made no effort to understand me in particular,' she said quickly, hoping to take the attention off herself and onto her stepmother to stop any further probing. 'So it wasn't very Christmassy in our house, although she always made a nice meal. I'll say that for her – she was a good cook. I think that's the main reason why Dad kept her on. He knew we'd all be well fed.'

'Talking of being well fed, here's the waiter with our food,' Brad said. 'Let's eat and then if you want to tell me anything more about what happened with that stepmother of yours, you know you can. It will never go further.'

The fish pie was delicious. Esme hadn't realised how hungry she'd been until she forked the last shreds from her plate and took another sip of the wine. Brad had made short work of his and had already finished.

'Are you okay?' he said.

'Yes. I'm feeling better.'

'Good.'

The air between them stilled – as though waiting to see what either of them would say next. If it might be something more intimate even. He felt it, too – she knew he did by the way he was looking straight at her. He wasn't acting like a married man at all. Did Stella really get it so wrong? She gave an inward sigh. They knew so little about one another.

'Whereabouts do you come from in America?' she asked, needing to break the spell.

'Denver, capital of Colorado.'

'That's west, isn't it?'

He nodded. 'To be really accurate, it's part of the Mountain West and known as the Mile High City.'

Her eyes widened. 'Is it really a mile high?'

He grinned. 'When you reach the thirteenth step of the State Capitol Building, that's exactly a mile above sea level.' His gaze was still on her. 'Isn't that amazing?'

'Amazing,' she repeated, catching his gaze, knowing she wasn't referring to Denver city's height.

'Ever heard of the Rocky Mountains?'

She shook her head, determined to look at an atlas at the first opportunity and see exactly where this city called Denver lay.

'It's beautiful,' Brad continued. 'A huge range of snow-capped mountains. The air is clean and crisp in winter – perfect for skiing. But it gets pretty hot in the summer.'

'It sounds wonderful. You must miss it.'

'Not at the moment. I'm too busy here to have time to miss it.'

'But you must miss your family.'

Half wishing she could bite back the words she hadn't intended to say at that moment, she wondered where this would lead. But it was obvious. Brad would ask about her own family even if it was only for the sake of politeness. She waited on the edge of her seat for his reply.

'My parents are elderly now but both doing well. They say they have to give the impression of being healthy to the neighbours because their son's a doctor.' He gave a rueful smile.

'Do you have siblings?'

A shadow passed over his face. 'I had a younger sister.' His hand clenched.

Had. That horrible past tense.

'What happened to her?' she asked softly.

She saw his Adam's apple move before he answered.

'She was driving her Ford – her pride and joy that she'd saved up for months to buy. That night a car shot round the corner on the wrong side – she didn't stand a chance. They found out the driver was *drunk*, but he got off without a scratch . . . after killing my sister. She'd just turned thirty with her whole life before her.'

Esme startled at the sound of his voice, the voice she loved was now harsh and filled with bitterness as he banged his fist on the table.

The couple sitting at a nearby table turned their heads to stare for a few seconds, but he didn't notice. Esme had never seen him like this. She hoped the couple didn't presume the two of them were having a row. Without thinking more than trying to quieten him, she took his fist, smoothing it open. He looked down at their two hands, hers on top of his, and brought hers to his lips, giving it the lightest kiss before letting it go.

'Oh, Esmeralda, I'm so sorry. I didn't mean to get carried away. It happened nearly three years ago but it feels like yesterday. It makes me feel so angry every time I think about it. Patsy was my little sister and I was the brother who she looked up to, yet I wasn't there when she needed me.' He took in a deep, jagged breath, and as though she'd unleashed the hatred inside him, went on, 'He killed another as well.' He lowered his eyes. 'I've not told anyone this, but Patsy had let me into her secret . . . I was going to be an uncle.' When he looked up, she saw his eyes were glistening with tears.

Oh no. Not that as well. Esme's eyes pricked. She must not allow her own tears to overflow.

She sat silently, not knowing what to say. She could hardly say she related to his despair or he would question her as to how.

'It was a terrible tragedy that needn't have happened,' she ventured.

He nodded. 'I was nearly as excited as Patsy because I'd always wanted to be a father and I still never have.' He momentarily closed his eyes.

Her mind felt it would explode trying to take in everything. She would need to be on her own to work out exactly what his outburst meant – not just to him but also to herself.

'But you don't want to hear my misery – you have enough of your own to deal with from the sounds of Muriel and the way she treated your father.'

'That's nothing compared with your sister.'

How badly she wanted to tell him about Anthony. *It feels like yesterday*, Brad had said, when he'd learnt about Patsy. The same as it had been when Anthony had suddenly died – heartbreaking and raw. That was, until she'd met Brad and fallen in love with him. So how could she tell him about her husband? He would be so kind and understanding, she knew, when all the while she loved another – Brad himself. Now, when she thought of Anthony, it was with guilt, piling on even worse that Brad might have a wife in America who loved him and was waiting for the war to end so he would come home to her. Esme tried to brush away the indistinct figure. But sooner or later she knew she'd have to ask about her – though definitely not here in the restaurant. Oh, why did everything have to be so complicated where relationships were concerned? She gave a deep sigh.

'What was that sigh for?' Brad said.

'I don't know. The world has gone mad. Sometimes I find I can't even think straight.'

'No one can these days.' Then he lightened his tone. 'Would you like a dessert or coffee?'

'No, the pie was just right, thank you, but you go ahead.'

'Not for me.' Brad caught the eye of a passing waiter. 'May we get the check, please?'

'The bill, sir?' the waiter queried. Brad nodded. 'Right away, sir.'

Now in Brad's car, Esme stole a glance at him every so often, taking in the contours of his profile – the slightly hawked nose, the strong outline of his jaw – and his well-shaped hands firm on the steering wheel. She couldn't help it. She liked everything about his looks. But he didn't speak. Once he turned to her for the briefest second as though to say something but refrained and fixed his eyes on the blackness ahead. It seemed only minutes later that he turned the engine off outside her house.

There was an awkward silence. She heard Brad clear his throat. He bent towards her in the darkness and put his arm round the back of her seat.

'Esmeralda, there's something I want to say to you that I should have told you some time ago. Whenever I tried, it didn't seem to be the right time.'

She didn't need to ask him if he had a wife. He was about to tell her. She knew it. Where her heart should be was only a dull ache.

'Brad, it was so kind of you to take me to dinner tonight. I needed that break from Muriel, and . . . well, everything. But I'm really tired. There's been quite a lot to do since Dad died and the funeral's only a few days away . . .' she appealed to him.

'Of course, dear. I'm being thoughtless, as usual. We'll take a raincheck. But can we make some time that we can have a proper talk?'

'Of course,' Esme said, not aware she was echoing him. 'I'll feel better when this is all over and I'm back at the Manor.' She opened the door. 'I can let myself out, Brad.' Without thinking, she twisted round and kissed him on the cheek. 'Thank you for such a lovely evening. You've been a true friend and you don't know how much I appreciate it.'

'My absolute pleasure,' he said, but his words were drowned as Esme was already on the pavement, giving the car door a firm slam.

Chapter Twenty-Four

On a bitter, cold December afternoon, the day before the funeral, Esme stood on the platform at Bath railway station, with Christmas presents she'd bought that morning: soap for Muriel and bath salts for Freda and Stella. She watched as the train from Reading pulled to a screeching, shuddering halt. Among all the heads sticking out of the windows, she recognised Freda's hat, an arm outstretched waving to her. With the help of a soldier, Freda jumped down and hurried towards her sister and gave what she considered a hug but was merely a brief moment of physical contact.

'Hmm. You're looking a bit wan,' she said, staring at Esme. 'When did you go back to the house?'

'At the last minute,' Esme said, giving a rueful smile. 'Not until yesterday afternoon.'

'Good for you.' Freda tipped the porter and turned back to Esme. 'Let's find a taxi. I can't wait to hear all the news.'

'So what's Muriel been up to, then?' Freda said as soon as they were sitting in the back of a cab.

'She's actually not been too bad at all.' Esme took her purse out, ready to pay the driver.

'Hmm.' Freda sounded unconvinced. 'Do you think she's up to something?'

'I'm not sure.' She looked at Freda. 'Put that purse away – I'm paying for this and I insist.'

'How nice to see you, Freda,' Muriel said with a rare smile as she came from the kitchen to greet them when Freda had used her own front-door key. 'How are the boys? You haven't mentioned them lately.'

'I wonder if that's because you never ask,' Freda shot back.

Muriel's smile faded. Esme sent Freda one of their warning signs when they were children – she touched the corner of her mouth with her forefinger. Freda appeared to take notice as she added quickly:

'But since you have, Bobby's much better after a bad cold, and Felix is about to leave school and thinking of joining up.' She paused. 'Not at all what I want and thank goodness he has a few months still to think about it.'

'You must be relieved,' Muriel said, her tone measured. 'Supper's almost ready. Go into the sitting room and I'll call you when I'm ready.'

'I see what you mean,' Freda said when they were alone. 'I don't think she realises she's not included in the division of our parents' house, or why would she act so pleasantly towards us? She's not usually like this unless we're bringing her a birthday or Christmas present.'

'Maybe she finally realises how fragile life is,' Esme said, 'especially now there's a war on, but I don't want to keep talking about her as we never seem to get anywhere.' She paused. 'Let me go over the arrangements for tomorrow.'

Bernard Grant had requested a simple cremation, and in the end only a dozen or so people attended the service. It was a miserable rainy day with gusts of wind that threatened to blow people's hats off. Esme wished Mr Wallace had been there. He wasn't just their solicitor. He had been such an old friend of her father's, and a frequent visitor in her youth. It would have been a comfort to see him, but he was still in the sanitorium. But at least she had her sister with her. She was too numb to cry at the funeral, although she was surprised to see Freda wipe her tears away more than once.

Now in her childhood home, Esme clung onto the idea that later, when she was back at Redcliffe Manor, she'd be able to think about her father quietly in her room. Remember him. Try to picture him with her mother when she was little. When the four of them were a proper family. But not here. Not with so many vivid memories growing up under Muriel's thumb.

She'd half wondered if Brad might have come, seeing as he'd met Dad, though they hadn't exactly had much of a conversation, but of course he wouldn't. It was a family affair and he was incredibly busy at the hospital with all the new patients that had poured in recently.

Now, the last of the friends and neighbours had left, and Muriel was making yet another pot of tea. She brought the tray into the sitting room with a slice each of her ginger cake. Esme had hoped she could sit and chat quietly with her sister on her own, but after Muriel had poured the tea, she sat in her husband's armchair by the fire.

'Now we're on our own,' she began, 'I have something I need to discuss with the two of you, and I'd be grateful if you'd let me speak and finish without interrupting.'

The two sisters sent a startled glance to one another.

'You don't need me to remind you that I gave your father twenty-four years of my life – promising to look after the two of you, especially Esme who was only seven.' She looked at them as if to check they were concentrating on her words.

'Go on,' Freda said coolly.

'And I kept my promise. I cooked and cleaned and made sure you were not neglected.'

'Except the one thing you neglected and what we needed most of all – especially Esme,' Freda said, her eyes fixed on their stepmother. 'And in case you don't know it, Muriel, it's love . . . with a capital "L". You gave neither of us a shred of love.'

Muriel's lips almost disappeared in her grimace. 'I did my best – and your father was more than satisfied. And he wanted to show me his gratitude.'

Where is all this leading? Esme stole a glance at Freda, whose eyes were firmly fixed on their stepmother.

'This may come as a shock to the pair of you, but he changed his will not long before he died . . .' she paused as though to let such an astounding fact sink in. Freda sat bolt upright and Esme found herself swallowing hard, nervously waiting for what was coming. '. . . and removed both your names as the beneficiaries of this house. He inserted *mine* instead.'

'WHAT!' Freda exploded. 'He would *never* have done that and left us out.'

'I'm afraid he did,' Muriel said, with a distinct note of triumph. She stared at them. 'And when you think about it, it was the right thing for him to do.'

'Mr Wallace is away on sick leave,' Esme said quietly. 'So how did this happen?'

'Your father wasn't very good on his legs so Mr Lake from the firm came to us. It's all signed – with a witness – and it's what your father wanted. And in case you say different, he was in full possession of his faculties.'

'If you're lying, Esme and I can soon put this straight,' Freda said, walking over to where Muriel sat and putting her face close to her stepmother's. Muriel inched back in her chair. 'But if it's the truth, I assure you we'll contest it. We're his daughters. He's always assured us that the house he and our *mother* bought – mostly with *her money* – would one day be ours.' She put her index finger up to Muriel. 'He was too ill to know what he was doing. You *made* him.' Freda's eyes flashed. 'You probably threatened to leave him if he didn't sign over the house, and he was terrified.'

Muriel half rose from her chair. Freda waved her down.

'Just a minute, Muriel. You're going to look very foolish when Esme and I go to the office and see that you're telling a pack of lies. Because that's what it is.'

'By all means go and see him,' Muriel said, with a curl of her lip. 'He'll show you. Your father left this house to me . . . it's there in black and white . . . and there's nothing either of you can do about it.'

'We'll see about that.' Freda's tone was steel. 'Esme and I will contest it with every bone in our body.'

'You'll be wasting your time.' Muriel's eyes gleamed. 'I already asked Mr Lake if it could be contested by his daughters and he told me . . . these were his very words: "It's all above board – signed, witnessed and dated. There's no chance it can be altered . . . by your stepdaughters or anyone."'

'Let's have a bit of supper out,' Freda suggested to Esme an hour later. 'I can't eat in the same room as her.' She looked at her sister. 'What do you think?'

'It'd be a relief,' Esme said quickly. 'We can walk into town. Like you, I need to get out of here and breathe some normal air, blackout or not.'

Freda plumped for a small Italian restaurant in one of the side streets of the city which the owner, who miraculously hadn't been interned, had thoughtfully painted the pavement outside in white stripes that showed up in the blackout.

'I'll ask the waiter for a private corner,' she said when the two of them stepped into the room, Freda with her overnight case so she could catch the train after supper. 'Somewhere we can talk without being disturbed, for a change.'

Soon the sisters were shown a table at the back of the room. Being near the kitchen, it was noisy with the clattering of plates and cutlery, but Freda remarked that it would make a good cover for their conversation. Esme sank gratefully onto the upholstered dining room chair, still trying to digest Muriel's momentous news.

After Freda had ordered spaghetti and had chosen the wine, she said: 'Esme, we should go and have a look at the will. See if Muriel's telling the truth.'

'Oh, I don't doubt she is,' Esme said. 'It's a waste of time. She's too cunning to pretend, knowing we'd hotfoot it over to the solicitors. No, I think we should wait until Mr Wallace returns. I know it's not for several months but that's how long probate will take anyway.'

'We could be too late contesting it by then,' Freda said.

'I seem to remember that you can contest a will even after probate has been granted,' Esme said.

Her sister raised an eyebrow. 'Where did you learn that?'

'Someone in the library once borrowed a book about wills and he happened to mention this. His wife was contesting a will.'

'Hmm. Interesting. We need to make sure that's a fact because the last thing we want is that we're on the wrong side of the deadline.' She brought out a packet of Players Please. 'It's hard to believe that Father would simply hand over our family home because he was so worried she wouldn't stay and look after him when he first became ill.' She shook out a cigarette. 'That was the crux of it.'

'I know. But there's nothing we can do at the moment.'

Freda rolled her eyes. 'We have to contest it. We're his daughters.' She fixed the cigarette in her holder to light it, then inhaled deeply. 'Oh, I needed that.' She waved the cigarette holder in the air for emphasis. 'Anyway, let's change the subject.' She fixed her eyes on Esme's. 'Did you ever find out about your Dr Brad – whether he has a wife or not?'

Esme's heart turned at the mention of Brad's name.

'No. And just to remind you, Freda, he's not *my* Brad. But he did mention a tragedy that happened to his sister the other night when we had supper out in Bath. It wasn't the time to question him on any wife as he was really upset and bitter about it. Poor Patsy. A drunken driver killed her on the road.'

'Oh dear. How frightful. But he must trust you for him to confide in something so sensitive.'

They finished their meal, Esme diverting her sister off the subject of Brad. 'I wish you'd stay the night,' she said.

'Not while Muriel is there.' Freda stood and buttoned her coat, attracting the attention of the waiter with the bill. She glanced down at it.

'I'll get this,' Esme said, quickly taking the bill out of her sister's hand. 'You go before any German planes arrive. And have a safe journey home.'

Freda adjusted her hat. 'Goodbye, Esme dear.' She bent and lightly kissed Esme's cheek. 'I hate to leave you with all this to deal with, but I'll give you a day or two whenever I can. Keep in touch.' She stopped abruptly and searched in her handbag, pulling out a key on a ring. 'You'd better have this as you'll be going backwards and forwards to the house and Muriel may very well not be there – on purpose,' she added pointedly as she handed the key to Esme.

Muriel would have gone to bed by now, Esme thought, as she let herself in and went straight up to her old bedroom.

She'd tidy the house in the morning before she went back to Redcliffe Manor so Muriel couldn't grumble. As for today, she could only thank God the funeral was over. Dad would at last be at peace.

Chapter Twenty-Five

'Good, you're back and here to stay, I hope, for the foreseeable future,' Sir Giles said three days later when his eyes alighted upon Esme as she came into his study.

'I'll try to stay as long as you want me,' she said.

'Then I'll have to keep finding you work, so you can't ever leave.' Sir Giles gave a rare grin and Esme smiled in return.

'What would you like me to do today?'

Sir Giles cleared his throat, not quite catching her eye. He looked towards the typewriter, then turned to Esme.

'I've thought deeply about what you said regarding that climb,' he said. 'Maybe you're right. Maybe it would be more honest to include it in my biography.'

She was touched that he trusted her judgement.

'Oh, I'm so glad, Sir Giles. I think you might even find it's a cathartic exercise and feel better having written it out.'

'Hmm, I'm not so sure about that, but I agree, it wouldn't be complete without it, though who would be interested in my life, I have no idea, especially as I have no children to hand it on to.'

'You'd be surprised.' Esme took the cover off the typewriter and sat at the machine. 'If it had come into the library where I used to work, I would definitely have asked to borrow it.'

'You're not like most – that's all I can say.' He put a sheaf of handwritten notes fastened together with a green tag onto the desk. 'Anyway, if you're really intent on doing this, you can put it in after the bit about George and Gerald, in the Boer War—' He broke off and cleared his throat.

Warmth crept up her neck as she still felt a spike of guilt that she'd already read of this in his father's private letter.

'I haven't come to that bit yet,' she managed. 'It must have been awful for you . . . and your parents.'

'I didn't know them that well as they were a lot older than me. But I do remember my parents being devastated. My poor mother couldn't stop crying and Father went to pieces. He shut himself up in his study and wouldn't come out. Mother had to have all his meals delivered. I was only a young lad at the time and they were in their twenties, so I didn't really know them as I'd hardly ever seen them. I acted more like an only child, but I had to pretend to Mother that I was grief-stricken too, though I didn't know the meaning of the word. I just didn't want her to think me completely heartless. And I was sent immediately to boarding school which I hated but couldn't complain because my parents had enough to cope with.'

What must it have cost him to speak in such a personal way, Esme wondered, when Sir Giles left the room.

She carried on with the memoir and after a few more pages she came to the part where Sir Giles had written of his brothers' deaths. He'd described it almost completely devoid of emotion. She supposed it was a typical Englishman's way of dealing with such tragedy. Then she recalled Sir Giles saying they were much older than him, so he was never really that close to either of them. Well, it was probably more honest of him this way.

Suddenly giving a yawn and then another, she rose up and gave a good stretch. She needed a break. Her back ached and for once the room felt stuffy and airless. She'd make herself a cup of tea and help herself to a biscuit or two – that is, if Cook was in a good mood.

Early the following morning, Esme walked back to her room having just enjoyed her twice-weekly bath – all they were allowed because of the war, and then only up to the red line of exactly five inches. Nevertheless, the hot water had warmed her, but now, upon entering the bedroom, she immediately felt the chill on her damp skin. Little heat emanated from the one electric bar on the fire in the hearth that was only allowed on for a short time if the radiator wasn't yet warm. Mrs Morgan had warned her she was not allowed to run the second bar. Esme stood in front of it for a few moments, a feeling of rebellion surging through her, and was about to switch on the second bar when she saw a slip of paper slide under the door.

Curiously, she picked it up and unfolded it. She read:

I saw you kissing Dr Parker that night. I should have reported you to Sir Giles. If he knew what was going on under his roof he would sack you on the spot. He doesn't want an old woman like you. You are disgusting.

Esme startled at those last words. She'd forgotten all about her and Brad being interrupted by the door opening that night. All she had ever thought about was the magic of his kiss. But now it came flooding back to her. The gasp. And then the door closing very quietly. Warmth flooded her cheeks as she relived the embarrassment of being discovered.

She quickly read the note again, giving a wry smile at the 'old woman' bit. She was only thirty-one, for goodness' sake. Then her smile faded. That had come from a child. One of the schoolgirls. She would seem ancient to fourteen-year-olds. She sighed. It didn't need working out who it could be. There was only one girl who had shown such open dislike from the beginning. Bertha.

But why? All she could think of was that Bertha had a schoolgirl crush on Brad. Well, there was nothing she could do about an angry schoolgirl. Also, she didn't know for sure it was Bertha. But whoever it was, it was best to ignore it.

Later that morning, Esme caught sight of Hilary Fenton taking a dozen of the older girls out for what looked like a long hike with their backpacks and walking boots. Bertha was among them, her plaits drawn away from her face even more fiercely than usual. As the group passed by Esme in the Great Hall, Hilary Fenton looked through her as though she didn't exist and marched on, while Bertha threw her a look of utter contempt and began whispering to another girl. The girl spun round and regarded Esme with interest. Esme simply smiled at her and the girl abruptly turned back to Bertha.

Forget it. It was time to get cracking with her work.

She planned to continue with Sir Giles's memoir this morning and finish the next stage of cataloguing the books in the library in the afternoon unless he had other plans. He looked up as she entered.

'Good morning, Esme. Colonel Parker has just telephoned. He says they're planning to put on a jazz evening next Saturday and they've invited some of the older girls and their teachers.' He stopped short and smiled. 'Oh, and you and Stella, of course.'

'Will you be going, sir?'

He shook his head. 'It's not my kind of music. And I get too tired at night. But I think you'd enjoy it.' He pressed some tobacco into the bowl of his pipe and struck a match, making little popping noises until it took. He looked up. 'Would you let the appropriate powers that be – Miss Fenton and the teachers – pick out those older girls who can be trusted not to let the school down?'

'Yes, of course.'

Could he possibly be alluding to Bertha? No. She didn't think he had any interest in the schoolgirls other than as he'd once mentioned – that he quite liked having them in the house and hoped some of the works of art and the beautiful surroundings would have some influence over them in the future. But now, not only might Bertha be part of the team to help decorate the hospital, but also as a guest at the jazz evening.

It was another two days before Esme came to the point in Sir Giles's mountain accident when he and his fellow climbers had almost reached the peak and the weather turned. She braced herself as she looked at the page of his script and began to type:

From what had been the start of a triumphant descent, with the sun glinting on the snowy caps, that morning suddenly changed in the afternoon, Sir Giles had written. *Dark clouds rolled in and I could tell we were in for a storm. As we neared the top I sensed we were all going to be caught in it. Walter and I were roped together and we gave each other the thumbs-up. But minutes after, the weather became worse. Wind was howling around us and Walter's hat was torn off his head. Then the snow. It fell suddenly and thickly. I couldn't see in front more than a yard.*

The two of us trudged on for maybe half an hour. I hadn't heard the voices of the others for the last ten or fifteen minutes and realised Walter and I had become separated from the party. And then I felt a tugging on the rope. Walter must have slipped! I peered down, but the snow was too thick to make out anything. I pulled hard to help him regain his foothold. It seemed to work and I thanked God. But the next moment the rope tugged again. I called down and heard a faint reply, but it was lost in the storm.

'Louder,' *I yelled.*

And then I heard him shout, 'Feel sick. Can't go . . .' *and his voice trailed off.*

'Hold on,' *I shouted back, bracing my legs to pull the rope again.*

'Rest a moment.' But whether he heard me or not, I'll never know. And what I heard next made my blood turn to ice.

'Cut the rope!'

'NO!' I bellowed. 'Hold tight. I'll help to pull you up.'

For a few seconds the snowfall eased and I squinted through the opening. To my horror, Walter was swinging in the air below, waving his arms and shouting, 'Cut the bloody rope!'

My feet slipped, one and then the other. I was nearing the edge of the deep gulf below me. I started to overbalance with his dead weight.

'Cut . . .'

That was the last word I heard my friend utter. It struck me he had altitude sickness and was too exhausted to go on. He was trying to tell me he wanted to save me. If I didn't cut the rope we would both go down. Even if I managed to pull him back again, would he be in such a bad state that he would likely die of hypothermia?

Before I could think further – before I could change my mind – I cut the rope. All I heard was a faint sound, like a cat hissing, and then even that was gobbled up by the roar of the storm. I was frozen, not only my hands and feet, but my very soul. Walter had saved my life – but in doing so I had to let him drop to his death. And I have never forgiven myself.

Tears rolled down Esme's cheeks. When he'd related the accident to her, he hadn't bared the depth of his emotion but only hinted how he'd felt all these years. Poor Walter. And poor Sir Giles. Guilt had plagued his life. No wonder he'd wanted to skip over that part of the memoir. But he'd listened to her. He'd included the tragedy. She'd changed his mind. The rest of the words blurred in front of her. She put the cover over the typewriter. It was impossible to type anymore today.

Chapter Twenty-Six

Esme settled into Redcliffe Manor as soon as she walked into her yellow-rose bedroom. In fact, she realised she felt more at home here now than she did in her childhood home.

She spent an hour typing another chunk of Sir Giles's manuscript, then rising from the typewriter, stretched her arms and glanced at her watch. Nearly eleven o'clock. Time for a coffee, but first it might be prudent to clear her idea of allowing some of the girls to help decorate the wards with Hilary Fenton, the housemistress, being a third teacher and senior to the other teachers. If she agreed, then Esme would have a word with Anita Lonsdale and Russell Kingsnorth to ask if they would be able to release some of their pupils.

She wasn't looking forward to a conversation with Miss Fenton. She'd only met the woman briefly at Sir Giles's dinner party, and she'd looked down her nose and barely acknowledged her.

Talk of the devil.

Hilary Fenton appeared on the landing and glided down the grand staircase in a plum-coloured dress, nipped in at the waist, and matching jacket. Esme had to admit she always looked in the height of fashion, the few times she'd seen her in the distance. The woman was about to sweep past when Esme put out her hand.

'Oh, Miss Fenton, would you have a minute?'

The housemistress frowned.

'I'm on the way to my office.' Miss Fenton's voice was low and modulated, her words crisp. 'You'd better come with me.'

With an imperious gesture she led the way to her office, where she pointed towards the upright visitor's chair, then settled into her seat behind her desk. Esme felt like a naughty schoolgirl about to be reprimanded.

For heaven's sake, stop acting like one then.

She straightened her spine and looked the woman in the eye. Miss Fenton silently waited until Esme had explained the reason for her visit.

'Hmm. I don't much like the sound of that,' Miss Fenton said, casually lighting a cigarette without offering Esme one. 'Picking only four out of thirty is bound to cause friction. And some of the girls are difficult to control.'

'Bertha being one?'

'Afraid so, but she's not the only one.' The housemistress inhaled deeply, then blew out a stream of smoke rings.

If she's trying to impress me, it hasn't worked, Esme thought, by now thoroughly irritated.

'Are you dismissing the whole idea?' she said.

'Have a word with Russell and Anita. If they agree, then by all means, go ahead.' Miss Fenton half rose from her desk, a sure sign that the meeting had ended.

Esme was about to take her cue when Miss Fenton said:

'Oh, one other thing, Mrs Donaldson—'

'Do call me Esme,' Esme interrupted. 'Most people do.'

'I'm not "most people",' Miss Fenton said coolly, stubbing out her half cigarette in the ashtray. 'But while we're on the subject of the girls, I should mention there's gossip spreading among some of the older ones about you and I need to put a stop to it – for everyone's sake.'

Warmth crept up the back of Esme's neck. What the devil was

the woman on about? Willing herself to keep her voice calm, she said: 'About me?'

'I'll be blunt.' Hilary Fenton looked her straight in the eye. 'I'm sure you're not hiding a dark secret but . . .' she paused for what seemed like dramatic effect, '. . . as far as we're aware, library work – even a fully-qualified librarian, which I don't believe you are, but correct me if I'm wrong – is not a reserved occupation.'

Esme forced herself not to lower her eyes. She would not let this nosy housemistress get the better of her.

'What exactly is your point, Miss Fenton?'

'Well, there's talk among them,' the housemistress went on, 'questioning the reason why you haven't joined the forces or been called up to do factory work– in other words, you've never mentioned any children so presumably you don't have any dependents.'

That bombing raid destroying my life. Destroying my cherished baby.

Giving no time to think, Esme shot from her seat and bent over the desk, her face only inches away from the smug expression on Hilary Fenton.

'How *dare* you, Miss Fenton! It's none of your business why I haven't joined up, and as housemistress it was your job to stop such gossip. Don't ever speak of my private affairs to them again or allow them to spread rumours. If I hear to the contrary, I'll make sure you face the consequences.'

'Do not threaten me, Mrs Donaldson.' She lit another cigarette. 'I was merely trying to make things more pleasant for you.'

'Things are more than pleasant here for me,' Esme said. 'And as long as Sir Giles is happy with me, that's all I ask.' She paused. 'But thank you, Miss Fenton, for your interest.'

With that, she swept out of the office and made straight for the staff room, waves of fury rolling through her shaking body.

For heaven's sake, don't let that woman get to you – it's what she wants.

She set her jaw. She'd weather this after all she'd been through. She wasn't going to allow herself to be bullied by the likes of Hilary Fenton, or anyone else, let alone those girls.

Feeling calmer, Esme hurried up to her room and rinsed her face in the washbasin, tidied some stray tendrils which had escaped from her victory roll and renewed her lipstick. She was ready to face anyone – or anything. At least the ghastly housemistress hadn't put a stop to the girls helping to decorate the wards. Now to find Anita Lonsdale. They'd never had much of a conversation as the teacher seemed on the shy side, so it would be nice to get to know her a little better.

'Anita, may I have a word?'

The young woman stopped in her tracks in the Great Hall, surprised. 'Oh, Esme, are you back to stay?'

'I am now.'

'I hope you don't mind but Sir Giles mentioned about your father. Do accept my condolences.' She pushed her rimmed glasses up her nose. 'What can I do for you?'

'It's more a question of what the girls can do.' Esme smiled as she explained what she was looking for and wondered if Anita could think of four girls who would take the job on seriously and at the same time be cheerful, but not overly so, around the patients.

'I certainly can,' Anita said with enthusiasm, then frowned. 'Have you spoken to Miss Fenton?'

'Yes. She wasn't enamoured of the idea, but she said if you agreed, then you could go ahead.'

Anita smiled, lighting up her eyes. 'Oh, good, but the only difficulty will be to choose which four as I've a feeling most of them would love the chance. I might have to end up putting names in a hat and someone picking them out.' She hesitated as though reluctant to ask, 'What about Russell's class?'

Esme had already gleaned there was a certain amount of competition between the girls in Anita's class and those in Russell's, but she was determined to bring them all together in the spirit of Christmas.

'I'll ask him about putting four names forward as well,' she said.

The only name she hoped she wouldn't see was that awkward little minx, Bertha. She didn't trust her at all.

Esme caught sight of Russell later that day in the staff room.

'This is a pleasant surprise, Esme. I'm sorry to hear about your father but are you now back for good?'

'I hope so,' she said, wanting to keep her arrangements vague where he was concerned.

When she asked him about the girls decorating the hospital wards, he looked doubtful.

'I wouldn't want anything to interfere with their lessons,' he said. 'How long will this take, do you think?'

'I've no idea. I haven't had a grand tour of the hospital since it's taken in patients, but I thought eight girls altogether – four from both classes – would get the job done in a couple of days. We can't send more as they'd start to get in the way.'

'Hmm. I'm not sure of the whole idea.' Russell grimaced. 'There are a couple of girls – one in particular – who'd go barmy if they weren't picked and they can be difficult to control.'

'Would Bertha be one of them?'

Russell raised his eyebrows. 'Why, have you come across her before?'

'Yes, and for some reason she's taken a dislike to me.'

He nodded. 'She's not the most popular in class. But she's

come from a difficult home background. Her father's not a commissioned officer but in the Great War he was promoted to a second lieutenant for an exceptional act of bravery. Most of her class know this and some of them shun her because in their view, she doesn't deserve a place in their school.' He sighed. 'Children can be very cruel. But I think I'd have to include her and give her the responsibility as it might be the making of her to see the patients having a much worse time than herself – that is, if you have no objection.'

To Esme's relief, Bertha didn't take part in the Christmas decorating at the hospital as the schoolgirl was laid up in the sanatorium with a bad cold. Apparently, she didn't make a good patient, so Cook said as she spread the gossip the nurse had told her. Bertha was peeved because she'd wanted to help with the trimmings – it was only a cold, she kept telling them – but Russell had put his foot down. He didn't want any of the other girls ill over Christmas.

Esme, tempted though she was to join the eight girls at the hospital, stayed in the Manor. It would look more natural not to be rushing over to the hospital. Instead, the girls worked under Stella's supervision and were in high spirits when they'd finished at the end of the two days, singing Christmas carols and making themselves useful so that Stella was able to give a glowing report to Hilary Fenton on their conduct the next day.

'Brad Parker is delighted with the result,' Stella told her that evening in the staff room when she'd popped over to see Esme.

'Oh, that's good.' Esme's voice was non-committal. 'I'm sure the patients will enjoy a little Christmas festivity this year.'

Stella stared at her. 'Brad seemed surprised you didn't join us, Esme. Why didn't you?'

Warmth spread to Esme's cheeks. Thank goodness they were

alone. But how she'd love to have known if he'd been disappointed that she wasn't there.

'Oh, I was caught up with something of Sir Giles's,' she said. 'And it would have been a case of too many cooks and all that.' She made herself look Stella in the eye. 'You're the artistic one so I know you will have done a great job, besides keeping the girls focused.'

Stella gave her a quizzical look. Then to Esme's amazement, she said: 'Esme, it's as plain as that most attractive nose on your face that you're in love with our colonel.'

'What on earth are you talking about?'

Stella grinned and fished out a small mirror from her handbag. She held it up to Esme. 'Have a look at yourself.'

Esme blinked. Her face was flushed and her eyes had a soft, luminous appearance that she'd never noticed before.

'And that was only by my mentioning his name,' Stella giggled. 'Heaven knows how you'd be if he walked in right now.'

'Don't be ridiculous, Stella. I'm not—'

Stella held up the palm of her hand.

'Esme, listen to me. I do . . . *did* . . . have a bit of a pash on Brad, but when I saw how disappointed he looked when I said you weren't coming, and he asked if anything was the matter and he hoped you weren't sickening with something – I realised that not only *you* are head-over-heels—' she broke off as though for emphasis '—but so, my dear Esme, is *he*!' She stared at Esme as though to challenge her that it wasn't true.

'B-but you said he had a wife,' Esme stuttered, her heart almost jumping from her chest at Stella's proclamation.

'Yes, I know I did. Brad mentioned it himself, just in passing. I can't remember what the conversation was that brought it up. But he is one of the most decent chaps I've met in a long time, and I don't think he'd allow himself to fall for another woman – you – if he were truly happy. He wouldn't want to hurt his wife or you, or indeed himself. You just have to find out the state of play there. And just to be clear, I'm bowing out – not that there was ever anything going on for me to bow out of . . . unfortunately,' Stella ended with a chuckle. 'But what I *am* going to do is drag you to the jazz evening on Saturday whether you like it or not.' She stared at Esme. '*D'accord?*'

Esme couldn't help smiling at her friend's nonsense. '*D'accord*, Stella. I wouldn't dare do anything else but agree.'

Stella grinned. 'And you're going to wear something stunning to make sure Brad remains as soppy about you as you are about him, so have you got something really dressy?'

Esme shook her head. 'Not here. I don't often go out in the evenings and I didn't think to bring anything like that with me.'

'That explains why you didn't dress up much for Sir Giles's dinner party that night,' Stella said.

Esme shrugged. 'Yes, I suppose it does. As it was, it didn't matter when I read the telegram that my father was so ill.'

'Brad took you home that evening, didn't he?'

'Yes. He was very kind and watched over Dad through the night. And because he was a doctor he could tell what was going on.'

Stella gave a knowing smile. 'It shows he's in love with you.'

'No, Stella. You just said yourself what a decent man he is. He would have helped anyone in that situation.'

'You'll see I'm right and I can't wait to say "I told you so." But to get back to the jazz evening – are you going home between now and Saturday so you could have a search in your wardrobe for something gorgeous?'

'I don't intend to go back to the house. I had a bit of a falling out with my stepmother.'

'Oh dear.' Stella shook her head. 'Not always easy with parents.'

'Particularly if they're not your own flesh and blood,' Esme flashed.

'Yes, that's more difficult.' She looked Esme up and down. 'We're about the same build but you're quite a few inches taller than I am so I can't lend you anything.' She frowned. 'I know this sounds crazy, but I've just thought of something. Lady Carmichael – Sir Giles's wife – had some fabulous cocktail dresses. And she was almost as tall as you and certainly as slim. She always wore designer dresses and they never go out of fashion so why don't I ask him if he would lend you one?'

'Please don't, Stella. It would be an imposition. And anyway, as far as I understand, it's going to be quite informal.'

'Well, I'll have to have a rethink.' Stella went silent for a few moments.

'Honestly, Stella, don't worry. If I'm not good enough for wearing something simple, then it's just too bad.'

Chapter Twenty-Seven

The following evening when Esme was writing to Freda in the small staff sitting room, Stella bounced in wearing a scarlet dress with low-cut neckline and swinging hemline at her calves, a white belt showing off her waist.

'Ta-da.' She spun round to show the dress from every angle.

Esme set her pen down and gazed at her.

'What do you think, Esme? It's for the jazz night on Saturday.'

'It's a lovely colour on you with your blonde hair, but I think it would look better shorter – just below the knee is more fashionable.' She paused. 'Would you like me to take it up a few inches?'

'That won't be necessary.' Stella beamed. 'It's not for me – it's for *you*.'

'*Me*?' Esme's lips parted in astonishment. 'I wouldn't wear a dress like that. Or that colour.'

'Why not?'

'Because it's not my style.'

'What *is* your style, Esme?' Stella didn't wait for an answer. 'Oh, I suppose it would have to be something fit for a librarian.'

'Thanks, Stella.'

'Sorry, I didn't mean to be rude. But you need to come out of yourself sometimes, darling. Do something a little daring.' Stella hunched her chin to her chest to look at the top of the dress. 'If you're worried that it's too risqué, it's not sexy enough to show any cleavage . . . well, it might give the soldiers a thrill if you bent over low enough,' she giggled. 'Anyway, I want you to try it on.'

'Why aren't *you* going to wear it on Saturday?'

'Actually, I've never worn it. I bought it before the rationing and keep meaning to have it altered. It's a bit too big on the bust for me but you'll fill it out nicely. And because you're a good few inches taller, you won't have to take it up.'

'I could easily alter it for you so you can wear it yourself.'

'No,' Stella said. 'I want *you* to wear it and make Brad sit up and see another side of you.' She grinned. 'Go on, Esme. Humour me. Let's go to your room and you can try it on. Even if you still don't think it's right, at least I'll know you gave it a go.'

'All right, just to please you,' Esme sighed.

In Esme's bedroom, Stella peeled off the dress, not seeming to worry in the slightest that she stood in her cami-knickers and brassiere, so Esme decided not to make a fuss either. She hated the way Stella had hinted she was a prude. She'd been a married woman, for goodness' sake. But perhaps having had a husband didn't necessarily prove anything in this new topsy-turvy world.

Reluctantly, she pulled the dress over her head and Stella smoothed it down over her bust and hips and zipped up the gap at the waist. Stella was right. She filled it out perfectly.

Her friend stood back. 'I was right. It looks stunning on you. The colour is gorgeous with your chestnut hair. You should wear red all the time.' She pursed her lips thoughtfully.

'Do you have some heels? Preferably red.'

Esme shook her head.

'What size are you?'

'Six-and-a-half.'

'Hmm. I'm a five so that's no good. Let me see what you have.'

Esme opened the wardrobe door. Immediately, Stella pounced on some white open-toed sandals with a wedge heel.

'Not ideal, but they'll have to do,' she said, laughing, 'and they'll go with the white belt.' She tossed the sandals over to Esme. 'Well, that's got you sorted, so I need to decide what *I'm* wearing now.'

'Thanks, Stella. You've gone to a lot of trouble but I'm not going to wear it.' Esme began to unzip the side.

'Hang on. You've not even looked in the mirror yet. Put the sandals on to see the full effect.'

Esme stepped over to the mirror, the dress skimming her knees as she moved. No, that couldn't be her reflection staring back at her. Where was Esme, the librarian? This one was Esmeralda, the glamorous girl in a figure-hugging red dress, ready for dancing.

'Looks good, doesn't it, Esme?'

She swallowed. 'Well . . . yes, I suppose it does.'

'We're agreed, then. I'll have to put it back on as I can't trip outside semi-naked,' Stella laughed. 'I didn't want to bring something else to wear because I didn't want you to guess what I was up to.'

'No chance of that,' Esme couldn't help laughing, too, as she took the dress off and handed it to her. 'If you're sure it looks all right and you're not going to wear it, then thank you. It's very generous of you to lend it to me.'

'Glad to help,' Stella said, pulling the dress over her head.

'You know, I would never have tried on anything like this in my wildest dreams.'

'I'm sure when Brad sees you he'll think you've just stepped out of *his* wildest dreams,' was Stella's last retort as she sailed out of the room.

In her head, Esme crossed off the days until Saturday, aware she was acting like one of the schoolgirls. Stella had brought the red dress back the following morning before she started work at the hospital, this time wrapped in a sheet so no one would see it. When she'd disappeared, Esme had held it up against herself and looked in the mirror again. She couldn't imagine what Anthony would have said. Probably, 'Isn't that a bit too revealing, my dear?' Would Brad think the same? Did she look like a scarlet woman in her scarlet dress?

Esme shook herself. If she was going to think like that, she might as well stay at home because she wouldn't have the confidence to carry it off. Or she'd be doomed to wear something smart but not eye-catching. Was Stella right? Did she really dress like a librarian? Unobtrusive, reserved, understated? She was sure they were the words Stella was thinking.

A scene from *Gone with the Wind* popped into her head. Scarlett O'Hara, in rebellious mood, had appeared at a charity ball in a bright red dress instead of her black widow's weeds she should, by tradition, have worn. Not only that, but she'd been made an outcast with rumours that she'd been in the arms of her cousin, Melanie's husband, Ashley Wilkes. The town's society had been abuzz with gossip. Only Rhett Butler had grinned admiringly. He'd offered an exceptionally generous bid for her for the first dance – to everyone else's utter affront and Scarlett's utter delight.

Esme couldn't help a grin as she put the dress back on the hanger. *Damn it all.* She'd wear it if it was the last thing she did! She couldn't help a wry smile. You never knew. At least Brad was the same nationality as Rhett Butler.

Bertha glared at Esme as she came into the dining room at lunch that day, then immediately looked away. In that moment Esme could have bet her life that the note was written by the insufferable schoolgirl. Not only was the girl disgusted about her kissing Brad, but it was almost certain she'd been the one to spread gossip about why she hadn't joined the forces to do her bit in the war. It was also clear that Hilary Fenton wasn't going to discipline her. Esme wondered if she should say anything. No, she mustn't. She was in danger of becoming an interfering busybody and was not in charge of Bertha. She had to shrug the whole thing off. There was bound to be fresh gossip about someone else sooner or later and they'd forget all about Esme Donaldson's personal life.

Until the day of the jazz evening, Sir Giles kept her busy, mainly in the library.

'I'm not sure I like my office crammed with all that stuff that was in the Muniment Room,' he said. 'We have plenty more rooms that could serve the purpose. I do think it should all be kept together.' He lit his pipe. 'Perhaps you'll have a think about where we should put it all, Esme.'

'Yes, of course, Sir Giles. But it might be easier to tackle when you have all your rooms back again.'

'We could wait forever for that to happen,' he said. 'And in the meantime, you have a jazz "do" coming up soon.' Sir Giles puffed on his pipe. 'I expect you have something special to wear for the occasion.' He smiled at her in a fatherly fashion.

She startled. He was looking for all the world as though he knew about her feelings for Brad.

'I've not definitely decided,' she said.

But the scarlet dress danced in front of her eyes as she spoke the words.

Chapter Twenty-Eight

For the second time that week, Esme put Stella's dress on. And this time she was really going to wear it. It was Saturday evening and so far she hadn't wavered in her decision to do something different. Be someone different. The dress had demanded a lipstick brighter than usual, but what about her hair? She'd started to pin it off her face as usual, when suddenly she ripped out the kirby grips and let her hair cascade to her shoulders in gleaming chestnut waves, sweeping up just the sides with Stella's two silver combs. She pushed her feet into the white wedge sandals she'd hardly worn, hoping they didn't look too summery, and grinned at the mirror. The glamorous woman in the mirror beamed back. Of course, the dress wouldn't change her radically but it might give her the confidence she needed knowing Brad would be at the jazz event. If there was any possible opportunity, she wanted him to open up about his wife – just to clear any air – in her mind, at least – that needed clearing between them.

Her heart beating a little more rapidly, she dabbed a couple of drops of Elizabeth Arden's Blue Grass perfume inside each wrist, then using her same scented fingers and another trickle of perfume, daringly pulled away the scooped neckline and patted them onto her décolletage. Before she could change her mind, and feeling more reckless than she could ever remember, she danced her way out of the room in a manner Stella would have been proud of.

The first person Esme set eyes on as she entered the music-filled room, transformed from one of the hut-like extensions attached to the main hospital, was Stella. The band was playing a piece she didn't recognise but had an irresistible beat that she immediately wanted to tap her toes. Four of the five musicians were black, including the singer, a glamorous woman in a bold orange-and-white dress with a deep side split. Several couples were already dancing. But not like anything she'd ever experienced. One of the Americans in his Army uniform was doing what seemed to Esme a crazy dance as he twirled the girl around him, lifted her high, then abruptly pulled her under his side-stretched legs.

Stella's eyes gleamed as she turned to Esme.

'So you dared wear the dress,' she said. 'And you have the perfect lipstick to go with it.' She took hold of Esme's hand, Esme as usual feeling like the younger friend to the sophisticated Stella. 'Come and say hello to a group of patients. It's their first night out,' she giggled.

'How long have you been here?' Esme shouted above the hubbub of conversation and the beat of the music – powerful, and like nothing she'd ever heard before.

'Twenty minutes or so. I began to worry that you weren't coming.' She looked Esme up and down. 'I must say you look sensational.'

'Thank you.' Esme tried to turn her head surreptitiously.

A delicious feeling swept through her at the thought of Brad seeing her like this, but before she could consider that thought, a voice from behind said: 'Would this be Esme with the chestnut tresses?'

She spun round, her heart pounding in her chest, as she gazed into a pair of warm brown eyes.

'Yes, it's me.'

There was a long pause. Then Brad gave a low whistle.

'But it's not Esme after all – it's Esmeralda. You couldn't mistake it.'

Does that mean he prefers the new glamour-puss to the everyday librarian?

She noticed Stella had just sat down at a table with a small group of men, some of them bandaged, chatting together. Suddenly, she wished she'd worn something simple and gone with Stella to join them before Brad had found her. It would have been much more relaxing. Not that she and Brad had parted from their last meeting in anything but a perfectly friendly manner. So why was she feeling awkward? Too conspicuous. Not herself.

'May I get you a drink, Esmeralda?' Brad smiled at her.

'Thank you. Just a small glass of port, if they have it.'

Maybe it would calm her nerves.

'I was sitting at a table with the teachers and some of the girls,' he said when he came back with two glasses, jerking his head to a table on the right of the entrance. 'Will you come and join us?'

Oh no. Seated at the same table was Bertha. And Hilary Fenton. This was not going to be the kind of evening she'd visualised.

'Would you mind very much if I don't?' she said.

Brad glanced over. 'Hmm. Perhaps you're right. The schoolgirls do tend to be rather excitable. Why don't we go and find a table to ourselves.'

'That would be lovely,' Esme said with relief as she followed him through the crowd. But every table seemed to be filling fast. There was nothing for two. Miraculously, he spotted a table with only one other couple.

'Ah, Cindy, would you and Larry mind if we joined you both?' Brad nodded to a platinum blonde, whom Esme vaguely recognised as one of the nurses. The man with her immediately stood.

'Sure.' Cindy beamed up at Esme. 'It's Mrs Donaldson, isn't it? How good to see you. Come and sit next to me so we can get to know each other better. This is Laurence Lynne, one of the surgeons.'

'Call me Larry,' the American said.

He didn't look remotely like a surgeon, Esme thought. More like a bank clerk. He was inches shorter than Brad with a receding hairline. But his grey eyes twinkled as he gave her a warm handshake and she immediately felt if she ever had to have an operation, he'd be the one she'd want to perform it.

'And I'm Esme,' she said, then glanced at Brad who sent her a subtle wink in return as he pulled out a chair for her, then took one opposite.

She hugged herself. It was all going to be all right.

'You'll have a ball dancing to our jazz band in that cute dress,' Cindy chuckled. 'I can see it flying up as your partners twirl you round.'

'I don't think so,' Esme said. 'I wouldn't have a clue how to do that sort of dancing.'

'It doesn't matter – so long as the man leads you.'

'Well, don't look at me,' Brad put in. 'I'm a conservative ballroom dancer and can't keep up with all these modern crazes. But I have requested them to play some blues and some Louis Armstrong, so we should have a variety of music tonight as well as jazz . . . which I like to listen to very much,' he added.

Cindy began tapping her feet to the band who were playing 'In the Mood', then shot to her feet and dragged Larry onto the dance floor. As soon as they started to jitterbug, the people nearby shuffled back to clear the floor for them. Esme watched in awe as Larry spun Cindy as though she were a spinning top, then grabbed her and threw her round his neck, back onto the floor with more intricate-looking feet and leg movements, all in perfect time to the beat of the band and both grinning. Larry threw her up in the air and brought her down to slide between his legs, pulling her upright and into a final spin where he finished by almost doing the splits.

Good grief. How on earth can they do that?

'Are you sure I'm not holding you back?' Brad said, turning back to Esme.

'Not at all,' she said. 'I'm relieved. There's no way I could possibly attempt that. It looks downright dangerous.'

'Do you like ballroom dancing?'

'Yes, when I get the chance. I wouldn't say I was as good as—' She bit her tongue. She'd been about to say, 'as good as Anthony'. They'd made competent dancing partners, although she had to acknowledge he was a perfectionist who wasn't that sympathetic if she slipped up. She remembered how he used to make her practise the next day in the living room again and again to get it right. It wasn't as though she'd minded improving, but sometimes she had to admit he overdid it.

'As good as . . . ?' Brad's tone was curious.

'Um . . . well, as good as a professional.'

'I wouldn't expect you to be as good as a professional. That's not what counts. What's important is if you genuinely enjoy dancing, particularly with the person you're dancing with.' He held her gaze. 'Do you agree?'

Just at that moment the music stopped. One of the musicians laid down his trombone and walked up to the microphone, dabbing the dark skin of his forehead with a white handkerchief. Most of the couples, including Cindy and Larry, stayed on the dance floor listening.

'We're changing to a popular song at the moment in the States,' he said. 'I don't know if you folks out there have heard it, but it's one of my favourites, sung by the great Louis Armstrong and equally great Ella Fitzgerald. But for tonight you'll have to put up with me singing . . . not Ella's part, I hasten to add . . .' He stopped for a few seconds to wait for the chuckles to die down. '. . . But me, Ed Harvey, and our lovely lady trumpeter, Miss Josie Fry. So please give her a warm welcome.'

Esme and Brad joined in the clapping.

Ed Harvey turned back to the band. '"Cheek to Cheek". Take it away.'

'Would you care to dance, Esmeralda?' Brad stood and put out his hand.

It felt the most natural thing in the world for her hand to be in his. Trying hard to ignore the tingling up and down her arm, she allowed herself to be led onto the dance floor. As the band began the introduction, Brad put his arm around her waist and it felt as though he were caressing her bare skin. She gave a little shiver as she put her left hand on his shoulder and he pulled her towards him, linking his other hand with hers.

'*Heaven . . .*' crooned Ed Harvey. '*I'm in heaven . . .*'

She looked up at him, catching his eye. He smiled, drawing her a little closer.

'*. . . dancing cheek to cheek.*'

It was as though the singer had given them permission for Brad to hold her so close she could hear his heartbeat – even with the music playing. She laid her cheek against his. Heard him give a soft intake of breath. Was she being too forward? She drew slightly back but he pulled her more firmly this time to his chest and rested his cheek against hers.

The steps and rhythm weren't slow, but Brad was an assured

dancer, though he took some risks with some of his turns and she matched him perfectly.

'Fred Astaire had to sing this one at the same time he danced with Ginger Rogers in *Pal Joey*,' she laughed, when the song finished and she'd reluctantly left the warmth of his arms to clap the two singers. 'Did you see it?'

'Yes. Those two on the floor are pure magic.' Brad regarded her seriously. 'But *you* felt like magic in my arms.'

She didn't know how to answer. She couldn't say, 'You did, too,' because he still thought she had a husband. But that's how she'd felt. She'd never wanted it to end.

'Esme . . . Esmeralda . . .' His voice was deep, husky.

'Yes, Brad?'

It was as though the crowd had melted away and they were the only two on the floor.

'You never speak about your husband.'

His unexpected remark startled her. Desperately, she tried to think what to say. Was now the time to tell him she was widowed?

He looked down at her and she imagined she saw herself mirrored in his eyes. 'Because there's something I want to know – I know it must be very difficult for you with your husband away, but . . . I'm not sure how to say this as it's very personal, but are you still happily married?'

Unaware, Esme's hand went to the locket round her neck.

'Why do you ask?' she said in a shaky voice.

As soon as she said it, she realised how stupid the question was. If Stella was right and he was in love with her, of course he'd want to know the most important thing between them. Just as she wanted to question him about his wife.

But in her nervousness about how to answer, she pulled on

the fine gold chain and the locket fell to the floor. He bent low to retrieve it.

'The chain's broken,' he said, handing it to her.

'I don't have a pocket.'

'Shall I take it?'

She nodded and with trembling fingers, handed it to him. He put it in his inside jacket pocket.

'You don't need to answer my question.' Brad gave a half-smile. 'But to complicate things, I wanted to tell you that I'm in—'

The rest of his words were swallowed up by one of the musicians.

'And now we're going to turn down the tempo even more,' he announced. 'So stay right where you are, folks, and let's show the rest of 'em some slo-o-ow–' he drawled out the word, '–ja-a-zzz.' He gave a toothy grin and winked at the crowd.

'Would you care for another dance?' Brad said.

Her mouth was too dry to speak. She could only nod in agreement. He'd hardly taken her right hand in his, with her left hand lightly on his shoulder, a little self-consciously this time, when seconds later, someone pushed between them, forcing them apart.

'Dr Parker, why did you leave our table?' a young girl's voice demanded.

Bertha! Esme couldn't believe her cheek.

'Bertha!' Brad's voice was tight. 'Where are your manners, pushing in front of Mrs Donaldson like that.'

Bertha snorted. 'I just want to know when you're coming back.'

'I'm not.'

'Why aren't you?'

'Bertha, go back to your table like a good girl. Or try out one of the new dances with a friend when they change the music.'

'Huh. *They* don't know the American ones any more than I do. I thought you'd show me, Dr Parker,' Bertha wheedled.

'I don't know them either. But go and ask one of the patients who keeps up with the latest.'

Bertha's mouth downturned. 'I've tried but no one wants to dance with me. They think I'm just a schoolgirl.'

'Perhaps if you weren't quite so rude all the time, they might enjoy teaching you,' Esme said mildly.

'You monopolise him,' Bertha spoke under her breath so that Brad couldn't hear. 'You're disgusting.'

The same words. No doubt about it – Bertha wrote the note.

The music started again. Brad held out his arms.

'Shall we, Mrs Donaldson?'

Bertha's face contorted with fury. 'Don't forget – I've got something on you, *Mrs* Donaldson.'

But her words meant nothing to Esme as she floated away in Brad's arms to Ella Fitzgerald's huge hit: 'Bewitched, Bothered and Bewildered'. The song could not have been more appropriate.

It was only in bed that night that she realised she'd forgotten to ask Brad for the locket back. Oh well, it would have to wait until morning.

Brad was already in bed when he remembered he hadn't given Esme back her locket. Too bad. It would have to wait until morning. But perhaps he should make sure it was still safe. It obviously meant a lot to Esme as he noticed she always wore it. Tossing the bedclothes aside, he leapt out and went to the chair where he'd slung his jacket and felt inside the pocket. His fingers closed round the heart and he drew it out and placed it on the table. Now for the chain. He switched on the overhead light to inspect it. The chain itself hadn't broken but the link that fastened the ends together had split. He'd get it mended before he gave it back to her. Then, as though someone were urging him to open it, he found himself pushing his nail into the opening seam. It sprang apart. And there was the tiny photograph of Esme looking a little serious on one side and her husband in his Royal Air Force cap on the other, grinning widely. Quickly, he snapped the little gold heart together again. It felt as though he'd snapped his own heart in two.

Chapter Twenty-Nine

Esme had been spared the need to answer Brad's question fully on the dance floor last night. He'd appeared to intuitively know that she didn't want to speak about it and didn't mention it again. She was being a coward, Esme knew, by not just coming out with it, but she was terrified he'd then say he had feelings for her, but that he was married. If she didn't explain about Anthony's death, she wouldn't have to listen to words from Brad she'd rather not hear. It would only cause misery for everyone. Thankfully Christmas was around the corner, which gave her some distraction.

The American hospital was looking Christmassy but as Stella commented, Redcliffe Manor hadn't undergone the same festive treatment.

'Sir Giles doesn't care for Christmas,' Esme told her. 'He says it's for children, not grown-ups.'

'Yes, Sir Giles can be a bit of a misery,' Stella said. 'Grown-ups are children at heart and you should hear how the patients enjoyed having their wards decorated. Said it reminded them of home.'

In the end, Esme had persuaded Sir Giles to agree to a Christmas tree in the Great Hall only if she and Stella decorated it, but he did at least allow the girls, under the supervision of their teachers, to decorate their own classrooms.

'I've noticed one thing,' Stella told her when they were having lunch together in the dining room, 'there are no books for the patients. Brad has a comprehensive library for the staff – all non-fiction, I might add – but the patients need some escapism.'

'Have you spoken to Brad about it?' Esme said. There'd been an unspoken agreement between the two women that Colonel Parker – or Dr Parker – was now 'Brad' for both of them.

'No. He's got more than enough on his plate. But that's where you come in.' She looked at Esme. 'You're the obvious person to resolve the problem.'

'I can't interfere with what goes on at the hospital,' Esme protested.

'Oh yes, you can.'

'How? I can't suddenly tell Brad I need to create a library especially for the patients. He wouldn't have a spare room, for one thing.'

'No need,' Stella laughed delightedly. 'You just ask Brad for a few shelves in his staff library kept for the patients' use, but I bet some of the nurses would be really grateful to see something a bit lighter than the latest in medical science of how to amputate a leg or whatever. And the patients confined to their beds can tell you the sort of books they're interested in and you can find them something suitable and take it to them.' She gave a sly smile. 'Brings you in touch with Brad a bit more often.'

'I'll ignore that,' Esme smiled back. 'Let me think. What about if I bring them round on a trolley so they can choose the books themselves? We can call it the Trolley Library.'

Stella giggled. 'Perfect. I wish I'd thought of it myself.' She laid her knife and fork neatly together on her plate. 'Mmm. That meat pie was good even though I couldn't find any meat in it.'

'I could maybe start tomorrow on my day off,' Esme said, warming to the idea of the library on a trolley. 'I was going to do a bit of Christmas shopping today and buy Sir Giles something – I thought a desk diary – but this sounds more important.'

'It is, and ideally they should have it by Christmas Day.' Stella dabbed her mouth with her napkin. 'I'm happy to help you choose some books, if you like?'

'Yes, I would like.' Esme lightly touched Stella's hand. 'Stella, I really appreciate your friendship.'

'That makes two of us,' Stella chuckled.

'Do you think I should mention this to Sir Giles?'

'Not really. What you do on your day off is up to you. But if you did tell him, I think he'd be delighted. He really likes and deeply respects Brad.'

A warm feeling stole through Esme's heart.

'I think I'll ask Sir Giles if he has some books in his library that he wouldn't mind lending. After all, he'd get them back when the war's over – whenever that might be.' She hesitated. 'But I'll speak to Brad first as he might not allow it.'

'He's there all afternoon, so go now – strike while the iron's hot!'

'Can I tell him this is *your* idea?'

'It's *our* idea.' Stella beamed. 'We concocted it together – you named it, remember?'

'Oh, all right.' Esme grinned back. Stella really was incorrigible.

Esme knocked on Brad's office door, sure he wouldn't be there. But to her surprise, he opened it and his face lit up when he saw her.

'Oh, do come in, Esme. This is a nice surprise.'

Giving a wry smile, she noticed she'd become 'Esme' again having shed her more glamorous self.

'Take a seat.' Brad gestured towards an easy chair and took the other, pulling it close by. 'What can I do for you?'

Esme quickly explained that she and Stella had got chatting about the patients' needs and had come up with the idea of a trolley library. To her delight, his eyes sparkled with enthusiasm.

'That's a very good suggestion.' He looked directly at her. 'I'm surprised none of the nurses didn't think to mention it to me.'

'They're busy,' Esme said. 'Stella says they hardly have time for a cup of tea, let alone worry about the patients' reading material.'

'But this is right up your street – as you English say,' Brad chuckled.

'Well, it is. Not so much with Sir Giles's library as he has very few novels, but I think I can put something suitable together.' She hesitated. 'But first, if you approve, I'd like to meet some of the men and get an idea of the sort of books that might appeal.'

'Excellent idea.' He stood up. 'I presume you'd like to get this organised in time for Christmas?' She nodded. 'Then why don't we go right now.'

As she walked with him down the corridor, Brad said, 'Some of the patients aren't well enough to read, but most of them in this first ward are – even if they're not mobile yet.' He opened the door for her to pass by. One of the nurses who was taking the temperature of a pale, pinched-looking young man, turned round, and grinned from ear to ear.

'Well, if it isn't Mrs Donaldson come to see us,' she said with a slight inclination of her head to where the patients were sitting or lying in beds lined up against each side of the room. 'What can we do for you?'

'Nurse Cindy.' Esme smiled delightedly. 'I hoped you might be on duty.'

'I'll leave you ladies to it,' Brad said. He glanced at Esme. 'I'm in my office catching up on some administrative work, so come and see me after you've done the rounds and let me know if there's anything I can help you with.'

'Thanks, Colonel Parker,' she said formally. He gave her a wink and disappeared.

'Nurse Cindy, can you take me round to the patients who are

well enough to read, as I'm trying to set up a mobile library with books they can borrow?'

'Oh, great idea. Yes, of course.'

There was enormous interest from the patients as the two women went from bed to bed. Esme had had the forethought to bring a small notebook, and she wrote down the names and preferences of all who were interested and able. They were a cheerful lot, she thought, often making light of their wounds, even though many, Cindy muttered, were serious, some being noticeably disfiguring.

She'd finished the last person Cindy introduced her to, when a patient she'd already spoken to, Bob, said:

'What about Lloyd Taylor?'

Cindy bit her lip. Esme watched her curiously. Why was the nurse looking so uneasy?

'Don't worry – we won't leave him out,' Cindy said, then glanced at Esme. 'He's in the ward next door.'

'I feel sorry for him, all on his own, that's all.' Bob propped himself up on the pillows and reached for his glass of water. 'It must be very dull for him . . . and lonely, though I do have a few words with him at the doorway when I can.'

'Oh dear, is he infectious?' Esme asked.

'No, it's because he's black,' came Bob's short reply.

'I don't understand.' She gazed at Cindy for an answer, but the nurse just shook her head.

'He's black,' repeated Bob, 'and that's the only reason he's not allowed to be in the same ward with us. He can't sleep or eat with us either. And when he comes out of hospital he'll go back to his all-black unit.' He looked at her. 'It doesn't make sense, does it? Not to mention he's a thoroughly nice guy.'

Esme's skin crawled with horror. She had read reports in the *Chronicle* about the Jim Crow laws in the States, which demanded segregation. But she couldn't believe the American Army would enforce them here. *Surely not. This couldn't be allowed just because of the colour of his skin.*

A patient sitting in a chair by his bed called out, 'We don't want no negroes in here. It's agin' the law and a good thing, too.'

'I'm afraid it *is* against the law, Esme,' Cindy said under her breath. 'They have to be segregated throughout the forces. And it's not just the forces. At home it happens in restaurants and hotels, buses – lots of public places where they're not welcome. Even the latrines are separate.'

Esme was almost too shocked to speak. She swallowed hard and licked her lips. She had to say something or she'd never forgive herself. She looked at Cindy. 'But surely you agree it's wrong.'

'I certainly don't think it's right,' said Cindy. She looked miserably towards the door separating the two wards.

'Does everyone in here feel the same way as that charming gentleman?' Esme asked the nurse.

But before Cindy could answer, a voice piped up from the nearest bed.

'No, ma'am,' a boy who could be no more than eighteen or nineteen spoke up. He had been listening to the exchange with interest. 'It's our law. It ain't right, but it's the law. Ain't nothin' we can do about it.'

'One can always do *something*,' Esme shot back. 'I think I'll go and meet Mr Taylor now.'

There was a silence as all eyes watched her walk across to the door. Cindy looked as though she wanted to curl up and sink through the linoleum floor.

Chapter Thirty

There had been so much to take in next door that Esme hadn't noticed how stark the wards were until she and Cindy entered Ward 5. A strange black netting was fixed on the windows – extra camouflage in preparation for the blackout each afternoon, Cindy explained, making a face. The room looked dismal, made worse by the total lack of chatter and laughter found in Ward 4.

A nurse on the far side of the ward, her back to them, was standing on a chair looking in a tall cupboard. At their entrance she turned, and Esme noted she, too, was dark-skinned. The nurse immediately stepped down from the chair, her expression tense.

'Oh, Nurse Veasey,' Cindy said with a smile, 'I've brought Mrs Donaldson from the Manor. She's setting up a trolley book service and would like to know Mr Taylor's preferences.'

Nurse Veasey raised her eyebrows but gestured towards the only occupant.

The soldier who'd been lying on top of his bed, his right arm in a sling and a huge plaster on his forehead, now tried to hoist himself up. Nurse Veasey hurried over to tuck some extra pillows behind his back.

'Mr Taylor, I've brought Mrs Donaldson to see you,' Cindy began. 'She's setting up a trolley library and wants to know what books you like.'

'At least they think I *am* able to read,' he said with a cynical edge to his voice. He glanced at Esme and quickly looked away. 'Sorry to be sarcastic but I get rather bored in here on my own – except for Nurse, of course.' He sent his nurse a smile and she nodded back, a hint of a smile on her lips.

Esme put her hand out for him to shake hands. After some hesitation, he took hers awkwardly in his left hand, but no longer than a brief moment.

'Good to meet you, Mrs Donaldson.'

'Please call me Esme.'

He nodded. 'I'm Lloyd and I'm desperate for something to take my mind off lying here just thinking. All I hear next door is conversation and laughter, but I don't know what they're talking about.'

'It's not fair,' Cindy unexpectedly burst out. 'You're a soldier, the same as they are, trying to keep us safe, so you shouldn't be kept separate.'

Esme noticed Nurse Veasey listening intently.

'We're not the same in their eyes. Or in the eyes of the US Army,' he said, then smiled at the two women. 'Didn't they teach you at school that life isn't fair?'

'More or less,' Esme said. 'But this is very different.' She smiled back at him. 'Anyway, we can do something positive for you if you'll give me an idea of the books you like.'

'Let me see.' He put his good hand up to tap the side of his cheek. 'As I'm in England and laid up for a couple of weeks or more, I'd be glad to read any of your English poets like Keats or Wordsworth or if you might have one of the Shakespeare plays – it doesn't matter which one. I've only read a couple, but this guy gets into the human heart and all their foibles like no other. He's the master, in my opinion.'

'He's a bit ancient now,' Esme chuckled. 'But I agree.'

Not one of the other patients had asked for any classic works, Esme thought, or for that matter asked about any English author. As far as Sir Giles was concerned, Lloyd Taylor would be luckier with his choices than the others in the next ward who had asked mainly for cowboy books and detective stories by American authors she'd never heard of. All except Bob, who'd requested any Ernest Hemingway, if possible, but was willing to read anything else on offer *except* Westerns.

'I'll see what I can do, Lloyd,' she said. 'And I'll be back as soon as I can get some books together for all of you.'

'Appreciate that, ma'am,' he said, then closed his eyes. A moment later he opened them and gave Esme an apologetic smile. 'I beg your pardon, Miss Esme, but the medication they give me makes me sleepy.'

'You rest,' she said, nodding to Cindy they should go. 'I hope the next time I see you that I'll be wheeling in a trolley of books.'

They said their goodbyes to Lloyd and Nurse Veasey, and it was only when they were outside Ward 5 that Esme realised the nurse hadn't spoken one word while they were there.

'Cindy, about Nurse Veasey,' she muttered. 'Don't tell me—' Esme wasn't able to voice the rest of her incredulity.

'I'm afraid so,' Cindy whispered. 'White nurses aren't allowed to attend coloured patients, so they had to bring a black nurse in.'

'For just one patient with a darker skin tone,' Esme said bitterly. 'It makes it even worse, the trouble the American authorities go to keep black people segregated.'

'I agree,' Cindy said with a sigh. 'And I feel bad that I learnt more about Mr Taylor just now than I have in the whole week he's been here.'

'Let's hope we've broken the spell and you'll get to know him even better,' Esme said, putting her hand lightly on the nurse's arm. 'But Cindy, I'm so glad you think the same as I do – that it's totally unfair to a human being to isolate him like that, just because of the colour of his skin.'

'Oh, I do,' Cindy nodded vehemently before she hurried back to Ward 4.

Esme knocked on Brad's office door. Her heart was beating slightly out of kilter. Why was she so nervous?

Because you're going to tackle him on this segregation issue and you have no idea how he'll react, her inner voice told her.

It was true. If he didn't hold the same values as herself, he wouldn't be the man she'd thought.

Brad opened the door and smiled.

'How did it go?' he said, after she was seated.

'It went well, I think. A few weren't interested or were too poorly, but most of them were pleased and have put in their requests, but they were all asking for American authors so I don't think Sir Giles would be able to help with this, but I will ask him.' She hesitated. *Here goes.* 'But one of the patients asked for some English authors which I've seen in Sir Giles's library and I'm sure he'd be only too pleased to lend them.'

'That's great. Maybe I can drum up some American novels from the staff for the rest of them. I've probably got a couple of my own here.' He paused. 'Who asked for the English authors?'

'The patient in the ward next door.'

'Ah. Lloyd Taylor. Yes, nice guy.'

Esme watched him closely.

'He seemed to want to take advantage of being in England and read English authors like our poets and Shakespeare.'

'Really? The classics?'

'Brad, I need to talk to you about him.'

'Esme, I can guess what you're going to say.' He looked directly at her. 'You're going to tell me he should be in the ward with the others.'

'Yes, he should. It's a disgrace to let a human being be put into isolation when he's done nothing wrong. He risks his life the same as the others.'

'I wouldn't argue.' Brad gave a deep sigh. 'But I'm afraid it's the US Army. They set the rules and we have to obey them.'

'They're rules that have no logic at all,' Esme shot back.

'I know. But in the US forces we have to abide by them. It's military law.'

'Thank goodness our military law is not the same,' Esme stormed.

'Maybe not as far as the military goes. But there's still a certain amount of racism here, though not on the scale of the States, I admit.'

'I've never seen it.'

'You may never have seen a black person in that situation before, but that doesn't mean it doesn't happen.'

'I don't go around with my eyes shut,' she told him crossly. 'Don't forget I worked in a public library for the last two years and we saw people of all shapes and sizes and colours. And Bath isn't that far from Bristol, which is home to people from all over the world. But our libraries are for everyone who's interested in learning or just wants an escape from this horrible war. It isn't just for white people.'

He started to speak but she stopped him.

'Please, Brad, let's not argue. I just want to know if you'll bring him into the ward with the others.' When he didn't answer, she said, 'There's only one patient who's opposed and he's downright ignorant. The others seem to be perfectly all right about it – that there's no need for this separation business.'

Brad stood up and came round to Esme's side. He touched her arm, but she flinched.

'I think it's wrong just as much as you do, Esmeralda, but it's one thing I don't have the power to change. I'm sorry to disappoint you.'

She lifted her eyes to his. 'What would happen if you did anyway?'

'I could be court martialled. It would ruin my career. I might even find it difficult to work as a doctor in civilian life as my record would be sullied. All my training would be wasted.'

Esme was silent, her stomach churning.

'You do understand, don't you, Esme?' He waited. 'Esmeralda?'

'No, I don't,' she flashed. 'He's a human being with feelings and thoughts and blood that flows through his veins exactly the same as you and me. He's risking his life the same as the others. It's a wicked law to inflict upon a human being. And may I remind you that you're not in America now – you're in *England*, and ought to be abiding by *our* laws.'

Tears threatening because he wouldn't even consider it, she jumped up from her seat and rushed over to the door, then tore it open. A moment later she was out in the corridor, her heart empty, sapped. It was as though whatever feeling she'd had for him was now trapped in his office when she'd pulled the door shut behind her.

Determined to track down Sir Giles, she went straight to his study, but it was empty. So was the library. She glanced at her watch. Maybe he was having a late lunch in the dining room. He did that occasionally when the girls had finished their meal and he could be served in peace.

Her guess was correct.

Sir Giles smiled as he wiped his mouth with his napkin. 'Come and join me, Esme,' he said, putting his knife and fork together.

'I was just debating whether I should have some of that ginger pudding and custard when they told me it had all gone.' He grimaced. 'Probably just as well.'

She forced a smile. He studied her closer as she sat down opposite.

'What's the matter? Your eyes are all red. Have you been crying? If it's because someone's upset you, then I'll see about it.'

'It's not quite like that.' Esme sighed. 'If you're finished, Sir Giles, could we go back to your study where we can be private?'

'It sounds serious.' Sir Giles thanked the dinner lady for his meal, then followed Esme out.

In the study, when they were sitting in the two easy chairs, he said: 'Tell me everything so I get the complete picture as to why you're so upset.'

He sat very quietly while she related the ugly scene in the ward, and then in Brad's office.

'Hmm. I must admit I hadn't realised the extent of the difficulties with mixing any black soldiers with the others,' he said. 'But the colonel is right. Their laws are different from ours, so his hands are tied.'

'But who would know if he just allowed Mr Taylor to go into the main ward?' Esme demanded. 'No one's going to report him.'

'You'd be surprised. That patient who was adamant about not letting him in, for one. People snitch on one another. People you'd never think. It happens all the time in war. It did in the last one and it does in this one.'

'But where are Dr Parker's principles?'

'You said he didn't like it. But he could be in deep trouble with his superiors if they found out about it. And it's quite likely to be leaked, it's that serious a violation of the law.' He looked at her. 'I'd like to be able to change this – help in some way, but I cannot be seen to be interfering. What the US Army does is purely their business. You probably aren't aware, Esme, but our relationship with the US military is often far from amicable within the top ranks. Our two countries are apt to be suspicious of one another, which doesn't always bode for a smooth and united path.' He looked her straight in the eye. 'As far as I can see, the problem you're presenting on racial issues is impossible to surmount.'

Brad watched with sinking heart as Esme flung out of the door. Surely she must understand that his career would be in jeopardy if he was found to have flouted the military law of keeping all coloured people separate. He'd been perfectly truthful with her. He didn't agree one iota with the law. It made no sense. As Esme had rightly pointed out, young Lloyd Taylor and all his comrades in the all-Black 92nd Infantry Division were fighting just as hard, risking their lives, exactly the same as all the other soldiers. He'd also heard some excellent reports about the 92nd Infantry Division and how professional and brave they were.

He lit a cigarette, but after a few puffs he ground it out in the ashtray. He had to turn his attention to the latest job in hand. Giving a report to his superiors about this first significant influx of patients. Sighing, he took the file from the cabinet but as soon as he saw his superior's name, he scowled. Brigadier General Maxwell Thomas. He stuck to the rulebook like a leech and gave the severest penalties to anyone who was in breach.

There would be hell to pay if I even tried to discuss what nonsense it was about segregating the soldiers in a hospital – or anywhere else for that matter, Brad thought grimly.

'*No discussion*,' Brad could hear Thomas's curt tones, the palm of his hand in the air.

No, Esmeralda, much as I would like to, I can't risk it.

But what if it meant losing her? his inner voice whispered. *She's the woman you love. It would mean the world to her if you could find a way around this problem. In less than a minute, you lost her respect.*

In despair, he put his head in his hands. What a conundrum it all was. And there seemed no solution.

Chapter Thirty-One

The following morning, bleary-eyed from a disturbed night mulling over both Brad's and Sir Giles's words that nothing could be done to change America's laws, Esme washed and dressed in a haze. Desperate for a cup of tea, she hurried down the magnificent staircase and into the breakfast room. It had only just opened and no one else was there except Lil, who was preparing the tables for breakfast.

'Mornin', madam.' Lil smiled. 'What would you like for breakfast?'

'Tea, please, and would it be possible to have a poached egg on toast?'

'Yes, I can allow you an egg. We don't do too bad with eggs as Cook has a friend with chickens.' Lil grinned, putting a packet of cornflakes on the 'cold' table.

Five minutes later Esme collected her tray. She sat down and took the first wonderful swallows of strong tea and was in the process of salting her egg when suddenly the last words she'd told Brad before she'd left his office flashed through her mind:

You're not in America now – you're in England, and ought to be abiding by our laws.

Maybe it wasn't impossible. Maybe there *was* a way that Sir Giles could help.

* * *

She'd been in the library for three solid hours working on what she hoped was the third of the way towards categorising Sir Giles's thousands of books, when the very man she wanted to speak to came in.

'I've ordered coffee for us to have in here,' Sir Giles said, beaming at her.

She smiled. She knew him well enough by now that he was pleased with himself to have been so thoughtful.

Stretching up and rubbing the small of her back, she said, 'Perfect timing. I'm dying for one.'

They talked about the different categories she was working through when Dolly appeared with the tray of coffee and biscuits.

'You don't seem very happy this morning,' Sir Giles remarked when the maid had disappeared. 'Are you still upset about that young man who's on his own at the hospital?'

'Yes, I am.' She hesitated. 'You know you said it was impossible to change their laws and I'm quite sure that's true,' she began.

Sir Giles nodded.

'But I believe you hold the answer to the problem which even the highest-ranking officer in the American forces can't deny.'

Sir Giles leaned forward, steepling his hands under his chin.

'Go on.'

Esme took in a breath. 'Would I be awfully rude if I ask how permission came about for an *American* hospital to be built in the grounds of a private country estate?' She looked at him. 'But please don't answer if you'd rather not.'

'It's not really a secret,' Sir Giles said. 'Well, it is as far as the enemy is concerned. But I was actually approached by the Army itself.'

'The British Army?'

'Yes. One of their chaps was a liaison officer to the USAAF.'

When Esme looked puzzled, he said, 'The United States Army Air Forces. So that's how it all came about.'

He lit his pipe. 'I talked it over with a friend of mine as to whether I should allow it and how much land it would take up. He thought ninety acres should do it and advised me to have it in writing that the nearest building to the house would be three hundred yards away. I reckon they've overruled that one by about sixty per cent, but I'm not too worried. As you can probably see, the buildings are only temporary for the duration of the war.'

'Well, at least you can use any rent for the general maintenance of the house,' Esme ventured to say.

He threw his head back and laughed. A harsh sound with little humour.

'I don't receive any rent from the school or the hospital.' His laughter faded as he studied her. 'The Ministry of War requisitioned Redcliffe Manor for the school, same as they have with several of the neighbouring estates and there's little compensation although some people were told they'd get it. But we all have to do our bit and thank God they can't call me for active service, so the least I can do is provide space inside and outside my home – and that seemed more than welcome to the powers that be.'

Esme gave an inward smile.

'So the hospital was an absolute favour with no strings attached.'

'Yes, I suppose you could call it that.'

'Do you have any paperwork to verify this?'

'No, it was just a gentleman's handshake.' He looked at her. 'I've never worried about it.'

Esme sat back in her chair with a smile of satisfaction.

'Well, then, all it would need is if you would go and see Brad—' She broke off, flushing a little at the slip.

Sir Giles didn't appear to take any notice of her use of the colonel's Christian name. 'And then what?' he said.

'Remind him of the favour you did to allow him to build his hospital on your land. And then point out that the hospital is built on British soil, and the address is in England. Therefore, although the hospital is for Americans, it's only there at your discretion. You could actually give him notice.'

He gave a start of surprise.

'I'm not going to threaten him, Esme.'

'Of course you wouldn't do that, because the British and the Americans are all in it together. But offering ninety acres for their benefit on your land must require them to abide by *our* laws.' She looked directly at him. 'Our laws don't mention segregation. We don't like the term or the actions imposed upon black people. Lloyd Taylor's only crime is to be black. Just by being in the forces should give him the right to be in mixed company, and that goes for the wards. You could tell Colonel Parker you'd like him to personally see that this is carried through.'

Esme felt almost breathless. Had she gone too far?

'I need to think about this,' Sir Giles said finally. 'You know desegregation is a serious offence in the US military, and also, there's strict segregation in the whole country. I'm not sure if you realise that.'

'Yes, Nurse Cindy mentioned it, but this is important. It's an American boy's life and how he spends it in the hospital. It's his future. Besides, he's the only patient who asked me for some English authors – he'd like English poets such as Keats and Wordsworth and any Shakespeare plays.'

'Hmm. Interesting.' Sir Giles tugged at his tie. 'I should be able to help you on that, at least.'

'And will you speak to Brad Parker about my suggestion?' Esme asked worriedly.

'Let me think about it,' he repeated, catching her eye, 'while I sort out some books for the chap. If the hospital doesn't have a spare trolley, I daresay Mrs Morgan will find you one.'

She had to leave it at that.

'Sir Giles, may I also have a look to see if there's anything for the other patients? They're asking for American writers, but I don't remember noticing any in particular when we moved the books.'

'There are a few,' he said. 'I'm quite a fan of American novelists. There's *The Great Gatsby,* for one.' He looked at her. 'Have you read it?'

'No, I keep meaning to. I've tried twice but never managed to finish it.'

'Mean it seriously the next time,' he said with a smile.

It was the first real smile she'd had from him that morning.

'And by all means take anything you see that they might like. Just make a list so you can check they come back. But no first editions.'

'No, of course not,' Esme said firmly. 'I'll be most careful.' She looked at him. 'I'll give them to you to have a look anyway before I take them over.'

'No need for that,' Sir Giles said. 'I trust your judgement. Just help yourself.' He took up a sheaf of papers. 'Now, we'd better get on with the work. I have another twenty or so pages of my memoirs which I'd be grateful if you would type and give me your opinion as to whether I should stop where I have.'

Esme gave an inward sigh. As frustrating as it was, Sir Giles was right. It was a big thing to ask him to do and he needed time to work out how to approach Brad and the way to say it – not threatening or ordering him, but friendly yet firm. As she had every faith that Sir Giles would strike exactly the right note, she forced herself to concentrate on the next extract of his life.

After a solid hour, she stretched her arms above her head. It would be Christmas Day the day after tomorrow. The perfect day to visit the patients with her trolley of books.

Chapter Thirty-Two

When Esme awoke on Christmas Day her first thought was that she was going to see the patients and let them choose their books. She'd spent an enjoyable hour yesterday picking out a dozen or more books by American authors and as many English classics for those who she hoped might like to try one. But she'd have to tell them that not surprisingly there were no cowboy books lurking on Sir Giles's shelves. However, Sir Giles had pulled out several English poetry books for Lloyd Taylor and a couple of Shakespeare's plays and sent his best wishes to the boy.

Esme took in gulps of the damp cold morning air as she struggled with two bags of books, feeling a little self-conscious in her new trousers she'd bought recently, and hoping she'd see someone who'd come and help her with the larger box. Sir Giles had offered but she'd turned him down. He was much too frail. There were no gardeners about at this time of the year but there could be a maintenance man or one of the porters who might help her. But there was no one in sight. That was, until she was almost at the entrance door when a familiar figure emerged: Brad. As soon as he spotted her he strode towards her.

'Merry Christmas, Esmeralda, and I do like those pants . . . very much,' he added, smiling.

'Thank you.' She gave him a brief smile back. 'They're practical for these sorts of jobs.'

His eyes fell to her bags. 'Here, let me help you with those.'

Her insides melted at the sight of him – the sound of his voice. But she was determined to keep herself in check.

'That's kind of you.' She made her voice neutral – not unfriendly, but it had none of the usual warmth she reserved for him.

He took the bags from her, trying to catch her eye, but she pretended not to notice and turned her head.

He glanced at the two bags. 'Are these all the books?'

'No, they're all I could carry. There's another box waiting in the hall.'

'I'll go and fetch them.'

'No, you're too busy.'

'I'm not.' Brad smiled but it didn't appear to reach his eyes. 'It's Christmas. A more relaxed day for the staff as well as the patients.' He opened the entrance door and gestured her in. He followed and dropped the bags on the floor, then opened a store cupboard and pulled out a trolley.

'It's one of the medicine trolleys,' he said. 'Do you think it will be okay?'

'Yes, it's perfect.'

But the aura between them felt awkward. It hadn't improved, even with his smile.

'Come into my office and you can stack the books in there.'

When they were in his office, he said: 'I'll go and fetch the other box.'

Although it was warm and cosy in the room, Esme didn't remove her coat as she rubbed her sore arms, then stuck her hands on the radiator. What bliss radiators were, she thought, as the hot metal permeated her gloves and warmed the cold skin underneath. Still keeping her gloves on, she neatly arranged the books on the lower shelf.

Brad was back in minutes with the box of books and set it on the floor. At the same moment the telephone rang.

'Colonel Parker here.'

Esme started towards the door, but he waved her back. There was a long pause.

'Right,' he said. 'Keep him calm. I'll be there immediately.' He turned to Esme. 'There's an emergency. Can I leave you to it?'

'Of course.'

He nodded and disappeared. For a few seconds she heard his footsteps hurrying along the corridor. Hoping he wouldn't find a patient who was seriously ill or injured, she bent to open the box and piled the books on the top of the trolley. There were about forty altogether so it should give the patients who were up to it enough reading material for several days, if not a week. *Good.* She was ready to walk round the ward and offer the books.

Her hands and feet now warmed up, she wheeled the trolley along the corridor until she came to Ward 4. No, she'd go next door and give Lloyd his books first and have a chat. She knocked on the door and quietly opened it in case he was asleep. No sign of Nurse Veasey or Lloyd. His bed was empty, the covers flung back as though he'd left all of a sudden. He must be having an X-ray or something. Should she leave his books by the bedside? No, she wanted to have a little chat with him. Just to make him feel he wasn't alone this Christmas. She'd be his visitor as he probably rarely had one.

I'd better go to Ward 4 then and maybe when they've finished choosing, Lloyd will be back.

The shouts of laughter and singing assailed her ears before she'd even opened the door to Ward 4. At first no one noticed her standing in the doorway. She went right into the ward and closed the door behind her. The girls had certainly done a good job giving the ward a festive atmosphere. Coloured paper chains were looped across the ceiling, wrapping paper festooned the beds and pillows, cards were strung up over the beds of those who had to stay lying down, and two or three men still had presents to open by the look of the unwrapped parcels on their lockers. Most of the patients were sitting up in bed, leaning over to talk to those next to themselves.

Two nurses, one of them Cindy, caught sight of her and came over immediately.

'Hi, Esme. Merry Christmas. Glad you could make it. It's all happening in Ward 4, isn't it?'

'It certainly is.' Esme grinned. She turned to the patients. 'Merry Christmas, everyone.'

Just at that moment, she heard the curtains surrounding one of the beds being swished back and Nurse Veasey stepped out. She caught sight of Esme and smiled. Esme blinked. It couldn't be. There was Lloyd, sitting upright against the pillows, beaming at her.

'Looks like y'all have a visitor, Lloyd,' Nurse Veasey said in a distinctive Southern drawl.

Brad! How wonderful! He listened to me after all. He risked any dressing down from his boss so that Lloyd wouldn't have to spend Christmas alone.

Warmth stole round her heart. Oh, how she loved him. She wanted to rush back to his office, tell him how proud she was that he'd done the right thing. But she must see Lloyd first. She wheeled the trolley over to his bed, aware of Buddy who'd objected to having a black man in the ward, tracking her with his eyes.

'This is a welcome surprise,' she said, smiling at Lloyd as she took his good hand to shake.

This time he held hers for a fraction, then drew it hastily away as though he didn't want her to think he was taking advantage of her kindness.

'Good to see you, Miss Esme.' He gestured to the trolley. 'What have you brought me?'

'Almost exactly what you asked for,' she said. 'I've got a poetry book of Tennyson and one of Keats, and one of general English poets, compliments of Sir Giles, the owner of Redcliffe Manor. He says you can keep the English poets as he has another copy.'

Lloyd's liquid-brown eyes sparkled.

'That's just hunky-dory, Miss Esme. Please thank him for me.'

'*And* I have *Macbeth* for you.' She handed it to him.

'That's swell.' Lloyd eagerly opened the cover. 'Printed in 1842!' His tone was full of wonder. Looking up, he said, 'California hadn't even joined the other thirty united states in America at that time.' He turned a few of the flimsy pages. 'It's wonderful, Miss Esme. I'm really going to enjoy reading this.' He hesitated as though wondering if he should say more. 'I don't tell many people this as they usually say it's impossible for a black guy, but I want to be an actor. And when I have enough experience – probably years but I'm prepared for that – my dream is to become a Shakespearian actor.'

'That's a wonderful dream to have,' Esme said warmly, 'and you have such a beautiful speaking voice. I can just imagine you on stage.'

'When the war's over, I'm determined to go to drama school and learn everything I can.' His eyes were wet with tears as he looked up at her and Esme's heart contracted. 'I can't thank you enough, Miss Esme.'

'Just call me Esme like everyone else,' she told him, lightly squeezing his good hand.

'If I can interrupt your *personal* conversation and get a word in, some of us would like to see the rest of the books – *if* you can spare us a few minutes of your *precious* time.'

Esme swung round to see Buddy glaring at them. Ignoring his sarcasm, she said: 'I'll be doing the rounds to everyone shortly.'

'He's not too happy about my being here,' Lloyd said under his breath.

'Well, that's his problem, not yours.'

They were interrupted by Nurse Veasey.

'Lloyd, sorry to break in but I need to take your temperature.' The nurse popped a thermometer under his tongue.

'I'll go,' Esme said, then added softly, 'I'll come and see you again soon.' She turned to his nurse. 'Thank you, Nurse Veasey, for looking after him.'

The nurse smiled directly at her, the deep brown eyes glowing with warmth.

Lloyd mumbled something but she couldn't distinguish the words through the glass tube in his mouth. She nodded and wheeled her trolley over to Bob, who was grinning from ear to ear.

She thoroughly enjoyed helping the men – most of them not much older than boys – to select a book, deliberately keeping Buddy waiting until last.

'I know what yous is up to,' he drawled.

Esme feigned innocence. 'If you mean leaving you until last, you never mentioned you wanted a book.'

Buddy scowled. 'You gotta cowboy book there?'

'No, I'm sorry. Dr Parker said he'll ask around the staff if they've brought any American books with them that they don't mind lending.'

He looked at her. 'Don't bother, ma'am. I only read the funnies at home.'

'Well, I might be able to find you a *Beano*.' Esme grinned at his bemused look. Then she said to the others, 'I'll be back in a few days with a few more books but there aren't going to be that many to choose from.'

'Don't worry, ma'am,' Bob called out cheerfully. 'We'll swap among ourselves. Then test one another that we've read them.'

'Good idea,' Esme said, smiling. She glanced over at Lloyd. 'I hope you enjoy reading the poetry and Shakespeare's *Macbeth*, Lloyd. I don't think you'll be disappointed.'

Lloyd broke into a wide grin and waved.

Esme couldn't wait to see Brad to thank him for moving Lloyd. How she wished she had a Christmas card to give him. She smiled to herself. Everything was going to be all right between them now. Hoping he'd be back from his emergency, she knocked on his office door, but there was no answer.

Oh well. She'd speak to him at the very first opportunity.

She was in the corridor, just about to leave, when she saw him striding towards her.

'Oh, Esmeralda, good. I've been looking for you. Can you come into the office?'

Esme smiled at him happily. 'Yes, of course. I needed to speak to you, too.'

He took the trolley from her and wheeled it in.

'Before you say anything,' Brad started, 'I want to explain—'

'There's nothing to explain, Brad,' she interrupted. 'I can't tell you how pleased I am that you changed your mind and put Lloyd in with the others. It was so lovely to see him there and he looked chuffed to bits, too. You did the right thing and no one, I'm certain, will get you into any trouble. It *is* Christmas, after all.'

Brad heaved a sigh. 'Yes, that's the problem.'

She frowned. 'What do you mean?'

'I've taken a chance and allowed him to be with the others for Christmas until New Year's Day. But then, I'm afraid, it's back to normal.'

'You mean you've let him onto the ward because it's Christmas and you're going to send him back when it's all over?' Esme could hardly contain her frustration as she glared at him. 'And it's *not* normal – it's the most *ab*normal thing to do to a human.'

'I know it is. But I wish you would understand.'

'No, I'll never understand. And I'll never understand you either.'

For the second time in succession, she stormed out, leaving the trolley behind. Not until she was walking over to the Manor did she let rip with a few choice words that only a blackbird sitting on the fence could have heard. He stared at her with his yellow-edged, shiny black eye, then fluttered away as though he'd heard enough. Esme dashed the tears from her cheeks with her hand, feeling even more upset, if it were possible, than when he'd told her the first time he couldn't allow Lloyd to be in the same ward as the other patients.

But Sir Giles would fix it. She had every faith in him.

Chapter Thirty-Three

Cook had told Esme she wouldn't be back until the 28th and Sir Giles had requested his meal in his room.

'All the maids have gone home to see their families, so would you take his lunch?' Cook said, 'because I want to catch the two-fifteen bus and it's the only one going this afternoon into Bath.'

'Of course.' Esme realised she knew nothing about Cook's private life. Cook was stern but she decided to take a chance. 'Do you have family there?'

'My brother. He's recently lost his wife and is no cook, so I said I'd see him for a few days.'

'Oh, I'm sorry.'

'Don't be,' Cook said surprisingly. 'He never stops moaning. And it's not just because he's on his own. He's always been like it.' She removed her pinafore and hung it on the hook behind the door. 'I reckon he sent her to her grave.'

Esme gave a start. 'Oh, I'm sure—'

'You don't know him like I do.' Cook handed her Sir Giles's tray.

'Good luck,' Esme said, smiling. 'I hope you find your brother not too difficult.'

She carried the tray along one of the passages to Sir Giles's bedroom, telling herself not to ask him his decision until he'd finished his lunch. Cook had made a roast chicken for Christmas dinner, as there was only a handful of people remaining at the Manor, but it smelled delicious.

Sir Giles was sitting up in bed, reading the newspaper. He laid it down when he saw her.

'Have you had yours?' he said.

'Not yet. Cook's left ours – those that are here – on hot plates in the dining room.'

'Well, I won't keep you,' he said. 'But come back afterwards – I need to talk to you for a few minutes.'

Good. It sounded as though he was going to tell her how he'd approached Brad about Lloyd. Or how he intended to if he hadn't already. And it would be the right time to give him his Christmas present.

Her mouth still watering from the sight of Sir Giles's delicious-looking Christmas lunch, Esme opened the dining room door to see there were a couple of schoolgirls who hadn't gone home, and Russell. *Drat!* There was no possibility of sitting quietly on her own today. She deliberately made straight for his table, and it was only when one of the girls with hair down her back turned round that she noticed it was Bertha without her pigtails. The schoolgirl wrinkled her nose as though there was a bad smell under her nostrils as Russell patted the chair next to him.

'I was beginning to think you were avoiding me,' he said in an undertone.

'Not at all,' she said untruthfully, then turned to say hello to the two girls. 'It's nice that you have each other with everyone gone.'

Bertha snorted but said nothing.

'I don't know your name,' Esme said to the other girl.

'Faith.'

Yes, Faith suited her, Esme thought. She seemed a quiet girl though her eyes were red as if she'd been crying.

'Were you not able to go home for Christmas?' she said, hoping she wasn't putting her foot in it. For all she knew, Faith could be an orphan.

'No, they're in India.'

'Do they live there?'

'Yes, and so did I until I was sent to boarding school.'

'I expect you miss your parents.'

'Not particularly. They couldn't get rid of me quickly enough.'

Esme noticed Bertha was quiet all this time, seeming to listen for once.

'Oh, I'm sorry.' Esme regarded the girl. She had pale eyes of no particular colour behind metal-rimmed spectacles. But her crowning glory was her hair – shiny copper ringlets fell around her elfin face with its pointed chin. 'Maybe we can play some games tomorrow.'

She noticed Russell looking at her hopefully.

'What sort of games?' Bertha demanded.

'Oh, I don't know. I'll have to think about it.'

They ate the rest of their meal and a small slice of plum pudding, when Esme pushed her empty plate away.

'That was delicious, but I couldn't eat another thing if you paid me,' she told Russell.

The two girls had devoured theirs and already left the table, only Faith saying, 'Merry Christmas.'

'Will you come and have a drink with me in the staff room after supper?' Russell said. 'I think it's going to be a "help yourself" tonight after such a big lunch.'

Esme hesitated. She didn't really want to spend a whole evening in Russell's company, but there wasn't anything much to do for the rest of the day, and the evening might feel long and lonely with Sir Giles in bed and no one else around.

'All right,' she said before she could stop herself. 'That sounds nice.' She glanced at him. 'Shall I meet you just after six?'

'Yes, I'll have some drinks ready and see if I can rake up some cheese and biscuits.'

Esme looked at her watch. 'I'd better go.'

'Go ahead.' Russell smiled at her. 'I'll be there at six.'

Esme picked up the desk diary she'd managed to get him and hurried to his room. She knocked and went in as he'd always told her to do, regardless of whether he called out to enter or not. He was sitting up in bed reading.

'Come in, my dear, and pull up that chair. Now,' he regarded her, 'I want to talk to you about that young man, Lloyd Taylor.'

Good. He'd brought up the subject himself. That was far better.

'I've thought over what you asked me to do most carefully . . .' He paused. 'And I'm afraid there's nothing I can do. I can't interfere with American law.'

'Oh, but—'

Sir Giles raised his hand. 'Listen, Esme, not only is Brad Parker a senior doctor, but he's a colonel. Both are highly respected titles so we shouldn't compromise him in these two positions that he's worked so hard for. He'd like to help, I know, but he can't. It's the military and they're not going to be swayed by one black chap on his own in the next ward, however lonely he is.'

Esme swallowed.

'I'm sure if you really thought hard about it, Esme dear, you'd come to the same conclusion, disappointed though we both are.'

'I understand,' Esme said miserably. Well, she'd tried – she really had. Her shoulders slumped. She couldn't fight the entire American military.

'Before you go, I have something for you.' Sir Giles pointed to a small box on his bedside table. 'That's for you. I'm sorry it's not wrapped in gift paper, but I did put some string round it.' He smiled.

'Oh, you shouldn't have—'

He waved off her protestation. 'Don't open it now. You can do that later. I have to warn you that it's not new. I'm not one for shopping.'

'You're very kind, Sir Giles. Thank you. And I have something for you.' She gave him the diary that the assistant in the stationery shop had kindly gift-wrapped for her.

'Oh, you shouldn't have,' he chuckled, deliberately echoing Esme's reaction, causing her to smile.

'That's better.' He beamed. 'You have a delightful smile, so go and enjoy the rest of your day.' He put the gift on his bedside table. 'I'll open it when I've had a nap.' Then stroking his beard, he said, 'I'm sorry again, Esme, that I've had to disappoint you on speaking to the colonel.'

It was more than disappointment, Esme thought, when she later went to sit in the empty staff room with the box Sir Giles had given her. She linked her fingers behind her head and sighed. She simply had to resign herself to the fact that Brad couldn't change American law any more than she and Sir Giles could. But at least she'd expressed her opinion.

A knock at the door made her startle. *Strange.* It couldn't be one of the staff because they'd have just come in. She opened it to see Brad standing there with his briefcase. He gave her a tired smile.

'Hello. Merry Christmas,' she said, feeling suddenly shy.

'Merry Christmas. May I come in?'

'Yes, of course.'

'I kept meaning to give you back your locket,' he said, when he sat on the chair near her and handed her a small envelope.

'I kept forgetting to ask you.' She looked at him. 'I must get the chain mended.'

'It's done.'

She gave a start. 'Really?' He nodded. 'How much do I owe you?'

'Nothing. I didn't need to take it to a jeweller's because the chain itself was intact, but the fastener had come apart. A pair of pliers soon sorted it.'

She opened the envelope and shook the contents out into her hand. It was only then that she realised he must have looked inside the heart. Her cheeks flushing, she said:

'So now you've seen a photograph of my husband.' It was a statement rather than a question.

Brad had the grace to look sheepish.

'I'm sorry, Esme, I—'

'Don't apologise. I'm sure I would have done the same.' She licked her lips and opened her mouth. It was time to tell him about Anthony.

'He looks a nice sort of guy.' Brad cleared his throat. 'But I didn't come to talk to you about the locket – I wanted to give you a gift.'

'I didn't get you anything,' Esme blurted.

Brad smiled. 'I didn't expect anything.'

'Sir Giles gave me something' – she nodded towards the table where she'd set it to answer the door – 'but I haven't opened it yet.' She held it out to him.

'Do it now, ' he said, taking a penknife and cutting the string, 'and then you can have mine.'

She opened the box to find a slim navy-blue leather case with a yellowing white card on top. She opened it and read:

To my dear wife, Beatrice, on our wedding day, with all my love, Giles XX.

She looked over at Brad in amazement. 'It's something he gave his wife on their wedding day and now he's given it to me.' She opened the box. Inside, gleaming in its snowy bed of cotton wool lay a beautiful string of pearls. 'I can't believe it.' She removed the necklace, carefully holding it up for Brad to see.

'You said he didn't have any children, so Sir Giles rightly thought you were the one to inherit it – probably because he sees you as a daughter.' He gave a rueful smile. 'Oh dear, my gift for you is going to look very meagre compared to that.' He drew from his briefcase a festively wrapped package, quite obviously a book, and handed it to her.

'It's a record,' she joked.

He grinned. 'I knew you'd guess. And I'd better admit right now that it's also second-hand.'

'I'm beginning to like presents that have already been loved.'

It was so nice to banter like this instead of having to argue about serious matters as they had done recently. Unwrapping the paper carefully and folding it back into its creases, she turned the book over, then couldn't help a chuckle.

'*The Great Gatsby*. Sir Giles told me to read it.' She suddenly grew suspicious and stared at him. 'Tell me the truth. Did he say I'd tried to read it twice but gave up?'

'He might have done.'

'Hmm, I thought so.'

'I didn't say definitely . . . but then it *is* recognised as being the great American novel.'

'Just as well.'

And then he stood and pulled her to her feet. 'Friends again?' he said, hugging her.

'Friends again,' she echoed, hugging him back.

The door opened and they both looked round as Russell came in with a bottle of wine. He stared at them both.

'Ah, I see you already have company,' he said, as he left the room, quietly closing the door behind him.

Chapter Thirty-Four

January 1943

Blustery showers brought in New Year's Day. The beginning of the fifth year of the war. Esme could hardly believe how long it had dragged on and still it continued. The BBC and Sir Giles's *Telegraph* that he always left for her when he'd finished with it had made noises that there'd been a turning point since the North African landings in November when the longed-for victory at El-Alamein had finally happened.

She'd seen nothing of Brad since he'd come to the Manor on Christmas Day evening. He'd invited her and Stella and Sir Giles to a New Year's Eve party, but she'd declined. Instead, she'd made a flying visit to see Freda and her boys for a few days, feeling guilty that she hadn't even given Brad a card. Not that she'd given out many. Just to Sir Giles and Stella and one to Freda and the boys and at the last minute sent one to Muriel.

So much had happened before Christmas. Her father's funeral, then Muriel dropping the bombshell that would change all their lives, and poor Lloyd Taylor . . . It was no wonder that she wasn't exactly in a Christmas mood.

But then common sense took over. She was naïve if she thought she could change American law. Neither Brad nor Sir Giles could do either – it was for the US government to change.

A wave of remorse swept through her. It had been utterly inappropriate to ask either Sir Giles or Brad to break the rules and she hadn't been very gracious in the way she'd treated Sir Giles when he'd told her he wasn't going to interfere. She needed to apologise to both of them. Sir Giles first. Pulling her mouth in a determined line, she finally found him having a cup of tea with Hilary Fenton in the staff room.

'Oh, I'm sorry,' she said, acknowledging the housemistress who barely nodded, then turning to Sir Giles. 'I didn't mean to disturb you. I was just going to the study.'

'I'll be there in a few minutes,' Sir Giles said, putting down his teacup.

True to his word, he appeared in the study doorway five minutes later.

'Sir Giles, I want to apologise. I should never have asked you such a thing about putting Lloyd in with the others when I knew it was a strict American rule. It was way beyond my duties, so I apologise.'

'Don't. I admire you for standing up for what you believe in, just as I did when I was a conscientious objector in the Great War.' He looked at her. 'I would love to have waved a magic wand over the whole thing, but Brad's hands are tied as well.'

'I realise that now,' Esme said quietly. 'Can we forget it?'

Sir Giles smiled. 'Of course, my dear.' He looked at her directly. 'And I hope you will not allow this to come between you and Brad Parker either. It would be a shame if you did.'

'No, I'll tell him the same. I need to clear the air.'

She went up to him and kissed his cheek.

'What was that for?'

'Because I haven't even thanked you for the pearls. I'll wear them with pride and gratitude, so thank you for trusting me with them. And . . .' she smiled, 'because you're the nicest man I've ever worked for.'

He beamed. 'And that's one of the best things anyone has ever said, so I thank you.'

Oh, the relief. Now she had to face Brad. Get that over with. But she wasn't looking forward to it one bit.

'I do have something very interesting to tell you,' Sir Giles said, breaking into her thoughts.

'Oh? What's that then?'

'A telephone call from the Palace.'

Esme's eyes flew wide. 'Goodness. What did *they* want?'

'Somebody rather special is coming to pay us a visit this Tuesday.' He paused for several seconds. 'It's a member of the royal family.'

'How exciting. Is it one of the princes or princesses?'

Sir Giles looked at her and winked. 'Perhaps I should let it be a surprise.'

'Oh, please don't.'

'Just teasing, my dear. It's Queen Mary herself.'

Esme startled. 'Queen Mary?' she squeaked. 'Goodness, that *is* exciting. Is she just coming for an afternoon tea or something?'

'Not quite. It's all been arranged between one of the officers of the Royal Household and me through Miss Fenton. She's coming Thursday morning with her lady-in-waiting and inevitable entourage. She's staying overnight and will leave Friday morning. She's interested in meeting the schoolgirls. Apparently, it's the kind of thing she relishes.' He paused. 'Anyway, that's what I was talking to Miss Fenton about.'

'Have you told Mrs Morgan?'

He grimaced. 'No, I'm about to tell her now. I hope she doesn't go to pieces.'

Esme hesitated. Maybe this was an ideal opportunity to soften the prickly housekeeper. It was difficult enough to keep on the right side of Cook.

'Sir Giles, it will mean a lot of extra work for her. Could you spare me to help her?'

His expression was that of relief. 'You know, Esme, I'm sure Mrs Morgan would really appreciate it. But leave it for half an hour after I come back before you offer – just to let it sink in. She's not really dealt with famous people before. The butler always managed them but of course with the war, we had to let him go – as we did most of the staff.'

Sir Giles was back in less than ten minutes, his face crestfallen.

'Was Mrs Morgan all right?' Esme said.

'Hardly. I thought she was going to have an apoplexy.' He blew out his cheeks. 'I think it might be wise for you to make your generous offer right away, Esme – before she packs her bags! And I must inform our colonel. He'll need to contact his superior to invite him, as Her Majesty will doubtless want to see the new military hospital.'

There was a firm knock on Brad's office door. It would be Sir Giles, Brad thought, as he stood to let him in. Sir Giles had already telephoned to make an appointment to see him about something important, he said. It could only be one thing. Esme must have had a word with him. He was going to try to persuade him to alter the ward arrangements.

Heaving a sigh, Brad shook hands with his host.

'Good to see you, sir,' he said. 'Let me take your raincoat and have a seat.' Brad gestured to one of the comfortable chairs by the window where the rain was falling more heavily, streaking the pane and obliterating any view.

Sir Giles went over and sat down and Brad took the second chair.

'I think I know what this is about.' He looked at Sir Giles intently.

'Go on.'

'About the coloured patient in the room next to the main ward.'

Sir Giles stroked his chin with rasping noises like a nail file.

'You've guessed that Esme approached me,' he said. 'She had it mapped out quite clearly how I could persuade you to break the rules. But I told her I couldn't.'

Brad's eyes narrowed. 'Is that how you left it?'

'More or less.'

'What did she say to you?' Brad watched Sir Giles's expression.

'I think she sees things a little differently now. But I have some other news that you might want to discuss with your boss – we're soon to have a royal visit.'

Brad felt his shoulders relax. It didn't seem as though Esme was still angry that he was powerless to change US military law. She hadn't mentioned it when they'd last spoken on Christmas Day evening anyway.

'That sounds a very special visit.'

'It is.' Sir Giles pulled out his pipe and Brad nodded for him to go ahead and light it. 'It happens to be Queen Mary. She's taken an interest in the school here,' he said in between setting the bowl alight, 'but as soon as she found out there was an American hospital in the grounds, her interest was piqued further. Apparently, she wishes to visit that as well.'

'She told you that?' Brad's tone was incredulous.

'Not to my face,' Sir Giles chuckled. 'But her lady-in-waiting approached Miss Fenton, the housemistress.' He paused. 'I'll leave it with you, Brad, but keep it under your hat as far as your staff and the patients go. It's all rather hush-hush and we wouldn't want it leaked to the Germans – they'd have a field day if they had that kind of information, the way they've targeted Buckingham Palace on several occasions.'

'I understand,' Brad said with a nod. 'When is she due?'

'I don't know the hour – I don't think anyone knows until she arrives, but it's Thursday and she's returning to Badminton House where she's staying for however long the war lasts, the following morning.'

'I'll see that the patients are looking their best,' Brad said, smiling. 'They're going to think they're living history. Something to tell their folks back home.'

When Sir Giles had left the office, Brad leaned back in his chair and pulled out a packet of Lucky Strike and lit one. He drew on it deeply, then allowed the smoke to stream out. He should get onto the general right away. There'd be hell to pay if there was a royal visit and the general wasn't told about it – and invited Brad inhaled again. He'd finish his cigarette first.

While Esme hurried to find Mrs Morgan, she was wondering how to put it to the woman without sounding as though she didn't think the housekeeper was up to the job. She gave an inward sigh. You could never tell how Mrs Morgan would react. Probably best to be natural and play it by ear.

'She's in the kitchen, madam,' one of the cleaners told her.

Esme opened the door to Cook and Mrs Morgan having a heated discussion.

'It's the last thing we need here with all the comin's and goin's,' Mrs Morgan declared.

'And how do I find enough rations to make dishes fit for royalty, I don't know.' Cook's face was red, as usual, from one or other of the ovens.

Neither woman took any notice of Esme as she stepped into the kitchen, hiding an amused smile as both kitchen maids looked up at her and grinned. They were obviously enjoying the two women's disapproval at Sir Giles's announcement, and the extra work a visit from the Queen would undoubtedly bring.

'And you want to watch her like a hawk,' Cook said. 'A house like this with all its treasures – why, she'll have those beady eyes of hers on what she can claim.'

'I'm well aware of that,' Mrs Morgan said stiffly.

Esme had heard enough.

'Sorry to intrude, but I've come to offer any extra help you might need,' she said cheerfully. 'Perhaps more at Mrs Morgan's disposal than in the kitchen, as I'm not that much of a cook.'

She caught the surprised glance between the two older women.

'Well, that's very nice of you, I'm sure,' Mrs Morgan said. 'Perhaps you can help me fold the napkins how Sir Giles likes 'em.'

'It would be a pleasure, Mrs Morgan.'

'And we'll need the table laying more fancy-like.' Cook folded her arms over her chest, not to be outdone. 'Are you up to that?'

'I'm sure I am,' Esme said. 'And anything else you can think of.' She smiled at them. 'May I just ask one question, Cook?'

Cook nodded.

'What did you mean by your remark about the Queen and having to keep an eye on her?'

'Don't you know?'

'Know what?' Esme asked, puzzled.

Cook brushed her hands down her apron and snorted. 'They say that if the Queen takes her fancy to – well, it could be some unusual ornament or painting, anything of that nature – in someone's home, particularly in grand houses like this one – she'll point it out and admire it, until they're *forced* to give it to her. She always receives the item as though she's surprised at the owner's generosity.'

'And apparently, she's always extremely gracious,' Mrs Morgan chipped in, 'but the one who owns – or *did* own it – no longer does.' She shook her head. 'And it's often somethin' meaningful to them. But they all know what the rule is – if she admires it, it's the sign she wants it, and won't leave until they hand it over.'

'What sort of things might she want? I mean, she must have everything, being a Queen.'

Cook pursed her lips. 'It could be somethin' as small as a beautifully cut vase, or something much more valuable. You never know with her what might take her eye.'

'But that's not right,' Esme blurted.

Mrs Morgan and Cook both smirked.

'No, it's not,' Mrs Morgan agreed, 'but she in't like the rest of us.' She sent Esme an ironic smile. 'What Queen Mary says goes and no one – it don't matter who it is – can argue with her with that lovely smile she has. 'Course that's only what we've been told. To be fair, we 'aven't witnessed it ourselves. But that in't all.' The housekeeper took in a breath. 'The powers that be are always on the look-out that she might be kidnapped by the Nazis, so wherever she goes, even if only for a night, she takes all her jewels – and her tiaras, no doubt – in three extra suitcases, no less.'

'Goodness, it sounds as though very rich people have an added worry that we mere mortals aren't aware of,' Esme said, hoping this was just a myth. 'But I must say, I'm really excited that we'll all have a chance to meet her.' She smiled at the two women. 'Aren't you both?'

'I don't suppose for one minute I'll get the chance,' Cook said. 'And probably just as well – I'll be too busy cooking for Her Majesty.' She glanced at Mrs Morgan. 'You'll meet her, Joy,' she added, 'so no doubt you'll tell me all the goin's on.'

'I'd better go and see about laying the table,' Esme said, hiding a grin that Mrs Morgan's Christian name was Joy.

'Well, well, our librarian in't so hoity-toity after all,' she heard Mrs Morgan say to Cook as she closed the kitchen door behind her.

So that was why the two of them were always so snippy with

her. They'd got her completely wrong, but it seemed her offer of help had thawed them out a little. Esme gave a wry smile. Her plan to kill them with kindness had worked. And she'd certainly plenty to think about with the forthcoming royal visit, she decided, on her way back to Sir Giles's study.

'May I speak to you a moment, Mrs Donaldson?' Hilary Fenton's strident tones came from behind.

Esme spun round, surprised. 'Of course, Miss Fenton. What is it?'

'Perhaps you'd come to my office.'

Oh, not another confrontation.

Reluctantly, she took a seat opposite the housemistress.

'I'm sure you're now aware of Queen Mary's visit to our school.' Hilary lit a cigarette without bothering to offer Esme one, and sat back in her chair, with her eyes narrowed against the smoke.

'Yes, I am aware,' Esme answered coolly.

Hilary Fenton nodded. 'This is an important event so I wonder if you might be able to help me with something.'

Esme waited, wondering what was coming.

'You're obviously well educated by your accent and your literary knowledge,' the housemistress went on.

What on earth is the woman on about?

'So I just wondered if you were ever taught to curtsey.'

The question was so unexpected, Esme didn't know how to control a burst of laughter.

'Are you asking me to teach *you*?'

'Of *course* not.' The housemistress drew on her cigarette again. 'It's obviously for the girls.'

'Ah, I see.' Esme looked across the desk, biting the side of her tongue in her effort to fight her amusement. 'Well, no I wasn't . . . taught to curtsey at school.'

Miss Fenton's mouth turned down unattractively.

'Oh, that's a shame.'

'I might have thought the same of you.' Esme made a point of relaxing in her chair, a glint of mischief in her eyes.

'What do you mean?' the housemistress snapped, viciously stubbing out her half-smoked cigarette.

'You speak as though you've also been well educated.' When the woman didn't answer, Esme continued, 'Stella is the one to ask. She's a cousin of sorts to the family here.'

A frown appeared between the housemistress's brows. She shook her head.

'Oh no, not Miss Stratten. We don't get along at all. I couldn't ask her.'

Interesting. Not just me, then, who the woman has taken against.

'*I* could ask her.'

Relief cleared Miss Fenton's face.

'Would you do that?'

'Of course.' Esme's mind raced. 'You're right, that this is an important event for the girls and *I* need to know the correct way to curtsey as well. Stella could give the girls lessons in deportment at the same time. I've noticed several of them slouch and I'm sure it's because they hunch over their desks as we all do when we're studying and writing. But she's the right person. She'd also teach them how to reply to the Queen when she speaks – and she must *always* be the first one – and those other little niceties.'

Hilary Fenton sat back in her chair looking thoughtful.

'Why would you want to help me?'

Esme looked the housemistress directly in the eye. 'We all have to live together. Being pleasant is essential for a happy household. And anyway,' she added, 'I want us all to give the best impression possible to the Queen, so she always remembers her stay here. And the girls will always remember the honour of meeting Queen Mary. It will be something to tell their children.'

'So I can depend upon you,' Hilary Fenton said, fixing her eyes on Esme.

'On one condition.'

'Oh?' the woman's eyes narrowed with suspicion. 'What would that be?'

'That you stop calling me Mrs Donaldson and I stop calling you Miss Fenton.' Esme looked at her and grinned. 'It's all too silly for words when we're roughly the same age and under the same roof.' She paused. 'Do you think you could manage that, Hilary?'

Hilary Fenton cleared her throat. 'Yes, I think I could . . . Esme.'

Esme smiled. 'Then you may depend upon me to put forward your request to Stella.'

'But don't tell her I asked you to.'

'Happy household.' Esme rose to her feet and gazed down at her, a friendly smile hovering over her lips. 'That's what we're aiming for, isn't it?'

Chapter Thirty-Five

Esme decided not to waste any time in speaking to Stella. Both she and the girls would benefit from Stella's lessons in deportment and, of course, the curtsey, which must be performed with perfection under the critical eye of Queen Mary.

Stella's usual lunchbreak on the switchboard was from one o'clock until a quarter to two, but she usually managed to stretch it out until two. That would give them plenty of time to eat and discuss Hilary Fenton's surprising request.

I might see Brad.

Crossly, Esme brushed the idea away. She had one purpose and it didn't include him. Then something Mrs Morgan had said crossed her mind.

What Queen Mary says goes and no one – it don't matter who it is – can argue with her.

Esme momentarily closed her eyes. Could she, dare she, put into words what she was thinking? After all, she had no right to approach Queen Mary, whose son was now on the throne. If Mrs Morgan and Cook were right, the old Queen was a most formidable lady. Esme lifted her head. She wouldn't baulk. She'd just have to wait for the right moment, that was all. Closing her lids and trying to picture the scene – what she would say, how she would say it – she knew there was no possible way she could go up to the Queen, curtsey, and make her request. There must be another way.

She opened her eyes and blinked. There was. But she'd have to see Brad after all. Persuade him to allow her to escort Queen Mary round the wards, particularly the ones where the patients were recuperating from their operations – including Lloyd Taylor.

She'd go and see Brad right this minute. She had to apologise to him anyway.

Wondering quite how Brad would react, Esme, dripping with rain, knocked on his door.

He opened it immediately, his expression one of astonishment.

'Happy New Year, Brad.'

His features relaxed as he smiled at her. 'Happy New Year, Esmeralda. It's good to see you. Here, let me take that wet raincoat.'

'Oh, I won't be long.' She remained on her feet, not quite catching his eye. 'Am I disturbing you?'

'Not at all.' He drew on his cigarette, then went to his desk and stubbed it out in the ashtray. 'What can I do for you on this brief visit?'

Esme shifted from one leg to another. Then, she looked straight at him.

'Brad, I didn't say anything on Christmas Day when you came over in the evening, but I should have.'

He said nothing, just raised an eyebrow.

'I've come to apologise when I was so angry that you wouldn't allow Lloyd to stay in the main ward after Christmas. It was unforgivably rude of me and—'

He put his hand up. 'Stop! There's no need to apologise. I understand completely why you were upset. I feel the same way myself – I told you so. But I have no power at all to change the laws of the military. Unfortunately, it's no different in the civilian world back in the States.' He looked at her. 'You do understand my position, don't you, Esmeralda?'

She gave a slow nod of her head. 'Yes.' Then she tilted her chin a fraction. 'I'm sorry I acted so childishly.'

He smiled. 'I admire you for standing up for what you believe is right. And I believe it's right as well. I don't want you ever to forget that.'

'I won't.' She hesitated. 'That wasn't the only thing I came in for, but I wanted to get that bit over with.'

'Then why don't you take that wet coat off and sit down for a minute.'

She did so, then said, 'Has Sir Giles spoken to you about Queen Mary visiting the Manor – and that she wants to see the hospital as well?'

'Yes, he did. It's a great honour so I need to tell the patients and the staff so we can get everything ship-shape before she comes.'

'Well, I wondered if you would be the one to escort the Queen round the wards.'

He gazed at her. 'Yes, it will be me and the general showing your Queen round, and I'd been about to call him when you came in just now.' He gave a brief grin. 'I don't think he will let such an opportunity slip by.'

Esme smiled back.

'I wondered if you might allow me to go with you all – just round the wards where I do the trolley library,' she added. 'I think it's something positive to show Queen Mary that the patients are recuperating well from their operations.'

She felt Brad's eyes on her. Did he realise why she was suggesting this? She could almost see his brain ticking over. And then with relief, she realised what conclusion he was coming to. She suppressed a chuckle as she saw the warmth of Brad's admiration in his eyes.

After another moment's hesitation, he said, 'I don't see why not. You're the one who thought up the trolley library idea, which I might tell you has gone down a storm. I'll have a word with the general when he arrives.' He grinned at her. 'I suppose you don't trust two Yanks to escort your Queen and her lady-in-waiting.'

'Oh, it's not that,' Esme said quickly. 'The Americans I've spoken to here are always most polite. But the Queen might feel pleased to learn that we have a good relationship with one another.'

'Are you referring to yours and my good relationship?' Brad's eyes danced with merriment. 'Because if so, I'm all for it.'

Esme's cheeks reddened slightly. 'You know what I mean.'

Brad's grin spread wider. 'Yes, I do, and I promise not to embarrass you anymore.'

'I'm not embarrassed.' She stood. 'Well, I won't keep you any longer, Brad.'

He came from behind his desk.

'Of course I know what you meant,' he said as he went to open the door for her. 'But I still hold to my deliberate misinterpretation that I'm ready to renew our good relationship which isn't – wasn't – just friendship. I hope you're ready, too, but perhaps this will convince you.'

Before she could protest, he took her in his arms, then cradled her head as he kissed her firmly on her lips. The now familiar masculine smell of him filled her senses. Just as the last time, she couldn't help responding, her lips softening under his. Letting one arm drop, he still remained in contact with her other.

'Have I convinced you that's what I *really* meant?' He looked down at her, his eyes searching hers.

She didn't answer. But almost in a trance, she gave his arm the lightest touch before she left.

Her senses intoxicated, Esme couldn't help thinking: *kiss number two*. Recalling how he'd deliberately misunderstood her remark that she now realised had been badly formed and open to ambiguity, she couldn't help smiling to herself. Typical man. But his kiss had cheered her up immensely. He still found her attractive. He obviously hadn't liked having to say no to her about Lloyd. But there was something *she* knew that he didn't.

He thinks I'm going to talk to the general – beg him to change the rules, just this time, just for Lloyd. No, Brad, I'm not doing anything of the kind. All I need do is accompany Queen Mary and let her see the situation for herself. I doubt I'd even have to say anything.

She nodded to herself. Yes, it was by far the most diplomatic solution. Not at all sure to whom she was appealing, Esme crossed her fingers as she walked along the corridor to where Stella worked and said out loud:

'Please let this be third time lucky.'

Stella swung round on her chair when she saw Esme enter the telephone switchboard room.

'Why, this is a nice surprise. Happy New Year, Esme.' She gave Esme a kiss on the cheek. 'I can't believe I'm working on New Year's Day after last night.'

'Did you have a nice time?'

Stella smiled and sent her a wink.

'That's an understatement, darling. It was simply spiffing as we used to say at school.'

Not at my school, Esme thought. They'd have ribbed us like crazy if we'd used that sort of language.

'Well, I'm glad,' she answered, though noticing Stella's eyelids now drooped with tiredness, and she had bags under her eyes that weren't normally there.

'Why didn't you go?' Stella demanded.

'I'm not good with late nights.'

Esme refused to admit that she hadn't wanted to see Brad on

New Year's Eve when perhaps he'd kiss her, but only just for show, at the stroke of midnight. But this time hadn't been like that at all, she couldn't help thinking, reliving the memory of his lips on hers only minutes ago. They still tingled. Her cheeks warmed and she was glad when one of the circuits on the switchboard lit up and Stella excused herself to insert a phone plug, then announced:

'Redcliffe United States General Hospital.' She turned to Esme and hissed: 'Wait here.' Esme nodded. 'To whom do you wish to speak?' After a brief interlude, Stella said: 'Just connecting you now to Mr Robbins.' She turned to Esme. 'Sorry about that. You were saying . . .'

'Can't remember,' Esme laughed, 'so it couldn't have been important.' She waited while Stella swivelled right round in her seat. 'I do want to talk to you about Queen Mary though.'

'Ah.' Stella gave a triumphant smile. 'It's exciting, isn't it?'

'Yes, and I'm wondering if you can help.'

'In what way?'

'I don't want to make an exhibition of myself for doing something out of order,' Esme said.

'So you think I can rehearse you on how to address her when you first set eyes on her.'

'And the rest.' Esme smiled.

'Do you have any idea how to do these things?'

'No. Very little. I want to learn as much as I can.'

Stella swung off her stool and grabbed Esme round the waist in one quick, fluid movement.

'Don't tell me that's the preparation for a curtsey,' Esme said.

'Maybe not, but I'm warming you up, so watch me carefully.' Stella came closer. 'Hold out your skirt like this.' She whipped up the edges of her skirt on either side and spread the material in front of herself. 'Cross your legs with one leg back for balance, then bend your body slightly sideways at the same time – then bend down further, like this.'

'I could never do it as elegantly as you,' Esme giggled when she almost fell over with her effort.

'And again,' Stella's voice pealed out. 'Then again.'

'I must have done this twenty times,' Esme grumbled when Stella said it still wasn't quite right.

'I don't care if it's a hundred times, you're going to do the most beautiful curtsey in front of Queen Mary, who's a perfectionist and will be most impressed, though I doubt she'll make any comment.'

Ten minutes later, Stella announced:

'If you keep practising, you'll be fine.' She grinned. 'Come on, let's have some lunch and you can tell me all about the forthcoming royal visit. I presume she'll want to meet some of the schoolgirls. If so, they'll need to learn as well. And also their deportment and when not to address her.'

'Sir Giles wants *all* of them to have that opportunity.'

'How many are there?'

'Around fifty.'

Stella wrinkled her brow. 'Hmm. I'll have to divide them up into two or three sessions.'

'When's the best time for you to rehearse them?'

'I'd say mid-morning break. Then there's the opportunity to practise throughout the day.'

'I'll report to you if that's all right with Anita and Russell,' Esme said. 'Oh, and Hilary Fenton said she'd be grateful for your help, Stella.'

Stella frowned. Then a wicked smile crept over her lips.

'I expect she would say that. She likes to think she's above everyone, but really she's no woman of the world that I can see.' She gazed at Esme. 'Why didn't she come and ask me herself?'

'I think she feels awkward about it,' Esme replied. 'But all that will change, I'm sure, when she sees what a good tutor you are.'

'Hmm.' Stella pursed her lips. 'We'll see about that.' Then she caught Esme's eye and she sent her a sly grin. 'I have an idea. *You* teach Hilary to curtsey and I'll take on the fifty girls. I think that's fair, don't you?'

Chapter Thirty-Six

Esme drew back her bedroom curtains and glanced out of the window. She'd heard it pouring with rain again during the night, crashing and splattering onto her windows, the wind rushing down the fireplace, keeping her from having a good night's sleep. It didn't look as though the rain had shown any respect for Queen Mary's visit this morning, as the heavy squall hadn't abated one bit. Such a shame, Esme thought, as she slipped the new midnight-blue dress over her head. She'd had barely enough clothing coupons saved to buy it in the January sales only two days ago. Smoothing the soft wool material down her body, she zipped it at the side, pleased that it fitted so perfectly. With a boat-necked collar, the skirt just over the knee, it looked like a two-piece with its defining hip-length second hem and the narrow matching belt at the waist. Yes, she thought, as she glanced in the mirror above her sink. The top half she could see looked dignified, even elegant, but she had to admit, a little dull.

Of course! She opened the dressing-table drawer and took out the navy-blue leather case, then removed the string of pearls Sir Giles had given her. After fastening them round her neck she glanced in the mirror. It made all the difference. Her skin glowed. She was now appropriately dressed for the royal visit.

Queen Mary was due to arrive at eleven o'clock, just giving time for her driver to take her cases upstairs, ready for her strict time for coffee at quarter past, so her lady-in-waiting had informed them. Esme could sense the excitement both staff and girls exuded in the Manor as she looked round at them all, congregated in the Great Hall to meet the mother of King George. Sir Giles had insisted she stand next to him at the entrance and dwarfed by his height, she realised what an impressive figure he cut with his snowy-white hair and beard in charcoal morning suit with contrasting blue waistcoat and tie. He caught her eye and then his glance fell onto the pearl necklace.

'They suit you, my dear,' he said very quietly so only she could hear, 'and my wife would have approved.'

For once, the younger girls weren't sniggering and giggling and looked charming in their gymslips as they occasionally turned to whisper something to their neighbour. Anita wore a cream dress, looking more fashionable than usual, and Russell's unruly mop of red hair gleamed under a heavy-handed coating of Brylcreem. Hilary, elegant in a cherry-red wool dress, stood next to Mrs Morgan, who looked like Mother Hen in a brown tweed costume. The only ones who had no change of costume were the maids and kitchen staff but they, too, were looking particularly spruced up and smart.

But someone was missing – Stella! Where on earth was she?

The time drew nearer to eleven. There was an air of expectation. Heavy logs burned in the grate of the enormous fireplace, but the Great Hall still felt chilly and Esme wished the dress had come with a jacket. Stella was going to miss it if she didn't turn up soon. But just as Esme heard a crunching of wheels up the gravel drive, Stella rushed down the staircase in a beautiful coral suit and pushed her way to stand next to Esme, then turned to Sir Giles who was frowning and sent him an apologetic smile.

Sir Giles had told her Queen Mary always arrived everywhere in her famous green Daimler, driven by Fred

Southgate, the chauffeur, and now Sir Giles opened the heavy front door where Esme had a perfect view. She watched as the chauffeur slammed the door shut and stepped round in the teeming rain to where the Queen and her lady-in-waiting were sitting at the rear. He opened her door, holding out a huge black umbrella ready for the two women to alight. He escorted the two ladies up to the entrance porch where Sir Giles and Esme were waiting. As Queen Mary approached, Sir Giles gave a brief bow from his neck and Esme gave a practised but somewhat diminished curtsey in her straight skirt.

'Welcome to Redcliffe Manor, Your Majesty,' he said. 'I'm sorry I didn't manage to arrange better weather.'

'I'm sorry, too,' Esme heard the Queen answer with a rueful smile.

'And I believe Lady Margaret,' Sir Giles said.

Queen Mary's lady-in-waiting gave a slight nod to acknowledge her host.

A sleek black motorcar drew up behind the Daimler and the driver and another younger man emerged, then opened the rear door to help a modestly dressed young woman whom Esme presumed to be one of the lady's maids. She watched both men pull from the Daimler's boot three expensive-looking trunks and several smaller suitcases from the second motorcar.

Esme shook her head in wonderment. This was a different world. She couldn't wait to be part of it, if only for a day, and was delighted Sir Giles had insisted she accompany him throughout the royal visit.

Sir Giles took Lady Margaret's soaking rain cape from her, giving it to Dolly who was standing by to shake it out and hang it up, then he instructed the maid to show the lady's maid their rooms, and help her to unpack Queen Mary's trunks. Sir Giles led the tall, elegant Queen, still wearing her grey wraparound leather coat with fur collar, into the drawing room, with Lady Margaret close behind.

'Would you and Lady Margaret care to sit by the fire?' Sir Giles said, nodding towards the two richly upholstered, rose-patterned armchairs near where Dolly had managed to goad the fire into leaping orange flames.

'Thank you, Sir Giles,' Queen Mary said, and her lady-in-waiting nodded as they settled into the two chairs.

'Coffee should arrive very soon,' he said.

The Queen's eyes sparkled. 'That would be most welcome.'

Esme couldn't take her eyes off Queen Mary. She tried to be surreptitious but once or twice caught the Queen watching her with raised eyebrow and a slight uplift of her lips as though she were thinking:

You can't believe it's me, can you? You're pinching yourself having the Queen only feet away from you. Did you ever imagine such a thing?

Yes, Queen Mary was every inch a queen, Esme had to admit. And it wasn't just by the quality of her clothes. It was by her very stature and stiffly held back, her hair in tight silver curls framing a determined face under a fashionable hat in a plaited design with a chiffon, fan-shaped decoration standing to attention at the back. Two rows of pearls adorned the neck of her light-grey blouse with rolled collar, and in the centre was pinned a magnificent diamond brooch. Alert blue eyes gazed back at her, then turned towards Sir Giles.

'I should like to pay a visit to the Royal School for Daughters of Officers of the Army,' Queen Mary stated.

'Certainly, Ma'am,' Sir Giles responded. 'And I believe you've enquired about the American military hospital in the grounds.'

The Queen nodded. 'Indeed, I would like to visit it after lunch.'

'Yes, of course, Ma'am. What time would you like to visit?'

There was no hesitation.

'A quarter past three. The patients should be rested by then and ready to receive me.' She turned her attention to Esme. 'I imagine some of them are in a bad way.'

'I'm afraid so.' Esme's tone was grave.

'Do you have much to do with them, my dear?'

'Only that I run a trolley library service to those who aren't too badly injured by the war and who miss reading.'

'From where do you acquire your books?'

'Some from Sir Giles's library and others from Bra . . . that is . . . Colonel Parker's own book collection.' Warmth rose to her cheeks with the way Queen Mary sent her a sharp look.

For goodness' sake, the Queen's asked you a question and she wants a full reply. She's not interested in you and your romantic inclinations.

'Very interesting, my dear. I should certainly like to visit those wards.'

There was a knock at the door and Esme leapt up to open it. Dolly, smiling from ear to ear, came in with a beautifully laid tray.

'Thank you, Dolly. Can you put it on that table, please?'

Dolly set it on the table, looked in Queen Mary's direction, gave an awkward little curtsey, and keeping her attention on the Queen, bowed out of the door.

'Would you like to have a rest before lunch is served, Ma'am?' Sir Giles said.

The answer again came without hesitation.

'No, Sir Giles, I don't need to rest. I'd like to meet some of the schoolgirls after coffee. I have something important to ask them. A challenge, actually.' What looked like a sly smile crossed the Queen's face. 'But I intend to reward the most successful pupil.'

'That's very generous of you, Ma'am,' Sir Giles said.

'But Sir Giles, I insist *you* take a rest.' The Queen turned to Esme. 'Perhaps, Mrs Donaldson, *you* would like to accompany us.'

'I'd be delighted, Ma'am,' Esme said, secretly thrilled she could watch the Queen in action.

'That's settled then.' Queen Mary stretched out her arm to take the cup and saucer from Esme, who put down a plate of biscuits and the sugar bowl and hot milk. 'That shortbread looks delicious.' She dropped two sugar lumps into her cup and swirled in some hot milk, then sipped her coffee.

Half an hour passed pleasantly. The Queen wanted to know Esme's official position at Redcliffe Manor and if she enjoyed her work.

'Very.' Esme's tone was emphatic. 'We've recently moved the library from the attic to the ground floor.'

'It sounds like an enormous undertaking.' The Queen reached for a fourth shortbread. 'I'll just have this one and then we'll go.'

Voices filtered through Russell's classroom door when Esme knocked and stood aside for Queen Mary and Lady Margaret to enter. Immediately, everyone hushed and stood to attention. Even Bertha looked suitably impressed, Esme noticed, hiding a smile.

'Good morning, girls,' Queen Mary said. 'Do be seated.'

There was the shuffling of feet and clattering to unfold the seats.

'I would like to spend more time with all of you than I'm able, but I have something important to ask you.' She paused. 'Hands up if any of you collect salvage for the war effort.'

There was a mutual puzzled look from the girls. Esme saw Russell's eyebrows rise.

'Nobody?'

A few shook their heads.

'We've never really discussed it, Your Majesty,' Russell said, looking as though he wished he had.

'Well, I'm giving you all a challenge. I want everyone to take part as you're all old enough to contribute. I want you to search for old bottles, old tins, any scrap iron, paper, newspapers – anything you think possible that the Ministry of Supply can use.' She gazed round the classroom, her blue eyes missing nothing. 'That doesn't mean normal rubbish.' She glanced at Russell. 'Your teacher will guide you if you're not sure.'

'I certainly will, Ma'am,' Russell said.

One of the girls put her hand up and rose to her feet. 'Excuse me, Your Majesty, but how is all that stuff used?'

Russell looked horrified at the girl's interruption, but Queen Mary smiled.

'A worthwhile question,' the Queen said. 'Tell me your name?'

'Joan Masters.' The blushing girl sat down, ignoring the look of contempt on Bertha's face.

'Well, Joan, the Ministry is particularly desperate for scrap metal which you can find in all sorts of places – old barns and coach houses, garden sheds, rivers and ditches . . . They need it for making Spitfires. And paper is pulped for books and stationery. Bottles can be used again when they've gone through a cleaning process. And you'll have the satisfaction of doing something for the war, and I will arrange for the one who collects the most salvage to receive a prize . . . and a medal.'

There was a murmur of excitement at the mention of a prize. Highly amused, Esme noticed Bertha sit up straighter. The Queen had raised a level of competition in the class.

'Now, are there any further questions?'

Bertha's hand shot up.

'Please, Your Majesty, what will the prize be?'

Queen Mary's lips curved into a slight smile. 'And your name, my dear?'

'Bertha Newman.' Bertha's tone was impatient.

'Well, Bertha, I haven't quite decided. You will have to wait.'

'Is it money?' Bertha said, obviously not willing to let it go.

The class sniggered as they turned to stare at her. Bertha glared defiantly back at them.

Russell frowned. 'That will be all, Bertha, thank you. We will allow Her Majesty to come to her own decision in her own time without any prompting from you.'

Her mouth taking a sulky downward turn, Bertha folded her arms stiffly in front of her but made no more comment.

After a few more minutes, Queen Mary said:

'I must take my leave of you for the time being. But before I go, do you all promise to do as I ask?'

Bertha's voice rose above the rest in affirmation and with that, the Queen swept out of the door, nodding to Russell who was holding it open.

'My goodness, she's a determined woman,' he muttered under his breath.

'I admire her,' Esme said, smiling. 'She gets things done.'

Chapter Thirty-Seven

Sir Giles had requested Mrs Morgan to prepare the private dining room on the other side of the kitchen for more privacy, particularly as not only were they entertaining a Queen, but Brad Parker and his general had been invited to join the small party. Sir Giles had told Esme he would escort Queen Mary and Lady Margaret to lunch but that the Queen would be the last to enter when everyone was in their place and seated.

'There will only be seven of us,' Sir Giles had already primed her. 'Queen Mary will be seated at the head of the table with Lady Margaret on her left and you will sit next to *her* left opposite the general. Then I've put Stella next to him and the colonel will sit by the side of you – if you don't mind, of course,' he'd added with a sly grin. 'Just to break up what would have been a row of men on that side.'

Esme couldn't help smiling as she studied the table at midday, checking everything was in order by making a few minor adjustments. Extra attention had been given to the table setting and the centrepieces.

Stella's touch, Esme thought. *She's certainly kept that secret, but the table looks stunning*. She only hoped Stella would not arrive late and embarrass everyone. Thankfully, a few minutes later, Stella breezed in.

'Are we all ready?' she said.

'Yes, and you never let on that you sneaked in yesterday, I suppose, to do the table.'

'I wanted it to be a surprise.' Stella grinned. 'Right, now do we all know where we're sitting?'

'Yes, and if there's any complaints, speak to Sir Giles,' Esme laughed.

'Where are you and I?'

When Esme pointed to the two chairs, Stella said:

'And our lovely colonel?'

'Here.' Esme couldn't stop her cheeks warming.

'I see.' Stella gave her a knowing smirk.

'And you'll be entertaining the lovely general.' Esme grinned. 'At least I hope he'll be lovely.'

'So long as he's good-looking, we'll both be happy,' Stella chuckled.

At twelve-thirty, the door opened and Sir Giles strode in, his stick nowhere in sight, accompanied by whom she now knew was Brigadier General Maxwell Thomas. The general looked impressive in his uniform with the silver star on his broad shoulders gleaming under the chandeliers above, but Stella might be disappointed, Esme thought, hiding a smile. He was considerably older and several inches shorter than Brad, with steel-grey hair, prominent forehead and deep hooded eyes, though she was immediately aware of his stature within the US Army. Mouth set in a grim, resolute line, he surveyed the two women as though he were inspecting his soldiers on parade, then gave a nod that Esme hoped was approval and turned to make some comment to Brad.

The two officers came purposefully towards her and Stella.

'Mrs Donaldson, Miss Stratten, may I introduce General Thomas,' Brad said.

The general proffered his hand and Esme found it grasped in a strong handshake.

'I'm very honoured to meet you, sir.'

He greeted Stella in the same way. She gave him a beaming smile and Esme was amused to see the general's mouth twitch at the corners before releasing her friend's hand.

Sir Giles showed the two senior officers their seats before he excused himself to fetch the Queen and her lady-in-waiting.

The general chatted about his satisfaction at the way the new hospital was operating, but Esme was conscious that the four of them were waiting expectantly for the very special guests to arrive.

Finally, the dining room door opened. All eyes turned as Queen Mary regally swept in, her lady-in-waiting behind her, followed by Sir Giles. He pulled out the beautiful carver with its embroidered upholstery at the head of the table, and when the Queen was seated, did the same for Lady Margaret. Then he nodded for everyone to now take their seats and introduced Her Majesty to Brad and the general.

'I'd like to take this opportunity to show my country's appreciation for the important part your soldiers are playing in our fight against Nazism,' Queen Mary said, giving the general a charming smile.

'We couldn't stand by and let the British carry on alone, Ma'am.'

The discussion about the war went on for a minute or two until the waiter who had been hired for the occasion came to serve them with salmon and hollandaise sauce, boiled potatoes, spinach and carrots. It was a simple meal because of the rationing, but perfectly delicious.

While the Queen was talking to Sir Giles, the general caught Esme's eye.

'I believe you're giving the patients a taste of your English culture,' he said.

Esme smiled. 'I do try to find them books they could be interested in, but I wouldn't dream of forcing them to read a book by an author they've never heard of.'

'Isn't it your job to educate them?' The general raised a sardonic eyebrow.

'No, not really. They're all a bit vulnerable coping with their injuries. Something familiar that reminds them of home is probably better for their morale . . . except one young man who loves Shakespeare. In fact, he admitted his dream was to become a Shakespearean actor.'

Maybe she shouldn't have mentioned anything about Lloyd. But it had slipped out. She stole a glance at Brad sitting next to her. His mouth tightened for a second, but then he carried on eating. She was gratified Queen Mary turned her attention to the conversation.

'He sounds like an educated young man to me,' she said. 'Be sure to let me meet him this afternoon.'

'Yes, Ma'am, I certainly will.' Esme replied, hugging the thought.

Brad might be eating but she noticed he'd been listening intently.

At ten past three, Queen Mary emerged from her bedroom, erect and immaculate, having changed into a blue velvet dress, a matching hat perched on her head, as she seemed to glide down the grand staircase, followed by Lady Margaret, carrying a soft leather case. Esme was already waiting for them in the Great Hall.

'Will Sir Giles be accompanying us?' the Queen enquired.

'I'm so sorry,' Esme said. 'He's asked me if you would be kind enough to excuse him. In his words, he's had to succumb to a nap, but he'll be pleased to join us later for tea.'

'That's understandable,' Queen Mary said, 'and I'm sure you know the way, my dear.'

'Yes, Ma'am, and I'm pleased to report that it's finally stopped raining.'

'Excellent. We shan't be needing any cumbersome umbrellas.'

Lady Margaret held the Queen's leather coat open so she could slip her arms through the sleeves and after tying the belt firmly, Queen Mary said:

'Then let us go.'

Esme's boots sank into the wet, muddy grass leading to the bridge. As they crossed the lakes, she noticed the water had risen noticeably over the last few days.

'Do be careful,' she said over her shoulder to the two special visitors who were picking their way over the slimy wooden floor, Lady Margaret holding Queen Mary's arm firmly. 'It's really slippery.'

Thankfully, they arrived at the hospital entrance without any mishap. It was Stella who opened the door to them. She smiled and curtsied to Queen Mary who nodded graciously as she and Lady Margaret stepped in, with Esme following.

'I'll go and fetch Colonel Parker and the general to accompany you over the hospital, Your Majesty,' Stella said.

'There is no need, my dear.' Queen Mary smiled at Stella. 'For the moment, I'm particularly interested in the wards Mrs Donaldson mentioned, so if you ladies would like to accompany me, I should be most grateful.'

'Yes, of course, Ma'am,' Stella said.

Good, Esme thought. She wanted to speak to the Queen without the presence of the two officers.

Dear Nurse Cindy was on duty today, Esme saw with relief when they entered Ward 4. All the patients who could raise themselves in their beds sat up smartly. Bob and two others had been sitting on their bedside chairs and now stood to attention. The chief nursing officer, whom Esme had never met, stepped forward, her starched white uniform with its dark cape rustling as she gave a small neck bow to the Queen. Esme wanted to giggle when Cindy rolled her eyes, then jerked her head towards her superior.

'Welcome to our hospital, Your Majesty,' the CNO said in a precise though strong American accent that sounded as though she'd been rehearsing all morning, 'and of course Lady Margaret.' Gesturing the space of the ward with her arms, she declared they were in Ward 4. 'And next door is Ward 5 – these are two wards where the patients are recuperating.'

Queen Mary nodded and with her lady-in-waiting walked towards the furthest bed. Esme was amazed to watch as Lady Margaret opened the leather case and took out a packet of cigarettes, a pair of socks and chocolate. Then she handed them to the Queen who gave them to the incredulous soldier.

'Oh, Ma'am, thank you.'

The Queen smiled and spent a minute or so talking to him before moving on, stopping at every single bed, giving the same welcome gifts to all the patients.

'Thank you very much, Ma'am,' became almost a mantra around the ward.

'I have something else which might interest you, too,' Queen Mary said to the awed soldiers, then murmured something to Lady Margaret, who delved into the bag again and brought out half a dozen newspapers. 'It's the most current *New York Times*,' the Queen said triumphantly, 'though you'll have to pass them round as these were the only ones I could lay my hands on.'

There was a loud cheer as she gave them to Bob, who was standing. Grinning from ear to ear, he said, 'Ma'am, you can't know how much this means to us – a little bit of home – even though I don't think there's one of us here who actually comes from New York state.'

There was much laughter and the Queen beamed back. She sat on a vacant chair – the CNO's, Esme was amused to see – in the middle of the room and pulled out a gold cigarette case from her handbag. To everyone's astonishment she removed one and placed it between her lips.

'I had better be the first to light up so anyone can follow,' she said, lighting it with a gold cigarette lighter, inhaling deeply, then blowing out a half dozen perfect smoke rings.

There was a stunned silence. The CNO's jaw dropped open. A senior nurse, who'd just come into the room, halted in her tracks. The whole ward whooped and clapped, and soon there was smoke curling from every bed. The CNO coughed loudly, looking towards the Queen with unconcealed disgust. But to Esme's delight, she was either oblivious or took no notice.

'What about Lloyd?' It was Bob again. 'I'm sure he'd like cigarettes, same as all of us—' He looked pointedly at Buddy. 'And, of course, to meet Her Majesty,' he added quickly.

'Is he not here?' Queen Mary enquired.

Another hush.

'Er, no, Ma'am,' Bob said.

'Where is he?'

'He's next door,' Esme said, feeling the need to take control of where this was leading. 'In Ward 5.'

The Queen took a tiny silver ashtray from her handbag and stubbed out her cigarette. Lady Margaret put it into a brown paper bag and tucked it into her own roomy handbag.

'It sounds as though he's on his own.'

'He is, Ma'am.' Esme's heart began beating fast.

'Then we must pay him a visit.' Her tone was imperious as she rose to her feet, every inch of what must be her six-foot height, a true queen.

'Esme, would you take him this newspaper?' Bob said. 'I'll have it back when he's finished. 'Oh, and take some of my cigarettes.'

'Please be assured we have some spare packets,' Queen Mary said.

As the Queen and Lady Margaret, the latter looking anxious, followed her out of the door, Queen Mary said:

'Does this patient have something infectious?'

'Oh, no, Ma'am.' Esme opened the door and hung back to allow the Queen and Lady Margaret to pass through.

'Ah.' Queen Mary nodded as she looked towards the lone figure. 'I see.'

Lloyd Taylor was reading a poem from the book Esme had brought him. He glanced up, then gave a look of startled surprise when he saw who his visitors were.

'Ma'am, this is Lloyd Taylor,' Esme began. 'He has a complicated broken arm and was also wounded in the head. But it hasn't hurt his love of reading whatsoever.' She smiled at Lloyd.

'Good afternoon, Your Majesty,' Lloyd said, trying to straighten his back with his one good arm. 'I'm sorry I can't greet you in the proper way.'

'You just stay where you are,' Queen Mary said. 'What happened to you?'

Lloyd told her briefly how he'd been caught under fire and had been separated from his division.

'Your fellow patient, Bob, I believe his name is, asked me to give you this.' Queen Mary handed him the newspaper.

'The *New York Times*.' Lloyd's eyes were wide in astonishment. 'How wonderful.'

'And these are also for you.'

Esme was elated to see Lady Margaret pass the Queen not one, but two packets of cigarettes, two boxes of chocolates and two pairs of socks which he gratefully took with his good hand.

'I can't thank you enough, Ma'am,' he said, eyeing such luxury items spread on his counterpane.

After another minute or two chatting about poetry, Queen Mary said:

'I've very much enjoyed talking to you, Lloyd, and I wish you a speedy recovery.'

'Thank you, Ma'am.' He hesitated. 'I want you to know I will never forget meeting you as long as I live, and I will be sure that when the time comes, if I'm lucky enough to marry and have children, I will tell them, too.'

Queen Mary took his good hand in hers.

'And I thank you for coming to help Britain in her hour of need and risking your life in doing so.' She shook his hand. 'With the help of the Americans we will win this war for freedom against tyranny – no doubt about it.' She held his hand another moment or two before she let it go. 'It's been a pleasure and an honour to meet you, Lloyd,' she continued, 'and I wish you the very best of luck in the future, and also to that lucky girl you're yet to meet.'

She smiled at him and he flashed a wide grin in return.

Esme could hardly hold back the tears, and when she glanced at Stella, she noticed her friend's eyes were moist.

'I think I'm ready for a cup of tea,' the Queen announced as they left the ward.

Esme glanced at her watch. 'It's all laid on in the staff room here, unless you'd prefer to go back to the Manor, Ma'am.'

'Oh no, we'll have it here and it will give me the chance to have a word with General Thomas and Colonel Parker.'

Esme only just managed to restrain herself from hugging her.

Sir Giles had already joined the two officers who stood up, hastily stubbing out their cigarettes, and gave a neck bow as Queen Mary with Lady Margaret swept into the staff room where a table had been specially laid with refreshments. Esme's lips curled in amusement to see it looked exactly like an English country house tea-time with a Victoria sponge and plain scones with jam and cream, and sandwiches with the crusts cut off. She wondered if Cook had given the Americans any tips about how to provide tea fit for a queen. On second thoughts, this was more likely to be Stella's doing.

Queen Mary commented on the hospital and how the patients who were on the mend were enjoying Esme's trolley library service.

'So I'm told,' General Thomas commented, a blob of cream unknowingly stuck in his moustache. 'Great idea, Mrs Donaldson, and I'm sure it cheers up our fighting boys.'

'It's cheered one patient in particular,' the Queen said pointedly.

Esme saw Brad stiffen. He knew what was coming, she was sure of it. She also noticed Sir Giles's eyes were trained on the general.

General Thomas turned to her. 'Who would that be, Ma'am?'

'The coloured soldier in the ward next door.' Queen Mary focused her gaze on the general. 'He seems to be a very educated young man, although, I sense, lonely.'

'Ah, yes.' The general stopped eating his scone and looked at her. 'I know you British don't have segregation, but it's the law in the United States.' He hesitated as though wondering how to finish an uncomfortable conversation. 'I'm afraid other matters far more important in the war must take priority.'

'I'm not sure I agree.' Queen Mary's voice was noticeably cool, but General Thomas appeared not to notice. 'Doesn't the young man risk his life in the same way as all the other soldiers?'

He shook his head. 'It's our law, Ma'am. And the military are very strict that we keep it.' He paused but didn't quite meet the Queen's eye. 'Maybe one day things will change, but I'm afraid I have to say that time is in the future. For now, we must concentrate with all our might on the war and how to beat the Nazis.'

Ten minutes later, the Queen brought the meeting to an end by rising to her feet. Everyone stood while she proffered her hand to the officers. Brad thanked her for her gifts to the patients and the general added his heartfelt thanks.

'You couldn't have brought them anything more welcome, Ma'am,' Brad said.

Queen Mary gave him a gracious smile but only a brief nod to the general as he opened the door for the four women and Sir Giles.

Outside, out of Sir Giles's hearing, Queen Mary looked straight at Esme:

'I believe I can guess what you are thinking, my dear.'

Esme felt her face flush and the Queen nodded.

'I, too, cannot agree with that practice of segregation,' she continued. 'I only wish I had the power to allow that young man in with the others. But it's their law and I'm forced to respect it. An American hospital on British soil is rather like a foreign embassy. The country of the embassy, while it exists, has all the rights of their own laws. And, of course, that same applies when we're on *their* land.' She paused. 'So I would think the same pertains to this hospital.' She looked Esme in the eye. 'Besides, we don't want to do anything to cause any ripple when they're our allies and risking their soldiers' lives to help us fight the Germans.'

'I do understand, Ma'am,' Esme said miserably. 'But I think it's totally illogical and unethical.'

Queen Mary gave her a sympathetic smile. 'It will change one day, my dear. You'll see. I won't see it, but you're young – *you* will.'

If Queen Mary didn't have that sort of influence, then there was nothing more she could do, Esme thought. She'd have to be content with the Queen's parting remark. But it still rankled.

Chapter Thirty-Eight

Sir Giles was most interested to hear how it went at the hospital. Esme filled him in with the gifts the Queen had for the patients, and he roared with laughter at the picture of her lighting up a cigarette, defying the CNO's full disapproval, made worse when all the patients followed suit.

'Even *she* couldn't tell the Queen she mustn't light up,' he chuckled.

'By then the ward was filling with smoke,' Esme grinned. 'You should have seen her face. And the senior nurse's. Neither could believe what was happening in the ward and the CNO started coughing loudly. Queen Mary didn't take a scrap of notice and coolly as you please, blew out perfect smoke rings in a most unladylike way.'

'Oh, I do wish I'd been there,' Sir Giles said, still chuckling, lighting his own pipe.

Esme's smile faded. 'Yes. But you *were* there when we had tea and Queen Mary showed her disapproval – in a very polite way, of course – of Lloyd being in an isolated ward.'

Sir Giles nodded. 'I know. But we have to accept it, I'm afraid.'

'I won't ever, but Queen Mary seems to think it will change one day.'

'I'm sure it will.' Sir Giles was silent for a few moments, then asked, 'Where are our two ladies now?'

'Queen Mary said they were going to their rooms, so I imagine they're resting.'

'Then why don't you have a couple of hours to yourself before dinner,' he said.

Esme went to her room and wrote a letter to Freda, telling her of the royal visit, and how Queen Mary was organising the schoolgirls into doing their bit. When she'd finished her letter and addressed the envelope, she glanced at her watch. Nearly half past six. She hoped Mrs Morgan had sent the message to Lady Margaret that dinner was served at seven-fifteen sharp.

At dinner that evening in the private dining room, Queen Mary wanted to discuss how the war was going.

'They try to protect me at Badminton,' she said, using her fork to section off a piece of cheese soufflé, 'but having decided to make my home there with the Duchess of Beaufort – that's my niece – until this dreadful war is over, I don't wish to be ignorant of events.'

Eventually the Queen put her knife and fork together, saying she did not care for a pudding, and calmly lit a cigarette. Esme gave an inward smile to see Sir Giles looking at the cigarette enviously. The Queen caught Sir Giles's eye and nodded; he must have taken it as his cue that he could follow suit, she thought, because he immediately took out his pipe and lit it.

The rest of the evening passed quietly although Esme felt it quite a strain to be in the Queen's presence for so long at a time. Stella had primed her that you didn't start eating until the Queen did, you must stop eating immediately she stops, and you mustn't be the first to leave in her presence. Another half hour passed. Her watch showed almost eight. Then to Esme's utter relief, Queen Mary finally nodded to Lady Margaret and picked up her bag. Esme rose to her feet a fraction after the two of them.

'May I take you to your rooms?' Esme said.

'Thank you, my dear.' She glanced round. 'And thank you all for making me so welcome. I have really enjoyed my time here.'

Sir Giles leapt up to open the door and the three women disappeared.

Queen Mary, although a formidable-looking woman, was approachable, Esme thought, when she'd finally said goodnight to Stella and Sir Giles.

Her mind drifted to what would happen when the war finished, as it surely had to sooner or later. She needed something to distract her. Maybe now was the time to start reading the book Brad had given her and this time to stick with it right through to the end. She'd turn in early and have a nice long, relaxing read.

Esme had just learnt that Nick, narrating the story, is at a dinner party given by his cousin, Daisy, when he first hears the name of Jay Gatsby, a new and mysterious neighbour, when she heard an eerie sound. A wailing – a high-pitched scream . . . She shot up from her chair. *What on earth . . . ?* Dear God, it sounded like the air-raid siren! And Queen Mary was under their roof! Sir Giles was responsible for her well-being, but he slept so deeply, he might not have heard the alarm go off. Even if he had, he couldn't move quickly, hampered by his walking stick. All this was rushing through her mind as she hastily shoved her coat over her pyjamas and thrust her feet into her outdoor shoes. Just then she heard the sound of pounding footsteps, dozens of them. A girl screamed and someone urged them on. Then a shout and a bang on her bedroom door.

'Everyone to go to the cellar IMMEDIATELY!'

It was Stella's voice. *Oh, thank goodness.* Unaware of how odd she looked, Esme flung open the door.

'Stella. Wait!'

Stella turned round.

'Have you seen Sir Giles?' Esme gasped as she rushed up.

'No, I was just going to check he'd heard. You go and make sure the Queen heard it.'

Keep calm, Esme kept telling herself while the siren was still sounding that terrible wailing. *But we only have two or three minutes before the bomb drops*, tore through her brain. She must alert the Queen and make sure everyone was accounted for in the cellar.

Hilary Fenton appeared in a towelling robe looking pale and anxious. 'Going to help the teachers with the girls,' she muttered before she dashed off in her slippers.

Esme flew to Queen Mary's suite. She knocked. No answer. She tried the handle. It gave way and she opened the door, calling out, 'Your Majesty. Please come with me.'

No answer. Esme ran through the room to the bathroom, but there was no one. She flew next door where her lady-in-waiting had been allocated, not bothering to knock, and burst in.

Lady Margaret, still in her dressing gown, was putting her shoes on.

'Lady Margaret, we must go down to the cellar – NOW!'

Esme's reply was swallowed up by a loud cracking noise above them as though the ceiling was about to fall in.

'I must find Her Majesty!' Lady Margaret's voice was shrill. 'The Germans may be trying to kill her!'

And then the two women stood riveted as the drone of aeroplanes, hardly registering as a hum in the distance, were suddenly overhead. *BANG!* The room lit up – a harsh light, far brighter than daytime. Esme was about to step over to the window to find out what was happening when the beautiful Georgian pane crashed into the room. Crying out, she jumped aside as the glass shattered over the floor. It had missed her by seconds. She could feel the Manor shaking under her feet. A roar of guns. And then the room was plunged into darkness. A minute later the room filled with black smoke.

'Lady Margaret, where are you?' Esme coughed out the words, putting her hand to her mouth.

'H-here.' The voice trembled.

'Are you hurt?'

'I don't think so.'

Esme turned slowly as though she were in space, treading like a blind person, one arm out in front, the other keeping her hand over her mouth, towards Lady Margaret's voice. The glass eerily tinkled under her shoes. With relief she felt the woman's arm.

'Have you seen the Queen?' Lady Margaret's voice sounded as choked as her own.

'No. She's not in her room. But she's very sensible. Someone will have helped her.' Esme gave the woman's arm a pull. 'We'll die of this smoke if we don't get out of here now.'

'I'm responsible for her,' Lady Margaret said, coughing. 'I must look up here first.'

'No, we have to get to the cellar. Someone will have helped her,' she repeated.

With Lady Margaret still protesting, Esme grabbed hold of her arm when another bang caused them both to jump.

'Come on, Lady Margaret, I don't intend to die up here.'

Esme opened the door to the landing. Straining her eyes in the dim light, she could just about recognise where they were. But to her dismay, feathers of smoke were curling up the main staircase. Something – she wasn't going to stop to look – was already on fire.

'We'll use the back stairs,' she said, roughly grabbing the woman and running her back along the landing, then wrenching open the door leading to the maids' staircase.

Thankfully, the narrow curving wooden steps carried on

down to the cellar where three schoolgirls clattered in front of the two women. And there in the main room sat Queen Mary in her blue velvet dress, hatless now, but her pearls still strung round her neck, looking as regal as ever and as though she were receiving visitors. Esme half expected to see a tiara perched on her upswept grey curls as she looked up from her crossword puzzle.

'There you are, Margaret – and Esmeralda, too. I was beginning to worry about you both. These air raids are such a nuisance.'

But the Queen's next words struck fear into Esme's heart.

'Is Sir Giles with you?'

Esme's stomach gave a sickening lurch.

'No, Ma'am. We thought he'd be here.'

Queen Mary shook her head. 'No one appears to have seen him.'

'Stella was going to find him when the siren first sounded,' Esme said. 'I don't see her either.'

More schoolgirls descended into the cellar together with Mrs Morgan, Cook, the maids, Hilary Fenton, Russell and Anita. The two teachers were busily checking against the register that all the pupils were present. Still no sign of Sir Giles. Esme swallowed hard. He was her employer. He'd given her the job. But she was very fond of him for himself. Then to her relief, she heard Sir Giles's voice coming down the stairs, followed by Stella's lighter one.

'He was phoning the fire brigade,' Stella said, gasping for breath, 'so they should be here shortly.'

Sir Giles nodded towards Queen Mary in the now-crowded cellar, the girls all talking at once.

'I'm so sorry you've had to go through all this, Ma'am, but I trust you haven't come to any harm.'

'None at all,' was the Queen's gracious comment. 'But we're very relieved to see *you* . . . and Stella.'

One of the girls suddenly shouted above the din:

'Has anyone seen Bertha?'

The room hushed.

'Bertha!' called Russell. 'If you're hiding, come out. It's not a game and you know it.'

But nothing stirred. No one spoke. Esme held her breath. Surely Bertha wasn't being so foolish as to horse around when this was a real air raid.

'Anyone have any idea where she might be?' Russell said, his voice now thick with alarm.

One of the other girls in Bertha's class called out, 'She told me not to let on – she made me promise.'

'Linda,' Hilary's voice was stern. 'Tell us where she is.'

Linda's reply was muffled by a sob. And then Esme's blood ran cold when she heard the girl say, 'She said she was going down to the lakes.'

'Oh, that silly child,' Hilary Fenton burst out.

A split second later there was an almighty explosion! The cellar trembled. Everyone except Queen Mary jumped and several of the girls let out a scream.

Esme didn't hesitate. She made for the door.

'Stop!' Queen Mary raised her hand. 'Where are you going, Esmeralda?'

'To find Bertha, Ma'am,' Esme tossed over her shoulder.

'You will stay here,' the Queen demanded, but Esme had already shot out of the door. She flew up the cellar stairs and into the Great Hall where the smoke was thicker than ten minutes ago. Her eyes stinging, she tried to pull the solid oak entrance door towards her. It didn't budge. Now using both hands, she tugged with all her might and with what sounded like a dying groan, the door gave. *Oh, thank God.*

Esme tore down to the lakes and even though she wore her

sensible shoes, they kept getting stuck in the rain-sodden grass. Once, she almost overbalanced. Frantic now, and cursing under her breath, she twisted her head right and left as she ran, desperate for a glimpse of Bertha. But there was sign of the schoolgirl. Finally, gasping and coughing, Esme reached the bridge spanning two of the lakes.

'Bertha!' she shouted. 'Where are you?'

No sound. Nothing.

She flew onto the bridge – and then it happened. The wooden floor was slippery and with a cry she fell in a heap. Agonising pain tore at her ankle as she tried to struggle up. Dear God, had she broken something? From her slumped position, she shouted again. A rustle through the long grass. She cocked her ear. What was that? It sounded more like an animal in distress than a human being. The whimper came again. Human. It must be Bertha. But where was she? Esme managed to pull herself upright, trying to ignore the knife-like stabbing in her ankle as she did so.

'Bertha! Where are you?' she bellowed.

'Help me!' The voice was thin in the cold, damp night air.

Dear Lord, she was in the water.

'Hold on, Bertha, it's Mrs Donaldson. I'm coming.'

'Help! Please help!'

Esme squinted through the dark. The voice was coming from her right. Not caring, she flung off her coat, yanked off her shoes, and jumped in. Immediately, the freezing cold water penetrated her pyjamas as though she was naked. Trying not to think, not to feel, to ignore the pain in her ankle, she swam towards the voice. Thank God. The outline of Bertha's head bobbed up but then disappeared. She *must* get there in time. Sick with worry that the girl hadn't emerged, Esme grimly struck out more forcefully. Oh, there was her head! She reached out to seize Bertha's arms, but the girl slipped through her fingers and went under again.

Esme took a gulp of air and dived down into the lake that was much deeper than she'd realised. She *had* to grab hold of her this time or Bertha would surely drown. She felt a limb and clutched it. The leg kicked and thrashed as Esme hung on, using every ounce of her strength to push them both up to the surface.

'Stop wriggling and hold onto me,' Esme told her. 'We're not far from the bank.'

Bertha felt like a dead weight with her outdoor clothes weighing them both down. Gritting her teeth, and with all the strength she could muster, Esme hauled Bertha onto the lake edge, dragging her a few feet to safety and cradling her head. Bertha was silent but her chest was heaving. Esme was shivering violently but managed to roll Bertha onto her side, then, her ankle protesting, bent to thump her on the back. A gush of watery vomit spewed from Bertha's mouth. Esme felt her go limp.

'Bertha, speak to me! Are you all right. Just say "yes".'

And to her joy Bertha gave a grunt that sounded like yes.

'Can you stay there while I fetch someone to carry you back to the house?' Esme said.

'Yes.' This time the word was distinct.

'I promise I won't be long.'

Esme straightened up then suddenly felt light-headed. No, she mustn't faint. She had to get help. But as her world collapsed on top of her, she imagined she heard Brad's voice calling her name – 'Esme. Esme, darling, where are you?'

She screamed his name, but it was lost in another explosion. A heavy black blanket was smothering her. She was powerless to struggle under its weight. With a deep sigh, she gave herself up to it.

Chapter Thirty-Nine

What . . . where on earth am I? What's that smell?

TCP – or was it disinfectant? Esme gingerly turned her head to the right on the starched white pillowcase. A wall was bearing down on her. She closed her eyes again and slowly turned to the other side where a nurse sat close by. A nurse who looked vaguely familiar. She immediately rose from her chair.

'Esme, you're awake at last.'

'Wh-where am I?'

'In hospital.'

'Oh. I know you, don't I?' Esme shook her head as though to shake through her memory box.

'Yes, you do. It's Cindy.'

'Ah, yes. Nurse Cindy.'

Every bone, every muscle ached. Her ankle was throbbing.

'Have I had an accident?'

'Yes.'

'What happened?'

Cindy frowned. 'You rescued that foolish girl in the Manor from drowning . . . and then you fainted.'

Esme rubbed her forehead. 'Oh yes, Bertha. There was a fire . . . but she was in the lake.' She closed her eyes, trying to remember what happened. It was all so confusing.

Her lids flew open. 'Is Bertha all right?'

'She is, thanks to you,' said a dear familiar voice. A husky masculine voice with an American accent.

Cindy sprang from her chair. 'I'll leave you to it, Dr Parker, but please don't overtire the patient.'

'I'll be sure not to, Nurse.' Brad smiled at Cindy. 'Perhaps you could fix us a tea?' He looked at his watch. 'Breakfast will be over, but if you can rustle up a couple of slices of buttered toast.'

'Coming up, Doctor.' She vanished.

Brad looked down at Esme. 'How are you feeling?'

'I'm not sure,' Esme said. 'I've only just this minute woken up.' She looked at him, noticing his eyes were full of concern. 'How long have I been here?'

'Since last night.'

She tried to sit up and would have fallen back onto the pillow if Brad hadn't put out a restraining hand. He held his hand on her back while he plumped up the pillows behind her, then gently eased her into what felt like a comforting embrace of billowing clouds.

'What time is it?'

He glanced at his watch. 'Nine thirty-five.'

'Oh, no, I must get up.'

'Just relax, Esme. You're in no condition to go anywhere just yet. You've had quite a shock and need to rest. I'll sign you off tomorrow if I'm satisfied you're completely well.'

Esme sighed as she settled back on the pillows. 'But Bertha's safe.'

'Yes, she is, thanks to you.' Brad frowned. 'But she nearly had you both drowned.'

'Where is she now?'

'Back at the Manor. I sent one of the doctors to check her and make sure she was all right.'

'Thank goodness,' Esme said. She looked at Brad. 'We mustn't go on at her. All children that age are foolhardy.'

'She's not a child – she's old enough to know better so let's hope she's learnt her lesson this time.' Brad's tone was sour as he sat on the chair Cindy had vacated. 'I'd just like to know what she was doing going out after hours on her own to the lake.'

'I expect Russell will ask her for an explanation,' Esme said mildly. And then it struck her. When Brad had heard the air-raid siren, was it possible he'd come to see if she was safe? But instead of her being in the Manor, he'd come across her and Bertha on the bank of one of the lakes. He was the one she'd heard call her name. He'd come to the rescue. And just now she'd been defending Bertha and not even mentioned thanking him. Then her face felt hot. He'd called her 'darling'. She was sure of it. Or was it simply wishful thinking? Just her imagination running wild.

'Brad?'

'Yes?'

Esme swallowed hard. 'You found us. How can I ever thank you enough?'

'Think nothing of it.' He grinned at her. 'All in the line of duty.'

She stared at him. 'Perhaps. But what made you come out in the first place?'

His grin faded. He caught her gaze. She felt she could read what he was thinking.

'I heard the siren. I was worried that there might be someone trapped in the house who would need medical help. You had your Queen staying. It wouldn't have looked too good if anything had happened to her. Or' – his eyes didn't leave her face – 'someone might be missing. And I was right. *You* were missing. And I was determined to find you. But when I ran across the bridge, I stumbled upon the pair of you on the bank. You'd fainted and Bertha had recovered enough to tell me how you'd saved her life. Apparently, she was trying to pull something out of the lake – I can't imagine what – and fell in, coat and all. That was what was weighing her down. I'm assuming she can't swim. And you pulled her to safety.' He hesitated. 'Do you remember?'

'I do now.'

'You were taking a risk.'

Esme's eyes widened. 'No, Brad. I'm a good swimmer. There was no risk.' She sighed.

'Hmm. I'm not so sure. The water was freezing.' He studied her. 'The main thing is that you're safe. But there is one thing I must talk to you about, Esmeralda.'

'You sound serious.'

He hesitated. 'I am concerned as to why you fainted.'

'Wasn't it from the explosion?'

'I don't think so.' Brad paused and glanced at her. 'You got Bertha to safety but couldn't summon the energy to get to the Manor. You were obviously in shock not just with plunging into such cold water, but it was as though your body couldn't take any more stress.' He shook his head. 'Most people's adrenalin would see them through the emergency and they might possibly feel they would need to rest afterwards from the shock, but it's always wise to do a test if they actually pass out for longer than a minute. You *did* come round, but it was quite a bit longer and then you went into a normal sleep. That's when I ran some tests.'

Esme waited in silence, guessing what was coming next.

'Your heart shows there's some scarring of your heart valves which leads me to believe that you've had rheumatic fever.' He looked at her. 'Am I right?'

She nodded.

'Esmeralda, it's not the best time to ask you, but as your doctor, were you ever warned there's a weakness there and it might be wise not to do certain things?'

'Yes.' Her voice was a whisper.

'You don't need to tell me now, but perhaps tomorrow we can have a private chat.'

'All right.'

What could she tell him? Dear God, if it hadn't been for that bomb, things might have been so different. Esme closed her eyes against the vision of her lifeless little dark-haired daughter the nurse had briefly shown her before she was whisked away. She swallowed hard. Was this going to be how she would have to come clean that she'd been warned never to get pregnant again? In what would be a strictly clinical conversation? But maybe that was the better way with no emotion attached.

'Have Queen Mary and Lady Margaret gone home today as they'd planned?' she said, mostly for something to say to hide her confusion.

'Yes. She asked about you, but you were out like a light.'

Esme clicked her tongue. 'Oh, I do wish I'd known. I would like to have thanked her and said goodbye.'

'It can't be helped. You'll have to write her a note. I'm sure she'll be relieved to know you're okay.' He smiled. 'I really liked your Queen. She was quite something. You wouldn't want to be on the wrong side of her, but she demanded respect. All the schoolgirls were in awe of her – even that little brat, Bertha.'

'So was I,' Esme smiled back. Then her smile faded. 'Oh Brad, I haven't asked you about the Manor. The beautiful staircase.'

'Sir Giles acted fast and called the fire department and the fire trucks came in record time. It was barely touched. Those houses were built to go through all sorts of upheavals.'

Esme bit her lip. 'You'd think I would have heard all those clanging bells.'

He shook his head, then held her eye. 'You were already well out of it, my love.'

Esme startled. *My love.* Then it hadn't been her imagination. He *must* have called her 'darling'. Everything was becoming too complicated. Her heart hadn't wanted to take any further strain when she'd been so frightened that Bertha was in danger in the

326

freezing-cold water. She just hoped to God she hadn't caused her heart any further damage.

Looking up at Brad, she saw for the first time what she'd thought was simply warm concern in his eyes, but she saw something more. It was a question. She didn't dare put into words what the question might be.

Her voice sounding to herself a little shaky, she asked, 'Was there any other damage from the bombs?'

'Unfortunately, yes. A bomb dropped onto the coach house, and it needs substantial repairs.' He gave a heavy sigh. 'The war felt a tad too close yesterday evening.'

Esme shivered. 'It's not the first time the war has felt close.'

He gave her a sharp look. 'What do you mean?'

She hesitated, then said, 'I was caught in a bombing raid in London during the Blitz.'

Brad's eyes widened. 'Dear God. I didn't know. Were you hurt?'

'Not much at the time.' She heaved a sigh. 'It doesn't matter now. So many people have had worse to put up with.' She parodied the words she'd said so often. 'I'm just worried about how Sir Giles will cope,' she added.

'Luckily, he'll be well insured,' Brad said. 'And I've told him our builders here are pretty well finished, so I've already sent two of them over to assess the damage.' He stood up. 'I have to go, Esmeralda, but I'm so relieved to see you've come through fairly well unscathed.' He bent over to brush his lips to her cheek. 'They're keeping you in tonight and if all goes well, you'll be back at the Manor tomorrow. But don't forget we're going to have a serious word tomorrow.'

'I won't forget.' She gave him a thin smile. 'Thank you for coming to see me.'

'You're more than welcome.' He turned and waved at the door. 'Just rest. Do as I say – as I am now your official doctor. If you don't behave yourself, you'll have *me* to deal with.' He tapped his chest with his fingers. 'Get some sleep now and I'll see you in the morning.'

Esme fingered the place where he'd kissed her. Had he noticed how hot it felt when his lips touched her skin? She was almost certain he had the same feelings for her that she did for him. But that didn't stop him from being a married man who had no business to be falling for another woman even if he wasn't particularly happy with his wife. Everyone goes through bad patches in marriage but that didn't mean it excused infidelity.

She shook herself. She might have it all completely wrong. Maybe he really was just a concerned doctor doing his duty. After all, they were the words he'd used a few minutes ago when he'd told her how he'd gone to find her. Sighing, she felt her eyelids closing. There was nothing more she could do or think until she saw Brad tomorrow.

'Hope I'm not too early for you,' Stella said that afternoon, bending to kiss Esme's cheek. She dumped a canvas bag on the nearest chair. 'I've brought some clothes for you, so you look decent when you leave here. Oh, and your handbag. A woman is lost without that.'

'Oh, thanks. It's lovely to see you,' Esme smiled as her friend pulled up a chair.

'You gave us all a dreadful fright,' Stella said. 'Thank goodness Brad thought to telephone us from the hospital. He didn't tell us much more, only that he'd brought you here to rest and keep an eye on you.'

Esme filled her in with as much as Brad had told her.

'How terribly romantic,' Stella exclaimed.

'Stella, get romance out of your head. He was doing his duty. In fact, when he first heard the alarm, he was worried about the Queen.'

Stella grinned. 'I can just imagine Brad dragging Queen Mary out of bed, though she'd probably love it,' she giggled. 'Instead, there she sat, fully dressed, her pearls still round her neck, not a hair out of place, doing the crossword as cool as you please.'

'I know. I saw her . . . totally calm and collected.' She glanced at her friend. 'You know, Stella, she is rather marvellous.'

'I agree, but enough of the Queen,' Stella said. 'How are *you*?'

'I'm all right now.' She wouldn't mention the heart issue or Stella might let it spread to Sir Giles's ears and he might think she should perhaps give up her job. It was different with Brad. He was now her doctor.

'Well, let's hope our Dr Parker will sign you off after a day or two's rest,' Stella said. 'By the way, I asked Sir Giles for Freda's telephone number and let her know about the fire and that you're all right.'

'You're a pal.'

Stella grinned, then glanced at her watch. 'I'd better go. They'll be wondering where I've got to.' She jumped up, blew a kiss at the doorway and was gone.

Esme drifted in and out of sleep and woke up to Cindy bringing her a cup of tea – lukewarm and weak. She swallowed it quickly before it went stone cold. Cindy had apologised she needed to go to the other patients and now Esme was in the small room on her own.

This is how poor Lloyd must feel all the time.

She sighed, wondering when Brad would come in to check on her. It was so quiet just lying here thinking. If only Stella had brought her a book to read. *No wonder the patients had pounced on the trolley library*, was her last thought before she once again fell asleep.

Chapter Forty

Next morning, after breakfast, Brad came in. He had the same serious look as he'd had yesterday evening when he'd mentioned her heart. *Oh, please don't let it have developed into anything more serious.* She braced herself as he came towards her, and to her relief, he smiled.

'Did you sleep?'

'On and off, but yes, I did.'

'Good. I can only stay a minute as I'm in the theatre this morning, so if you feel up to it—'

'Yes, please tell me the results.'

'They showed me what I suspected yesterday – that the rheumatic fever you had has left a scar on your heart. But nothing more ominous than you already know. You don't need undue strain or stress, but you can live a perfectly natural life – swimming, playing tennis – whatever your hobbies are, though I'm afraid you'll never be the girl on the flying trapeze.' He kept a straight face.

'Another dream that won't come true then.' She chuckled.

He grinned. 'I shall want to know all about those dreams, but not now . . . I must go, but I'll be back later today and we can have a proper talk.'

He kissed her mouth this time and hesitantly, she responded.

He stood and smiled down at her. 'That's better. All you need to do now is rest.'

Esme hoped Brad would come and see her that evening to continue where they'd left off. But he didn't have the right to kiss her again. Nor did she by responding when she should have pushed him away. But her lips had felt so right under his – just as they had done before. Waves of remorse washed over her as she sat up in bed, sipping her cup of coffee. She didn't like herself very much where Brad was concerned. He was married and that should have been the end of it. And to boot, she was beginning to feel like a fraud. It was time to get dressed and go back to the Manor – immerse herself in work. At the thought, she felt a little better. Draining her cup, she put it in the saucer and onto her bedside table when she heard someone come in. Elated at the thought Brad had come back sooner than she'd expected, she jerked her head round to see a dark-haired woman in a pristine white coat walking towards the bed.

'Mrs Donaldson?'

'Yes, that's me.'

'Dr Parker's been called away on an emergency and I'm afraid it's going to be a long one.' The woman's accent was distinctly American. 'He's asked me to pass you the message that he'll see you tomorrow.'

Esme swallowed her disappointment.

'I'm Dr Lorrimer, specialising in cardiography.'

Esme immediately felt the culprit – her heart – plummet. Dr Lorrimer's expression on her pleasant features struck her as serious.

'I want to examine you,' the doctor said.

'I understand Dr Parker already did that last night when he

first brought me in.' She felt her cheeks warm as she pictured what a spectacle she must have made in a dead faint in Brad's arms.

'Yes, I know.' Dr Lorrimer's voice was impatient. 'But he wants me to do it again, so if you'll allow me . . .'

Without bothering to hear any reply, Dr Lorrimer put the headset of her stethoscope to her ears, adjusting it, and placed the chest piece on Esme's upper body. From time to time she moved the chest piece around, all the while listening intently. When she'd finished, she removed the stethoscope without speaking.

Esme pulled in her stomach to prepare for an answer she wouldn't like. 'Is it all right, doctor?'

'As expected.'

Esme stiffened. 'What did you expect?'

'Why do you ask? Do you have anything further to report? Any symptoms of breathlessness, dizziness . . . ?'

'No, nothing.'

'Good. And this rheumatic fever—' Dr Lorrimer looked Esme in the eye. 'Did any doctor ever tell you not to conceive as it might strain your heart?'

'Yes,' she muttered.

'And did you keep to that?'

'No.'

'So you had a baby. When was that?'

'Two years ago.' Esme's voice was hardly a whisper. 'It was stillborn.'

Dr Lorrimer scribbled something down in her notepad. Then she looked up.

'Did you try for another one?'

'My husband was already d-dead before our baby was born,' Esme said, desperately trying to keep it on formal terms, 'and I never met anyone else I wanted to spend the rest of my life with.'

Other than Brad. She forced the thought away.

'I'm sorry to hear about your husband.' Dr Lorrimer was still writing in her pad. She looked up. 'Was he killed in the war?'

'Not exactly,' Esme said shortly. 'He was in the RAF, but he died from a brain tumour.'

'How tragic.' She stared at Esme quite openly. 'Well, if you *do* meet someone else, I advise you to carry on with that doctor's advice and not risk becoming pregnant again.' She snapped her pen back on the clipboard. 'There are other ways of becoming a parent. You might adopt, for instance.'

Esme flinched. Adopting a child would be a wonderful thing to do, but she couldn't help worrying that it would always be a reminder that she would never have her own baby. She swallowed the tears that threatened.

'Thank you, doctor. I will bear it in mind.'

'See that you do.' Her gaze softened. 'I don't mean about adopting, but about trying for a baby.'

Esme felt her heart beat fast. 'May I ask you one thing, Dr Lorrimer?'

'Yes.'

'Please don't say anything to Dr Parker about the baby. I don't want him to know.'

'You have my word.' That piercing look again. Then with a crackle of her starched white coat, Dr Lorrimer spun on her heel and disappeared, leaving Esme in an emotional whirl.

Esme awoke after a restless night and looked at her watch. Twenty past six. Her stomach gnawed with hunger. She sat up in bed, remembering the way Dr Lorrimer had spoken to her so matter-of-factly. For a few moments, she allowed herself to wallow in self-pity.

Stop this at once, her inner voice reprimanded. *The doctor was being professional – doing her job. Concentrate on today. Just get dressed and let Sir Giles see you're up and about and ready to do what you're paid to do – work for him.*

Impatiently, Esme flung back the covers and was about to thrust her feet into her slippers when there was a tap at the door. A young, smiling nurse she hadn't seen before came in.

'Good morning, Mrs Donaldson. I'm Nurse Fisher. It's real nice to see you're awake. Are you ready for breakfast? If so, I can bring it before you get dressed.'

'I'm more than ready,' Esme smiled, getting back under the bedcovers.

'But first, I want to take your temperature.' She popped a thermometer under Esme's tongue. After a minute she peered at it. 'It's regular.'

'Do you mean "normal"?'

'Exactly.' She smiled. 'I'll be back shortly with breakfast.'

Nurse Fisher was back in minutes with a breakfast tray containing not one, but two peeled boiled eggs loose on the plate, two rounds of buttered toast and a saucer with a good teaspoon of jam. What a treat when eggs were rationed at only one a week! And although she would have preferred tea, the coffee was much better than at the Manor. She tucked into her meal and gratefully poured a second cup of coffee from the pot.

'Can you please let Dr Parker know that I'm going home this morning?' Esme said when the nurse came to take her tray.

'I will, but he'll have to sign you off. He won't be along until midday.'

Esme wasn't going to wait until then. But she wasn't going to tell Nurse Fisher that.

When the nurse had disappeared, Esme washed and dressed in record time and put her toiletries together. She buttoned her coat, retrieved her handbag from the cupboard in the bedside table and guiltily, stealthily, let herself out of the side door, thankful she was able to walk at quite a speed in spite of her stiff ankle.

Sir Giles looked up from his desk where he was awkwardly writing with his deformed hand.

'Esme! How delightful to see you up and looking – if I may say so – much better than the last time I set eyes on you when Brad took you to the hospital.' Then his voice was one of concern as she came towards him. 'What happened to your leg?'

'Oh, just a sprained ankle. It's much better now.' She sat on one of the visitors' chairs.

He gave an ironic smile before lighting his pipe. 'Join the club.'

She smiled back.

'Do you remember Queen Mary and me coming to see you?'

'No, I don't remember anything until I woke up in the hospital room not knowing where I was, let alone what I was doing there.'

'Well, Russell carried Bertha back here – she's in the sanatorium with a nurse looking after her – and Brad carried you back to the hospital. We've all been terribly anxious about the two of you.'

'Don't be with me. I'm well now. But do you know how Bertha is?'

Sir Giles stroked his beard. 'I haven't seen her. Wasn't sure it was my place. But Russell's been. Apparently, she's developed a bad cold and they're worried about it turning into pneumonia.'

'I wouldn't be surprised.' Esme grimaced. 'It might not be my place either, but I think I'll go and look in after a couple of hours on your memoir – if that's all right with you, Sir Giles?'

'Yes, of course, but why not go now.'

Chapter Forty-One

As Esme made her way to the West Wing, she tried to work out the best way to handle Bertha.

Hilary and Russell need to know why she disobeyed school rules and went out after supper when she was supposed to be in bed asleep, Esme thought. The accident should not have happened because Bertha would have heard the air-raid siren and rushed down to the cellar with her class.

She came to the door marked *Sanatorium*, knocked and opened it to a room with six narrow beds. Only one was occupied. Bertha. A nurse was standing by her bed, peering at a thermometer, then shook it. Twisting round, she nodded an acknowledgement, but not before Esme had seen the nurse's frown.

'Won't you come in, madam.' The nurse looked down at Bertha whose face was flushed as she sat propped up on several pillows. 'I'll leave you both for a few minutes.' As the nurse passed Esme, she muttered, 'I'm rather concerned as she still has a temperature so don't stay too long.'

'I won't,' Esme murmured.

'What were you whispering about?' came Bertha's wheezy voice as the nurse left.

'Just that I shouldn't stay too long as you need your rest,' Esme said as she pulled up a chair near the bed to face her.

'What's the matter with your leg?' Bertha's tone was more petulant than concerned.

'Oh, I twisted my ankle.'

'When?' Bertha narrowed her eyes.

'Oh, the other day.'

'I saw you fall on the bridge.'

Esme's eyes widened. 'You did?'

'Yes. At least from that distance I saw someone fall – so it was you?'

'Yes, it was. But that's over and done with.'

'Why have you come then – is it to tell me off? Because if so, I don't want to hear it.' She dug her fingers in her ears.

Esme gave an inward groan. Bertha didn't have a chip on her shoulder – she had a chunk out of it.

'Stop being such a child, Bertha, and take your fingers out of your ears. And no, I haven't come to tell you off.' She looked the girl in the eye. 'Why would I?'

Bertha ignored the question. Instead, she said, 'Did they tell you to come here?'

'No, I came because I wanted to see how you were. Miss Fenton and the teachers are worried about you – we all are.'

'Miss Fenton hasn't been anywhere near.' Bertha's voice was coated with bitterness. She pulled a plait forward and momentarily sucked on its end, then let it swing back. 'Mr Kingsnorth came. I suppose he wants me to thank you for saving my life.' Bertha rolled her eyes. 'He thought I couldn't swim. But all I had was a bit of cramp. I'd have been perfectly all right.'

'I'm not so sure about that,' Esme said mildly. 'When I found you, you were calling out for help.'

The girl's cheeks reddened. 'I'd have managed,' she muttered.

'Well, there's no harm done,' Esme said, 'so let's forget it.'

'It was all *her* fault anyway,' Bertha erupted.

Esme gave a start. 'To whom are you referring?'

'That Queen.'

Esme's mouth dropped open. 'Queen Mary?'

'Yes, her.'

'What has the Queen got to do with you floundering in the lake?'

'She wanted us to collect metal for the war effort.'

Esme waited for Bertha to continue, not really following how this tied up with the accident.

'The lake's a good place to find old iron and metal – I got a piece of metal bench the other day. Anyway, I could see a bicycle in there with the handlebars sticking up. Well-off people are disgusting – they chuck all sorts of things out so they can buy a new one.' Bertha gave Esme a contemptuous look as though she were challenging her for being one of those 'well-off' people.

'But I couldn't quite reach it,' Bertha rushed on as though there was now no stopping her. 'I stretched my arms out as far as I could and my fingers just touched the handlebars when I overbalanced . . . and that's when I fell in.' She bit her lip. 'And then the bloody air-raid alarm went off . . . and then I got cramp and couldn't move so I went under.'

About to reprimand Bertha for swearing, Esme heard the child's voice wobble.

Dear God. She must have been terrified.

'I'm not surprised with your heavy coat and shoes on,' Esme said, giving her a half-smile. 'And the shock of suddenly being in the cold water would have been what gave you cramp.' She tried to catch Bertha's eye, but the girl was pointedly looking away. She had to say something positive. 'You can be proud of yourself, Bertha, for wanting to do something for the war effort.'

'I didn't do it for no war effort.' Bertha swung round and glared at Esme. 'I did it to *win*. The Queen said she'd give the winner a prize for collecting the most, though she didn't tell us what, but I hoped it was money.' She sniffed. 'I wanted to beat all of them and come top. Now that drippy little creature, Yvonne, will win.' A lone tear ran down her cheek.

Curbing her instinct to put an arm round the girl, Esme said, 'Why was winning so important to you?'

Bertha rounded on her. 'Don't you understand *anything*?' Her voice rose. When Esme didn't answer, she burbled on, 'I don't speak like the other girls in case you haven't noticed. They all come from la-di-da families. I wanted to show them I was as good as them.'

'But you are anyway.'

Bertha shook her head. 'No, I'm not. I come from working class. Then my dad won a lot of money on the horses and he bought a house. Mum was so proud of it, but a year later he lost the lot gambling again so we had to sell it. And from that day, all Mum and Dad's new posh friends dumped us, so now we don't have no *suitable connections*.' She impersonated the last two words in an exaggerated, upper-class manner. 'I was lucky... or unlucky, depending on which way you look at it, that my dad fought in the Great War and was sent home an invalid. He won a medal for Bravery in the Field. They were short of officers and someone high up made him an officer. That's how the Army took me as a pupil at the school.' She drew in a breath and fixed her eyes on Esme. 'Yes, they allowed me to mix with their hoity-toity daughters of their stuffy fathers.' She sneezed three times without bothering to put her hand to her face and Esme reared back. 'I don't have one proper friend here. They all hate me because I'm working class and they're above me.'

So that's why she was a rebel. Why she showed off. She wanted to be someone. To be noticed.

Before Esme could say anything to the contrary, Bertha put her head in her hands and began to heave great sobs which turned into a coughing spasm.

Esme jumped from her chair and bent down to the girl, putting her arms round her, cradling her. For a few seconds, Bertha rested against her, then stiffened and pulled away.

'I don't want no pity.'

'I'm not pitying you,' Esme said. 'But I do now understand some of the problems you're facing. And I can assure you your classmates don't hate you. And you're not inferior in any way.'

'That's all you know.' Bertha sniffed, staring at Esme with swollen red eyes. She wiped her cheeks with her sleeve. 'You don't know anything.'

'Oh, but I do,' Esme said. 'I can see you're hurt and upset and I'd like to try to help, if I can.'

'I don't want no help from you, Mrs Donaldson. You're like all the rest of them.' She lay down and turned her face the other way. 'The only one I like in this whole place is Dr Parker. He always treats me nicely even if he don't have much time for me because he's so busy helping the soldiers.' She broke into fresh sobs.

Esme unbent from her squatting position and looked down at the troubled girl. There was no point in trying to talk to her further because she obviously wasn't feeling well if she still had a temperature.

'I'll leave you to rest,' she said.

With the words 'suit yourself' echoing in her ears, Esme let herself out of the door, almost colliding with the same nurse coming in.

'How was she?' the nurse said.

'Not very cooperative,' Esme said. 'She seems to think we all hate her, which is nonsense.'

The nurse's smile was kind. 'I'm sure she'll be fine when her fever breaks.'

Esme walked towards Sir Giles's study feeling quite shocked at Bertha's outburst. She let out a long sigh. There didn't seem any way to get through to the child that a posh voice and a public-school education were not necessarily the prerequisites for finding fulfilment and happiness in life. But how to convince her?

She looked at her watch. She'd been gone less than ten minutes. She passed the dining room where she could hear the girls on their morning break. Impulsively, she opened the door and to her relief saw Russell standing and chatting with Hilary. They stopped and Russell smiled at her as she walked up to them.

'So you're back on your feet after your unexpected excursion,' Hilary said.

Why did the woman always have to sound prickly, Esme wondered. Then to her surprise, Hilary added:

'Well done, anyway. It could have ended in a disaster.'

'I'll second that.' Russell's smile was broad. 'Let's go and sit at a table on our own. Let the girls have a natter without us around for a change . . . and I'll get us some coffee.' He darted off towards the hatch opening into the kitchen.

Hilary looked at her watch. 'I've only got a few minutes because I must get back. Anita's not in today and I need a bit of time to go through the lesson she's left me.' She looked round at the tables. 'Let's take that one.'

'I managed to cajole them into giving us a few biscuits,' Russell said, grinning as he came back with a full tray and set out the steaming cups. He glanced at Esme. 'I don't suppose you've seen Bertha, have you?'

'Yes, just now.'

'And?'

'She wasn't very cooperative to start with, but the nurse said she still has a temperature, so I think she's feeling particularly sorry for herself.'

'Oh dear.' Russell took a swallow of coffee. 'She's not an easy child and can be very disruptive. Quite frankly, I don't know what the answer is.'

'She thinks everyone hates her – including her classmates.'

Russell and Hilary both turned to her in surprise.

'Does she really believe that?' Hilary said.

'Yes, and I now understand the reason.'

When Esme explained why Bertha had gone to the lakes in the first place, and why she so badly wanted to win, the other two fell silent.

'It doesn't appear that she's had any visitors except you, Russell,' she said.

'Well, several of the girls wanted to see her, but I wouldn't allow them to. I didn't want them to end up with bad colds or worse.' He blew out his cheeks. 'At least we now know the reason.' He glanced at the two women. 'But what next?'

'You've just said that some of the girls wanted to see her,' Hilary said. Russell nodded. 'Then I have an idea. Why don't I get them to make a giant get-well card in the Orangery tomorrow when we have our next art class.'

'That's a really good idea,' Russell said, his face relaxing with relief.

'And not just sign their names,' Hilary said, warming to her theme, 'but putting a special note underneath that they've missed her, or wish her a speedy recovery, or something like that. And I'll pop in later and see her. I'd planned to go earlier but I'm standing in for Anita.'

'I think she'd appreciate it, Hilary.' Russell gazed at the housemistress as though about to say something more but closed his mouth. Instead, he beamed at her. 'Thank you.'

Mmm. Esme hid a smile. Maybe Russell was seeing Hilary in a new light.

Esme felt happier as she went back to Sir Giles's study, hoping he'd be there so she could tell him about Bertha. But it was empty. Maybe he was in the library. She put her head in the door but that was empty too. While she was there, she thought she'd tidy up the shelves, not for the first time thinking how generous Sir Giles was to let the schoolgirls and anyone else interested borrow books except those under lock and key. Some of the authors in the fiction section were out of order and she automatically righted them.

Little Women had been put on the wrong shelf. She clicked her tongue as she made to put it with the 'A's when it occurred to her it might be the perfect book for Bertha. Just then the door opened and Sir Giles lumbered in with his stick.

'There you are, Esme,' he said. 'Come and sit down and tell me how you got on with Bertha. Was she awake?'

'Yes, but she does have a temperature, so I didn't stay long.' Once again, she recounted to him Bertha's problem.

'It sounds as though she's lost all confidence,' he said with a wry smile. 'Rather like me not wanting to do any more mountaineering.'

Esme threw him a sympathetic smile.

'I thought I'd take this book to her to read,' she said. 'It's *Little Women*, though I just hope it won't give her any more ideas when she reads Jo's escapades.'

Sir Giles smiled. 'Yes, she really was a tomboy, wasn't she. But it's a wonderful classic. I think she'd enjoy it.'

Esme's eyebrows shot up. 'You know it?'

'Yes, from that one you're holding. It's pretty ancient. I read it when I was eleven because I longed for a sister and that was the closest I was ever going to get!' He looked at Esme. 'Talking of mountaineering . . . or rather *I* did . . .' Sir Giles hesitated. 'You know, Esme, I thought I'd finished my memoirs, but I changed my mind and added another piece.' His tone was almost apologetic. 'I think it's a fitting conclusion. But I don't know what you'll think – whether I should include it or not. If you say not, I won't.'

'Sounds intriguing,' Esme smiled. 'The last time you didn't want to include something, I practically forced you to do it. Are you saying I've got to do the same again?'

He gave her a shadow of a smile.

'No, no. You'll know what I mean when you read it.' He refilled his pipe. 'It's in my desk. I don't want you to bother with it until you've finished typing the main manuscript which I realise might not be for another week or so.' He studied her for a few seconds. 'But first – have you eaten, because it's lunchtime?'

Esme's stomach rumbled in response. The two biscuits hadn't assuaged her hunger.

'I suppose I should have something.'

'Then we'll have some lunch brought here. I'll ring the bell to order it.'

Chapter Forty-Two

After lunch, Sir Giles decided he would have a nap. Esme settled at the typewriter and worked her way through another ten pages. She was coming to the end. Only thirty or so pages to go and that would be it. It was always slow-going to read Sir Giles's awkward handwriting even though she was getting more used to it. After two hours solid, she stood up for a few minutes, rubbing her neck, trying to get the circulation back in the chilly room. She went over to feel the radiator. It was barely lukewarm. No wonder she felt cold. She licked her lips. *Oh, for a cup of tea.* Well, she'd give herself a break for half an hour. As Sir Giles mentioned, she wouldn't be able to finish the main body of his memoir for several more days. And she'd have her tea in the library for a change of scenery.

To her relief, no one was in the kitchen although an enormous saucepan on the stove emitted a lovely smell of cloves and apples. Cook must be making her famous apple purée – so delicious on porridge. She and the assistants usually started again just before five. Esme boiled the kettle on the enormous stove which one of the kitchen maids had assiduously blacked that morning. She poured the water over the scant amount of tea leaves in a small teapot, conscious of the severe rationing of tea – now only two ounces of tea for one person a week. It was a good thing Cook couldn't accuse her of using up the sugar allowance as well, Esme thought wryly, as she helped herself to a couple of plain biscuits from the tin marked: *DO NOT TOUCH*.

Balancing the tea tray with one hand, she opened the door to what had been the Munitions Room, startled to see Brad sitting in the leather visitor's chair. He shot to his feet, giving her one of his smiles that made her heart melt like wax, but the lines round his eyes had deepened and he looked weary.

'Sorry I wasn't able to warn you when I was coming, but it's been a pretty hectic day and I'm done in.'

'You don't have to apologise. Dr Lorrimer was very efficient.'

'Yes, she is.'

Don't let her have said anything about my baby. I want to tell you myself when it's the right time.

'Here, let me take that tray.' He set it on one of the display cabinets and glanced at her. 'Any chance I could join you?'

'Er, yes. I'll just go and get an extra cup . . . and some more biscuits.'

'May I come with you?'

Cook wasn't there. It wouldn't matter.

'If you'd like.' She hadn't meant to sound so abrupt, but her jangled nerves were getting the better of her.

As they walked towards the kitchen, Esme said, more for something to say:

'Did Dolly say Sir Giles was still on his nap?'

'"Indisposed" was the term I believe she used.'

Esme tapped on the kitchen door and opened it to find Cook, her face furrowed in concentration, behind the pine table, spooning the apple purée into the waiting jars. Immediately she saw Brad, her expression relaxed into a smile of welcome.

'Dr Parker. How nice to see you. Was there anything you wanted?'

Esme bit back a smile at the difference in tone Cook used for the doctor.

Brad grinned at the cook. 'Good to see you, too, Cook. I was wondering if we could have an extra cup for the tea.'

'Fetch the doctor a cup and saucer – one of the blue sets – and bring me the special biscuit tin,' Cook ordered a girl Esme didn't recognise. She turned back to Brad. 'I thought you Yanks only drank coffee.'

'Not since I arrived in England,' Brad smiled. 'I've quite taken to tea.'

'Much more sensible.' She looked at Esme. 'Where are you?'

'In the new library,' Esme said.

'Then Janey will bring it to you with a fresh pot.'

'Where's Lil these days?' Esme asked.

Cook sniffed. 'She's gone and joined the Land Army, leaving us short again.'

Esme gave her a sympathetic smile and hurried back to the library. She took a chair facing Brad and he reached over and took her hand.

'I'm sorry for the intrusion, Esme, but I felt we had some unfinished business.' He gazed at her. 'Esmeralda, we are friends, aren't we?'

What is he getting at?

'Y-yes, of course we are. Why are you asking?'

Was he going to reveal his wife and say all the platitudes that she'd heard married men say – that their wives didn't understand them? They probably understood them only too well, she thought, grimly.

'I want to know why you didn't trust me enough to tell me that your husband had died – that you were a widow – at least that's what Marilyn Lorrimer told me.'

Esme swallowed hard, then forced herself to catch his eye.

'I wanted to,' she said quietly. 'But it never seemed to be the right time.'

'Why was that?' His voice was gentle.

'Because . . . because—' She broke off.

'Yes, because what?' he encouraged softly.

'Because I didn't want you to think I was . . . oh, I don't know how to say this.'

There was a tap at the door and, relieved, she jumped up to answer it. Janey gave a bob of her head as she came in with the fresh tea tray.

'Shall I pour, madam?' she asked.

'No, that won't be necessary, Janey, but thank you.'

Janey bobbed her head again and scurried out. Esme noticed Cook had thought Dr Parker was special enough to warrant a couple of chocolate biscuits.

'Let's have a cup of tea,' Brad said, picking up the pot and smiling at her. 'I'll be "mother", as you British say.'

'You seem to know quite a lot about the British from the short time you've been here,' Esme remarked, desperate to take hold of herself.

'We were all given a pamphlet right before we came over as to how we must interact with the British. What we should and shouldn't say. Never to brag about our country that everything there is bigger or better – which, of course, it isn't always – or how much we earned . . . that sort of thing.'

'I hope you all took it to heart,' she said lightly, relieved to change the subject.

The tea warmed and revived her, but she could tell Brad had *not* forgotten his question by the way he suddenly became silent, staring at the floor. How could she tell him she didn't want to leave herself open in case she was vastly mistaken? And anyway, there was his wife to think about.

'You were worried I didn't have the same feeling for you as I'm arrogant enough to think you have for me,' Brad said, putting his cup back into the saucer and gazing at her. 'Am I right?'

She could only nod wordlessly.

'So where does that leave us?'

'What do you mean?' She felt her pulse quicken.

'I mean that I love you – more than anything in the world. And I think you love me. That's what I mean.'

This time she trembled, not like the same shock of seeing Bertha struggling in the lake, or even the pain of losing her precious baby, but that Brad had said the unthinkable – the impossible – that he loved her. Brad pulled her to her feet. She gave a soft moan as he wrapped his arms around her.

'Am I right?'

'Yes.' There didn't seem to be anything to add as he moved towards her to kiss her.

After seconds tasting the bliss of his mouth on hers, she suddenly came to her senses and jerked away.

'Haven't you forgotten someone?' she demanded.

'My wife?'

She sent him a sharp look. He'd voiced those two dreaded words so easily. No apology, nothing, for not having mentioned her before.

'Yes,' she managed without her voice cracking. 'The person you married . . . the woman who loves you,' she added shortly, feeling she might choke.

He shook his head. 'No, that's where you're wrong, dearest. She doesn't love me. She's in love with another man – has been for a long time. Our divorce is imminent and she can't wait to marry him. He's far wealthier than I am, and also ten years younger . . . much more exciting than me at thirty-nine with only a doctor's salary.'

A divorce? Something that had never crossed her mind. She supposed it was a more common occurrence in America than it was in England.

'And if you're wondering,' Brad continued, 'she dangled the evidence in front of me – hotels they'd stayed at, expensive jewellery he'd bought her that she'd pretended was worthless but was actually worth tens of thousands of dollars . . . In the end I had no alternative than to file for adultery. And as soon as I'd put it in motion, I was so relieved, and happier than I'd been in a long time.'

'Why didn't you tell me sooner that you had a wife but were getting a divorce? I would have understood.'

'Because I wanted to be completely free when I told you I loved you so you wouldn't think you'd instigated any kind of break-up.' He brought her close again and kissed the top of her head. 'But I have never been able to resist you.' He laughed softly. 'We have a lot to talk about, darling, but I want to hear something from you. Something I've been longing to hear from those beautiful lips.'

Barely knowing what she was about to tell him, she said, 'Are these the words you're longing to hear, Brad – that I love you, too?'

He gave a long sigh. 'If it's true, that's all I wanted to hear.' He gazed into her eyes. 'Is it?'

'Yes,' she whispered.

'When did you know?'

'When . . .' She hesitated. She couldn't tell him it had been love at first sight. That would sound terribly forward. But so what? She wasn't some starry-eyed young girl, but she knew now that she'd fallen in love with him the moment they'd met. She smiled at him. 'I felt I was in danger of falling in love with you when Stella introduced us and you called me "Miss Donaldson" and she corrected you. You said, "my mistake" but then you added so only I could hear, "I'm really sorry." I took it to mean you weren't apologising because you had my title wrong, but because you were disappointed I was married.' She met his gaze. 'Was that how you meant it?'

'It was exactly how I meant it,' he said, smiling back. 'And I knew you realised, even though I didn't know how you felt about it.' His smile widened to a grin. 'But of course the first time we met was in the Pump Room.'

'Why didn't you tell me you were one and the same person?' Esme demanded. 'You gave me your handkerchief and melted away before I could thank you.' Her tone was almost an accusation.

'I wanted you to work it out. But you never did – or if you did, you didn't mention it to me.'

'I sort of suspected once – no, twice – but told myself it was just a coincidence that the last two initials were yours.' She paused. 'So now you can tell me what the "J" stands for.'

'Hmm. I suppose you'll have to know sooner or later. It's Jackson.' He grimaced.

'What a strange first name.'

'I'm named after a town in Jackson, Mississippi. It's where my parents met.'

'Well, if *my* parents had followed that pattern, I'd be called "Bath",' Esme laughed.

'Then they made a wise decision to call you Esmeralda.' Brad grinned. 'So does that answer all your questions?'

'More or less,' she said. 'But I wanted to tell you I never forgot how kind you were to come over and offer me a crumb of comfort.' She looked straight at him. 'You must have thought I was an awful cry-baby.'

'No, my darling. Aside from having the most adorable face, I think you're the most wonderful woman I've ever met and I want us to be married – start a new life in Denver.' He kissed her forehead. 'Oh, darling, I can't wait to show you round and introduce you to my parents and friends.'

When she didn't answer, his smile became uncertain.

'I suppose this has all come as rather a shock to you, but tell me you feel the same, my darling.'

Only then, at the mention of Denver, did she realise what this meant... that she'd have to move to America after the war. Live in this strange place nicknamed the Mile High City in Colorado. Brad had told her it was in the West – sometimes known as a Mountain state – and she remembered how she'd looked it up in one of Sir Giles's atlases. It had seemed so far away from dear old England, and she knew nothing about Colorado except for the range of Rocky Mountains. She might hate it. She might feel lonely, or worse – a misfit. Did she love him enough to uproot – give up everything she knew – go so far away from Freda and her boys, her only remaining family whom she might never set eyes on again? Oh, why had she fallen in love with an American?

Her only remaining family.

She drew away from him and sat down again. The family she thought she'd created with Anthony had been snatched away from her. She gulped. Brad had told her he longed for children and she could never give him any. She could never fulfil his dream. She could never divulge her secret – the secret she'd kept from everyone. But was she being fair to him?

Say it, Esme. Tell him now. Be honest. That's the main thing holding you back.

He'd sat down, too, and was gazing at her.

She stared numbly back, not having the foggiest idea how to answer him.

Chapter Forty-Three

Now in her bedroom, Esme threw herself onto the bed and wept. Her dearest dreams had come true – Brad wanted to spend the rest of his life with her, hoping she felt the same, and she hadn't been able to give him a proper answer. All she'd done was nod feebly and tell him she'd better go and see whether Sir Giles had finished his nap and needed her before supper. She'd made her getaway quickly, but not before she saw a shadow of doubt pass across his face. His expression had almost made her stop in her tracks, turn round and rush to him, telling him she loved him and if he was proposing, then she'd respond with all her being, 'Yes, Brad, oh yes, please.'

Thoroughly ashamed of herself, she went to the sink and splashed her swollen eyes with cold water. But there was something else looming which would be even more unfair to him. She could never give him the babies he craved. She swallowed the bitter taste in her mouth. He would make such a wonderful father – and the dearest husband to some lucky woman. Blinking to stop the tears from flowing, she knew on that reason alone, she had to let him go. Let him go with a generous heart to find an American woman who wouldn't have to emigrate to another country – and the right woman to give him children.

But she loved him and he loved her. But supposing he said it didn't matter and meant it now, but later . . . She put her hands to her head . . . Later, he might resent it. And when she added it up, they hadn't spent much time getting to know one another. If she threw caution to the wind and went with him, supposing their relationship didn't work once they were in his own country? She'd be trying to learn and accept a different culture such as the cruel segregation issue. And she would have upped sticks to an unknown country where the only person she knew was Brad and he would be attending to his patients, so she'd be left on her own. She heaved a jagged sigh. There were so many things that told her she would be a fool to leave England.

Why on earth hadn't this all occurred to her before? She supposed it was because it had been so far out of the realms of possibility that it hadn't needed mulling over. Her head began to ache. She pulled the cover over the typewriter and scrawled a note to Sir Giles, leaving it on his desk for his return. Upstairs, she flung on her coat and walking shoes. The fresh air would help clear her head to make a common-sense decision. A practical one.

As Esme was about to open the front door, Hilary waylaid her.

'Are you going anywhere in particular?' she said.

'Not really. Just for a walk.'

'Have you seen Bertha today?'

'No. But I could see her when I come back.' She glanced at Hilary. 'Why do you ask?'

'Because I think you're the right person to tell her,' Hilary said somewhat mysteriously. 'She detests me.'

Esme chuckled. 'She's not that keen on me either. So what is it?'

'Tell her that she's neck-and-neck with Yvonne on her salvage collection. The bad news is that Queen Mary only left one medal and one five-pound note, as she didn't bargain for a tie.'

'Well, they can split the money,' Esme said, 'but I admit the medal is more difficult.'

'Anyway, can I rely on you to tell her, and that we expect her back to class tomorrow?' Hilary said.

'Yes, I'll explain.' A thought came to Esme. 'When do you think the get-well card will be ready?'

'Linda and Faith are taking it to her after school today.'

'That's marvellous. She's sure everyone hates her so it will cheer her up. But I won't say anything about it – let it be a surprise.'

The sun dappled yellow-gold light through the mostly leafless trees in the crisp winter air. Esme breathed it in as though it were nectar – hanging onto every breath as long as possible. Her shoes made a crackling noise on the gravel drive, still spattered with fallen leaves between muddy patches where the small stones were sparse. Not really having any particular walk in mind, she found herself going in the direction of the lakes. What if she could find the bicycle Bertha had coveted? If it was in a bad state, it could still be useful to someone for spare parts, but whatever the condition, it would make Bertha the outright winner.

Pleased with the idea, she walked on the grass, relishing the silence. She was completely on her own except for a blackbird that flew past with a rush of wings, another in hot pursuit. Carefully, she made her way over the bridge, remembering when she'd slipped on it that frightful night. She found the spot where she'd first seen Bertha and hunched down on the opposite bank. But apart from some paper litter, there didn't seem to be any sign of something bulky. She gazed across the water for several minutes . . . and then she saw what looked like a set of bicycle handlebars caught in the undergrowth on the opposite side from where she'd come. Good. It would be much easier to retrieve now it was so close to the bank.

She stretched up and crossed the bridge again, then bent once more and closed her hand round the metal bars, knowing she was at a difficult angle to heave such an object. But she'd give it a go.

Bracing herself and with a deep breath, she pulled with all her might. Grimly hanging on for dear life, she stumbled backwards into the grass as the wreck had been so much lighter than she'd expected. She stared down at her hands and laughed aloud. The handlebars, unless she was very much mistaken, were all that was left of what must once have been an expensive ladies' Sunbeam bicycle – some woman's proud possession. Bertha was in for a disappointment there wasn't a whole bike, but she hoped the girl would forget it when she was told she and Yvonne had risen to Queen Mary's challenge to find the most salvage for the war effort.

Picking up the dripping handlebars, Esme carried them back over the bridge and to the side door that led into the scullery. As she closed the door behind her, Cook came to see who it was.

'What on earth have you got there, Esme?'

Esme grinned. 'Bertha's addition to her salvage collection – or so she thought, but someone will snap them up for their own bicycle, I'm sure.'

'Just as well.' Cook sniffed. 'Just don't bring it in here – or your muddy shoes.'

'May I leave the handlebars in here for the time being?'

'S'long as they're gone by the end of the day,' Cook said firmly, as she turned back to her pie-making.

Good. Now for Bertha.

She found the girl sitting up and staring at the ceiling.

'Hello, Bertha. How are you today?'

'All right, I suppose,' Bertha mumbled, barely turning to acknowledge her.

'Do you think you should be returning to class?' When Bertha didn't answer, Esme said, 'You're missing your schoolwork and your friends miss you.'

'I doubt that.' Bertha's mouth took a downward turn. 'Only Faith came to see me.'

'That shows she's thinking of you.' Esme smiled. 'Look at me, Bertha. I do have something interesting to tell you.' She brought a chair nearer the bed. 'I went to the lakes just now to see where you fell in.'

There was no response at all.

'And I saw what you were trying to retrieve.'

Bertha still didn't say anything.

'Bicycle handlebars were poking out of the water near the opposite bank half hidden in the undergrowth.'

Bertha's back straightened. She twisted her neck to stare at Esme.

'You found the bicycle?'

'Part of it,' Esme smiled. 'Just that – the handlebars. No frame or anything else I could see.'

'That's no use,' Bertha said, turning her face to the wall.

'Oh, but it is,' Esme interjected. 'Your salvage collection is at a tie-breaker with Yvonne.'

'So what?' Bertha mumbled.

'So everything.' She glanced at Bertha's back. 'Turn round, Bertha, and look at me.' Slowly, Bertha did so. 'That's better. Listen to me. You and Yvonne have collected the same amount of salvage, but Queen Mary only imagined one winner. It would have been difficult to divide the prize. But now you've got the handlebars to add to your pile, you must have won!'

There was a stunned silence.

'Are you sure?'

'Yes.'

'Did you know about this when you went to rescue it?' Bertha demanded.

'Yes. Miss Fenton told me about the tie between you and Yvonne. I was just on my way out for a walk and thought I'd go and see what you were trying grab hold of. When I saw what I thought was a bicycle, I had to retrieve it. And it doesn't make any difference that it's only the handlebars – it's the metal that counts.'

Bertha chewed her lip.

'You went to the lakes again just for that?'

'Yes.'

Bertha put her head in her hands and sobbed. Esme jumped up and put her arms round the girl.

'Don't cry, Bertha. You should be proud of yourself. You will have done your bit for the war – and not only receive a medal from Queen Mary but she's offered five pounds too.'

Bertha looked round with tear-stained eyes.

'I'm not proud,' she said. 'I've behaved badly sending you that note and hiding the library plans to try to get you into trouble. You knew it was me all the time, didn't you?'

'I suspected,' Esme said, smiling to soften her words.

'But you still went and found the bit of bike I was after so I could win the prize.' She shook her head. 'No, I'm not very proud. And y-you s-s—' She broke into fresh sobs. 'You saved my life, Mrs Donaldson, and I never even thanked you.'

'It doesn't matter.' Esme handed her a handkerchief. 'All this takes nothing away from the fact that you are the winner of Queen Mary's challenge, and one day when you have children of your own, they're going to be very proud of their mum.'

Bertha sniffed, then gave the glimmer of a smile. 'Do you really think so?'

'Yes, I do,' Esme said firmly. 'Come on, wipe your tears.'

Darn it! Too late, Esme watched as Bertha peered at the blue embroidered initials. 'These are Dr Parker's initials. I know that, even though they start with the wrong letter.'

'That handkerchief has done the rounds,' Esme said.

Bertha studied her curiously. 'You two should get married.'

Chapter Forty-Four

Esme had worked solidly on Sir Giles's memoirs this last week, marvelling at the small details Sir Giles had crammed into this last section of his life. He'd brought it right up to date with the start of the Second World War, admitting that he was thankful he was too old to fight in this one – even if he'd wanted to. The memoirs were rapidly coming to an end. Only another sheet left to go of his writing and there didn't seem to be a proper ending to the memoir. He'd finished by saying he was sure the Ministry of War would requisition the house for its own purposes. As an example, he mentioned that Lord Booth, owner of one of the estates between Bath and Bristol, had been made homeless within two days flat because the War Office said they needed it for top secret training. They couldn't accommodate him and his wife, so Lord and Lady Booth had been obliged to move in with a niece and her husband. Esme quickly typed the remaining paragraph.

I will just have to wait until I receive any letter from them, Sir Giles ended, *but I'll be prepared to do anything that will help us through what looks to be another very long conflict.*

Esme sighed as she rolled the last sheet out of the typewriter, then fastened the loose pages together with a green treasury tag. She sighed. It wasn't a satisfactory ending, in her opinion. Then she remembered he'd put the extra bit that he wasn't too sure about in his desk drawer. She walked over to his desk and was about to pull the middle drawer open – the one he never kept locked – then abruptly stopped. He'd seemed slightly hesitant when he'd mentioned he'd written a final part. No, she'd wait for him to give it to her himself, but she'd remind him it was there.

Esme's thoughts now turned to Brad. She'd have to give him an answer to his proposal when he was back. He'd sent her a message he'd been called to another hospital and might not be back for a week or two, so hoped by then she would have had enough time to give him an answer. He'd return any day now and it wouldn't be fair to keep him waiting any longer. Her father had told her she must always follow her heart, but that had sometimes misled her. This time, she told herself she must look at it more practically. But for now she'd go and find Sir Giles and tell him she'd finished typing his memoirs.

She tracked him down in the old attic library where he'd kept a small overflow of books that he hadn't looked at for decades but was now walking round the nearly empty shelves peering at the titles. As she came in, he looked round and gave her a wan smile.

'Just checking there's nothing here I want down in the new library,' he said, pulling out a heavy volume. 'You know, Esme, these have been like old friends to me.'

'I know exactly what you mean,' Esme said fervently. 'I feel the same with some of my books. And by the way, I haven't told you I finished *The Great Gatsby* Brad gave me.' Her voice cracked as she said his name, and she saw him give her a sharp look.

'And?'

'I'm glad I read it. I was struck by how it warned readers not to value certain relationships, and I think I can see why it's known to be the great American novel.'

'Well, it's good that you persisted. It doesn't hurt to have our values examined.' He cleared his throat as though to give himself time to work out what he was going to say next. For some reason, her stomach lurched as he waited a few seconds then said: 'But you didn't come just to tell me that.'

'No. It's to say I've finished your life story except for the extra you've added so I wondered if you'd like me to get started on it.'

Was there a mist of hesitation in his eyes?

He looked directly at her. 'Esme, it's rather personal.'

What on earth does he mean?

'Is it too upsetting for you?' she said, picking her words carefully. 'Because I don't want you to feel pressurised if you'd rather keep something private.' She tried to lighten the moment with a smile. 'Have you decided you'd prefer not to include them?'

He shook his head. 'It's not quite like that. You'll understand when you read it.' He fumbled in his trouser pocket and handed her a tiny key.

'It's in the bottom right-hand drawer. But you've done enough typing today. Just leave it for now.' He paused. 'I'm going to London tomorrow to see an old friend of mine in the hospital – he was one of the team on the mountain,' he added gruffly. 'I'll be staying at my club for a couple of nights so that might be a good time for you to have a think about it.'

'Shall I read it first and then discuss it with you before I type it?'

'No, but I would read it first. Then you'll know whether I should include it or not.'

But how would she know? She didn't want to be responsible for putting something out there in the public – if indeed it were published – if he wasn't entirely happy. She stole a glance at him, but he caught her eye and gave an almost imperceptible nod. Maybe he was making something out of nothing. But something told her she should brace herself for this final piece of his memoir.

Esme kept busy in the library that day deciding how to tackle the deterioration of so many valuable editions, but the mystery of Sir Giles's last piece of writing hung over her. The key, minute though it was, seemed to weigh heavily in her skirt pocket. But she would abide by Sir Giles's suggestion to leave it until he'd left for his visit to see his old friend.

The next day, while the taxi waited, she saw him off, giving him a peck on his cheek. She was rewarded with his smile, showing his large, stained teeth that had somehow become endearing. He looked down at her, his expression unfathomable.

'I wish now I'd asked you to come with me.' He dropped his stick, and she quickly retrieved it. 'I'll miss you, Esme.'

He was only going for two days, but he'd made the words sound as though it would be longer. Or was he simply being polite and she was once again letting her imagination work overtime?

'I would have accompanied you if I thought you needed me,' she said impulsively, then added, 'Are you sure you'll be all right, Sir Giles?'

'Yes . . . but I want you to know you're very important to me, my dear, so do look after yourself.'

He gave an embarrassed grunt before he limped away to the taxi where the driver hurried towards him to help him safely into the rear seat.

Esme's thoughts turned to Brad. Just now, seeing Sir Giles go off – a lonely figure – she realised he would be her excuse as to why she couldn't marry Brad. She'd tell him Sir Giles depended on her too much. And she owed it to him as her employer and friend not to desert him. She'd say that if the war ended this year, they'd be off to America and she would never see Sir Giles again. She drew in a breath that was half a sob. Yes, that's what she would say to him.

But oh, how her heart would break to tell him so – especially as it wasn't the reason. But she must never let Brad suspect anything different.

As she walked back into the house she heard the telephone ringing in Sir Giles's study. He'd always told her to answer it if he was indisposed, so she ran to catch it before the caller rang off.

'Sir Giles Carmichael's residence.'

'Esme, is that you?'

'Oh, Freda, I was going to ring you today. Are you coming down soon?'

'Unfortunately not.' Her sister's voice sounded jerky. There must be something wrong with the line. 'Felix . . . he . . . well, he's joined the Army.'

'But he's only seventeen!'

'He's seventeen and a half – the minimum age to join up. I couldn't stop him. He wants to go with his friends, but he's still a child.' Freda's voice rose.

For a moment, Esme was at a loss what to say.

'He's not a child any longer, Freda. This war has forced us all to grow up fast, including Felix . . . you just haven't noticed. I'm afraid you have to let him—' She broke off, feeling the tears running down her face. 'You have to let him go – and with your blessing.'

'I know,' Freda said, 'but it's going to be dreadful worrying about him every minute of the day.' There was a pause. 'Let's change the subject. What's happening your end?'

Esme swallowed hard. How much should she tell her sister?

'Brad's asked me to marry him. His divorce is through any day. He didn't want to ask me until he could show me the papers to prove it, but things came to a head. And now I'm in a quandary.'

'Surely there's only one answer,' Freda said. 'Marry him! He's the best thing that's ever happened to you.'

'It's more complicated than that.'

'Only because you make it so.' The line crackled.

'Sorry, Freda, I didn't catch what you said.'

'You told me I have to let Felix go, and I know you're right, and I'm saying *you* would be a fool to let Brad go.'

After her conversation with Freda, Esme felt restless. Something else was niggling at her that so far she'd tried to ignore. She needed to talk to someone not in the immediate family. She'd give Stella a quick ring to ask if they could meet in the staff room at lunchtime.

'What's up?' Stella demanded, when they'd settled at one of the small tables. Being early, they were alone.

'It's about my job,' Esme said. 'I've finished his memoir – oh, there's a bit of tidying up, but in the main it's done, and my work in the library really doesn't warrant a full-time position.'

Stella drew her brows together. 'You're not thinking of leaving? Sir Giles is as fond of you as any favourite niece.'

'I know,' Esme said. 'But it will happen sooner or later. And I need enough to occupy me that will ideally help the war effort.'

'You're a bit more limited with your heart problem,' Stella said. 'And where does Brad come in?'

'He's asked me to marry him. His divorce is apparently imminent.'

Stella beamed. 'There you are then. The problem's solved.'

Esme looked at her. 'I can't marry Brad merely to resolve these problems. It would be terribly unfair to him. I want to be financially independent, not look upon him as my provider.'

Stella's face creased in astonishment.

'Don't be such a goose, Esme. He adores you. He doesn't care whether you have money or not.' She stared at Esme. 'Give the poor chap some integrity.'

Esme blinked. Stella was saying the same as Freda. But neither of them truly understood what was holding her back. And it wasn't their fault. She hadn't told them about Brad's overriding desire for children.

'And after the war, you'll go with him to America, knowing I'll be green with envy. But don't worry, I won't wait for an invitation – I'll just turn up and surprise you.'

Esme couldn't help smiling at her incorrigible friend. But nothing her sister or Stella had said had helped sort out the confusion in her mind.

After lunch, still thinking about Freda's and Stella's advice, Esme slowly went to Sir Giles's desk. With the drawer key in her hand, she was about to open it when the phone rang. She picked up the receiver and a pencil ready to take down a message.

'Esmeralda, darling, it's Brad. I'm back.'

Time stopped. Her heart stilled. For what seemed the longest pause, she was frightened it would never start beating again.

'Are you still there?'

'Yes, I'm here.' Her voice sounded wooden to her ears.

'Is it convenient for me to come over and see you?'

Best get it over with.

'Yes. Sir Giles has just left for a couple of days in London.'

'He mentioned it.' The line crackled. And then Esme heard him say: 'Is something the matter?'

'Um, no, not really.'

'Good. I'll be there in a heartbeat.'

Slowly, she put down the receiver.

Minutes later, Brad was being ushered into Sir Giles's study.

'Dr Parker to see you, Mrs Donaldson.'

'Thank you, Dolly.' She turned to Brad. 'Would you like some tea?'

'I'm okay, thanks.'

'Do sit down.' Dear God, she sounded so formal – as though they'd only just met.

He remained standing and held out his arms. 'Come here, darling.'

She stayed where she was. 'I have something to tell you that I hope you'll understand.'

'I don't like the sound of that.' He took a packet of cigarettes from his pocket and lit one. He gazed at her. 'Tell me straight, Esme.'

'I can't marry you,' she blurted.

Brad stiffened and slowly took a draw from his cigarette.

'Why's that?' He casually blew out the smoke.

She held her breath. She hadn't been sure until this moment what she was going to say.

'Because . . . because Sir Giles needs me.'

There, she'd said it without making an idiot of herself and breaking down in front of him.

Brad stared at her, his jaw dropped in astonishment.

'Because *Sir Giles needs you*? Are you actually saying you're prepared to forfeit your happiness for a man who's not even your family?'

'Yes.' She wished she could stop her stomach from trembling.

'I don't believe it. There's something else behind this and I want to know what it is.'

'He depends on me, Brad. I'm fond of him and I can't just leave him on his own.'

Brad narrowed his eyes. 'What do you mean – *fond*?'

Warmth spread up her neck. 'Nothing like you're hinting,' she said sharply. 'It's just that I've almost finished typing his memoirs. He's quite a complex character, and still feels guilty over something that happened ages ago and wasn't his fault.'

'When he cut the rope of that guy he was tied to in the mountains?'

It was Esme's turn to be surprised.

'Yes,' she muttered.

'He did ask my medical opinion. I've been talking to him over the last few weeks.' He gazed at her. 'I can assure you he's a perfectly capable and healthy individual. And you don't need to leave him on his own. We wouldn't be going back to the States until the war's over. That could be years yet.'

Numb, she shook her head. This wasn't going how it was supposed to.

'You're using Sir Giles as an excuse.' His eyes glinting, he fixed them on hers. 'Are you saying you *can't* or *won't* marry me?'

Esme swallowed hard. 'There's not much difference, is there?'

'There's all the difference in the world.' He took another puff of his cigarette, then viciously stubbed it out in Sir Giles's ashtray. 'All I can think of is that you don't love me enough – simple as that.'

He moved towards her, then stopped. 'I'll leave you in peace, but if you change your mind, you know where I am.'

Brad shut the study door quietly behind him, his face grim. He needed a coffee – no, he needed a stiff drink. Back at the hospital he went to his office, took off his jacket and poured himself a whisky, then sat in his armchair pondering over the recent conversation. Why had Esme changed so quickly? Why was she putting her boss before her and his happiness? Could it possibly be that Sir Giles had also proposed to her and she knew she wouldn't have to worry about money again? She'd told him about Muriel now owning her and her sister's family home and was upset to think she'd lost her independence. He flung the thought aside. She'd denied his hint of the word 'fond' and he'd believed her, but now he began to wonder.

He lit a fresh cigarette. There was something deeper. Her heart condition had ramifications and one of them was . . . Suddenly, his back stiffened. Like a thunderbolt it flashed across his mind. He nodded to himself. Now he knew the real reason she'd said she couldn't marry him. He shot up and stubbed out the cigarette. Grabbing his jacket, he rushed outside and darted back over the bridge, then over to the Manor. Standing for a moment at the main entrance to catch his breath, he rang the bell.

'Hello, Mrs Morgan,' he said as the housekeeper glowered, then realised who he was and turned it into a smile of welcome.

'Are you expected, Dr Parker? Because if so, Sir Giles is away for a few days.'

'I've come to see Mrs Donaldson.'

'Oh.' She took a step backwards. 'Well, in that case . . .'

'Thank you.' He smiled back. 'I left her in his study a few minutes ago and forgot to pick up some paperwork.'

'Then I'll get it for you if you'll wait—'

'Please don't bother, Mrs Morgan. I know my way.'

Chapter Forty-Five

Desperately trying to put the scene with Brad to one side, Esme unlocked the drawer and removed the thin sheaf of papers. Sir Giles had told her to read them through first before typing them – the new ending of his personal story. She glanced at the top sheet, noting the date – then stared in wonderment. It was the date she'd started working for him. Strange, it was only four months. For all that had happened, it felt much longer. But why would he include it in his ending? Well, he said she'd know, so she'd better start reading it. But when she came to the part where he wrote that Mrs Esmeralda Donaldson had changed his life, made it more tolerable – even, dare he say, happier – and that she had become the daughter he'd always wished for, she put her head in her hands and wept.

She didn't hear the door open.

'Esmeralda, what is it?'

She turned and raised her chin to see Brad standing at the doorway. Oh, why had he come back so quickly? Dear God, she couldn't face any more argument.

He rushed in and hunkered down beside her, then touched her lightly on her arm.

'I think I know why you won't marry me, but I'd appreciate hearing it from you.' When she didn't speak, he prompted her, 'Sir Giles isn't the real reason, is he?'

She shook her head. 'Not exactly.'

'It's to do with not being able to have children, isn't it?' He kept his eyes fixed on hers.

Esme gave a start. How had he guessed? Well, it was high time to be completely honest with him. She took in a jagged breath.

'Yes.' She hesitated, wondering how to explain when she barely knew herself. Nervously, she licked her lips. 'You said you longed for children of your own and when you lost your sister, you lost the child who would have been your niece or nephew at the same time. And I kept thinking I mustn't ever fall in love with you because I can never give you children.'

Brad raised his eyebrows. 'Let's start at the beginning, my love.' He stood and gently pulled her to her feet. 'Come and sit with me and tell me in more detail about your rheumatic fever.'

Esme allowed him to take her to the sofa. He pulled her onto his knee and she snuggled up to him.

'How old were you when you were diagnosed with it?'

'About seven.'

He nodded. 'Muriel, I believe, was looking after you at the time?'

'Yes. But she used to think I was putting it on when I was too tired to go outside and play with the other children. She wanted me out of her way. I was a nuisance because I was only a child. It wasn't so bad with Freda being so much older and working away from home. I think Muriel felt she'd been saddled with a child invalid and that hadn't been part of what she'd imagined as a housekeeper, so she was resentful.'

'How were your teen years?'

'Not too bad. But I rarely went to a dance. If I did, it was only when the band played a slow ballroom dance.' She looked up at him and said truthfully, 'I could never have done this American jitterbug even when I was younger.'

'What about when you were engaged to be married. Did the doctor talk to you about a family?'

This is it.

'Yes.' She'd have to come out with it. Get it over with. 'He told me it would be unwise to have any children.'

'Did you take his advice?'

'No.' Her answer was barely audible.

Brad put his hand gently on hers.

'Tell me what happened.'

'Anthony and I started a baby. It came too early.' She swallowed hard. 'It was stillborn.'

He hesitated. 'Was it anything to do with that bombing raid you were caught up in?'

'Yes.' Her voice felt strangled in her throat. How had he guessed?

He ran his finger along her jaw, then kissed her forehead. 'Oh, my love, I'm so sorry. I wish I'd known all of this. It might have saved us both some heartache.'

She was close enough to see his eyes fill with tears. This time there was no mistaking him. She was as sure as she'd ever been in her life that he loved her.

'Did the doctor say anything more afterwards – maybe when you were stronger?'

'Yes.' Her voice was low as she began to explain. 'He said I must never try for another one. It could have serious consequences.' She looked up at him, the tears dripping down her cheeks. 'Do you know the worst thing of all? I put my arms out to hold her just one time, but all the nurse told me was that it was a girl and held her up to me for no more than a couple of seconds.' Esme swallowed the tears, feeling they were choking her. 'And then she took my baby away. I just saw her little heart-shaped face, her dark hair . . . But I have no photograph, nothing. I named her

Amelia. No reason. I just liked it.' She broke off with a sob. 'I've never told anyone all this.'

'You've bottled it up too long,' Brad said quietly. 'Take your time.'

She bit her lip. 'Poor Anthony died before he saw her, though at least he knew she was near to being born but of course he didn't know if it would be a girl or a boy.' She stopped. Brad waited silently, not taking his eyes off her. 'And because of my heart,' Esme went on, 'the doctor strongly advised I should never become pregnant again.' She swallowed hard. 'She was so perfect – a little angel.'

She began to sob uncontrollably. He put his arm round her and pulled her closer.

'Don't cry, my darling. Please don't cry.'

He took out a handkerchief and softly wiped her face. When she'd managed to halt the tears, she looked straight into his eyes, and with a tremor added, 'I have a piece of paper with her name on it when I had to register her, but that's all I have to tell me my precious baby girl ever existed.' She gulped. 'Oh, Brad, I'm so frightened I'll forget her.'

Brad bent his head and kissed the tears from her eyes.

'Don't cry, my love. Of course you'll never forget her.'

He drew her close . . . so close she could feel his heart beating. Strong and comforting, she let her head fall on his chest and heard him say:

'Later, when you feel like it, I want you to tell me about her. I wish I could have seen her. And we'll always remember her birthday. But we'll adopt a baby and we'll love her or him just the same as though born from us.' When she said nothing, he added, 'I don't need to see a tiny version of *you*, darling. The children will be their own persons – just as it should be.' He smiled. 'So what do you say?'

This dear, darling man. Before she could think further, he was kissing her again.

'You know where this will lead us,' he said, when after long minutes they finally drew apart. He kissed her quickly again.

She briefly closed her lids, letting the words warm her to the core. Was this really happening? She opened her eyes to find him looking at her with so much love it took her breath away.

He gave her a little shake. 'Darling Esmeralda, you must know what I'm saying. I want to spend the rest of my life with you . . . and our children, of course.' He smiled at her. 'Are you feeling better now, my love?'

'A bit,' she admitted. 'But I truly *am* worried about leaving Sir Giles. He looked awfully . . . well, fragile is the only word I can think of, when he left, after telling me how important I was to him. And I've just been reading the very last missing piece of his memoirs about my being the daughter he'd always wished for. And then I'll be gone thousands of miles away.'

'Would you mind if I take a look?'

'Of course not. I hadn't read all of it before you arrived.'

She went to the desk and handed him the last few sheets. He led her back to the sofa and read the pages without saying a word, then flipped the bottom sheet over.

'Esmeralda, this one's a personal one to you.'

'What do you mean?'

'It doesn't seem to be part of the manuscript.'

'Oh, I hadn't reached that far,' Esme said.

'Would you like me to read it to you?'

'Yes, would you?'

'*My dear Esme.*' He glanced at her. 'Are you sure you want me to go on?'

She nodded.

'*My dear Esme,*' Brad repeated, '*You probably know me by now, more than almost anyone, having transcribed my life story, and you now know what you mean to me. So please listen carefully to what I want to say as I'm going to speak to you as a father would his daughter – not as employer to employee.*

'I would love you to stay here at Redcliffe Manor until the end of my days, but I'm not ready to meet my Maker just yet. So it would be extremely selfish of me to expect you to "see me out", so to speak. You are a beautiful woman, still young and with values that chime with mine. You've already made your husband happy, but it wasn't to be. He tragically died far too young.'

At this moment, Brad paused, and she could tell he was giving her some time to think about Anthony. He waited and when she nodded, he continued.

'And now I believe you have fallen in love with our American – namely, Colonel Bradley Parker.'

Esme gasped, and jerked her head towards Brad, but he kept his eyes fixed on the page.

'And he is very much in love with you, my dear.'

'Brad—' Her voice broke.

He quickly glanced at her, then back to the letter.

'I believe he will ask you to marry him. He is a fine man of whom I completely approve, but this will be a big decision for you because one day you will have to leave dear old England and cross the Atlantic to a new and completely strange country. It will mean leaving your sister and nephews and friends. But believe me when I say that your nephews will be thrilled they have an aunt in America and I am sure they will not let much time go by before they come to visit. And I am just as certain that you will one day have your own family with Brad. He is a doctor and will take care of you when the time comes.

'As I said, it's a big decision, but you have the common sense and strength to overcome any obstacles to be with your beloved.

As a father figure, I only want to say – do not follow what your head might tell you. The only true decision for your happiness – and Brad's – must come from your heart.

'There's nothing more I can say, except to believe me when I tell you I have written this letter with love.

'Giles Carmichael.'

The room was thick with the silence. Sir Giles had said the exact thing her father always told her – to follow her heart. Esme couldn't speak. She didn't dare move. She stole a glance at Brad. His head was still bent over the sheet of paper but as though he knew she was looking at him, he raised his eyes to catch hers. But still he didn't say anything. She knew he was waiting for her to be the first to answer such a personal letter.

Another minute ticked by.

'Esmeralda, are you okay?' Brad put his hand under her jaw and turned her tear-stained face gently towards him.

She nodded.

'Would you like a glass of water?'

She nodded again. He stood up and poured her a glass from the glass jug on Sir Giles's desk and gave it to her. She took a swallow, then another, and ran her tongue over her lips.

'Thank you.' She managed a smile. 'It sounds as though Sir Giles knows me better than I know myself.'

'Some people have that knack.' Brad returned the smile. 'He was rather like that with me.'

Esme gave a start. 'Did you tell him you'd asked me to marry you?'

'Yes. In so many words. He patted me on the back and congratulated me, then offered me one of his best cigars – a Cuban one. I didn't tell him you hadn't given me an answer or I might not have had the opportunity of enjoying such a marvellous cigar.' Brad's face was wreathed in smiles. Then he became serious. 'But

I think he knew you were hesitating or you would have given him the news.' He gazed at her. 'Esmeralda, darling, you realise what this means, don't you?' He waved the letter.

Slowly, deliberately, Esme removed her wedding ring and gently dropped it into one of Sir Giles's unused ashtrays, where it clinked as it struck the glass bottom. She turned and looked straight into Brad's eyes.

'Yes.' She beamed. 'It means I must follow my heart. And I will.'

Chapter Forty-Six

It was June and the war was finally turning in the Allies' favour. Tunis had recently been captured and the Axis had capitulated in North Africa. More than twenty U-boats had been sunk in a fortnight during the Battle of the Atlantic. But still the Nazis hadn't given up and nobody ever knew when the Luftwaffe would strike again. But at least any invasion seemed very unlikely now.

All this was on Esme's mind as she decided today's job was to be in the library sorting out books whose covers were in need of repair. Whether they could be done in wartime was anyone's guess, but the main thing was to keep them separate so when the opportunity came, they'd be together on a shelf marked *FRAGILE*. It was a satisfying job, knowing that one day all these valuable books would be strong enough to be handled and read once again.

Wearing white cotton gloves, she gently picked up a first edition of Charles Dickens' *Pickwick Papers* that had a split spine with some of the pages falling apart, when she heard the telephone ring in Sir Giles's study. She cocked her ear, waiting for a few moments, hoping he'd answer, but the ringing was insistent and she hurried to his room.

'Sir Giles Carmichael's residence.'

'I'd like to speak to Mrs Donaldson,' came a mature male voice whom she thought she vaguely recognised.

'Speaking.'

'Ah, Esmeralda. It's Neville Wallace, returned to the fold.' He gave a short bark of laughter. 'I'm sorry I've been gone rather longer than I expected. Truth to tell, I didn't want to leave.' He gave another bark.

'Mr Wallace! How nice to hear from you. Does that mean you're feeling better now?'

'Very well rested and ready to get down to business. But first of all, my dear, I was very sorry to learn about your father. He and I served together in the Great War – that's how we met and we've been good friends ever since.'

Esme sighed. 'It must have been a shock for you, too.' She hesitated. 'I suppose you've seen that Dad drastically altered the will when you were away?'

She heard a grunt.

'I want to call a family meeting in the office with you and your sister, and Mrs Grant – as soon as possible. There's something important I need to discuss. I'm in all this week, so if you could arrange a time to suit the three of you, then let me know and I'll make myself available.' He rang off.

Esme put the receiver back on its cradle, deep in thought. *There's nothing you can do about it*, Muriel's voice rang through her head. She'd tried to be philosophical. *If that's what Dad decided, there's no argument*, she'd told herself. But deep inside she'd felt a curl of resentment ever since Muriel had sprung it on them. She'd had to rent a cramped flat with other people's furniture that wasn't to her taste, with no way of ever earning enough money to put down as a deposit on a home of her own, let alone able to afford the payments.

Not that it mattered so much now she'd told Brad she'd marry him, but she'd hated to say that she had very little to contribute financially. He'd just laughed.

'I wasn't expecting any financial contribution, darling. I earn enough for both of us and any family we have.' He'd kissed the tip of her nose. 'Your love is the only contribution I need.'

But that didn't change her desire for independence. Freda and her husband had been able to buy their house when his property business was at its zenith long before the war started and fortunately, they'd escaped the Luftwaffe's attack on Reading in February. Their comfortable home on the outskirts, along with those of their neighbours, had thankfully remained unscathed.

Amiable as usual, Sir Giles allowed her to use the telephone to ring Freda and her stepmother.

'I suppose he's going to explain the situation to us,' Freda said. 'That it was Dad's decision and advise us that if we contest it, it will be a prolonged court case costing goodness knows how much if we lose.' She paused. 'I'm not sure if I could ask John to cough up for it as it will obviously be a risk as to whether or not we'd win.'

'It's the humiliation,' Esme said. She could just picture the scene: Muriel in court, purposely dressed in widow's weeds and Freda still managing to follow the latest fashion by making most of her own and the boys' clothes when the rationing had started. One looking in dire need of a home, and the other looking as though she'd just stepped out of a magazine.

'Oh well, let's see what he has to say.'

They arranged for late morning this coming Friday.

Now for Muriel, Esme thought, when she'd said goodbye to Freda. She dialled home.

'Mrs Grant speaking,' came Muriel's sharp tone.

'Muriel, it's Esme. I've just had a telephone call from Mr Wallace.'

'Oh, he's back then?'

'Yes, and he wants to see you and Freda and me in his office.

We've arranged for this Friday at noon to allow plenty of time for Freda to get here.'

'You didn't consult me first to see if I'd made any previous arrangement.'

'Muriel, for goodness' sake—'

'Yes, I can be there. But I don't know why it's necessary.' Her stepmother paused. 'Oh, yes, I do. It's to inform us that probate has come through. So I'm sure you and Freda will want to know what your father's left you – outside of the house, of course.'

Esme felt a bubble of irritation in her throat.

Don't rise to her.

'Well, we'll have to wait and see,' she said in as neutral a tone as she could muster. 'Anyway, I'm on Sir Giles's phone so I must go. I'll meet you in the lawyer's office on Friday.'

Chapter Forty-Seven

Esme was grateful she had plenty to occupy her in the next few days. The library trolley service was gaining momentum because more soldiers were now well enough to take an interest in books than there were soldiers being discharged from the hospital. But Friday couldn't come quick enough for the meeting with Mr Wallace. She just wanted to have the whole thing over and done with and Muriel's triumphant smile behind her.

Following the funeral, Esme had brought most of her clothes over from her old home – now Muriel's, she thought with a grimace – to Redcliffe Manor. That morning, as they were having an unusual warm spell after an undecided beginning, she took from the wardrobe the blue-and-white spotted dress that Freda had made her just before the war started, and the white wedge sandals. She smiled at the memory of the last time she'd worn them – at the jazz evening when she'd put them on to go with the flirty red dress and had ended up dancing in Brad's arms. Reluctantly, she pushed aside the delicious memory. She must focus on the task ahead. She would need to be ladylike in front of Muriel and hoped Freda would be the same and restrain from giving their stepmother some home truths.

It was only a ten-minute walk from the bus station to Wallace & Wallace Solicitors, just off the high street. Esme tilted her face to the midday sun, enjoying the warmth on her face after nearly a week of rain. She rang the bell on what had obviously been a substantial residential house and immediately the door opened. Mrs Day, the elderly receptionist who'd started life there as a young secretary, stood smiling.

'Come in, my dear. Your sister is here already.'

'And Mrs Grant?'

'She's not here yet.'

Mrs Day ushered her into a small waiting room where Freda, dressed fashionably in a pale yellow summer dress, was lighting a cigarette.

'Have you been here long?' Esme asked her sister at the same time the doorbell rang.

'Oh, I expect that'll be Mrs Grant.' Mrs Day hurried to open the door.

'Damn!' Freda muttered under her breath, inhaling another lungful of smoke. 'I wanted to have a word on our own.'

'Thank you, kindly,' came Muriel's strident tones as she set foot in the hall. 'I know where to go, thank you.'

'Mr Wallace won't keep you a minute,' Esme heard Mrs Day tell her.

Muriel was looking very modest in a charcoal button-through dress Esme had never seen before and a wide-brimmed cream hat. She sat opposite the two sisters and after a nod of acknowledgement, picked up a magazine and began flipping through it. Now and again she looked towards the door and gave a long sigh.

It was a full fifteen minutes before the buzzer went on Mrs Day's desk.

'Mr Wallace will see you now,' she said, gesturing the small group to follow her.

Mr Wallace stepped forward and planted a kiss on Esme's and Freda's cheeks.

'It's lovely to see you both, my dears,' he said. 'And, Freda, I haven't had the chance to say how sorry I am about your father. I expect Esmeralda told you he was my oldest friend.' He looked at Muriel and extended his hand. 'Mrs Grant, you're looking well.'

Muriel simpered and he let her hand drop.

'Do sit down everyone. I'll have tea brought in.' He picked up the receiver on his desk. 'And send Robert and Jim in, Mrs Day,' he added to the refreshment order.

Almost immediately there was a knock at the door and two men entered, one maybe in his fifties with a receding hairline and signs of a paunch, the other, though taller, looking hardly more than a boy.

'This is Mr Robert Lake,' Mr Wallace said, 'our senior clerk.' He gestured towards Esme and Freda, introducing them to the older man.

Mr Lake first shook hands with Esme and Freda, then turned to Muriel, giving her a warm smile.

'Nice to see you again, Mrs Grant.' He briefly shook her hand and she nodded.

Esme couldn't help noticing Muriel's eyes were gleaming under her hat and her mouth was strangely twisted as though trying to bite back a smile. A smile of triumph, no doubt, Esme thought, sickened to think that the woman who had called herself 'stepmother' would inherit their home.

'And this here lad, Jim Cook, is our trainee clerk,' Mr Wallace said. 'He accompanied Mr Lake to the family home when the changes to the will were made, which is why I wanted him to be here as well.'

There was a silence. Then Mr Wallace looked towards Robert Lake.

'Tell me exactly what happened when you and young Jim went to see the late Mr Grant and Mrs Grant?'

'I'm not sure I understand why—' Muriel began loudly.

Mr Wallace held up his hand. 'Be patient, Mrs Grant. I was away. I need to know what was said so I can begin the probate process.'

'I see.' Muriel seemed mollified as she sat still, her hands relaxed in the folds of her pleated skirt.

'Begin, please, Mr Lake. We'll talk about the terms of the will later, but for now, would you please concentrate on the property known as 25 Ridge Way, in Bath.'

Mr Lake thrust out his chest, his thumbs in his lapels, and cleared his throat.

'Well, Jim and I arrived at the property on the pre-appointed hour of three o'clock in the afternoon of the fifteenth of October. I know the date well as it happened to be my birthday,' he added with a broad smile. 'Mrs Grant showed us into the sitting room where Mr Grant was in an armchair by the fire.'

'So Mr Grant was expecting you?' Mr Wallace said, scribbling some notes in his pad.

'Yes, sir. He'd specifically asked to see us. We both sat down and I handed Mr Grant the amended will and told him to read it carefully to make sure he was satisfied with the new arrangement.'

'So he'd already told you what he wanted to change?' Mr Wallace said.

'Er, not exactly. Mrs Grant told me on the telephone that he wanted to remove his daughters' names as the beneficiaries of the property and that his wife's should be inserted.'

'So you amended the will in the office without actually having spoken to Mr Grant himself?'

Mr Lake smiled. 'I knew there must be nothing untoward, as it wouldn't be valid—' He broke off and sent Muriel what looked to Esme like an apologetic smile. 'Because I would be there with Jim witnessing Mr Grant signing it.'

'Why didn't Mr and Mrs Grant come to the office, which most people do?'

'He hadn't been too well, and Mrs Grant—'

Muriel sprang from her chair. 'I told Mr Lake on the telephone that my husband wasn't able to walk that far or go on a bus.' She paused. 'And we couldn't afford a taxi.'

'I see.' Mr Wallace bent his head, then looked up. 'And did Mr Grant read the will carefully in your presence before signing?'

'Yes, sir,' Mr Lake said, at the same time as Jim said: 'No, sir.'

'What does *that* mean?' Mr Wallace's voice held an edge. 'You can't both be right. Either Mr Grant read the will properly before signing or not.'

Muriel jumped to her feet. 'Mr Wallace, I'm not sure what all this is about but everything's above board. The will was signed by my husband, who was happy to acknowledge that I had been his wife and mother to his daughters for the last twenty-four years. Esmeralda was only seven when I first set eyes on her.' She pursed her lips. 'I saved her from going to the orphanage and Mr Grant always let me know how grateful he was.'

'It's true,' Mr Lake broke in unexpectedly. 'Mr Grant told me the same himself. And if I may say so,' he turned to Esme, 'Mrs Donaldson has turned out to be a fine young woman having Mrs Grant as her stepmother.'

'So I see,' Mr Wallace said drily.

Muriel, still standing, sent Mr Lake an appreciative smile, then turned her gaze on Mr Wallace. 'I can assure you, Mr Wallace, that my husband requested the meeting and Mr Lake, *on my husband's instructions*' – she emphasised the words – 'carried out the necessary paperwork. There *is* no argument.'

'I'm not implying that there is, Mrs Grant,' Mr Wallace said sharply. 'But would you kindly be seated.'

Muriel sat down, glaring at no one in particular.

Esme and Freda shot glances at one another. Where was all this leading? It was making her head spin. If only she could escape from this stuffy room.

'Is it possible to have the window open?' she said.

'Jim, open that window a fraction.' Mr Wallace turned to Esme. 'Can't have more than a crack, Esmeralda, as it's windy today and blows the papers all over the place.' He pushed his glasses up his nose. 'Now, where were we before all the interruptions? Oh, yes, I was asking about whether Mr Grant read the will thoroughly before signing it.'

'He did, sir,' Mr Lake said. 'Not all of it, perhaps, as it was only the property stipulation that was to be altered. Everything else was to remain the same.'

'Would you please produce the two wills, Mr Lake. The one Bernard Grant signed before the death of his first wife, the mother of these two sisters, and the recent one.'

'Of course, sir.' Mr Lake opened his briefcase and placed them both on Mr Wallace's desk, side by side. 'Obviously, this latest one overrides the original one.'

Mr Wallace pushed his slipping spectacles back onto the bridge of his nose and peered at the signatures.

'I can assure you the current one is of the same hand as the original,' Mr Lake said.

Mr Wallace opened his desk drawer and removed a magnifying glass. He studied both signatures for a whole minute, then said, 'Yes, they look the same, though the second one is a little shaky.' He looked up at his senior clerk. 'Presumably that comes from his gradual deterioration of health.'

'That's exactly right, sir.' Mr Lake's expression was one of relief.

'Mrs Grant did have to put her hand on her husband's to

help guide him when he was holding the pen to sign,' Jim added helpfully.

Esme's hand flew to her mouth and heard Freda gasp. A stony silence settled over the small group.

'Really?' Mr Wallace leaned over his desk, his stubby fingers hooked together as he peered over the top of his glasses at Jim, then over to Mr Lake, and finally, a lingering look at Muriel. Esme was close enough to see she'd turned ashen. 'That's *most* interesting.' He turned his attention back to Jim. 'What more can you tell me about Mr Grant's condition, my boy?'

Esme didn't miss the glare that Mr Lake threw to the young man.

Jim's face reddened. 'Well, sir, we could tell Mr Grant was quite weak.'

'How could you tell?'

'For one thing, he tried to stand up when we came into the room but began to shake and fall backwards. I had to steady him and set him back down again.'

'So you weren't surprised when Mrs Grant had to give her husband a guiding hand?'

'Not really, sir. It would probably have been illegible if he'd tried to do it on his own.'

Mr Wallace glanced at Mr Lake. 'And did you confirm directly with Mr Grant that it was his wish to change the name on the deeds?'

Muriel was a mask of fury. 'It was my husband's decision alone to renew the will. He signed it while completely in his right mind, if that's what you're getting at.'

Mr Wallace opened a file on his desk and removed a couple of typed sheets. He looked up.

'I've had this report from his doctor. Mr Grant was officially diagnosed with Parkinson's disease last September. The doctor states he'd had it coming on for years, but the symptoms were not that noticeable. However, in the last few months they quickly became worse.' He paused. 'Parkinson's can affect your mental attitude, the doctor said, to the extent that you don't always think things through logically and sensibly. With that evidence and *you*, Mrs Grant,' he turned to her, '*helping* him to sign the new will – I use that term deliberately – makes this will invalid.' He waved the papers in the air. 'I hereby declare that the only one valid is the one Mr Grant signed in my presence nigh on twenty-seven years ago.'

Esme let out a gasp. She surreptitiously glanced at Freda who touched the corner of her mouth.

Muriel gave a screech of protest. 'I'm his *wife*. I looked after him and his daughters – who were not easy, I can assure you. Esme caught rheumatic fever soon after I became the housekeeper. There I was, having to nurse a sickly child as well as running the household and cooking. I gave up everything for him.'

Muriel glared around the room. Esme struggled to keep her expression bland, afraid to show her relief. Freda's face was alight with elation. Muriel sent her a withering look, then cast her eyes back to Mr Wallace, her tone now desperate. 'I don't mind if we divide the property into three – that's fair, isn't it?'

'I'm afraid I can't do that. By law, the original will must stand.'

'But that was drawn up before I came to him as a housekeeper, and then his wife. I was a devoted—'

'Mrs Grant,' Mr Wallace held the palm of his hand towards her, 'perhaps when probate is through, and if you are able to contain your resentment, you may find that your husband's daughters will not let you go without some mark of recognition.'

'I'm sorry, that's not good enough. As if I should be expected to rely on those two.' She shook her head so hard that her hat tipped to the side. She snatched it off and set it on her lap, her lips in a grim line. 'Mark my words, I'm not letting this go without a fight. I shall contest it in court! And I will win when the judge hears me out.'

'I wouldn't do that, if I were you, Mrs Grant,' Mr Wallace said coolly. 'A judge would call this an offence under the Forgery Act 1913. You could very well be given a prison sentence of up to ten years, plus a substantial fine.' He turned to the sisters and beamed. 'Freda, Esmeralda, Number 25 Ridge Way will be shared equally between you, so I will now organise probate which shouldn't take too long. I'll ring you when it's completed.' He came from behind his desk and put his hand out politely for Muriel.

She thrust his hand aside, tossing her head as she stood up, then glared at Mr Lake who was jangling some coins in his pocket.

'You said there'd be no problem, Robert.' Her face was an angry red. 'I've already given you half the money we agreed and I want it back—' As though realising she'd said too much, she pursed her lips, furious tears streaming down her cheeks.

No one moved.

'"Robert", eh?' Mr Wallace's voice was ice. Before Muriel could answer, he said, 'I'm afraid, Mrs Grant, this is sounding more and more intriguing. I wonder how such an agreement came to be, not to mention how much money you agreed to pay Mr Lake for having your name illegally put on the will and your stepdaughters' names removed. A judge would want to add conspiracy to the charges.' He glanced at Jim, who was biting his lower lip. 'Jim, my boy, thank you for your honesty here and thereby ensuring the correct will is observed. You have helped us to avoid improperly administering Mr Grant's wishes.' He glared at Muriel. 'And you, Mrs Grant, may not realise how very close you've come to my reporting you to the police. If I hear one more word that you're contesting this will, I'll personally see you put in prison.' He turned to Esme and Freda. 'And being Mr Grant's daughters, you now have the right to call in the police and have Mrs Grant arrested.'

There was a deathly silence.

Muriel broke the spell. She whirled round to Robert Lake.

'You stupid man,' she stormed as she shot to her feet. 'I'd never have gone out with you if I'd known how useless you'd turn out to be.' She pushed by the still-seated Freda to the door.

When Muriel had vanished, Esme caught a slight upturn at the corners of Mr Wallace's mouth.

'Freda, Esmeralda, I believe we've reached the right conclusion.'

'You certainly have.' Freda stood up. 'And I want to thank you most sincerely for getting to the bottom of all this, Mr Wallace.'

'I second that,' Esme added.

'Just doing my job,' he said, allowing himself a proper smile, as he walked to the door with them. 'I'll have any of the necessary paperwork drawn up and forward you both a copy.'

The last the sisters heard was Mr Wallace's voice.

'You will stay behind, Robert. You've made a mockery of the profession and broken the rules regulating employees in a solicitor's practice. I need to have a serious talk to you to consider your future.'

'Phew!' Freda blew out her cheeks when she and Esme were outside. 'I wouldn't have wanted to be in Muriel's shoes for all the tea in China . . . or Robert Lake's, as any employer who uses that term "considering your future" means the employee is about to be sacked.' She chuckled. 'Mr Wallace made mincemeat out of Muriel, didn't he? She didn't know where to put herself. And can you believe she and Lake were having an affair. Ugh!' She looked up and down the street. 'She's disappeared. Good riddance.'

'How long shall we let her stay in the house?'

'Oh, we'll be more than generous.' Freda gave Esme a sly smile. 'But what I propose is to let the Government Evacuation Scheme know there's a family house vacant in Bath with a ready-made housekeeper in tow.'

'Oh, Freda, you wouldn't do that.'

'Oh, yes, I would. I think it's the right way to go. After all, we want to give our stepmother the chance to do her bit where the war is concerned, don't we?' She laughed uproariously. 'She should thank us for coming up with such a perfect opportunity to give shelter to a deserving family. And when the war's over, that will be it where the house is concerned. She can find her own place to rent.'

'Even though Dad would have been appalled at Muriel's conniving, don't forget he's left her a cash settlement,' Esme said.

'Yes, and we'll carry out his wishes.'

After extracting a promise from Esme to keep her updated with any events from this afternoon's meeting, a jubilant Freda caught an evening train back to Reading. It was already dusk. Esme felt drained from the meeting, even though it had ended up going in her and Freda's favour, and she decided to treat herself to a taxi back to Redcliffe Manor. She'd just approached the taxi rank where there was a long queue, when a familiar motorcar drew up. The driver wound down the window.

'Why, if it isn't Mrs Donaldson.' Then Brad added under his breath, 'Soon to be Mrs Parker.' He hopped out and kissed her in front of everyone in the queue who was staring at them, then opened the car door, tucked her in, and took the driving seat.

'I hope that gives them something to gossip about.' He chuckled, glancing quickly at her.

She smiled.

'You don't seem too upset about the meeting,' Brad said, as he signalled to pull out into the road.

'Well, it didn't go as I expected.'

'No, I suppose not. It was all settled before Wallace got back, wasn't it?'

'Not quite,' Esme said. 'I'll tell you all about it when we're back at the Manor but for now, I just want you to tell me if you've missed me.'

'I might have done.' Brad kept his eyes firmly fixed on the road. 'But you'd better wish you'd not challenged me unless you're prepared to take the consequences.'

'I'm more than prepared.' Esme chuckled.

In no time at all, Brad was steering the motorcar down the drive to the Manor. He switched off the engine.

'I'll park it over at the hospital later,' he said, his husky voice sending shivers across Esme's shoulders. 'But for now, I'm going to kiss you thoroughly and then you can decide if it shows whether I've missed you or not.'

After...

Denver, Colorado, USA
July 1950

Esme swung the Triumph Mayflower into the short drive and switched off the engine, grinning at the novelty of driving her own car. Brad had bought it in celebration of passing her driving test last month. How she loved the modern design and the two-tone cream upper and green-gold lower – so different from anything she'd ever seen in England. But most of all, she loved the independence it gave her. She slammed the driver's door shut and went round to the other side. Bending low, she eased out the little girl. After setting the small feet on the drive, Esme reached in for the basket of groceries.

'Stay in car,' the child protested loudly, tears streaming down her baby cheeks. At nearly two, Eleanora was going through a tantrum stage.

'We can't stay out, darling. Mummy has a lot to do before Daddy comes home.'

Eleanora's blue eyes were wet with unshed tears. 'Want quackers.'

'Yes, you shall have crackers and milk while I put away the shopping and make lunch.'

Esme recalled how dismayed she'd been when she'd first set

eyes on her baby – the strange yellow skin and the fuzzy hair which had covered most of the tiny body, making her look more like a little monkey than a human. But Brad had assured her that jaundice and excess hair was perfectly normal for a premature baby, and that it would all disappear within weeks. She smiled fondly. He'd been right.

It had been a miracle that she and Brad had conceived after all the warnings she'd been given, exacerbated by the decreasing likelihood of doing so in her late thirties. Three years ago, when they'd first moved to America, she'd had a miscarriage and Brad hadn't wanted her to become pregnant again, but she'd been determined. At his insistence, she'd stayed in bed for the first few weeks of the pregnancy, but despite taking it easy, the baby had still arrived a full seven weeks early and weighed less than five pounds. It had been touch-and-go as to whether she would survive, and quickly Esme had named her Eleanora after her own mother. Esme had needed more time to rest in bed after the harrowing birth. Brad sent his mother to look after them all, and true to form, Mrs Parker couldn't have been kinder.

My recovery was really down to my mother-in-law, Esme thought, as she shushed her daughter. Mrs Parker had made delicious meals, encouraged her, and generally used common sense as she showed her daughter-in-law how to look after the little mite when Esme was feeling stronger and spending more time out of bed.

Brad's mother had invited Esme to call her Mom, but if she didn't feel comfortable with that, then to call her Lou – 'Short for Louise,' she'd laughed, 'because I'm not crazy about that name.'

To Brad's delight, Esme had gladly taken to calling her Mom and Mr Parker had become Pop.

Yes, Esme told herself. *I've been very lucky. And yesterday I was thirty-nine. I can hardly believe it. So much has happened since that terrible war. Did it really last six years? Brad's release from the US Air Force and his partnership with Marilyn Lorrimer, the cardiologist who attended me at the military hospital after Bertha nearly drowned, is working well . . . and he and I are still so happy with each other and our darling Nora. And now we've filled out the adoption form to welcome a new baby brother or sister for her.*

It hadn't all gone smoothly. At first, Esme had been horribly homesick. She missed her sister, but Freda had written only last week that she and John and the boys – both strapping young men – were planning to come over in the summer holidays to visit.

My niece, Freda had written, *must be growing fast and I want her to know her Aunt Freda. Me with two boys, it's lovely to have a girl in the family.*

Even Stella had mentioned she hoped to come one day and visit. How strange it all was. If Mr Greenwood at the Bath Lending Library hadn't given her her notice and she hadn't met Stella and found her the position in the library, she would never have met Brad . . . or had Nora. And that would have been inconceivable. She couldn't help grinning at the unintended use of the word. And yes, she missed Stella, as well.

But most of all, she'd worried about Sir Giles, and if she were honest, she missed not only working for him but the man himself. He did write more regularly than anyone, but his handwriting, never the best because of his hand, was beginning to look worse. She sighed, imagining the years taking its toll on him. She couldn't expect him to keep up his once-a-week missive. But still she was anxious that she hadn't heard anything from him for a whole month.

Now, Esme checked the mailbox next to the gate and removed what looked like two late birthday cards. She put them together with a couple of bills on top of the basket and took Eleanor's hand again. In the porch, she saw the mailman had left a parcel. Unlocking the front door and making sure her daughter was safely inside, she picked it up and looked to see who had sent it. From Stella. Strange. They didn't normally send one another birthday presents.

'Mummy, Nora want quackers.'

'All right, darling. Mummy won't be long.'

Esme put everything on the kitchen table and lifted her daughter into her high chair, then swiftly poured a beaker of milk and took two crackers out of the tin, then set them on the little table in front of the child. She made herself a coffee and sat on one of the kitchen chairs, fingering the parcel.

Good. It feels like a book. And Sir Giles was aware of her taste in books.

She carefully broke the sealing wax and cut the string, then folded back the brown wrapping paper. The present was wrapped in pink crêpe paper and there was an envelope on the top with her name. She opened it and a newspaper cutting fluttered to the floor. She picked it up and turned it over to see the smiling face of someone familiar. Someone dressed in Tudor costume beaming at her. Her eyes widened as she read the headlines:

MAKING HIS STAGE DEBUT
LLOYD TAYLOR PLAYS OTHELLO TO RAVE REVIEWS

A warm glow stole round her heart. Lloyd had achieved his dream. Shown them all. Oh, she couldn't be more proud of him. Beaming back at his photograph, she put the article on the kitchen table to read and savour later, then unfolded Stella's letter. Sir Giles was now her concern.

My dear Esme,

I hope you are well and happy and will be pleased to learn that your favourite patient, Lloyd Taylor, also looks well and very happy!

Esme grinned, but as she read on, her smile faded.

I know this will come as a shock, but Sir Giles died peacefully in his sleep last night. I was with him a few hours before and he was perfectly lucid although he'd recently suffered a bad chest cold. He told me he wanted you to have a particular book and would I send it to you on his behalf. They were more or less his last words before I said goodnight to him. Anyway, here it is. I hope you receive it in time for your birthday. I'll write a proper letter as soon as I can, but there's a lot to do here at the moment.

Try not to feel too sad. You of all people know that he had a full life.

Much love,
Stella x

For a few moments, Esme sat rigid, stunned at the news. Sir Giles, her saviour, was gone. In a daze she tore the crêpe paper from the book and her mouth fell open in astonishment as she read the title:

No Shining Armour
by Sir Giles Carmichael

He'd done it! He'd had it published for all to see!

Momentarily, she closed her eyes. She could see him now, stroking his beard as he did when he was unsure of something or needed time to think, and saying he didn't wish to include the mountain accident. At least he'd lived to see his biography with all its ups and downs published for others to think on and perhaps be inspired by a very special human being. Holding her breath, she opened the hard cover and read on the frontispiece:

*This memoir is dedicated to
Walter Wheeler.
Forgive me, old pal.*

Hardly conscious of the tears running down her cheeks that he'd dedicated the book to his friend who'd died too young on a freezing mountain, she turned the page. Her heart leaped to recognise Sir Giles's scrawling handwriting.

*For my dear Esmeralda,
with grateful thanks always.
Yours, with my love,
Giles Carmichael*

Esme swallowed hard, brushing her damp face with the back of her hand. Slowly, she turned to the next page – the first chapter entitled: 'The Background to My Story'. It felt like only yesterday when she'd typed that first line. She pulled one of the sofa cushions closer behind her back, took a sip of her coffee, and began to read.

Acknowledgements

As I often mention to my readers, a writer doesn't scribble away in a garret – not these days, anyway. We need all sorts of contact, support and outside stimulation for the story to come together well before it hits the shelves. Below are the many people who have helped, advised and encouraged me to write this story.

My previous dear agent, Heather Holden Brown (sadly since retired), had the idea for me to set the next novel in a country house that had been requisitioned by the War Ministry for their purposes. But it was her colleague, Elly James, now my lovely agent, who discovered the ideal estate on which to base my fictional one, namely Longleat, near Bath. During the war, Longleat housed the Royal School for Daughters of Officers in the Army, which was evacuated from Bath, as well as a US military hospital in the grounds. Elly and I spent a wonderful day at Longleat, ignoring the safari park (post-war), and concentrating on the house itself.

I want to give huge thanks to the archivist, Emma Challinor, who took such an interest in my proposed novel and gave Elly and me a riveting private tour. As we walked round the house, Emma handed me two laminated plans to take away, showing the layout of the ground floor and first-floor rooms which had been occupied by the school. These helped me enormously when writing this novel. And as we were strolling in the grounds, admiring the wonderful country views, Emma pointed to where the US hospital would have been sited. I noticed the building would have been near some lakes, and immediately a dramatic scene flashed through my mind for *The Wartime Librarian's Secret*.

The name for my hero came quite unexpectedly. I met this tall, dark handsome American on a train going to Port Isaac where the Vestas (see below) were to spend a week's retreat for writing. He and I got chatting and he told me he came from Denver. Well, I lived in Denver for three years in the sixties. He said he visits Norwich every year to see the football – and I grew up in Norwich. When he told me his name, Bradley Parker, I said, 'If that isn't an American hero's name, I don't know what is.' I asked if I could use it for my American hero in my new novel, and that I would give him an acknowledgement. He was delighted and offered to swap emails in case he could help me with any further information on the American hospital. In case you're wondering, yes, he did email me the next morning saying how much he enjoyed our conversation and to feel free to contact him at any time. Oh, if only I'd been twenty years, no, thirty years, no, if I'm honest, forty years younger . . .

Avon at HarperCollins has been my publisher right from the beginning, and I couldn't be in better hands than with the friendliest and most professional, multi-times award-winning team that is Avon. Emma Grundy Haigh is my new editor, and she is everything you hope an editor would be – warmly approachable and hugely supportive, not to mention being a terrific editor. And it's the whole Avon team of graphic designers, media experts, marketing, public relations and sales who have seamlessly put everything together to produce a book I can't help being proud of.

A noteworthy friend in my writing life is Alison Morton, thriller writer extraordinaire. We are critique writing partners and my, are we blunt – red pens hovering, ready to pounce on the other's manuscript. We call it 'brutal love' and it works! Thanks, Alison, for coming up with such a cracking title!

Then I have belonged to the same two writing groups (both a foursome) for a decade or more. We're all published authors writing in different genres. The Diamonds are Terri Fleming, Sue Mackender and Tessa Spencer. We try to meet once a month in one of our homes for the day but Zoom if it's not always possible. We take it in turns to read one of our chapters for a critique, which can be daunting, but we often fall about laughing as well as coming up with an answer to whatever the problem. The Vestas are Gail Aldwin, Suzanne Goldring and Carol McGrath. We don't usually get the opportunity to meet in person more than twice a year (Zooming in between) but as it's a whole week, we really push out the word count and read our fresh chapters out in the afternoon over tea and cakes. And we can nab one another to ask for advice or help at any time of the day or evening. Someone is bound to sort it out.

Needless to mention, all six of them have become good friends over the years.

Finally, a big thank you to you, dear reader, for giving up your time to put your feet up and read my novels. Without you, my stories would languish in a drawer. I do hope you enjoy this latest one as much as I've enjoyed researching and writing it.

A small request – would you consider leaving a review on Amazon? It always makes my day to read a review from someone who's enjoyed my stories, and it encourages others to perhaps give it a go. Thank you so much. And if you would like to get in touch with me direct, please go to my website: mollygreenauthor.com

I look forward very much to hearing from you.

Reading List

The Country House: A Wartime History, 1939–45 by Caroline Seebohm
Longleat: House Guide
Longleat: From 1566 to the Present Time (published in 1949)
Mercury Presides: Formerly Marchioness of Bath by Daphne Fielding (another absorbing memoir)
Longleat: The Story of an English Country House by David Burnett
Our Uninvited Guests: The Secret Lives of Britain's Country Houses 1939–45 by Julie Summers
Plain Jane: Her Memoirs by Jane Donaldson (She was a delinquent in the Royal School for Daughters of Officers in the Army and this is a fascinating autobiography.)
Queen Mary: The Official Biography by James Pope-Hennessy

Author's Historical Note

During the Second World War, Queen Mary really did enjoy visiting schools and hospitals and was even known to take a turn serving meals to the British and Allied forces from canteens and rest rooms organised by the WVS (Women's Voluntary Service). And she really did get caught once on a visit to a country house that took a bomb and was discovered in the basement exactly as I described her in my novel – perfectly groomed and calmly doing the crossword.

On a final note – when my sister, Carole, was four, she was out one day with our grandmother in Kings Lynn (where Nana and Pop lived). Just as they were going into Jermyn's department store, a tall, elegant, dignified lady followed by another refined-looking woman were on their way out and passed close to them. Nana bent to Carole and said, 'That was Queen Mary with her lady-in-waiting. Don't ever forget you've seen the old Queen close to.'

All these decades later, Carole says she clearly remembers seeing Queen Mary looking just like the photograph I showed her on the front of the paperback biography I was reading (see Reading List).

To give me a certain amount of freedom in creating my story, I changed Longleat to Redcliffe Manor but used the same school and American hospital settings to give an authentic flavour.

**Read on for an exclusive extract from
Molly Green's next novel . . .**

Chapter One

September 1944
Mayfair, London

Deirdre Redgrave smothered a yawn. If only she could stay in her bed this morning after such a rotten night. Those blasted new flying bombs Hitler was sending over – doodlebugs, they were called – had been constantly exploding in the distance. You were safe when you heard them, everyone said, but when it went silent… That's when they were right overhead and there was every chance they'd get you. With a sigh, she glanced at the bedside clock. Seven minutes to eight. Oh, lor', she'd only just make it!

Flinging back the covers, she leapt out of bed and splashed her face at the sink in the corner of her room. The water was stone cold from the hot tap. Thankful it was still warm weather, she soaked a flannel and hurriedly washed. She prayed her stockings wouldn't ladder as she quickly drew them up, then buttoned a flowered blouse. Finally, she zipped up the same black skirt she wore most days. Thank goodness she always pressed it at night with the flat iron, so it was ready for the next day's shift. No time to do anything more than a rake through her unruly red curls and hurriedly apply a smear of her precious lipstick. Outside the lift, she hesitated.

Lift or stairs?

It was always a dilemma. She hated being in that rickety ancient lift on her own and by the time it whined and clanked its way up to the top floor, she told herself it was quicker to run down the four flights of stairs.

Stairs, she decided.

She gripped the banister as she hurried down the worn stairs. Even in the dim light she couldn't help noticing how the diamond and ruby ring seemed to wink up at her. It was one year ago today that Denis had slipped it onto the third finger of her left hand. Not for the first time, she wondered what being a wife would really be like. Was she ready for it? After all, she'd been engaged before and had broken it off only weeks before the wedding because she'd felt Colin was too possessive, too controlling. She'd been crazy about him but had finally realised any future life with him would be on his terms. And that wouldn't suit her at all. But Denis was different. He was such an amiable chap, two years younger than her twenty-three years, and was devoted to her. He'd wanted them to be married within a month following the engagement, but she'd put him off.

'Let's wait until the war ends,' she'd said. 'We can't plan anything until then. We won't see each other for months until you manage to get some leave. And we don't know from day to day, minute to minute, when it might be our last time together.'

'That's just it,' he'd said. 'We should grab our happiness while we can.'

As it turned out, her words were almost prophetic. In May, Denis hinted that something big was afoot and no one would be allowed any leave at all for the foreseeable future. Since then, he hadn't mentioned getting married in his letters. Deidre supposed things were too precarious for anybody to make any specific plans, although people you met in the street seemed to know about the forthcoming invasion of France – all except the date and location, she thought, and rightly so. At least some things remained top secret.

She finally reached the ground floor and hurried over to the reception desk where Ron Cragg, the night porter, made a great show of looking at the clock, then stared up at her with his strange coal-like eyes.

'About time,' he grunted. 'I didn't think you were ever turnin' up.'

Deirdre did her own exaggerated pantomime of checking her watch.

'Exactly three minutes and twenty-two seconds past eight, Mr Cragg.' She smiled sweetly at him. 'I don't see how that gives you a reason to think I wasn't coming. I only had one day off work, and it's not as though I was going anywhere.'

'That's as maybe,' he grunted, hoisting his bag onto his shoulder. 'I'll be goin' then – I've had enough of this place and all you women.' He threw her a look of pure contempt.

'See you tomorrow then, Mr Cragg – oh, and do give my regards to Mrs Cragg.' Deirdre kept her tone civil. She was used to his rudeness by now, although she felt sorry for poor Mrs Cragg. Fancy landing up with a man who thought a woman's place was in the kitchen looking after her husband. He seemed to think of working with women as a personal slight. More than once he had complained that women had no business in the working world.

Taking jobs from under the nose of good men when the poor devils were fighting for King and Country, he'd said just the other day to a taxi driver waiting for his fare.

Her thoughts were interrupted by Ron Cragg letting the hinged side to the reception desk crash down. What a nasty temper that little trumped-up man had. Thank goodness she didn't have to work with him. She could never understand why the members of the Mayfair Ladies' Club had hired him in the first place, considering how much he seemed to hate women. Why didn't he look for another job in one of the nearby men's clubs? There were plenty of them around – the Army & Navy Club in Pall Mall, for instance. It was a much bigger concern and would have suited him far better, she would have thought.

Trying to shake the feeling of unease that always accompanied even the briefest conversation with the man, she read his notes from last night, went over the dining room bookings by the members and consulted the calendar of events planned for the coming month.

Deidre glanced towards the door. Gloria should arrive at any second, which would allow her to whip downstairs and scrounge some breakfast. Soon, it would be too late.

Where on earth was she? Deirdre glanced at her watch. Almost nine. The minute hand seemed to have slowed to a crawl. Gloria should have been here half an hour ago. Deirdre's stomach gave an irritable growl. If Gloria didn't come soon to release her, the kitchen would close, and she'd miss the staff breakfast – something she couldn't bear to contemplate.

To distract herself, she flipped over the pages of the diary to check the week's bedroom bookings.

A shadow fell over the reception desk. Deirdre glanced up. A tall, fair-haired man – in his late twenties, she calculated – stood there in a smart navy-blue pin-striped suit relieved by a bright-blue tie. He must have chosen it because it perfectly matched his eyes. And now those blue eyes met hers. For a long, uncertain moment, she held his gaze. Where had he appeared from? It couldn't have been through the front door, or she would have seen him. He couldn't have come out of the lift, either. Men weren't allowed upstairs unless they were trade carrying out some repair or other. Something this man definitely wasn't.

Of course! He must be the newly appointed manager that Nina, the third receptionist, had excitedly told her about a week ago. It had been the morning after Deirdre had tripped on the curb while walking back from the theatre in the blackout and fallen into the road, bruising her bottom so badly she could barely sit for days.

Now, she remembered Nina saying he was a bit of all right. But then Nina said that about most men younger than thirty, as there was such a shortage with so many of them away fighting. At the time, Deirdre, still nursing the pain of her fall, had taken little notice of her colleague's rapture. But this time she had to admit Nina's impression was accurate. The man standing in front of her was more than 'a bit of all right' and was most likely well aware of it. Well, she smiled inwardly, she wouldn't let on that she realised who he was.

'Good morning, sir.' She looked up at him politely. 'Are you meeting someone here?'

'Not exactly.' He extended his hand. 'Maxwell Forster, the new general manager.' He held hers in a firm handshake. 'And you are . . . ?'

'Deirdre Redgrave, head receptionist.'

An amused smile tugged at his well-shaped mouth. 'You have probably heard it a hundred times before, but your name is most appropriate.'

His voice had a musical richness in its tone. *And do I detect a slight accent?*

'More like a thousand times.'

He nodded. Then without warning, he leaned slightly forward and peered at her.

'Are you feeling all right, Miss Redgrave?'

Deirdre gave a start. 'Yes, of course. Why do you ask?'

'It's just that you look a little pale.'

She was aware of his gaze steadfastly fixed on her.

'Probably because I haven't had any breakfast.'

'Oh. Why is that?'

She raised her eyes to his. 'I can't go until someone takes over – which should be Gloria – but she's late. I just hope she hasn't had an accident – or got caught by those doodlebugs last night.' Deidre shivered.

'Let me see if I can find out what's happened.' The new manager turned round to a smart rapping on the half-glazed door. 'Ah, would that be Gloria?'

Deirdre heaved a sigh of relief to see Gloria's grinning face through the clear panel.

'Yes, thank goodness.'

Maxwell Forster covered the few feet across the foyer in easy strides. He opened the door to let in a girl, her bright-green beret precariously placed on the side of her head, adding a spot of colour to the dull brown jacket. She gave him a beaming smile before she dashed up to the desk, lifted the side that was hinged, and joined Deirdre.

'Sorry, Red, you must have been worried I wasn't going to turn up.'

'Well, I did wonder . . . and so did Mr Forster, our new manager.' Deirdre gave him a glance. 'He was about to come and look for you.'

'Shame it wasn't necessary,' Gloria giggled, then endeavoured to look contrite. 'I'm sorry to be late on your first day, Mr Forster.' Her eyes were wide as she stuck out her hand. He took it briefly. 'I simply didn't sleep a wink last night,' she went on, 'what with those new rockets Jerry's sending, and when I finally drifted off, it was almost time to get up.' She looked at Deirdre. 'Sorry, Red, but did you manage to get breakfast?'

'No, I couldn't leave here until you came.'

'Well, I'm here now,' Gloria said gaily. 'So off you go.'

Deirdre pursed her lips. 'It's no good. The kitchen closes at nine. And it's already ten past.'

'Oh, no. I'm so sorry. Would you have half my sandwich?'

'No, Gloria, that's your lunch. I'll ask Cook later if she'd allow me a couple of biscuits to go with her awful Camp coffee.'

'I may be able to help,' Max Forster broke in. He glanced at Deirdre. 'Will anyone be in the kitchen at the moment?'

'One of Cook's assistants does breakfast, but she'll be packed up and gone by now.'

'If you'll stay here for ten minutes, Miss Redgrave, I'll go down and make you something.'

'It's not the manager's—' But Deirdre didn't finish the sentence. He'd disappeared. She looked at Gloria and shrugged. 'I was going to tell him it wasn't his job.'

Gloria gave her an impish look. 'It seems he was determined to have his way.'

'What, by cooking a lowly receptionist breakfast? He's just being kind.'

'*Very* kind, if you ask me.' Gloria gave her annoying chortle. 'Anyway, let's see who's booked in this week.' She flipped open the large desk diary. 'Oh, no, the Macbeth witches are here for supper tonight because of the committee meeting tomorrow.' That dreadful Edna Bulley and her two crones were down to stay two nights. She pulled a face. 'They give me the creeps – the lot of them. They're all sickly smiles, yet they treat us like dirt.'

'Bulley by name and bully by nature,' Deirdre said, peering over Gloria's shoulder. 'But what I dislike most is having to be polite when they're so offensive. Though it's more than our job's worth to come back with as rude a response as they give us.'

'Why the members don't get rid of them, I'll never know. I suppose it's difficult when Edna's the chairman and the other two are her stooges on the committee. They're trouble, mark my words.' Gloria gave an exaggerated sigh. 'Well, we'll deal with it – we have to.' She glanced at her watch. 'I reckon our lovely new manager should be about ready now to serve madam's breakfast, so you'd better run along.'

Deirdre gave Gloria a friendly rap on the arm.

'I'll ignore that,' she said. 'But I definitely won't ignore the offer of breakfast.'

Deirdre ran down the concrete steps to the basement and along the dimly lit corridor where the kitchen was located at the far end. Before she'd even opened the door the smell of toast wafted into her nostrils. Maxwell Forster, wearing a white apron tied round his waist and looking for all the world a chef, was standing behind the long pine table, deftly buttering two thick slices of toast. He looked up and grinned.

'Perfect timing.' He sliced the toast cornerwise and put it on a plate, then took a glass dish from the oven and spooned scrambled egg over two halves, topping it with a sprig of parsley.

'Careful, the plate is very hot,' he warned as he placed it on the kitchen table, then looked about him. 'Where are the trays kept?'

Deidre didn't relish going next door to the breakfast room. Everyone else would have left to go to their jobs. She dreaded sitting there alone in case a bomb dropped on her and buried her underneath the ground. No one would know where to look for her.

'It'll be quicker if I have it here,' she said, sitting at one of the kitchen chairs.

He nodded and took a steaming kettle from the stove to the waiting teapot. 'I'm making tea. Would you like a cup?'

'Oh, yes, please.'

'But you must begin your meal. Nothing is worse than cold

scrambled egg . . . even though it is the powdered kind,' he added with that charming smile.

He poured the boiling water over the leaves and stirred it, then placed the pot on the table with a cup and saucer, milk jug and sugar bowl.

'How is it?'

She'd always disliked the taste of powdered eggs but the way he'd prepared it . . .

'It's delicious.' She looked up. 'How did you make them taste like fresh eggs?'

He smiled. 'Ah. That is a cook's secret.'

'Does that mean you're a cook in another life?'

He simply smiled.

She wished they could talk more, but she couldn't even allow time for the tea to brew. Pouring herself a cup, she munched her way through breakfast. The clock ticked the minutes by, until she was taking her last gulp of tea.

'I must go,' she said, setting the cup onto its saucer, 'seeing as I'm in work time and I'm conscious you could report me.'

'Yes, Miss Redgrave, so I could,' he said soberly, but a smile danced in his eyes, 'though on this occasion, I think I can forgive you.'

Good. He had a sense of humour. He'd be easier to work with. She smiled in acknowledgement and took her plate and teacup over to the sink and rinsed them, then slotted the plate in the plate rack nearby, wiped her cup and put it on a shelf with the others.

'Thank you, Mr Forster. That was very kind of you.'

'Think nothing of it,' he said, and began clearing up around the oven.

'Enjoy our breakfast, did we?' Gloria asked, once she was back at the reception desk.

'Considering they were powdered eggs, they were surprisingly good.'

'They would be if *Max* made them,' Gloria chuckled.

'Oh, it's "Max" now, is it?'

'Yep.' Gloria gave Deirdre a hard stare. 'Too bad you're engaged to Denis, Deidre Redgrave.'

'I don't know what you're on about, but let's get on with our work before *Max* gives us both the sack . . . on his first day.'

The two of them burst into hoots of laughter.

But the next time Deirdre glanced at her engagement ring, it didn't seem to twinkle quite so brightly.

September 1939

London is in blackout, war has been declared, but Dulcie Treadwell can think only of American broadcaster, Glenn Reeves, who didn't say goodbye before leaving for Berlin.

Heartbroken, Dulcie is posted to Bletchley Park, where she must concentrate instead on cracking the German Enigma codes. The hours are long and the conditions tough, with little recognition from above. Until she breaks her first code . . .

But when a spiteful act of jealousy leads to Dulcie's brutal dismissal, her life is left in pieces once more. Is it too late for Dulcie to prove her innocence and keep the job she loves? And will her heart ever truly heal if she doesn't hear from Glenn again . . . ?

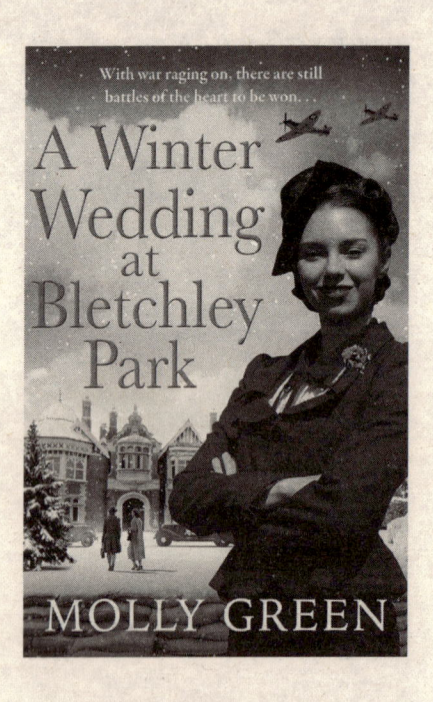

When Rosie Frost was jilted on her wedding day, she didn't think life could get any worse. But six years later in the throes of the Second World War, she is unceremoniously dismissed from her dream job after they discover her illegitimate child.

Thankfully, top secret war office Bletchley Park recognises Rosie's talent and recruits her to decipher their Italian naval signals. Happy to be doing her bit for the war effort, Rosie settles into her new life.

But when she spots a familiar face at the Park, Rosie's world threatens to come crashing down once more. Can she put her heartbreak behind her? And will wedding bells ring out across Bletchley Park before the year is out?

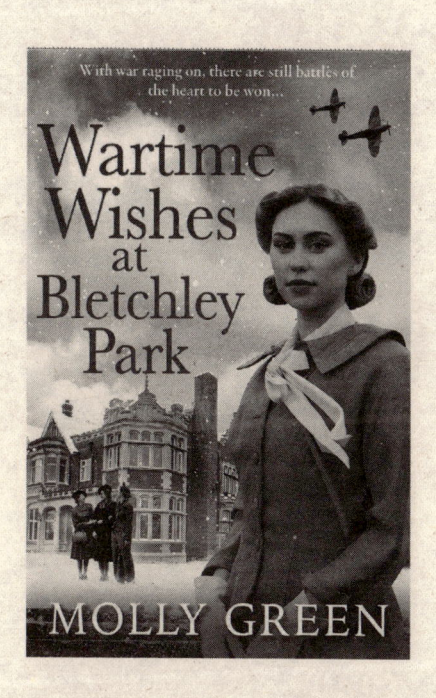

Munich. September 1938

When twenty-one-year-old Madeleine Hamilton is asked to smuggle two young pupils to Berlin, she nervously agrees. But, when they run into trouble on the train, it is Maddie's turn to be saved by a chance encounter with a handsome man.

Bletchley Park. September 1939

A year later, Maddie is undertaking training in Morse code when a familiar face shows up unexpectedly. The attraction between them is as deep as it is instant, but Maddie knows one person holds the potential to harm her country and her heart – and it is her duty to protect both . . .

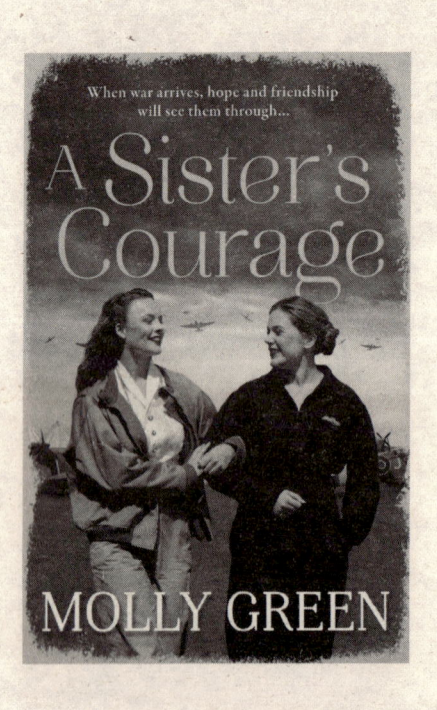

The most ambitious of three sisters, Lorraine 'Raine' Linfoot always dreamed of becoming a pilot. As a spirited seventeen-year-old, she persuades her hero Doug Williams to teach her to fly.

When war breaks out in 1939, Raine is determined to put her skills to good use. She enlists in the Air Transport Auxiliary, becoming one of a handful of brave female pilots flying fighter planes to the men on the front line.

Raine embraces the challenges of the job, despite its perils. But when Doug is reported missing after his Spitfire is shot down, she realises the war could tear apart not only her country, but also her heart . . .

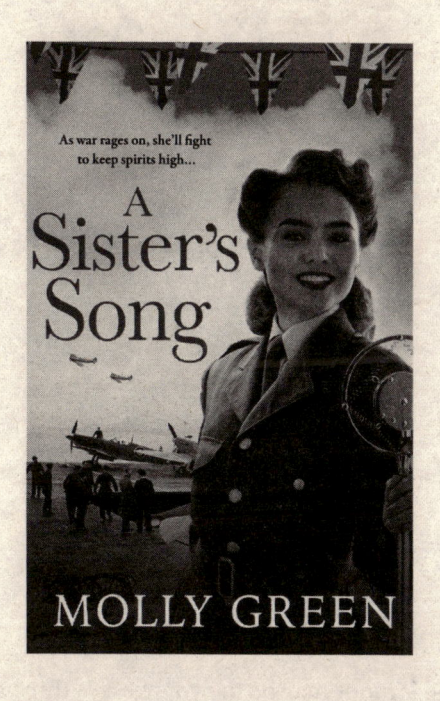

When World War II breaks out, Suzanne's dream of attending the Royal Academy of Music crumbles.

Determined to do her bit, she joins a swing band that entertains troops in some of the worst-hit cities of Europe.

Through singing, Suzanne finds a confidence she never knew she had, and she soon wins the admiration of Britain's brave servicemen.

But her heart already belongs to a Navy officer who is serving out at sea. The question is . . . will they meet again?

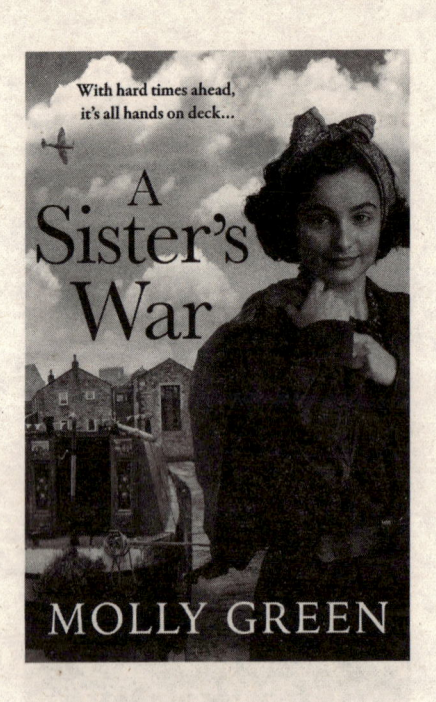

Britain, 1943

Ronnie Linfoot may be the youngest of three sisters, but she's determined to do her bit.

Against her strict mother's wishes, Ronnie signs up to join the Grand Union Canal Company, where she'll be working on a narrowboat taking critical supplies between London and Birmingham.

But with no experience on the waterways, she must learn the ropes quickly. She's facing dreadful weather, long days, and rough living conditions. At least she isn't on her own.

In the toughest times, will Ronnie and her fellow trainees pull together? For even in the darkest days of war, hope and friendship can see you through . . .

Liverpool, 1941

Haunted by the death of her sister, June Lavender takes a job at a Dr Barnardo's orphanage. June couldn't save Clara from their father's violence, but perhaps she can help children whose lives have been torn apart by war.

When June bumps into Flight Lieutenant Murray Andrews on the bombed streets of Liverpool, the attraction is instant. But how can they think of love when war is tearing the world apart?

As winter closes in, and the war rages on, can June find the strength and courage to make a better life for herself and the children?

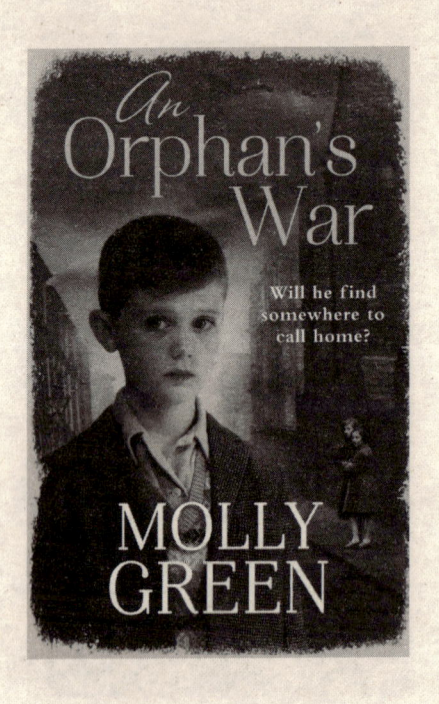

Liverpool, 1940

When her childhood sweetheart Johnny is killed in action, Maxine Grey loses more than her husband – she loses her best friend. Desperate to make a difference in this awful war, Maxine takes a nursing job at London's St Thomas's Hospital.

Maxine takes comfort in the attentions of a handsome surgeon, but Edwin Blake might not be all he seems. And as the Blitz descends on the capital, Maxine returns to Liverpool heartbroken and surrounded by the threat of scandal.

When offered a job at a Dr Barnardo's orphanage, Maxine hopes this is the second chance she has been looking for. And one little boy in particular helps her to realise that she needs the orphans just as much as they need her . . .

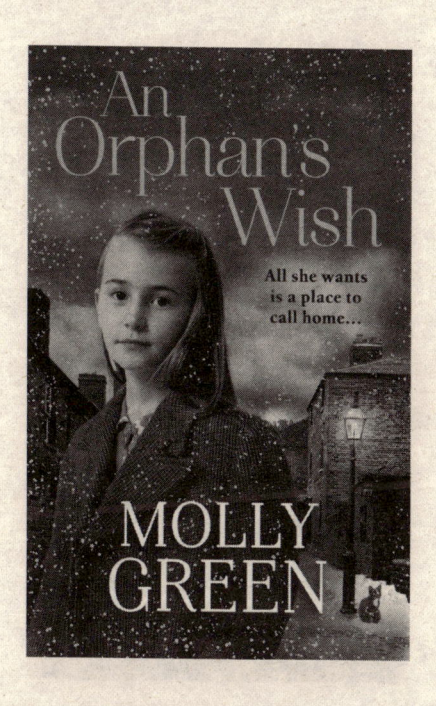

Liverpool, 1943

Yorkshire is the place Lana has always called home, but it's now filled with painful memories of her fiancé, Dickie, who was killed at sea. When she accepts the challenging position of headmistress at a school in Liverpool, she hopes a new beginning will help to mend her broken heart.

Not everyone at Bingham School is happy about her arrival but Lana throws herself into the role, teaching children from the local village and the nearby Dr Barnardo's orphanage. She thrives in her work, but soon finds herself falling for a man who she would once have considered the enemy – and is torn between what she knows is right, and taking a risk that might see her lose everything.

There are children that desperately need her help, and Lana must fight for everyone's happiness, as well as her own. But one young girl in particular shows her that there is a way through the darkness – because even when all seems lost, there is always a glimmer of hope to be found . . .

June, 1941

Britain is in the throes of war, but Katharina Valentine feels sidelined.

Employed as a shorthand-typist in the War Office, she is transferred to the basement below – having had no idea that this dark, airless, underground maze, home of the top-secret Cabinet War Rooms, even existed, let alone what her work will entail.

Unexpected staff shortages present an opportunity to work directly for Winston Churchill himself, and Katie jumps at the chance. And as she grows closer to Wing Commander Baxter Edwards, things start to look up . . .

But when a jealous colleague threatens to expose information about her family that could put her in violation of the Official Secrets Act, Katie faces serious repercussions.

Will she lose both the job and the man she holds dear?

Fern Britton
Picks
Exclusively for
TESCO

EXCLUSIVE ADDITIONAL CONTENT

Includes exclusive author content and details of how to get involved in *Fern's Picks*

Fern's Picks

Dear lovely readers,

I'm delighted to introduce our next pick, the brand-new uplifting saga novel from Molly Green – and I think you'll agree that it's her most engrossing and heartfelt story yet.

The Wartime Librarian's Secret takes place in a beautiful country estate at the height of the Second World War. The rich, historical detail has been researched meticulously, bringing the time period vividly to life. But, at its core, this novel is a timeless love story which will keep you turning the pages long into the night.

We meet Esme Donaldson, our heroine – and fellow book lover! – as she is reeling from the loss of her beloved husband. When she is employed at Redcliffe Manor as a librarian, she is soon thrust into a world that hums with whispers of top-secret activities. But Esme has a secret of her own, one that could cost her dearly…

With engaging and realistic characters that you'll enjoy spending time with, *The Wartime Librarian's Secret* is a gripping tale of love and loss that is sure to transport you this summer. I cannot wait to hear what you think!

With love
Fern x

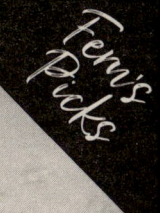

Fern Britton *Picks*

Exclusively for TESCO

Fern's Picks

Look out for more books, coming soon!

For more information on the book club, exclusive Q&As with the authors and reading group questions, visit Fern's website **www.fern-britton.com/ferns-picks**

We'd love you to join in the conversation, so don't forget to share your thoughts using **#FernsPicks**

Fern's Picks

Why, How and Where I Write Wartime Stories

The Wartime Librarian's Secret is my tenth novel for Avon HarperCollins, and at their request, and my delighted acceptance, they are all set during the Second World War. For years before I wrote novels, I was fascinated by this war as I wasn't born long after. My mother and father went right through the horrors of the London Blitz, though my father never said much about it. But Mum did sometimes talk about it, particularly the unfailing kindness of strangers. And I clearly remember my mother's ration books and her eking out of the meals as some foods were still rationed until 1954. Even when rationing stopped, the nation was conscious of the shortages and my sister and I were brought up never to waste food or neglect looking after our clothes and shoes.

I married Edward who was older than me and who had been in the RAF in the fifties, mending wirelesses and fitting them into aeroplanes. He was extremely knowledgeable about the war, and I always gave him my manuscripts to read and check before delivering to my editor. He would spot inaccuracies, anachronisms and Americanisms (probably a throwback from my decade living in the US). Sadly, he died five years ago, and I do miss discussions with him on plot holes (my computer changes this to potholes! – not much difference really) and scene settings. Whilst walking, he would invariably come up with the answer that perfectly fitted my story.

My interest in the war was furthered when 15 years ago Edward and I went to Bletchley Park and the following year to Churchill's Cabinet War Rooms. I've written a series of three heroines, each engaged in different work at Bletchley Park. Subsequently, I chose the Cabinet War Rooms for my heroine in *Courage for the Cabinet Girl*, who would become one of Churchill's secretaries. To have

Fern's Picks

Winston Churchill as a major character (well, he would be, wouldn't he?) and endeavouring to capture his volatile personality, was a real joy. And it was certainly no chore to revisit those important historical sites.

With all my novels, I need to do a huge amount of research reading. I say 'need to' but I adore this part of the writing process. The trouble is, I find books written on and around my subject riveting. I tell myself I only need to read certain chapters and can forget the rest. Then I read the first few pages just to 'set' the book in my mind, and before I know it, I'm spending the next month reading cover-to-cover yet another tome. Memoirs are especially absorbing and so valuable to a novelist to help create an authentic mood.

Visiting museums are key to my research. I try to go to the Imperial War Museum at least once a year. But the small museums devoted to one subject can really pay off. There's a museum for the Air Transport Auxiliary (ATA) at the Maidenhead Heritage Centre and above the museum's modest shop is a floor predominantly for the women in the ATA. One of the guides handed me a set of earphones so I could listen to several female pilots who had recorded their stories in the seventies, telling me just what it was like to fly planes during the war. Without exception, they were passionate about it! But it was personal incidents such as always applying their lipstick before a flight, their deep friendships with one another, and their fight (finally successful!) for equal pay with the male pilots that stayed with me. Then filled with trepidation, I stepped inside a Spitfire and managed to take off and carry out the instructor's orders to aim for the lighthouse some way away. At that, he asked me to touch down. Knowing this was the trickiest part of the test, I was so nervous, I couldn't land! All right, it was only a simulator in the museum, but it felt completely real to me and *A Sister's Courage* was born from that experience.

Another small museum is the London Canal Museum on the Grand Union Canal. I never knew that in the war women controlled 70-foot barges taking heavy cargo such as aeroplane parts, steel, iron and coal backwards and forwards along the Grand Union Canal

Fern's Picks

between London and Birmingham. It was back-breaking work and not surprising that only about 40 girls and women ever volunteered. But this museum boasted a three-quarter-size (in length) narrowboat you could step inside and walk through, marvelling that girls, often still in their teens, lived and worked in threes in such a confined space under the most primitive conditions. I couldn't wait to write *A Sister's War* where my tomboy 17-year-old heroine applies to join them.

I now come to where I write.

I'm not one of those writers who can only write in one place. I've written in planes, trains, other people's houses, on retreats, by the sea, in gardens . . . the list goes on. I find different environments can be stimulating. But I do like to have one set place when I'm at home and I feel incredibly lucky to have a separate office in the garden which happens to be a copy of a vintage railway carriage! And inside the genuine train door, I have my own First-Class compartment that looks as though it's come straight out of the Orient Express! This leads through to a long office where I have my computer, bookcases and more bookshelves, and an extensive worktop where I can spread out my research books and papers and any objects I collect that pertain to my novel-in-progress. My wartime heroines are always travelling by train, but unfortunately not in First Class. If they bag a seat, it's a miracle. They're usually found sitting on their suitcases, squashed in the corridor thick with cigarette smoke, as well as steam and smuts coming through the open window.

To see a photograph of my fabulous carriage, do visit my website: **mollygreenauthor.com**.

Questions for your Book Club

Warning: contains spoilers

- Which character in *The Wartime Librarian's Secret* do you relate to the most, and why? Did this change throughout the novel?

- Do you think the author had specific reasons for setting the main story in 1942? If so, what were they?

- What were your first impressions of Brad, and how did your sense of his character develop throughout the novel? Did you feel that he was a good foil to Esme?

- Esme holds several personal tragedies, including the birth of her stillborn daughter and the knowledge that another pregnancy could kill her. What was your reaction when this was revealed? To what extent do you feel that the author captured the pain that Esme must have felt, as well as the strength it would have taken her to confront her past?

- How could the experience of deeply personal grief such as Esme's be impacted by the context of wartime? When so many people are suffering, does it diminish the loss? Or does the tragedy add another layer of trauma?

- Discuss the role of the country house setting of the novel. How does it shape Esme's experience of the war?

- Do you feel that Muriel and Robert Lake got their due comeuppance for their scheming?

- Did *The Wartime Librarian's Secret* end how you hoped it would? Where do you think the characters would be ten years on?

An exclusive extract from Fern's new novel
A Cornish Legacy

CHAPTER ONE

North Cornwall, April, present day

Delia squinted through the windscreen, the sun ahead dazzling her. 'You'll see the turning on the right in a minute,' she said. 'Keep an eye out. I might miss it.'

Sammi tipped the last of the crisps into his mouth and sat up a little straighter. 'My eyes are peeled.' He pulled the sunglasses down from his head. 'Will there be some kind of landmark?'

'There's a big metal sign swinging on a post above the gates. Remember? You said it looked like a gibbet.'

Sammi chuckled. 'The gibbet! Yes, of course! Such a welcome.' He sat up straighter, alert. 'There!'

Delia saw the emerging gap amongst the tangled hedge of rhododendrons, with the rusted sign hanging from the post.

'Is that it?' asked Sammi. 'Can't read the name.'

Delia slowed, changing down through the gears. She wasn't smiling. 'Yep. This is it. Wilder Hoo.' The sight of the tatty sign that she had never wanted or expected to see again forced her stomach into a tight knot. Turning, she slowed the car and braked to a halt. 'I really don't want to be here.'

Sammi reached over for her knee and tapped it briskly. 'You're not on your own. I'm here, and those horrible people are gone. Come on.'

Delia put a hand to her chest and took a deep breath to control the old anxiety welling within. 'It's quite late. Let's go and find somewhere to stay tonight and come back tomorrow.'

'It's only half past four!'

'But it'll be getting dark soon.'

'Darling, it's April, not December.' Sammi's voice became soft and sympathetic. 'I know this is hard. But you can do it, and you will do it.'

'I don't want to do it.'

'The past is past. Dead and buried.'

Sighing heavily, Delia put the car in gear and slowly drove the winding tarmacked drive. 'Dead people can still haunt us.'

Stiff clumps of grass and dandelions had forced themselves between the cracked pitch, and in other places, huge potholes housed red, muddied puddles.

'It'll cost thousands just to repair the drive,' she said. 'Look at it.'

She knew that Sammi saw through different eyes. For him, this was an adventure. When Delia had first told him that the house had been gifted to her, he had been ready to celebrate, despite her horror of the whole thing. He seemed to feel only the thrill of an escapade.

Looking out of his side window at the ancient, rolling parkland with great oaks dotted across the scene he said, 'Delia, this is utterly captivating. Please tell me there's a lake. I'm expecting Colin Firth to stride forth in his wet breeches and shirt.'

Delia was scornful. 'If only. No lake, I'm afraid. Just a beach and all these acres of parkland. Do you know, it takes four men with a tractor each an entire week to cut all that grass? When they get to the end, they have to start again. It's a bloody money pit.' Her eyes flicked to the avenue of ivy-clad beech trees ahead, the bare branches forming a tunnel over sodden leaves. 'That ivy needs cutting back too. Argh. Who can afford all this, I ask you!'

Sammi was not listening. 'How long is this drive again?'

'It's 1.2 miles.'

'Very specific.'

Delia sighed. 'My father-in-law preferred to tell everyone it was two kilometres because that sounded longer.'

'And all this land belongs to the house?'

'Yup.'

Sammi was grinning. 'I'd love to jump on a tractor and spend a whole summer mowing all this.'

'You really wouldn't. Back in the day, there were sheep and deer to crop it.'

'Sheep and deer! Delia.' Sammi laughed. 'And all this is actually yours!'

She shrugged. She was weary and wretched. 'Not for long, I hope.'

They rattled over a cattle grid and onto a sparsely gravelled drive.

'OK. Here we go.' Delia swallowed hard. 'Round this bend, you'll see the house.' She took a nervous breath and added, 'I couldn't do this without you.'

Sammi tutted, 'I wouldn't let you come on your own, would I?'

Delia steered the last curve – and there, suddenly, was Wilder Hoo.

Available now!

Fern's Picks

The No.1 Sunday Times bestselling author returns

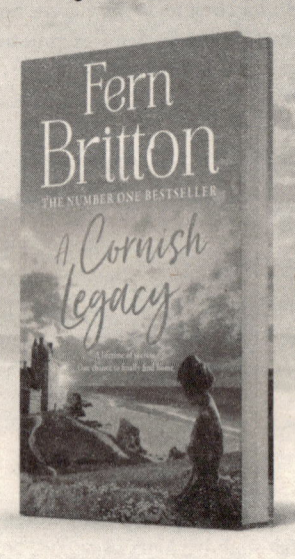

Wilder Hoo house holds a lifetime of secrets.

When Cordelia Jago learns she's been left the crumbling manor house Wilder Hoo, perched high on the Cornish coast, she wonders if it's one last cruel joke from beyond the grave.

Having already lost her marriage, her best friend and her career, she's at rock-bottom. Now she's inherited a house she hates, full of unhappy memories.

But as she fights with its echoing rooms and whispering shadows, the house begins to exert a pull on her. The wild Cornish landscape, the stark beauty of seagrass and yellow gorse against the deep blue sea, begin to awaken a connection Cordelia thought she'd buried for ever.

Could she turn around this monstrous wreck of a house – and, along the way, let go of the secrets of the past and heal her heart too?

AVAILABLE NOW!

Our next book club title

Fern's Picks

One night. One chance to be free.

Enya feels adrift. Trapped in a life she no longer recognises.

A loveless marriage. A distant son.

Until the night she saves a young boy's life – and upends her own.

Now to break free she must face the storm again.
And this time, she's fighting for herself.